D1029646

IMMORTAL

The Last of the Romans: II

Immortal

A NOVEL OF BELISARIUS

WILLIAM HAVELOCK

First edition October 2021

Book cover design by Dusan Markovic

Maps by Cyowari

ISBN 978-1-7379808-1-0 (hardcover)

ISBN 978-0-578-98896-2 (paperback)

ASIN: B097CC9GSG (ebook)

www.havelockbooks.com

For Anna

It was for him I chased

The Persians o'er wild and waste,

As General of the East;

Night after night I lay

In their camps of yesterday;

Their forage was my feast.

~Henry Wadsworth Longfellow (1807–1882 C.E.)

CHARACTERS

Aetius	Long-dead general of the Western Roman Empire, Attila's nemesis
Alaric	A junior officer amongst the Herulian *foederati*
al-Harith	Heir to the Ghassanid Kingdom
al-Mundhir III ibn al-Nu'man	Lakhmid Arab King, sworn enemy to the Ghassanids
Anastasius	Deceased Roman emperor of Varus' youth
Antonina	Young Roman aristocrat, daughter of Basilius, wife of Belisarius
Archelaus	A former *excubitor* and leader of the Thracian Army, killed in a trial by combat
Ascum	Alani ballista commander, serves the Cappadocian Army
Attila	Long-dead Khagan of the Hunnic Empire
Auria	A princess among the Mauri
Azarethes	Commander of all Persian armies
Baduarius	Ostrogoth, leads Belisarius' spearmen
Barzanes	An experienced cataphract under Bessas
Basilius	Former East Roman consul, chief advisor to Justin
Belisarius	General of the Roman Empire's Mesopotamian armies
Bessas	Armenian, leads Belisarius' cataphracts
Cassiodorus	Justinian's priest and personal advisor
Cephalas	Greek, former spearman of the Thracian Army, aide to Varus
Dagisthaeus	Ostrogoth, brother of Baduarius, a deceased tribune under Belisarius
Fulcaris	A young recruit to the Herulian foederati

Germanus	Justinian's cousin, general of the Thracian Army
Godilas	Deceased general of the East Roman armies and close friend to Justin
Hakhamanish	The magus, a priest of the Zoroastrian religion
Hermogenes	Imperial Minister and legate in the Persian War
Hypatius	The eldest nephew of Emperor Anastasius
Ildico	Attila's final bride
Irilar	A Herulian recruit, cousin to Fulcaris
Isaacius	A Jewish soldier in the Thracian Army, killed in battle against the Avars
Jabalah	King of the Ghassanids
Jafnah ibn 'Amr	A Ghassanid household guard
John	Belisarius' second-in-command and closest friend
Justin	Deceased Roman emperor, former master of Varus and Samur
Justinian	Justin's nephew and close advisor
Kavadh	*Shahanshah* of the Persian Empire
Kazrig	Khan of the Avars
Khingila	Warlord of the Hephthalites recruited by Kavadh
Liberius	A senior advisor to the Emperor
Marcellus	Lord of the excubitores
Marcian	Latin centurion, second to Solomon
Mariya	Princess of the Ghassanids, King Jabalah's daughter
Mundus	An experienced tribune of the Thracian Army, rumored a half-Gepid
Narses	Theodora's chief spy and advisor

Nepotian	A wealthy Roman senator and Solomon's father
Odoacer	Ostrogoth who overthrew the last Western Roman emperor
Opilio	Centurion of the Herulian foederati
Paulus	The Roman emperor's Minister of the Treasury
Perenus	An exiled Lazic prince and Varus' second-in-command
Perozes	Persian noble and general
Petrus	An aged Latin priest
Procopius	Imperial scribe and historian
Rosamund	A captured Gepid pagan and healer
Samur	A Herulian slave to Justin, Varus' only sibling
Sembrouthes	Commander of Aksumites guarding Princess Mariya
Sergius	Latin centurion under Belisarius
Shaush	Prince of the Avars, eldest son of Kazrig, slain in battle against Belisarius
Simmas	A commander of the Hun foederati, brother to Sunicas
Sinnion	An officer in the Hun foederati
Sittas	A Roman general in Armenia
Solomon	A young Roman aristocrat, son of Nepotian
Sunicas	A leader of the Hun foederati, brother to Simmas
Theodora	Senior Roman official, wife of Justinian
Tribonian	The Roman Emperor's Minister of Laws
Troglita	A centurion in the Thracian Army
Tzul	Kazrig's warlord, slain in battle against Belisarius

Uliaris	A Frank, a spearman of the Cappadocian Army
Valerian	A centurion in the Roman Empire's eastern provinces
Varus	The narrator, a Herulian, and a slave to Justin
Xerxes	Persian prince and commander of the Zhayedan, or Immortals

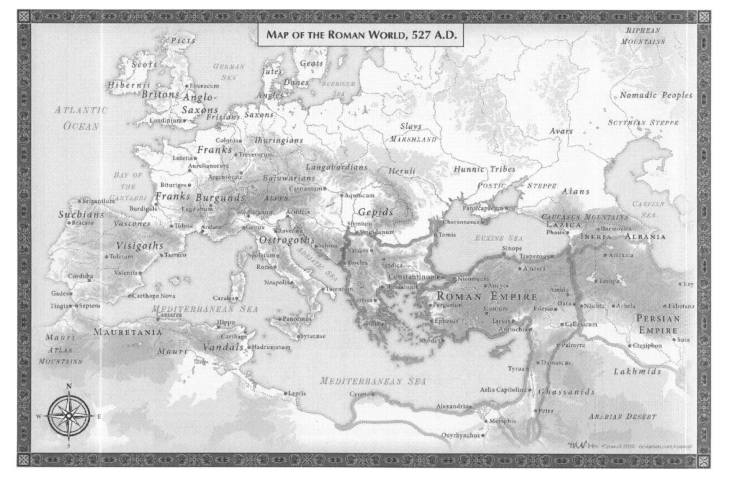

MAP OF THE ROMAN WORLD, 527 A.D.

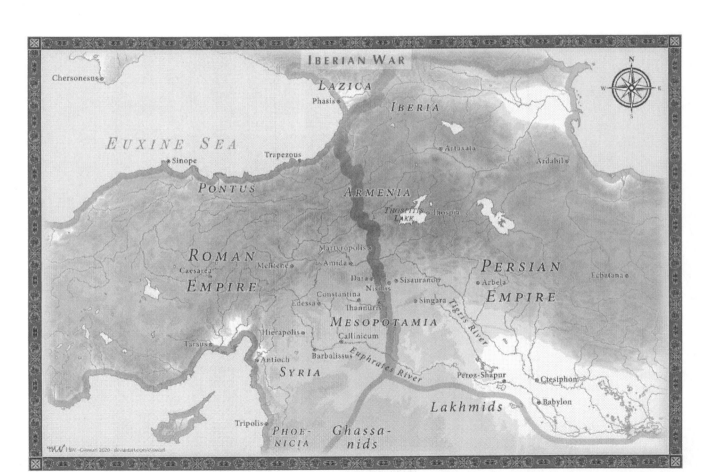

IBERIAN WAR

Chersonesus

LAZICA

Phasis

IBERIA

EUXINE SEA

Sinope

Trapezous

Artaxata

Ardabil

PONTUS

ARMENIA

THOSPITIS LAKE

Thospia

ROMAN

Martyropolis

PERSIAN

Caesarea

Melitene

Amida

Ecbatana

EMPIRE

Dara

Sisauranon

Nisibis

Constantina

Singara

Arbela

EMPIRE

Edessa

Thannuris

Tigris River

Hierapolis

MESOPOTAMIA

Callinicum

Tarsus

Barbalissus

Euphrates River

Antioch

Peroz-Shapur

Ctesiphon

SYRIA

Babylon

Tripolis

Lakhmids

PHOE-
NICIA

GHASSA-
NIDS

PROLOGUE:
THE FAVORED SON

AS A CHILD, THE FAVORED SON despised his brothers. They were older and far larger, vigorous with the strength prized by his people. They had teased and bullied, humiliating him on the training fields once he grew old enough to ride a horse and swing a sword. His father's love made the other children's taunting all the more vicious and unbearable. There was little reason for such partiality. Yet the father insisted that the favored son would carry on their lineage—it was foretold in the stars.

And so it was. Now the others were dead and gone.

The favored son was the only one left to carry his father's blade against the people's many enemies, to lift a shield before those who would steal all the people had amassed. Though it was strength, not entitlement, that they valued above all things, the warriors fell into line behind this designated heir and rode the plains with a renewed thirst for battle.

In spite of himself, the favored son felt a pang of grief for his lost brothers, even his eldest and cruelest brother, the chief instigator of his torment. Though some of his father's trusted advisors remained, the favored son had no blood relatives to enforce his will or share his trust, and the weight of leadership hung heavily upon his shoulders.

He would not make the same mistakes as those who had come before. The people had long respected his wisdom, and they did not balk at his orders for restraint. Though they raided and burned their neighbors, though slaves were taken and food stored to see the people through the deep snows of winter, the favored son courted no unnecessary risks, nothing that would place his people in mortal jeopardy.

Now, leading his people north, the favored son departed the lands of his father. Wind lashed the people's faces as they went, yet their bodies were unbowed, sturdier still for all the hardships of the past year. Many told stories, and their voices carried across the plains. Things would change now, improve, and his people would rise again, stronger and harder than before.

FROM THE ASHES OF DEAD MEN'S DREAMS

I NEVER KNEW MY FATHER, having been taken into slavery in that fog that clouds the dawn of childhood from later memory. After the death of the Emperor, I finally knew what it meant to be an orphan.

As a lower-ranking officer, I had not been granted permission to attend the Emperor's body prior to its internment in a predetermined Imperial crypt. No matter that Justin had once been my *dominus*—that pact had been severed nearly two years prior. No, the soft-skinned courtiers and patricians who skittered about the palace halls cared little for sentimentalities and even less for those of a former slave. All that mattered was decorum; any deviation from tradition would bring nothing but malicious gossip.

And so, rather than praying over Justin's cold body, I lingered in a dank centurion's quarters for nearly a week after returning from the carnage of Tauris. Upon my return to the ancient building, I discovered that a particularly voracious breed of rat had colonized the hidden nooks of the barracks walls, thriving within the filth and wasted food that naturally congealed wherever soldiers were idle. Frigid in the evening and sweltering in the heat of day, the barracks was a place where few in service to the Empire willingly wasted their days. Fewer still would ever find its moldering straw beds and unsteady tables an ideal setting to mourn. But middling infantry officers retained little leisure to complain about our plight, let alone sufficient coin to alter our fate, despite our victory over the Avars.

Brooding in the days leading to Justin's funeral, I sat in my cabin in the Imperial Barracks, attended only by my servant Rosamund and the occasional interruption from one of my men.

3

Bells rang in our training yard as they hailed the Emperor's memory. Even the grumbling of Constantinople's streets fell to a dull whisper, though whether this was out of respect for Justin or due to increased patrols of city guards, I did not know.

My naked sword lay across the bedframe, and I found my hands tracing its edge for the thousandth time. A gift from the Emperor—the third of seven gifts I was warned to expect—and it still did not truly feel like my possession. Other various arms lay stacked along the wooden barracks wall, including an Avar weapon that was half hammer and half axe, with a bitingly cruel edge along its blade. Next to it rested the second of my seven gifts, the dagger reputed to have been carried by Aetius in his many campaigns against the Huns for the salvation of Rome.

It was always the sword that called to me, just as it called to my former master. Its blue-green tinge shimmered even in the darkness, and its metal never seemed to rust no matter how much rain and mud I carried it through. It was a blade that had seen me through Rome's great stand against the Avars, where I, along with my brother Samur, came within a heartbeat of consigning our lives to the glory of Rome and our souls to God.

It was not to be. Leading his cataphract vanguard, General Flavius Belisarius had charged the Avar warlord and struck down our black-cloaked foes, saving my life in the process.

We were rewarded upon our return to Constantinople, though I quickly spent my allotted plunder caring for many in my ranks who had been grievously injured. Cephalas, one of my first friends as a recruit, lost the strength in his shield arm from an unlucky sword strike, and the injury reduced a good man to a sobbing wreck unable to return to service in the Army. Rather than condemn him to scratching and begging a living in the city's streets, I took him into my household as a personal messenger. Where Rosamund kept my life in order, Cephalas acted as a courier for the dozens of tasks that a centurion was required to perform on behalf of his men.

What other silver I earned slipped through my fingers like water. Although Rosamund cautioned against heady expenses, she never refused my orders to seek medicine and richer food for men whose bodies bore witness to the horrors of Rome's fight against the Avars. My own wealth was not all that dwindled; our ranks within the Thracian Army had become piteously few in number, and as autumn drew to a close, recruiters scoured the provinces for replacements to train up.

Now, sitting in my officer's quarters, the Emperor dead and my sword lifeless before me, all that remained to me from our victory beyond the Euxine Sea were yellow-green bruises and a litany of scarred wounds. That, and the nightmares.

My first nights back in the barracks had been haunted by visions of screaming warriors, some Roman and some Avar, their mouths belching blood and eyes wide with anger. I saw the great mace that had broken my ribs driving down into my body again and again, and thoroughly believed that I had been transported back into the Avars' final charge that shattered my lines and sealed my doom. Rosamund, frightened and roused by my screaming, had awoken me each of those first nights, cooling my sweat-drenched brow and wrapping her arms around my chest to guide me back into sleep.

Still, I never found the respite my body so desperately needed, and soon came the worst of the dreams: not merely marching north in Tauris, or fleeing a burning Gepid village as children shrieked, their flesh crackling, but the hazy sounds of my earliest years. A young woman pleading, screaming. A blade hacking at her exposed neck.

It was just this past night that had horrified me most. I had been lost in a lurid vision of our venture from Singidunum when Rosamund shook me awake. In the moments before my eyes adjusted to the darkness, I saw only the bone-white hair of a Gepid, an *enemy*, and I seized him by the throat. It was not until my fingers tightened and I heard my name choked out into the silence that I saw it was no enemy, but Rosamund, her face flush with panic and her white hair brilliant even in the dark. In a heartbeat, my senses returned, and Rosamund fell from my slackened grip, wheezing for air on the floor. I leapt to her side, babbling for forgiveness, but when I placed my hand upon her shoulder, she shrugged it off aggressively. I watched as Rosamund winced and breathed, her throat rasping as she sipped air. At last she stood and filled a half-empty wooden cup, her eyes distant as she let the cool water dribble past her lips, and all I could do was sit atop the bed until I could no longer bear the silence.

"I am losing my wits," I moaned. "In the dark, all I see are enemies."

Rosamund only nodded, rubbing at chafed skin, and set down her cup. A few more long moments and she sat beside me, so close I could see the hairs on her skin standing on end. She took my hand into her own, and I felt a shiver in the cool touch of her flesh.

"I have seen this before, in my village," Rosamund said finally, her voice slow to return. "An evil spirit, stalking survivors of raids and battle." She swallowed. "So I cannot fault you. You're all that I have left in this world, Varus. Any enemies that you may have are my own, whether they come from dreams or from blood. Wherever you go, you do not go alone."

Her words sounded almost like a lesson from Father Petrus, though within his teachings, it was God who joined each step. I never doubted Petrus—and I do not, to this day—yet that night, it was Rosamund's oath that yielded more comfort. Pagan and barbarian she was, but there was iron in her words. And God help me, those words offered the only measure of peace I could feel, and would for many years to come.

Sonorous church bells rang through vaulting barracks windows, marking the morning. I was alone in my contemplation; Rosamund was loath to leave me in my melancholy, but I insisted, and now she ventured into Constantinople's winding markets. The day I faced would have been like so many before it, blurred into a stream, with one inseparable from the next, had an interloper not broken my malaise at once, and forever.

A knock at the door broke me from my stupor.

"Who calls?" I croaked, coughing to clear my throat as I tore my gaze from my weapon. My thoughts were rooted in the past, where Justin still lived, and if any footsteps sounded beyond my doorway, I had been deaf to them.

The response was muted but unmistakable. "Your oath-keeper, Varus. Will you leave me waiting much longer?"

I gasped. "Lady?"

"Yes, Varus." Though I could not see Theodora, I could hear her smile. "And while I have voice enough to speak to you through this door, I would prefer the courtesy of your unimpeded company."

I scrambled for clothing, then lifted the bar of the door, opening it to Theodora and her retinue of palace guards. The Pope himself would not have been more out of place, surrounded by the century's worth of grime that coated the barracks walls. Women, too, were a rarity; besides Rosamund, the only ones who ventured here were a faceless collection of army slaves and a regular procession of aging prostitutes.

Yet there Theodora stood, bejeweled and austere in an olive dress that shimmered against rays of sunlight, her raven hair set with silver and pearls and tied up with an elegant onyx cloth. Chin high and lips pursed, she offered a curt nod, and I, mouth agape, gathered my wits enough to drop to a respectful knee. Theodora's gown billowed against my feet as she surveyed my diminutive stone and wood quarters—a stark contrast to the bright frescoes and marble-lined halls that shaped the Imperial Palace. Witnessing Theodora's gilded person, it was hard to see how rumors of her past as a lowly actress (or, perhaps, courtesan) could ever persist—had it not been for Theodora herself hinting that an inglorious past hardened her for the struggles of power ahead.

"It is good to see you, Varus," she said formally, her hands clasped before her thin waist. "May I come in?"

"Of course, Empress," I said, still kneeling as I averted my gaze.

At the sound of the noble title, her face broke into a warm smile, and she laughed lightly. "Not yet, but soon enough. And do get up. It's impossible to have a conversation when you are staring at the floor."

Hastening to my feet, I backed away to allow Theodora passage into my centurion's quarters. It was a modest wooden enclosure, with just enough room for a small bed, a table, and the stack of my weapons and armor.

Two palace guards stepped forward behind her, but Theodora waved them off. "Make sure we are not interrupted. Varus is a dear friend," she said, despite the guard leader's protests.

My quarters may have been somewhat cleaner surroundings than the hallway, but Theodora's brilliant silks were still a stark contrast. She ran a hand over the white wolf pelt at the foot of my bed, which had thankfully been cleaned of the blood and dirt that its previous owner, the Avar prince Shaush, had imparted before his death. Her eyes rose, taking in the large cloth pinned to one of my walls. She shuddered, recognizing it as a tattered black banner that the Avars followed into battle, but did not look away.

"I've heard tales of all the events of Tauris," Theodora began, gaze still fixed on the dark symbol. "Triumphs. And terrors. Some say these Avars were more beasts than men, gnashing at our soldiers and consuming the flesh of the dying."

I shook my head. "It was nothing like that. Vicious and pitiless, yes, but in the end they were no more than men—and boys, some of them. What they possessed in strength they lacked in organization."

"But the mists?" Theodora turned sharply to face me. "Men say that thousands under Godilas marched into a mist, but only hundreds emerged unscathed."

"That much is true," I said. "I was on the front lines. Tauris' weather was far from favorable, and the Avars took good advantage of that with their ponies. They caught us unawares." When Theodora said nothing, I reluctantly elaborated. "Chained javelins. Speared our men and dragged them into the mists by their guts."

If Theodora felt any revulsion at my blunt conversation, she gave no sign. Her eyes trailed back to the torn Avar banner, stepping close enough to touch it, and rubbed the coarse material with delicate fingers, her expression passionless.

"Did you see Godilas die?"

"Yes." A hard knot formed in my throat. "He was not himself, in the end. Liberius once said that his mind had been broken from a lifetime of bloodshed, and I believe he was correct. Godilas did not desire leadership over the expedition. The only relief I have is that the Avars slew him swiftly, and with no pain."

"His sacrifice will not be forgotten, I promise you." Theodora's voice was low, her stare fixed on the banner. Then, in the span of a few heartbeats, her attention swept to weapons displayed along my wall, from the Scythian axe to Aetius' dagger. But it was Justin's sword that held her gaze. She stilled and folded her hands to her chest as her eyes traced its lines and whorls. Only then did she sit, and nodded for me to alight beside her on the bed, her gold-covered fingers still clasped tightly.

As we sat in silence, I was close enough to observe her. Always a handsome woman, Theodora dressed formally since

Justin's death. Besides the decorations of her headdress, her earrings cascaded in an extended train of pearls, and circlets of jade and gold adorned her throat and chest. These, I knew, were not frivolities. The gems and precious metals revealed her status as an Empress-to-be—regal, yet always deferential to Rome and its emperor. Theodora played the part well, but she knew better than any the power of costume, and her jewels were a sparkling reminder of who had the true power in Constantinople.

"I hoped to see you sooner," she said after some silence.

I lowered my head. "I apologize, Highness. I have been... much occupied since returning from Cherson."

In truth, I retained little to do. Other men executed my purchases; my only role beyond furnishing coin was a brief, symbolic meeting with each man. The senior commanders, like Belisarius or Germanus, were the ones spending their days in the Imperial Palace, planning for our next war against Persia. I was left alone to ruminate in the growing chill of the barracks offices. Though I would witness unspeakable horrors in the years ahead, this had been my first taste of true battle, and I did not wish Theodora to know how the raw carnage had left me shaken. The horror I'd revealed to Rosamund had been bad enough.

But there was no concealing the truth from Theodora. She shook her head. "I mean no offense. I cannot imagine how Tauris has affected you."

Face burning with shame, I sat in respectful silence as she continued. "I've heard reports of what happened in Tauris, of the Avars... and of Tribune Archelaus," she said, stiffening slightly as she spoke of my former commander. "If the stories are true, I am considerably in your debt."

"Highness?" I could not read the intensity of her gaze.

"Between his actions against the Gepids and what he did at Scythian Neapolis, Archelaus' record is forever stained," she said.

"I should have known better than to trust him. I... I won't be so foolish again."

Theodora stood and examined my weapons, her eyes coming to rest upon the sword that I'd hastily stacked before her entry.

"We cannot build our future without the trust of the people, and Archelaus tarnished that for Cherson. We will not condone rape or abuse in the Empire any longer, for any reason," Theodora said. Though her voice was tinged with anger, her tone softened as she added, "It was the Emperor's will, and now it is my own."

Though my own recollection of our army's actions in Tauris was incomplete, Theodora's perceptions of Archelaus were undoubtedly true. Even before our voyage, Justinian's bride had already begun to craft new laws elevating the rights of women in the Empire, moving with elevated urgency in the days after Justin's death. Theodora continued, explaining that despite the justice of my actions, several former friends of Archelaus had decried me to Justinian.

"General Belisarius has asked for your transfer into his own army, but I wanted to speak with you first before approving it," she said. "And based upon your command against the Avars, it is within my authority to raise you to the rank of *komes*."

Komes. In a moment, Theodora snapped me into vitality. I held little desire to rush headlong into the shield wall, and such vaunted status would raise me into the Imperial Army's senior officers. A komes was given command over a *banda*, was a leader of hundreds of men in peace and in battle. More than that, however, a komes invested his men with a sense of meaning—where Archelaus had been a sigil for wrath and sorrow, I might deliver the promise that many entrusted onto me. But what had me nearly shaking with excitement was the knowledge that this rank was what Justin would have wanted for me above all things, and that this particular promotion would root me in the service of Belisarius, who shared the nigh impossible vision of a better life for all. A life where the Empire and its millions of citizens might know peace and plenty instead of destruction and famine.

For all these reasons, the honor was impossible to decline.

"Thank you, Highness. It will be a pleasure serving in General Belisarius' infantry." No sooner had I said it than I paused. This new rank would separate me from those who stood with me on the plains of Tauris—those who still lived, at any rate. The stab of guilt, especially at the thought of Perenus, brought me to question my good fortune. "But what of my men, Highness? What will happen to them?"

Theodora laughed lightly. "You may bring along officers of your choosing. Belisarius warned me this would be important to you." She spoke easily, yet her face lost its warmth as she continued. "But you will not be serving in Belisarius' spearmen."

I met her eyes, confused. "Highness, if not the infantry, then where would I go?"

Theodora leaned forward, folding her gold-lined fingers into an arch as she spoke. "We are forming a new foederati of Herulian horsemen to complement Belisarius' cataphracts. They are in need of Roman officers... and you are one of the few we have who can speak their language."

My heart sank as Theodora made her pronouncement. The foederati were martial units carved from masses of barbarian tribes that skirted the Empire's borders, eager for Roman silver and the promise of regular meals. Belisarius himself employed sizeable Hunnic and Alani formations, while a number of Goths rose high in his narrow band of trusted officers. Nevertheless, all foederati units were required to be led by Roman officers, but as the tribesman rarely mastered sufficient command of Latin or Greek, a knowledge of barbarian language was crucial. Moreover, though such a position was an honorable one, it demanded the appointed officer himself possess the skills the recruits were meant to learn.

And though I knew how to ride, only a child would mistake me for an experienced rider, and men of any age would laugh at my attempts at archery from horseback. Until now, I simply had neither need nor desire to master these skills beyond basic competency.

"Highness, I am not a skilled horseman and have no experience fighting in the saddle. Surely another would be more appropriate for this role?"

Theodora shook her head. "Heruli is an uncommon language amongst the Empire's officers, and your knowledge of the tongue makes you equally uncommon amongst officers. This is the easiest way for me to grant you a more senior rank," she said. "And we will need their soldiers in the wars to come... Rome does not have enough homegrown cavalry to hold the line against Persia, let alone across the Empire."

I struggled to disguise my displeasure. Honor notwithstanding, I would happily reject this promotion for a return to my life as a centurion, with little more than broken armor and a few silver coins to my name. I was no horseman; I had been trained to march and fight afoot, and I saw no reason that should change now.

I pled my case. "Highness, though I am Heruli, I have no memories of the tribes. I speak their language, but they will not know me."

"I understand, and I know what I ask is difficult," Theodora replied. "But you still are of their blood and can demonstrate how they might become both Roman and Heruli—honoring both, neglecting neither. Liberius' and Justin's teachings will flow into them through you."

I opened my mouth to protest further, but a stern glance from Theodora silenced me from pressing my luck. She favored me with an unorthodox private audience, but I doubted that such favor would remain if I refused her will. My years of service to scheming senators and princelings made me skeptical that anyone noble would elevate me for purely altruistic reasons, even Theodora. There was no outward reason to doubt her affections, of course, and compared to others of her rank, she displayed a remarkable and rare competence and sense of honor. Regardless, those as evenhanded as Theodora still possessed limits for disappointment, especially when they took pains or broke with tradition to extend an opportunity. I held little doubt that this formation of Herulian foederati was personally fashioned from my ancestral homeland by our Empress-in-waiting.

Theodora's deep-green eyes met mine, her sternness gone. She drew close, grabbing my hands and offering me a weak smile. "I know you may wish a different assignment, but our plans won't work without you leading the Heruli," Theodora said. "I will not force you to take this responsibility... God knows you deserve rest. But if you agree, I will take your service as a token of friendship that binds us together."

Her eyes grew wider, scanning the walls of smooth stones and gnarled wood that enclosed us. "Tribonian, Paulus, Cassiodorus... they use their influence at court to entrench themselves—and everyone else—in the past. You and I, we can build for the future. Justin and Liberius both told me to trust you, and I have not been disappointed thus far."

I lowered my head. Theodora and I had met only by a stroke of good fortune, yet that chance accident changed both of our lives forever. Her firm belief in my capabilities reminded me of my old master, whose words rang through the palace with a promise of better things rather than a slow death into history.

"Can I continue to trust you, Varus? Will you be my sword?" she asked, her eyes narrowing, unblinking.

God help me, but I could never refuse her—at least not deliberately. "Yes, Highness. Always." And so promising, I sealed my fate.

14

Theodora clapped her hands in delight. "Good! Now, do you wish to attend the Emperor's funeral?"

Another wild swing of raw emotion. The invitation tugged at the deep longing that had not left me since I had arrived at the docks of Constantinople. I knew I could not hope for one final conversation with my *dominus,* nor address the nagging questions that the dying Emperor promised to answer upon my return. Though I was nothing more than a slave, Justin had bestowed upon me privileges that even many patricians would never enjoy. He, along with Godilas and Father Petrus, granted me three priceless gifts, with the promise of four still to come. Deep in my soul, I yearned to learn the answers to Justin's mysteries, even to the point of shameful anger. For now, at Theodora's invitation, I found I wanted only to offer prayers over my fallen *dominus'* body. Theodora beamed; she seemed to know my answer before I opened my mouth, yet she waited patiently nevertheless.

"Absolutely, Highness. But low officers are not permitted at Imperial funeral rites." I spoke bitterly of my own station; I had at times even been tempted to sneak through the servants' passageways once again to share one final moment with my surrogate father. Theodora's smile shifted to bemusement, so I added, "Besides, I have nothing appropriate to wear. My armor was nearly destroyed in battle."

"Nonsense," she said. "None of the court will question your presence if you arrive with me. And don't worry about your appearance. If anything, the armor gives you a touch of rugged mystery." Rising to her feet, Theodora grinned once again. "Besides, it is to your benefit to socialize in court. There are quite a few ladies who would love to be on the arm of a handsome young komes!"

My cheeks burned as I shrank at the suggestion. Theodora was correct, of course; the daughters of wealthy merchants or impoverished patricians would happily overlook my humble beginnings to enjoy the rising status and Imperial privilege afforded to me. The established elite, whose members included Solomon and his father Nepotian, would forever view me as an upjumped savage, no matter my rank or how many gold coins I amassed. No, it was the directness of her statement that left me feeling awkward, awash with ambition and fear as I was, her suggestion disarming, especially so close to the funeral rites of a man who had been her husband's uncle.

Theodora raised fingers to her lips to stifle a chuckle. "Perhaps another time, soon enough. Gather your things, and we shall go to the palace."

With that, she left the room, and I knew I had but a scant moment to prepare myself. Though Rosamund had scoured my mail and polished its steel until it shone, there was no hiding the rents where swords had cut or the narrow hole where an arrow had pierced my shoulder. Several links in the chest area had been pushed inward, deformed by an Avar maul near the end of the battle. The armor looked ragged, but for now, it was all I had, and I could only trust Theodora's word that my appearance would be immaterial.

I threw open the door and joined Theodora's retinue, and the group of us exited the Imperial Barracks. Theodora's guards formed a dense square about their charge, their scaled armor glittering and spears raised as a warning to any who might approach without invitation. Theodora smiled to herself as she walked along patiently, her eyes taking sideways glances in my direction.

To my further discomfort, Theodora resumed her discussion of my prospects. "We really must get you married, Varus. There are many girls at court who would love a chance to wed a komes. You are what, twenty years? Maybe one or two more?"

"Thereabouts," I responded, not entirely certain of my age beyond the rough approximations that Justin had guessed at. "But I doubt any father would love a chance to wed his daughter to a freed slave."

Despite Justin's dreams of a more prosperous, equitable future, Roman society remained mired in its rigid social past, with soft-handed patricians rarely deigning to mix with the unwashed plebeian masses. Power resided in the hands of a few noble families, who looked upon merchants and craftsmen as necessary inconveniences regardless of their wealth or skill—to say nothing of peasants and freed slaves.

"I would not worry about that either." She grinned. "Would you prefer one of the Roman ladies? Or maybe even the daughter of a rich chieftain?"

Blushing deeply, I tried to hide my face as I thought of Mariya. My time with the Ghassanid princess had been brief, but its memory was enduring. Though I could only faintly recall the details of her face, I longed for it nonetheless. There was little logic in such desire, for Mariya rested far above any station I could ever hope for, and her hand was promised to Solomon, my boyhood rival. Even so, I ached to be merely in her presence, suffused with that pleasant, destructive madness so many poets described. But Theodora was unaware of my desire for Mariya.

"Ah, I see!" she said, tormenting me further as she glimpsed my reddening face. "Anyone in particular? Anyone that I would know?"

My gaze fell, and I shrugged. "It is someone who is not meant for me, Highness. That is all that matters."

Theodora slowed her pace. "Varus, I used to entertain men for copper coins to feed myself and my sisters, and now I am a breath away from the Imperial Purple. If you want this woman, and she wants you, then no law or custom need bar your way."

17

"As you say." I felt none of Theodora's certainty but could not outwardly contradict the future empress.

Blessedly, Theodora allowed the subject to drop. As the palace rose into view, I ventured one further question. "Highness, you mentioned speaking to Liberius. Is there any update of his whereabouts?"

She shook her head again. "We know he left for Judea, and then Palmyra, but could not obtain a clear explanation. His last message came from Dara, just before the Persians crossed the Tigris River into our Mesopotamian provinces."

I desperately hoped my old teacher escaped the advancing Persian army. Spies, organized in a ring created by Narses, reported tens of thousands of invading Persian soldiers at a dozen points along our eastern border, pushing deep into Armenia and Mesopotamia, and Dara, a fortified crossroads of regional trade, was perilously close to one of the Persians' initial targets. The approaching winter had slowed the Persian progress to a trickle, but there was no doubt they held an advantageous position for spring offensives in the new year.

Theodora and I approached the palace steps, waiting as two of her guards pried upon the high, iron-knobbed doors. A small crowd of city dwellers looked on, with some crying out blessings for the Emperor and the people of Rome. Many looked old, with hunched backs wrapped in drab wool and gnarled hands ruined by decades of tilling the field or spinning the loom, and though most were clean of obvious filth, all appeared unhealthily gaunt.

Worse, not all held honey in their tongues. As we advanced, faint hisses slipped through the murmur of the crowd.

"Usurper!"

"Your husband is crushing us!"

And, in an especially sonorous rasp, "Whore!"

My hand reached for my belt, though I'd left my sword at the barracks.

"Ignore them," Theodora ordered. I did so, and after mounting the steps, we swept into the cavernous halls of the palace, where we met a small sea of expensively dressed Roman citizens and senior army officers, all discontent left outside the heavy doors.

Most of the attendees wore black, with only foreign dignitaries and the Empire's own Imperial class in more fanciful colors. Presaging his confirmation as emperor, Justinian was adorned with flowing purple robes and golden chains, yet his close-cropped black hair was bare, still uncrowned by the Imperial diadem. Despite the somber mood, gossipy whispers echoed between arching columns and across the marble floor, and the heir to the Empire seemed visibly perturbed by his perceived lack of status at the previous Emperor's funeral.

Theodora's guards fanned across the sides of the room, taking their place with others entrusted with the palace's security. She beckoned for me to follow her through the crowd, which parted with curious stares and hushed whispers. Theodora remained aloof, her high cheekbones and thin nose held stern as she proceeded. Ahead, I spied Solomon and his father, the wealthy Senator Nepotian, engaged in a discussion of his battles against the Avars with several older statesmen.

"Complete savages, but we held them off in the end," Solomon was boasting. "I just wish General Godilas was here to rejoice in the glory — his last words in command were for me to lead our men to safety. And believe me, I paid back Godilas' death a hundredfold. Those maneaters won't come within a day's ride of Tauris for another decade or two, I'd wager."

As I passed, Solomon's gaze ran down the length of my torn mail and frayed boots. A smirk creased his lips, and it took all the reserve I could muster to keep from bashing a fist into his smug face. Even today, with my memory of Tauris clouded by decades of grief and struggle, I can still see Solomon: paralyzed in fear on the battlefield, then sulking in fear as our routed survivors ransacked

Scythian Neapolis. It was Belisarius, not Solomon, who preserved Roman control over Tauris' remaining towns—a fact that I wanted to scream at this sanctimonious, fawning bunch of patricians. Perhaps for the better, Theodora's continued progress forced me to scurry onward closely, leaving the braggart Solomon to soak in the adoration of his father's colleagues.

The Emperor's body lay across a marble slab, his frail skin masked by the layers of ornate armor that he once carried into battle in the name of Rome. Excubitores stood on each side of the body, armor bright and swords bared as they kept vigil over their commander during the wars of Zeno and Anastasius. By law, the elite guard of the Emperor's Sentinels was limited to three hundred of the Empire's most experienced soldiers, and nearly all guarded Justin's body that day. One conspicuous absence in their ranks was that of Archelaus, whom I had slain far to the north as punishment for his crimes against the Roman people.

The press of perfumed silken nobles thinned as we neared the Emperor's body. The excubitores' commander, Marcellus, stood at the Emperor's head with his sword drawn, and nodded to his men as Theodora approached, a silent order for the excubitor guard to step away from the marble slab. Justinian walked to Theodora's side and whispered in her ear, then returned to the gallery of his future nobles.

A lone black-cloaked figure stood over the Emperor's body, which I recognized as Father Petrus. Though Petrus normally demanded my presence for daily morning prayers, I had not been summoned to him since we both learned of Justin's demise. Thick tears ran down his weathered face as he muttered prayers of salvation for the fallen man. Seeing me, Petrus met my eyes and smiled feebly. He backed several paces away from the slab, standing silently but not leaving the enclosure. Far behind him stood skeletal Basilius, his face blank as he stood austere next to Marcellus and the excubitores.

Theodora walked to the Emperor's prone body, her silken dress brushing almost audibly against the marble floor in the reverent stillness. She lifted a hand in my direction, granting me permission to approach my master's body.

I nodded my acknowledgment but paused. Justin's face held a fitting expression of resigned determination, reflecting a life of hardship and service that had spanned nearly eighty years. I took in the lacquered armor and the debilitated body it protected, the man who had once been a terror to Rome's enemies, covered in the deep-violet cloak that dignified him as an emperor of Rome.

All week, night and day, I had yearned to attend Justin's body. Now that the moment had arrived, however, all I wanted to do was avert my eyes. Despite the simmering warmth of the hundreds of bodies gathered in the space, Justin's dais emanated a paralyzing chill, and I found myself unable to take the final step to the armored body.

"Please, Varus," Theodora whispered. "Justin would be very happy for your presence."

I raised my eyes and closed what distance remained. The air caught in my chest as my eyes traced the carefully tucked hands atop Justin's armor, the thick layers of soft ermine fur sprouting from openings between his gloves and vambrace. His arms, their sagging skin and wasted muscles masked by dark leather and iron lamellar, led a trail first to the intricately decorated chestpiece, and then to a heavy chain bearing the cross of our Savior. At last, I looked to Justin's face, its wrinkled skin and balding pate plain against such ornament.

"*Dominus*," I croaked, tears welling in my eyes.

All Justin's weariness seemed wiped clean. All that remained were closed eyes and the faintest scowl. It was a sight I had witnessed countless times in his service, yet now, as I gazed upon his lifeless features, my chest rose and fell, a thousand memories forging into a single moment of vigil over the fallen emperor. From my earliest recollection of the hulking giant who paid a visit during a winter illness, to the aging man who applauded my progress under Godilas' tutelage, to our final exchange, when Justin gifted me his fabled runed sword. Memories long forgotten fountained into my mind, and I felt close to fainting.

"I fulfilled my promise, Dominus," I sobbed. "I just returned too late."

As I reached out to touch the Emperor's armored hand, several excubitores moved forward, only to be halted by Theodora. She placed a hand on my back as we stood over the Emperor, ignoring the noise from the galleries beyond.

"He loved you, you know. It was obvious to all of us," Theodora said softly. "Now it is up to us to continue his dream of a better world."

I nodded, saying nothing. Seeing that I was calmer, Theodora left me alone to bid my master farewell.

"On my oath, I will achieve your vision and bring peace to the Empire." My throat was pained and constricted, and I made no effort to choke back my tears. "I promise you, Dominus. I just wish you were here to see it."

Soon thereafter, Father Petrus stepped forward once more, wrapping an arm about my shoulders to guide me away. With a deep breath, I bowed my head to the Emperor and backed away from the dais, leaving Petrus and the excubitores behind.

Still reeling, I walked into the sea of aristocrats, my nailed boots clicking against the palace floors. All were standing in wait for the Emperor's body to be carried to the Church of the Holy Apostles, where it would rest until Judgment Day, and with Theodora gone, few of the crowd deigned to acknowledge me. Alone, I stood awkwardly by a palace wall and anxiously wished for the proceedings to continue speedily and draw to a close. Even Belisarius had been called away with several of his officers, although he offered a quick wave as he passed by.

I found myself longing for Samur. My brother's grief for our dominus was far more muted than my own, however, and he doubtless preferred time in the training yard with Sunicas over a funeral. Even more, I realized, I missed Liberius, my old teacher. Standing alone, I wished for nothing else than to dart into one of the servant hallways and escape back to the barracks. I even considered dismissing myself from Theodora's company, slinking away to hide my discomfort from public view. I would hardly be missed; none of these patricians truly desired the company of a freedman as myself, even one freshly minted to the rank of komes. But my escape was thwarted by the arrival of a newcomer, rooting me to my private corner of the Imperial Great Hall.

All day, all week, my head had floundered in a maelstrom of emotions: emptiness after returning from Tauris, the Janus-faced mixture of giddy excitement and reluctant fear at my promotion, and just moments ago, grief clutching painfully at my chest. Besides the morbid satisfaction of seeing my dominus before his interment, I was certain I could feel no joy that day.

As I saw Mariya, however, I instantly knew that I was wrong.

Like Theodora, Mariya was exempt from black robes of mourning due to her blood ties to a royal family. But even for a woman of her status, she was uncommonly radiant. Her gown was a deep crimson, belted at her slim waist and shot through with thin threads of gold. Ruby-studded gold hung from her ears and neck, her black hair pulled into a graceful updo. A delicate black veil draped just below her eyes, which sparkled as she approached.

Seeing me, she smiled.

My mouth opened, but no words came. Instead, agape, I forced my mouth into a clumsy smile, realizing only heartbeats later how ridiculous I must look—to smile so at an emperor's funeral! How quickly I abandoned my mourning for Justin, I thought shamefully.

"Varus," she whispered. "I expected to see you sooner. I have heard many stories of the danger in Tauris."

I stiffened, puffing my chest. "Th-thank you, Lady," I stammered. "It was hard fighting, but the people of Tauris are now safe."

If death by embarrassment were possible, God would have stopped my heart at that very moment. My words seemed as if they were escaping the lips of a different man, lacking any tact that one such as Mariya undoubtedly grew accustomed to in a royal court. Mariya, however, only nodded, waiting for additional details that I struggled to produce.

God's bones, but it was painful to look at her. I knew so little of this woman—indeed, she may have been the same type of spoiled weakling that I despised in Solomon. Even if that were true, I simply did not care in that moment. It was not a question of beauty—there were many handsome women in the Imperial Court, bedecked in foreign silk and expensive fur. No, it was a desperate longing grown even more pathetic since our last meeting in Constantinople's marketplace, where Mariya gifted me a golden pendant in return for escorting her through a burgeoning mob. She did nothing to demand my allegiance, or likely thought little else of our unlikely friendship as a passing interest, but with the vaguest smile, she demanded my obedience. I am a weak man, God knows, and I make no excuses for it.

Mariya moved closer, her perfume wrapping around my head. "Is it true that you dueled your Army commander?"

"Archelaus was a replacement for our slain *magister militum*, but yes. He asked for a trial by combat to protest the charges against him, and he lost," I said, my mind wandering for only a heartbeat back to the windswept plains around Scythian Neapolis.

Mariya shuddered. "As I promised, I prayed for your safe return. I am glad to see that wish come true, despite all of your attempts to encourage the opposite result," she teased.

All I could muster was another awkward smile. Worse, my body swayed gently, my weight rolling from one foot to another, and it took deliberate effort to keep still. Panic rose like bile as I noticed growing attention from nearby patricians, their inquiring eyes disdainful of a Ghassanid royal consorting with no better than a bedraggled barbarian in broken centurion's armor. Mariya's eyebrows arched as she returned my smile, and she at last broke the silence.

"The Emperor, you were very close to him?"

My inane grin evaporated at the sudden pivot back to the Emperor's body. Whether from overexcitement or exertion, my throat seemed perilously dry as I fought to form words. In the end, I decided upon the simple truth.

"He was like a father. Everything I have is because of him."

Mariya beamed. "My father always spoke highly of the Emperor. Justin was fairer than most, and he treated my people with respect."

"From my experience, Justin treated his servants amiably as well," I agreed, "which I found is a rare characteristic amongst the Roman elite."

Mariya giggled, a hand over her mouth to muffle the sound. "Too true!" she said. "The only thing that I have found that the wealthy Romans disdain more than the Arabs are their own underlings."

A look of resentment crossed Mariya's face, so brief as to be imaginary, and was quickly replaced with forced deference and satisfaction. "I don't know Theodora well, but I now understand why she has passed laws to raise women in the Empire. If I were someone else, I might even be able to refuse a marriage that I did not desire," she said.

"Lady?" I asked in confusion.

"I am being offered to Rome as a symbol of peace and cooperation... my own wishes are secondary to such goals. My father gets the protection of Rome, and the new Emperor will receive a few thousand spears and horsemen. A mutually beneficial trade at any cattle market, wouldn't you agree?" she asked acidly, her visage of calm deference fading once again.

I sighed, and a rush of courage surged through me. "In our last meeting together, the Emperor told me that every person may forge their own path in life… no matter how great or small."

Mariya laughed again, drawing the ire of onlookers and an insistent hush from a nearby courtier. Though half blocked by marble columns and tucked to the side of the Great Hall, our every move was carefully monitored, and every word doubtlessly followed by the suspicious. Until the procession of well-wishers ended, there was little else to do in the uncomfortable and overcrowded hall than eavesdrop. In this, Mariya was no fool, muffling the volume of her voice to the faintest whisper. "Would that I wielded your courage, Varus. But I cannot disappoint my father, or my people."

I wished for nothing more than for time to stop in that moment. Soon enough, the excubitores carried the Emperor away in a casket that would transfer him into an Imperial sarcophagus. Theodora's chief courtier, Narses, began to ask the crowd to return to their business, demanding the attention of the hall as a dozen guardsmen rattled their spears against the floor.

"Romans," Narses bellowed, his high-pitched voice cracking as it rose in volume. "Our august Emperor has returned to the bosom of our Lord and Savior. His remains will be interred with those of his peers. My couriers will identify those who I wish to follow me to an adjoining room, while the remainder of you may depart the palace."

Immediately thereafter, a small army of clerks and secretaries hailed the attention of no fewer than fifty bejeweled and expensively attired patricians. Senator Nepotian and his son Solomon were counted immediately in their number, while the

Emperor's various ministers shuffled one after another alongside Nepotian's cronies. Theodora, requiring no invitation, followed Narses into the hall, leaving me to seek my departure from the palace grounds. However, as I neared the Hall's exit, a leather-collared slave tapped upon my shoulder.

"Varus the Herulian?" the man asked, his face lined with premature wrinkles and thin hair receding to a bald pate.

"Yes?"

"My lord Narses requests your attendance straightaway," the man droned, already weary of the subject. "I suggest you hurry before they bar the doors."

I frowned. "Bar the doors? For what cause?"

The slave sighed. "To unseal and read the will of the Emperor, of course. Now, if you please..."

Justin's will. Of course a man of his wealth and standing would execute a will, although until now its existence had slipped through my thoughts. As Emperor, Justin would surely bequeath many of his possessions to the state and the people of Constantinople—a practice dedicated to engendering goodwill amongst the plebeians of the new Emperor that would soon follow. Why Narses requested me, however...there, I possessed only confusion and an itching curiosity. Following Narses' slave, I entered a large antechamber whose marble frescoes glittered from a hundred flickering tapers. I passed Narses as I slipped through the doorway, his floral perfumes nearly bringing me to gag from their sickly sweetness. Narses nodded to me as I passed, a look of incredulity on his face. There was no time to investigate, however, for I was quickly directed to an empty wooden bench near the room's far corner. No dignitary or court minister deigned to sit within three paces of me, although I took no grievance against the obvious insult. Though it possessed soaring arched ceilings, the antechamber soon sweltered from the massed heat of so many present.

Procopius, the clerk who accompanied the Thracian and Cappadocian armies to Cherson, stood at the front of the room. Procopius was a squat, dour man, whose lip curled ever so slightly as he spoke. He carried himself with an importance that day as the flower of the Roman elite listened to his pronouncements.

In Procopius' ink-stained hands was Justin's written will. Since the time of Caesar, Rome's rulers had often left written instructions detailing the events to follow their eventual deaths. Normally, the execution of the wishes of the dying were relatively peaceful and unquestioned. However, when an Emperor's will is ignored, or does not exist altogether, the Empire can be thrown into the carnage and chaos of civil war. Though I had no doubt that the parchment's words were once spoken by Justin's lips, its script flowed from the hand of Justinian or Narses, for up until his death, my dominus remained illiterate. Unable to scratch more than his name, Justin insisted that I not repeat his lifelong limitation—a precious gift that I did not recognize until far later in life, and removed from the wicker canes of the palace's tutors.

Emperor Justin had known death was not far off, and so he planned well. His first order of business was to reaffirm his intended heir in Justinian, who'd already exerted Imperial power and privileges for several years. Others included an echo of the need for the Empire to reclaim its heritage in the west, and defend against the countless barbarian tribes that circled our provincial borders. Small gifts were awarded to members of Justin's household, from rich furs to obscure nieces and nephews and tracts of land to beloved friends, to grants of arms and armor to promising young officers in various provinces. The Emperor even bequeathed a small sum to the residents of Constantinople, including enough silver for a half month's wages for every adult man and woman. Though this would not go far to address the growing anger and desperation in the streets, even Justinian's miserly finance minister Paulus had to approve of such a maneuver, which bought the new Emperor Justinian time to placate the worst elements of the Roman mob.

The last name called, however, was the most shocking, for it was my own.

"… and to my longtime servant Varus, now an officer of the Roman Army, I entrust the remainder of my estate. The small land holdings, as well as my gold and silver not hitherto mentioned, will be granted to Varus as one of the seven gifts that he has earned by birthright, and through devoted service," Procopius said, his voice rising in shock as he read the extent of Justin's largesse to me.

At first, I did not react. Perhaps from confusion, but also perhaps from raw surprise. Gasps filled the hall, pierced by a high-pitched shout from one disgruntled senator. It was not until several heartbeats, as the enormity of the moment passed through the audience, that I could muster any response.

I giggled. Not from glee, for even then I did not truly understand Narses' pronouncement. All I know is that it began as a brief chortle, yet as the weight of Justin's gift crashed down upon me, I burst aloud with laughter, forced to cover my mouth as curious and angry eyes fixed upon my uncouth form.

It was likely expected that Justin's wealth would be divided amongst further relatives, or granted upon his heir Justinian altogether. Over the course of his extensive career, Justin amassed considerable treasure from his wars in the east and west alike. Even after his gift to the people of Constantinople, Justin left me a fortune that transformed me from a destitute infantry officer into one of the wealthiest men in the Empire. He further granted me the rights to a small estate in the Macedonian town of Pella, the ancestral homeland of Alexander the Great. Justin was born to a swineherd in those rolling hills, and rose to the highest peaks of the Eastern Roman Empire. And, to the disbelief of dozens of perfumed patricians, that legacy was now my own.

Immortal

RECONSTITUTION

THEIR GLARING EYES WERE JARRING. Half curious, half furious, the senators and ministers who comprised Justin's court whispered with distressed voices and wrinkled noses as they stole a glance at my disheveled armor. There was no pointing, or indeed any outright confrontation, for such gawking was underneath the dignity of patrician men. Even so, some stood involuntarily from their benches, unable to help against an uninvited glance at Justin's heir.

Tribonian, the Empire's Minister of Laws, ordered the Emperor's will into law. Commotion flooded the antechamber as observers milled about, with Solomon's mouth hanging open in bewilderment. With a single stroke of Tribonian's quill, I became an object of scorn and envy, wealthier than Croesus himself despite having no blood ties with my onetime dominus. Not that I took undue offense at their scorn—a slave armors himself each morning against the distaste of their betters. Though the rising incredulity bothered me little, the rapt attention of so many brought my eyes to fall to the floor, a bubbling mixture of embarrassment alongside a surging excitement as I fully comprehended my newfound fortune.

As Tribonian and Procopius called the gathering to a close, I was eager for escape back in the cocoon of the barracks. No sooner had I stood from my bench, however, than I was swarmed by a half dozen ministers who lacked the scruples of the disapproving patricians. One in particular jostled before the rest.

"Congratulations, Varus!" Paulus exclaimed with a grin that dribbled spittle upon his overlarge lips. "Entirely unsurprising, of course."

I had difficulty suppressing another nervous giggle. "Gratitude, Lord, but did you know the Emperor well? I do not believe we have spoken before."

Paulus' eyes narrowed, though the mirthless smile remained fixed. "The Emperor often spoke of your honor, and that only you could be trusted to fund his passions. I can see his trust is well placed."

I swallowed. My breath came only with difficulty. Though I'd stood firm against thousands of howling Avars in a field of death, something about Paulus' gaze left me feeling particularly unarmored and stifled. More, the impatient press of others lining behind Paulus made me desire nothing more than to dart to freedom, yet no open avenues remained to me.

"Lord, I—" I began, only to be immediately interrupted.

"Paulus, stop corrupting our young komes!" Theodora beamed.

The Minister of the Treasury bowed low, his head nearly parallel to the floor despite the persistent press of bodies. "Lady, I take offense at your insinuation!"

"That is your dilemma to bear, minister." Theodora shrugged. "Varus, you'll follow me now, unless you intend to entertain this mob?"

With a vigorous shake of my head, I tailed Theodora closer than a shadow. A chorus of irritated voices called my name, with Paulus' leading their chorus, yet all I yielded in return was a nod as I wove through the richly attired masses. In my urgency, I clumsily bumped into Theodora, nearly sending my savior toppling to the ground. Theodora's fingers clasped firmly upon the shoulder of one of her guardsmen, allowing her a moment to recollect her balance. Another guard glowered as I shrank inside my mail, sputtering an apology.

"Lady! Are you all right?"

"I am not made of glass, Varus." Theodora chuckled, beckoning to the nearby figure of Belisarius. "General, would you accompany me?"

Belisarius nodded. "As we discussed?"

"The very same," Theodora answered.

Though relief cooled my skin, I nevertheless felt exposed to the dozens of eyes that judged my every move. Theodora shielded against any aggressive suitor, though a mixture of requests and whispers followed my every step. I shuffled so impatiently toward the doorway that I nearly stumbled as my eyes caught upon another, far more welcoming gaze. Mariya smiled and waved, yet as she opened her mouth to speak, I was ushered into the hallway, unable to hear her parting words. As I turned to reenter the cramped room, a guardsman blocked my return, insisting that I proceed onward with Theodora. Raw excitement again turned to burning regret as I wanted nothing more than another stolen moment with the Ghassanid princess, even if her words were little more than the polite musings of another patrician. Alas, it was not to be so.

Theodora kept a brisk pace. Nevertheless, she allowed me to walk alongside her, with Belisarius two paces into the lead. As we hurried to the palace's upper floors, she offered her own words of congratulation.

"I did tell you that Justin loved you," Theodora whispered. "Now all the Empire knows this as well. Did you have any idea?"

"None," I answered. "To be honest, I don't understand why he gifted me so much."

Theodora nodded, although she did not lessen her pace. "Only Justin knew for certain, although I would wager that Liberius knew Justin's mind. I pray he is safe, wherever his insane travels have taken him."

When we reached our intended floor, we passed by rows of excubitores who had been dismissed from guardianship over

Justin's body. Theodora, Belisarius, and I paced toward a much grander hall than that which bore witness to Justin's will. Though dimming sunlight still flooded onto the broad wooden table that rested in the room's center, servants lit tapers along the richly decorated walls in anticipation of the darkness to come.

A half dozen additional excubitores lined the walls inside, all within a single lunge of Justinian's seated form. Justin's intended heir scowled at the head of the table, waving a hand toward Theodora and nodding at the empty seat at his side. Theodora obliged, leaving Belisarius and I to find our own position at the overfilled table.

Theodora took her place at the head of the table next to Justinian, talking idly as more dignitaries settled in for the meeting.

I should have paid greater attention to those around me. As a slave, I prided myself on such awareness—a slave who sees all and speaks little lives long enough to enjoy the fruits of discretion. Instead, however, I found myself exhausted, numb, and awash with more conflicting thoughts than at any point in living memory. As Belisarius guided me to a bench, I discovered my sword hand quivering, shaking me from a trance as I attempted to regain control of my overstimulated body.

Unawares, Belisarius clapped me on the back in congratulations. "Soon enough, I will be coming to *you* for funding," he joked, his eyes twinkling.

"Gladly, Lord, although I am not sure what I did to deserve this," I said, still absorbing the shock of the afternoon. So much of the past years made little sense—Petrus, who followed me throughout the army; receiving a dagger from Godilas or the Emperor's sword—and I yearned for answers about why Justin's fortune was granted to me. The Emperor had promised answers once I returned from Cherson, yet he died before I could be rejoined with him as the campaign ended.

Belisarius chuckled and shook his head, offering me further congratulations. "Justin was a good emperor, and a man worth following. Don't question this gift, but use it to better the lives of your loved ones," he argued.

We took our seats across a cushioned bench as Justinian called the meeting to order, leaving it to Procopius to take notes on its proceedings. The assembly comprised the Empire's leading generals and tribunes; one came from as far away as Alexandria, his skin darkened from the African sun. Procopius told of the status of our current field armies, as well as our border with Persia that pushed ever westward toward the Mediterranean Sea.

"Our Thracian Army is essentially destroyed, and recruiters are actively training new recruits that should be ready for battle by the coming spring," Justinian announced. He confirmed its leadership under Germanus and raised Mundus to the permanent rank of tribune as Germanus' second-in-command. Men rapped their knuckles against the table in support of the ruling as Germanus nodded in appreciation. Mundus still lay in the Imperial Barracks, healing from his wounds.

"Belisarius' Cappadocians are in better order, and I have been assured that gaps are being filled presently," Justinian continued, looking to Belisarius for affirmation.

"Yes, Lord, we will be fighting fit in another month," Belisarius answered, his voice ringing through the room. Most of Belisarius' senior officers filed into the meeting, and I overheard Bessas and John echo their commander.

Justinian continued. "In the new year, Belisarius shall have overall military command of the combined Roman armies in the East. The Persians have invaded over a broad front, and we will need to respond to them in Lazica, Armenia, and Mesopotamia," he said. Belisarius' officers cheered the announcement as others affirmed their appreciation for Justinian's choice for the geographically massive Persian war.

Justinian's details of the Persian army were sparse but shocking. Narses' spies discovered four distinct Persian armies operating across our borders, not including a separate force of marauders to the south under their Lakhmid Arab allies. Their armies already pushed far into Armenia and northern Mesopotamia, yet they had blessedly halted operations due to the increasingly harsh weather of winter. A separate army was forming around Ctesiphon, the Persian capital, which was estimated to contain forty thousand men by itself. The Persians outnumbered each of our formations, forcing the Empire's eastern armies to fall behind thick walls and mountainous terrain.

These efforts were supported by Constantinople, which sent orders and gold to pay for the construction of new fortifications at key crossroads near Dara, Theodosiopolis, and a half dozen other small cities. Despite his officers' resistance, Justinian demanded that these fortifications be battle ready within a scant year, making them key bulwarks in the war to come.

Theodora chimed in, her voice carrying over the dozen smaller discussions that had broken out across the table. "To meet the needs of our new army, we are commissioning new units. Some will be standard Roman spearmen, and others will be mounted foederati," she said, pausing to allow the pronouncement to sink over the room.

"We have reached an agreement with the Herulians, who will supply enough riders for a new contingent of foederati in Belisarius' army. Komes Varus…" she said, gesturing toward me, "… shall have the honor of command of that unit, and will select his subordinate officers."

Belisarius clapped at the announcement, with John and Bessas backing him. Others yielded a lingering stare, their faces a mask of confusion at the unfamiliar and disheveled newcomer.

The meeting continued for several more hours as finer details of the Empire's governance were laid out. Paulus gave a report of the treasury's finances, while Tribonian related the growing lawlessness and rioting in the streets of Constantinople and other major cities across the Empire. The cost of grain had risen to ruinously high prices as a tax to support the Roman Army. As a result, grumblings amongst the plebeians grew ever louder and more difficult to quench.

Cassiodorus, a plump clerk who began his service decades prior under Emperor Zeno, spoke of the need for religious reform to curtail the growing unrest amongst Rome's peasant class. The Church of Hagia Sophia, he noted, remained in ruin due to past rioting from races in the Hippodrome. More God, Cassiodorus reasoned, would convince the people to remain supplicant to our incoming emperor.

The mention of the ruined Hagia Sophia brought images of Perenus' victory in the Hippodrome, including the wanton violence that followed between the patrician Blues and plebeian Greens. From the vantage of the Emperor's box, the race certainly was thrilling, yet the fires and blood that followed left little room for celebration. For me, that day marked the first life I snuffed from this coil, the drunken attacker's blood spilled amidst the smoldering church that Cassiodorus now begged to be rebuilt from its ruin. Evil memories brought me to shudder, gaining a momentary glance by Belisarius before Cassiodorus' pleas were answered.

Theodora stood in anger, fingers splayed along the table before her as she glared at Cassiodorus. "You cannot feed starving families with religion, nor earn their love with taxation. We need to provide relief to the poorest families in the Empire... especially those whose loved ones have been killed in service to the Army."

Cassiodorus sputtered, while Paulus leered at Theodora. "The people will do as they are told," Paulus said icily, "and we will double the city watch to prevent uprisings from occurring in the future."

Theodora shook her head violently but said nothing aloud. Justinian was clearly intent that the conversation move forward. "Once the war with the Persians has come to a close, we will rebuild the Hagia Sophia to the design of Justin and his advisors," he said. Details of this feat were scarce, though Justinian assured us that it would be an architectural marvel that would be pleasing to God. Again, Theodora said nothing, only glowered.

Other points of business were addressed in turn. One that caught my interest was Justinian's affirmation of an alliance with the Ghassanid Arabs, who had already taken to arms at our frontier with Persia. In recognition of their fidelity, the marriage between Solomon and Mariya, the daughter of Ghassanid King Jabalah bin al-Harith, was to take place soon after the Imperial coronation. Justinian also ordered that other envoys be sent to other possible allies, from the Aksumites of Ethiopia to even the distant Göktürks along the Scythian Plains, who might be bribed into attacking the vast Persian Empire.

There was a hush, followed soon thereafter by acclamation. For me, it stung no less than the Avar arrow that dug into my shoulder on the fields of Tauris. One, unlike most of the nobles present, I would soon be sent to face the Empire's great enemy in Mesopotamia, having stolen but a few precious months of recovery from Belisarius' stand against Kazrig's horde. Two, my hated rival would be granted Mariya's hand, while all that was permitted of me was to shower praise and well wishes upon their union. Of both ill tidings, the latter is what drove me to despondency.

Senator Nepotian beamed his approval at the honor paid to his family, and assured Justinian that his son Solomon would be a noble representative of the Empire to Arabia. This was a hollow statement—the marriage would take place in or near the Roman capital, and Solomon would never have to step foot into the domain of his future bride. Most unions between great houses had been similarly conducted since the age of Agamemnon, and Nepotian appeared to bathe himself in the praise of his cronies from Constantinople's Senate and Imperial government.

A litany of other issues followed, yet the cascade of speeches and plaudits faded from my attention as I stewed in a confusing mixture of awe and resentment. Judging by how he slouched in his chair, Justinian shared in my eagerness for the tedium to end, though he still clapped at appropriate intervals and gave tentative nods when Paulus or Tribonian whispered guidance into his ear. Time slinked onward in what seemed like hours of increasingly uncomfortable discussion until, at last, we arrived at the final topic for the day. And for Justinian, it was enough to bring him surging upright, wide-eyed with newfound interest.

Justinian nearly leapt as Narses, aided by the ponderous stack of missives and scrolls from Procopius, explained how the Imperial coronation would come to pass. Narses confirmed, on the advice of multiple Imperial advisors, that the coronation would proceed within two months, a perilously short amount of time to produce an elaborate ceremony, although necessary in order to restore leadership in the midst of a war with Persia.

Not that the outcome of Justinian's anointing was uncertain, of course—through Basilius and Paulus, Justinian had distributed a small fortune of gold and silver coins to all the ministers and military commanders who possessed any power, let alone the inclination, to block his path to the purple. Still, Justinian soaked up each detail of the pageantry, lightly fidgeting in his seat as Narses assured the would-be emperor that nothing would be left to surprise or chance. After a battery of questions from Justinian, the meeting was at last called to a close, leaving many to dart for their escape to fresh air and privacy. Again I sought my escape, only to be denied by a friendlier face.

"A komes!" Belisarius lauded. "Well-deserved, Varus!"

I grinned, inwardly cringing at Belisarius' public praise. "Thank you, Lord. But how did you come to know so quickly?"

Belisarius stole a glance back to the far end of the room where Justinian's retinue privately chattered about further details of the coronation. "Theodora spoke to me days ago, asking if it was a sensible promotion. She made me promise to keep a secret, although you've been difficult to find in the past week."

My smile faded, replaced by a fleeting grimace and a nod. "Between Justin's death and returning from Tauris, I've been a bit melancholy."

Belisarius frowned, nodding. "Do you need to take leave? It is only natural to suffer an illness of the soul from loss, and you've supped of that bitter meal multiple times in the past few months."

"No," I replied. "If anything, leaving this city will do me a measure of good."

"If you're certain, although inform me if your opinion changes," Belisarius said. "If you've nothing occupying your time, you should join John and I for a meal—we've much to plan to ready ourselves for the expedition against Persia. In your new role as komes of the Herulian foederati, your men will be critical to our success."

"I'm grateful, Lord. But perhaps tomorrow? I am still in something of a daze, between Justin's funeral and will."

Belisarius smiled. "Of course, ridiculous of me to ask. Find me as soon as you are ready."

Relieved yet feeling somewhat guilty at escaping the trap of a formal dinner, I walked alongside Belisarius toward the palace exit. Guardsmen straightened as the freshly appointed magister militum passed by, though Belisarius seemed not to notice. From my experience at Tauris, what made Belisarius command respect had nothing to do with discipline or a haughty sense of honor, but instead a willingness to listen and care for those far below his station. While most of his words were cheerful, he parted from me with a warning.

"This war will be different," Belisarius mused. "If I lost at Tauris, Cherson would have fallen to darkness, yet the other provinces would have remained. But if our armies cannot withstand Persia, we might lose everything."

Belisarius' words numbed me, spurring a dangerous and hushed question. "Then why is the Palace giving you so few resources to fight?"

"They can't spare any more than we've scrounged up," Belisarius admitted. "God knows I don't want to fight so soon after the Avars, but our enemies rarely leave the timing of battle to our choosing. We all will have a part to play, and I'll be depending upon you and the Herulians for safety, just as much as I do with the Huns."

Again, my heart sank. Just as I was loath to disappoint Theodora, I could not bring myself to deny Belisarius unconditional support. "I'll make sure they're ready, Lord. You have my oath."

After finally escaping from the palace grounds, I found my way back to the barracks and threw off my armor, collapsing onto the bed. The final rays of sun faded into the early darkness that marked the coming of winter. Perenus pounded on my door, ignorant of the day's events and insisting that our small band leave for the taverns after dark. Grunting loudly, I pacified Perenus with what feeble answer I could muster.

"You'll wake the dead with your pounding!" I yelled as I pried open my door. "What is the urgency?"

"Wine." Perenus grinned. "And women, if we're lucky."

I groaned. "This couldn't wait for later?"

Perenus' grin widened. "Hardly! Be ready at dusk; you're coming with us. No moping and refusals this time."

He did not wait for any protest, leaving me to latch my door and fall again into a heap upon my cot. Sleep evaded me as I stared out of the high barracks window, listening to the buzzing cacophony of the city beyond. My stupor was interrupted by a slight creak of my door's hinges, which swung gently open to unveil two figures beyond.

"He's in here," Samur hissed.

A hooded figure walked inside with drab, loose-fitting garb, making the person shapeless in the dark gloom of my officer's quarters. It walked inside as Samur closed the door, leaving me alone in the entity's presence. My eyes darted to my weapons arrayed along a nearby wall, my muscles tensed at any malicious advance from a would-be attacker. Before I could decide on my best course of action, however, the figure reached an arm outward, latched the door shut, and removed its hood.

VIVAMUS, MORIENDUM EST

"LADY!" I EXCLAIMED, incredulous as Mariya shook off her peasant's robes and laid them across my desk.

She shushed me. "Keep your voice down," Mariya murmured. She shook her head, straightening hair that had gotten caught amidst the coarse robes.

"Lady, what are you doing here?" I asked. And a moment later, when my wild thoughts settled, I added, "And where are your guards?"

Mariya smiled. "A servant guided me through a hidden entrance from my rooms to the street—Sembrouthes will not check on me until the morning," she said, referring to the head of her Aksumite guards.

My mind spiked into panic. "If anyone from the palace finds you here, there will be hell to pay... for all of us," I said, attempting to sound calm. I did not want Mariya to know that my heart was nearly bursting in my chest, though whether it was from fear or desire, I could not know.

Mariya's eyes dropped to the floor. "Before I am handed over to Solomon, I just want one evening to enjoy the freedom of a normal Roman citizen. Several of your friends told me stories of your adventures out in the city... and I was hoping that you might take me along."

Yes. I wanted to say yes, and damn the fates. Mariya's revelation had robbed me of my senses, with only instinct governing my initial thoughts. Nagging fear soon reigned in such reckless behavior, both for Mariya and for myself. Mariya would be surely chastised, perhaps locked in a room until her wedding day, yet I would likely be hanged. Without a trial or an audience. Just taken outside the city, my head encased in sackcloth, and flaxen rope looped around my neck as my captors hoisted me up the nearest tree beyond the walls of Constantinople.

"Lady, this is too risky, and surely others from the palace could escort you around the city's establishments?" I begged. "I cannot guarantee your safety."

Mariya shook her head angrily. "Everywhere I go, I am shadowed by my father's soldiers or Roman guards. Since my father returned to Arabia, Nepotian has made me a prisoner in my rooms, despite all of his honeyed words and shallow compliments." Mariya's eyes began to flood with tears, threatening to smudge her kohl-lined eyes.

I opened my mouth to resist as Mariya surged forward, a hand gripping tight around my forearm. "Please, Varus, don't send me back," she begged. "I will wear whatever disguise you think is best... just let me enjoy this one night of happiness before marriage sentences me to seclusion forever."

Again, I hesitated. Everything about Mariya's request was wrong, from a blatant dereliction of duty to the Empire, to the torment that Justinian's jailors would happily inflict upon the purveyors of scandal. All the lessons I had learned had prepared me to resist such temptation.

But they simply were not enough. As Mariya's pleading eyes fixed upon mine, I surrendered to a longing that could easily lead many to ruin.

"Very well, but you need to follow my lead at all times. If I tell you to run, or hide, you do it without question."

Mariya's eyes crinkled with glee as she agreed. I left the room to grab another pair of sandals and clothing that were made available to my banda and found smaller sizes that would more closely fit her. When I returned and handed her the garb, she gave a muffled laugh.

"This is perfect!" she exclaimed.

I left the room to offer her a few moments of privacy, yet was interrupted by a crash of feet and boisterous voices that flooded into the hallway. I closed the door behind me, praying that Samur had not spread word of Mariya's arrival to the entire army.

Out in the barracks hall, Perenus and Samur bantered loudly to one another as they shared a wineskin. As they drew nearer to my rooms, their words became decipherable, and made me mortified for Mariya.

Perenus giggled to himself. "In Lazica, my teachers used to say that Zeus had sex with thousands of women. Think it's true?"

"Probably." Samur shrugged. "If you were king of the pantheon, what else would you do?"

"A few things." Perenus giggled again, his eyes going wide as he spotted me coming. He whistled and gestured to two other men behind him, and within moments trailed Cephalas and Ascum, the young Alan commander of Belisarius' archers and auxiliaries.

At last, he took a deep swig of his wineskin and handed it over. "Varus! Snap to, man! It's time to go!"

Rosamund ducked from outside another of the barracks rooms, smiling as she saw her friends. She deftly snatched the wineskin from Samur and guzzled its contents before throwing the half-empty skin to Cephalas.

I shook my head. "I need a few moments. Just be patient and wait outside. I will come to you."

Unfazed by my bravado, Perenus burst out laughing. Ascum egged him on.

"Get the splinters out of your arse, Varus, I'm thirsty!" Ascum bellowed.

"Give him time," Samur said, prompting raised eyebrows from Perenus and Cephalas. Even Rosamund looked skeptically at Samur, a half smile on her pale face. My brother was normally

45

happy to pursue mischief on others' behalf; for him to call for patience was wildly out of the ordinary.

"Hold on now, what is really going on in there?" Perenus strode closer to my rooms. I tried to block the door, only for my heart to sink as I heard its hinges groan open behind me.

My friends were instantly silenced, shock adorning their faces. Samur grinned slightly, while others looked on in confusion. Rosamund's eyes fixed on Mariya, her amusement erased as her face turned to stone.

"Sweet mother of God," Perenus said. "Is that the Arab princess?"

"Keep your voices down!" I hissed. With no alternative, I dragged the lot of them into my rooms and slammed the door. The small space was crowded by the press of bodies, and Mariya faced my friends, her lovely features sparkling with equal measures of concern and excitement. The army clothing hung loosely around her thin frame, and the worn boots had nearly convinced me that she would blend in with the common citizens of the Roman capital.

Ascum broke the silence. "So, what now?" he asked, amused at the drama of the moment.

I explained the situation, and that the princess would be joining us on our night out in the city's taverns. No one was to detect her true identity, I emphasized, and she would return to the palace at the conclusion of the evening. Perenus broke into a cackle, ribbing Cephalas with a joke I did not quite hear, but I hushed them silent nevertheless.

"I must swear you all to secrecy," I said. "Do you swear?"

A series of nods. Only Rosamund caught my gaze, concern in her eyes, until she, too, agreed to this caper.

"Just treat this as any other night out, and do not draw undue attention to our group," I said.

Perenus laughed. "So, not like any other night?" he said, drawing chuckles from Cephalas and Ascum—and to my surprise, Mariya.

"My sincerest thanks for the welcome to your group," she said. "I hope I—"

"Perenus, I'm serious," I said. "If Solomon's men discover her—"

"Ah, but they won't!" Ascum gave a hearty guffaw. "And if they do, I'll give them a good clubbing. Everything will be fine if you'll stop worrying so much."

Samur and Rosamund inspected her disguise, adjusting the loose fabric to better blend in with the city. Thankfully, Mariya had left her gold and jewels in the palace, but she protested when Rosamund asked her to wash her face of any cosmetics. Rosamund looked to me for support, yet I relented in Mariya's favor, arguing that kohl was common enough amongst many of the city's Greek and foreign residents.

Together, we departed from the barracks, forming a loose circle around Mariya as we flowed from small alleys and into the busier streets beyond. A cool breeze blew across the neatly lined stone streets, prompting many to clasp their cloaks shut for warmth. Mariya's excitement was palpable as she chatted idly with me, her eyes fixed on the rows of shops and inns that had normally been forbidden to her as a member of the Ghassanid royal family. Each word brought a giddy flutter in my stomach, although the ever-present taint of anxiety forced me to scan each alley and building for a potential onlooker.

Perenus led the group as always, pointing to our first destination on their preplanned route. He threw the door open, burst inside, and shouted a greeting to the owner of the building, who returned a warm and animated welcome to his recurring customer.

Cephalas grabbed a table in the corner of the tavern as the others grabbed unclaimed stools and benches. The *popina*, or tavern, was little different than dozens of others that littered the city, hewn with stone and decorated with simple wooden benches worn smooth from thousands of patrons. For centuries, the Empire's ministers of justice had sought to bring the more unsavory establishments to heel, either to prevent wanton gambling or limit the organized prostitution that inevitably sprung from gatherings of young men and excessive wine. Alas, they always failed, for the more cunning tavern-keeps and lurid destinations always found inventive ways to escape the eye of disapproving law-keepers. Bribery, in my experience, was the most effective tool of all.

Patricians spurned the popina, equally from the crude environment as much as the motley array of slaves, freedmen, and barbarians who frequented the stools of the *popinae*. One must have no desire for privacy or space, for the tavern owner sought to jam as many clientele as he could fit inside the building's walls. They were noisy affairs, prone to drunken grappling and boisterous arguments of some inane subject of the best chariot racers or most fearsome barbarian foes to ever face the Empire in battle. There could not be a more dissimilar place to the Imperial Palace, and God help me, I loved it all.

Normally, the sense of friendship within the popinae left me with a sense of contentment that I never found in the palace or upon the battlefield. Tranquility was absent from the current gathering, however, for no peace could be discovered while I monitored the press of unwashed bodies, sloshing wine, and overcooked meats for any sign that our gambit might be discovered. Mariya, however, seemed not to care at all for the grave danger we all faced, beaming as she struggled into a small bench that abutted an outer-facing window. Carefully manicured fingers patted the seat adjacent to her, and despite a nagging tug of worry, I again succumbed to foolish desire.

Ascum ordered several wineskins and carried the heavy contents back toward our table. About a dozen other Romans littered across other benches in twos or threes, only mildly interested at the arrival or our group. Eager hands grasped at the skins and a row of wooden cups laid out for us. Perenus heaped wine into each cup until it threatened to spill onto the table and passed them around to each of us. Samur took a seat to my left, while Perenus and Rosamund grabbed stools across Mariya and me.

"So, what shall we toast to?" Ascum chirped, red droplets falling over the lid of his cup and onto his callused hands.

Cephalas suggested the Army, which drew unenthusiastic assent. Perenus offered a cup to the late Emperor, which saw a few raise their cups.

Yet Mariya interrupted. "What about to Varus, our new komes? And the heir to the Emperor's estate?"

Ascum's face grew pinched. "What did you say?"

"Komes?" Perenus added.

"Heir?" Samur said.

Rosamund said nothing, only frowned.

Mariya tugged her hood tightly about her face as she spoke. "I assumed you all knew…Theodora named Varus a komes, and he was awarded the majority of the Emperor's estate at the will reading."

"Good God!" Perenus leaned forward, slapping me hard about the shoulder. "Right, man! Fortune favors you! Will you take Archelaus' old post, then?"

"No," I muttered. "Theodora is commissioning a new banda of Herulian foederati under Belisarius and asked me to prepare them for the coming war."

"Lord of the Heruli." Samur gaped. "It is a dream, Varus. Call it what you wish—fate, luck, reward—you will be rejoined with our people in a position of honor."

"It is," I admitted. "As long as I don't humiliate myself in front of them."

If any perceived my dour tone, none paid it any mind. Instead, Cephalas refilled each of our cups, while Perenus beamed with pride.

"Incredible... Komes Varus," he said with awe. He cleared his throat, giggling. "Although this means you are buying our drinks tonight!"

"Justin's estate," Samur said softly. "Varus, the old man had more wealth than we could ever count... and that was just in Constantinople! None know how he acquired it all, only that Justin could raise his own private legion if he wanted. This changes everything..."

"Congratulations!" Cephalas shouted. Again, Rosamund kept silent, but she raised her cup to meet Cephalas' own. Our cups smashed together, spilling wine onto the table, and we all drank deeply.

Mariya wrinkled her nose as she drew the cup away from her lips. "It's so sour!" Nevertheless, she raised the cup for another hesitant sip.

"Too slow!" Perenus reached across the table to tip her cup further.

Mariya's eyes widened as she gulped down the red wine, but she did not complain. Perenus laughed heartily as he cheered her on. "I promise you, Princess, it tastes better the more you drink!"

Rosamund elbowed Perenus in the ribs and mouthed "princess" with a shake of her head—he'd risked giving up Mariya's anonymity. The others, blithely unaware, joined in cheering as Mariya gamely choked down the remnants of her cup and slammed it, empty, to the table, a smile of victory on her lips. This, of course, only brought further cheers from Samur and Ascum.

The tavern door swung open again, and two fur-clad men thumped inside and out of the rising winds. Jovial voices grew hushed as the intruders entered, and even those inebriated to the brink of senselessness offered no comment as the scarred warriors plodded into the tavern and toward our little group. The tavern keeper frowned, though he did not demand that they leave. As the hulking figures drew closer, I made out the faces of Sunicas and Simmas, the Hunnic brothers who commanded the Hun foederati within Belisarius' army.

Ascum grunted in approval. "Ah, they've made it."

Sunicas and Simmas took their seats at the far end of the table, where Sunicas hailed the group and grabbed a cup from Ascum. "Sorry, had to sneak away from one of Belisarius' dinners with the other commanders."

More taciturn, Simmas merely shrugged and drank greedily from his overflowing cup. I shrank a bit, slightly ashamed at deflecting Belisarius' request.

The wineskins were nearly empty, so I withdrew several pieces of silver from a pouch at my belt and flagged down the tavern owner. When a new round of full skins hit the table, Sunicas cackled in delight.

"Our very own Crassus!" Sunicas barked, toasting me as he refilled his cup. "Honestly, though, congratulations to you, Varus. This will change the lives of everyone around you forever. It is no small blessing."

"And a well-deserved one!" Mariya shouted.

I blushed again.

"Varus had to win at *something*," Perenus remarked. "Everyone knows I'm funnier, smarter, and far more handsome."

Rosamund rolled her eyes. "And twice as useless."

Sunicas gave a throaty laugh while Simmas sat silently, frowning at Mariya's hooded figure beside me. He poured himself another cup, the deep lines of his weathered face creasing as he eyed her.

"Who's she?" he asked bluntly, nodding at her. Cephalas bumbled over an answer as Sunicas, too, looked to Mariya, and his eyes grew wide.

"I remember her from the Arab procession to the palace... she's Jabalah's daughter," he said. To Mariya, he said, "Aren't you supposed to marry that prat Solomon? I doubt he would appreciate you being seen with such... colorful company."

"Keep your voice down!" I hissed.

Mariya blushed and nodded. "You are correct, friend. But I myself... I quite appreciate the company."

"So just act like she's any other girl," I cut in urgently. "If she's caught, we'll all hang by morning."

Sunicas bared his teeth in a wide smile. "Brilliant! Fuck protocol and the stuffy nobility." He guzzled another cup of wine and pawed at one of the wineskins, winking at Mariya. "I'm Sunicas, and this lout is Simmas. If anyone asks, Lady, you're a foreign prostitute."

"Sunicas!" I cried.

"Fine, a courtesan, or whatever Romans consider a friendlier word for a whore! Point is, I'd rather not get flogged tonight." Sunicas grinned, and Samur giggled at my visible distress. "I don't know why you're such a prude, Varus. Prostitutes make the best of friends."

"It's true," Ascum chimed in. "I knew a whore in Sinope, made the best lamb stew you've ever had. Only charged a few coppers for a bowl and never took more than was owed, even if I was puking drunk."

Perenus laughed. "So, most every night?"

"Aye." Ascum frowned. "What of it?"

Our next round of wineskins emptied quickly, and true to my promise to Perenus, I ordered another round. Several others protested, with Mariya demanding to pay for the table, but I insisted, and our conversation grew happier for a rare moment of respite, the strong drink blurring the worries of the world that all of us carried in our own ways. Perenus in particular engaged our small band in stories of his homeland, which almost always centered upon past exploits with chariots or within drinking halls.

Mirth turned to general raucousness, and the tavern windows let in thin veins of cold air that cooled my back as I leaned against the street-facing wall. Mariya shivered from the chill and nudged closer to me, her dimpled smile never leaving her face.

Again the round of wineskins was emptied, and Perenus pounded on the table, somehow invigorated by the drink that otherwise muddled our thoughts and slurred our speech.

"Onward!" he cried eagerly. "Where next?" He was met with an enthusiastic response from all save myself.

"Why not stay?" I asked. I was reluctant to pry Mariya from a tavern that was relatively safe from dangerous eyes. "We're getting on well here."

Sunicas was already halfway to the exit. "I can suffer a prude, but not a bore. Besides, there's nothing we can't handle with enough wine and common sense. Just keep her hood down and stop whining so much."

Defeated, I joined the others as we gathered our cloaks and stepped onto Constantinople's stone streets once more. Blustery gales billowed through the wide avenues, threatening to blow over several of us as we tottered on uncertain legs. Though still early in the evening, few people roamed the streets alongside us, escaping the howling wind for a warmer shelter. Mariya edged closer to me as she shielded her face from the breeze, earning a curious glance from Rosamund. As we slowly edged forward to our next destination, Perenus came to my side.

"Truly, Varus, congratulations," he said, throwing an arm around my shoulder. "If I were a weaker man, I'd say that I'd miss you terribly."

Beaming, I yelled to him over the din of the gale. "You're coming with me, you arse, provided that you want to."

Perenus' drunken gaze drew suddenly sober. "What?"

"I'm naming you my second-in-command of the Herulian cavalry... God help them."

Perenus howled in jubilation and pumped an arm into the air. "I thought you were abandoning me!" He then clapped his arm clumsily around my shoulder once more, sending me bumping into Mariya as I fought to remain upright.

"I wouldn't dream of it," I said, my thoughts trailing back to the vast plains of the Tauric Peninsula.

We arrived at the second tavern, the wine flowing freely and our conversation growing more vulgar. The gleam of wine dulled my anxiety over Mariya's safety, though not over the potential offense to her sensibilities, and I stole a glance toward her, who I cannot imagine grew up around barracks talk. On this occasion, it was Cephalas who posed a nonsense question that spawned vigorous debate.

"Let's say a god comes to you with a bargain—you can choose between a guaranteed delicious hot dinner each night or sex with a beautiful woman. However, whichever you do not select is gone forever. What would it be?"

"Dinner," Perenus chirped, without any contemplation or delay.

"Food," Ascum grunted, "as long as it's delicious."

"Always dinner," Sunicas agreed.

Simmas nodded.

I attempted to steer discussion toward a less-offensive suggestion, yet was immediately interrupted.

"But why food over pleasurable company?" Mariya asked.

The men quieted slightly, eyeing one another to see who'd take the bait.

"Good dinner is hard to find on the march," Simmas said at last.

"Not just that." Sunicas chuckled, flashing yellowed teeth. "Because in all my years riding the steppe, Lady, I've been hungry and I've been desperate for a woman. But only one of those privations will eventually kill me if not satisfied."

"Sounds like you're doing it wrong, then," Rosamund said.

The group roared its approval, and Rosamund gave a small grin as the men around her hooted with laughter.

"Most likely!" Sunicas called out above the din. "Most likely. But you haven't seen Hun women. They've got faces like Perenus, full mustaches, and more bloodlust than their men. Not much to inspire a man to improve his skill."

"Is that why Attila never stopped campaigning?" Rosamund said airily. "Because he was afraid to go home?"

Another burst of wine-soaked laughter, including Mariya's, and even mine. The answers forked off into multiple drunken conversations and gluttonous descriptions of what would comprise the god-promised delicious meal. Mariya giggled at each declaration, and even I was starting to loosen up, not bothering to insist she replace the hood of her cloak when it slipped from her head. All was merry and raucous until Ascum broke the fun.

"I heard that Baduarius is returning soon, and will be marching with us into Armenia," he said, his voice momentarily sober. Baduarius served as the commander of Belisarius' spearmen and had remained behind as the Imperial Commander of Cherson's forces. Reports told of relative peace across the faraway province, with the Avars completely abandoning their invasion of Rome in favor of resettling in the steppes beyond.

"A shame about his brother. True shame." Simmas filled everyone's cup to the brim. "To Dagisthaeus... may he know peace in the afterlife," he said, raising his cup. The others murmured their agreement, the lightness of laughter temporarily replaced by somber memories of Baduarius' older brother.

By that point, many of our group became unstable on their feet, yet Perenus roared for a third—and final, as I insisted—destination. Sunicas met and matched Perenus' eagerness, and the rest followed in step. After a messy rummage for cloaks and settling of bills, we were running out into the blustery streets for a final time, the winds stiffer and colder as we half stumbled, half ran behind Perenus in the direction of the dockyards.

"Varus?" Mariya's voice behind me was clipped by her chattering teeth. "I'm sorry… but we have a problem."

I shielded my face from the biting cold, willing my vision to unblur, and slowly her uncovered face and bare, gooseflesh-riddled arms swam into view.

Panic sobered me. "Where's your cloak?" I hissed.

"I wasn't paying attention, and I must have dropped it!" she said. "Should I go back?"

"No!" Tensing, I looked around and softened my tone. "No." It was too risky. When I was certain no strangers were nearby to glimpse her, I threw my own cloak over her shoulders. It hung comically large on her frame, yet she gamely bunched the rough wool together and warmed her limbs.

"It is poor material compared to what you're used to," I said stupidly, watching as the others hustled off through the gale toward the waiting tavern.

Mariya shook her head, the drooping sides of the hood lapping against her wind-stung cheeks. "It's perfect. But won't you be cold?"

I smiled, though my own teeth threatened to chatter. "I've weathered much worse."

Her eyes softened. "You're kind to help me so."

Before I could move, Mariya stepped closer, rising upon her toes, and planted a kiss upon my cheek. It was swift and soft, little more than a peck that one might receive from a dutiful mother, yet in that moment I felt as though the ichor of the ancient gods themselves had suffused me, as though I could swim the Euxine Sea and back without tiring. At that age of my youth, I had not known such a feeling of raw triumph—not even after victory against Shaush in the shield wall. I was consumed by a fleeting moment, willingly swallowed whole into this speck of time where a freed slave might gain some measure of utter happiness.

Mariya immediately turned toward the group, rushing to a trot. I followed, raising my arms against a piercing wind that stung all the worse from a lack of covering. After a hundred paces, we found the intended stop and forced the door open against a violent gust of wind. Perenus had already procured a fresh stopper of wine, gulping and laughing all the while, and Mariya and I stumbled inside, greeted by the laughter of our friends. We took a seat along a nearby bench, and as we settled, I saw Rosamund's contentment melt into a frown.

"She shouldn't sit there," Rosamund whispered in Heruli.

Samur, just beside her, chuckled. "Why not?"

Rosamund rolled her eyes and looked pointedly to where Mariya was sitting a handsbreadth away from another group of revelers. "This is already dangerous," Rosamund said. "We need to make it more difficult for eavesdroppers to spot her face, so that means hooded and against the tavern wall."

Sunicas, who noticed our quiet conference, raised an eyebrow and nudged Samur for a translation into Hunnic.

"If Rosamund's worried, then it's best to pay attention." Sunicas elbowed his brother. "Make room. Our guest needs better disguising."

Simmas rolled his eyes before shuffling to allow space for Mariya—and me as well—to squeeze against the tavern wall.

Rosamund must have been satisfied, for she nodded, while the others immediately returned to their drink and japes.

I did not realize how long the evening had worn on until I spotted Ascum gathering a handful of bronze *nummi*. If we were down to the common coins that circulated amongst the Empire's poorest classes, we were due to be served particularly poor-quality wine—by that point, I doubted any other than Mariya would care or even notice. Even my own mind swam with the heat from strong drink, although an edge of fear lingered from Rosamund's warning, and I eyed the room for potential adversaries.

Despite my misgivings, Mariya and the others quickly fell at ease in their wine-befuddled state. The conversation grew nonsensical, increasingly riddled with declarations of friendship, emotion, and excessive bravado. As the cups were passed around, Perenus grew uncharacteristically melancholy and lifted his cup into the air.

"To Isaacius. He... he should be here with us today." Perenus tensed his jaw against a sob.

I lowered my head as he told of our fallen brother from the Thracian Army. Isaacius was a man as good as any and better than most who wanted nothing more than to be a Roman hero, yet all his commanding officer saw was a hidden Jew who retained no right to infiltrate our army. As our army collapsed in battle, Isaacius was sent on a suicide mission that he attended with the cool dignity of his character, even unto his own end.

We drunkenly thumped our wooden cups together, spilling a fair amount of wine in the process. Cephalas walked behind Perenus and grabbed him in a one-armed hug, his other, damaged limb hanging at his side. Perenus dragged a startled Rosamund into the embrace, and the three of them swayed unsteadily as they reminisced.

Others, however, quickly snapped back to good spirits, with Sunicas and Samur talking excitedly in Hunnic about an upcoming training exercise. Ascum leaned over toward Mariya, a wicked grin on his face.

"So, not excited for your wedding?" he teased. "With Theodora's new laws, you could always run away, you know."

"Ascum," I warned. "Don't."

Samur's nose wrinkled. "Why ruin a happy time with talk of Solomon?"

"He's a pig's arse," Cephalas added. "Apologies, of course, Lady."

If Mariya was offended or concerned, she was enough of a diplomat to show nothing on her face. Instead, with her hands carefully holding her hood in place, she peered at Ascum. "It is perfectly fine. I thought you would ask sooner." She pursed her lips, thinking. "To be honest, I've spent very little time with my betrothed. Mostly I've engaged with his father. Although, upon reflection, I wouldn't call our engagements conversation."

Ascum's eyebrows arched. "What do you mean?"

Mariya sighed. "I forget how different things are here. We Ghassanids are proud, wealthy, and bound to ancient custom. Women in our kingdom are held in great esteem so long as we are mostly silent of our wishes. Our value is in listening and doing as we're told, not doing as we wish. A princess most of all."

I all but reached for Mariya's hand but stopped myself. She had mentioned such restrictions in passing prior to my journey to Tauris, and I sensed that she expected a life of obedience: first to a father, then to a husband, and an especially uncaring husband at that. And though our stations in early life could not have been more opposite—she a princess and I a slave—our frustration at the shackles confining us was the same.

"So you wish something different?" I dared to ask.

"I have had many good things." Mariya shrugged. "I am my father's only daughter, and he could not deny me education in letters or in the world. He even allowed me to learn to ride a horse, although never far from the watchful eye of palace servants or guards."

"But in wealth and comfort, nonetheless," Rosamund muttered. I had not realized she was even listening.

"Yes, for which I thank God," Mariya replied evenly. "I am not blind to the advantages of my birth. But despite all the wealth of my father's people, I had—I have—no freedom. My friends were chosen by my father's ministers, and my movements were restricted to the silks and marble of our palaces. Every moment of every day was scheduled, and I hated it."

"So why didn't you run away?" Sunicas asked.

I would have kicked the man for the impolite question were I not too ill-positioned to execute the attack. Mariya, for her part, met the inquiry with a smile.

"But run away to what? I know little of how the typical Ghassanid makes a living, and I doubt I would last long in the sands of Arabia. Besides, my father would die of heartbreak." She shrugged, a simple gesture of resignation. "I may find the palace oppressive, but I know no other way to live than under the protection of my Aksumite guards and the care of an army of servants." At that, Mariya chuckled, shaking her head. "I sound like an impetuous child."

She sipped at her wine, her lips curling at its bitterness. In that lapse, Ascum leaned forward.

"So Solomon, then." His tone was more respectful than before, and I did not move to quiet him. "That was arranged by your father?"

"Or one of his ministers," Mariya replied. "For years, I thought I would be shipped to the household of an aged friend of the Ghassanids. It is not unusual for young girls to be promised to men with gray hair and round bellies. So when my brother spoke of my union with a young Roman patrician, I leapt for joy."

"Joy?" Samur said, incredulous.

"Incomparable joy." Mariya nodded. "The first day that I arrived in the palace was the happiest of my life. I love my people more than anything, but in a foreign land like the Roman Empire, I thought I might have a measure of freedom."

Her expression grew more distant, as though her amber eyes were watching the passage of unrealized dreams.

"After my first week, I realized that Constantinople was no different from my home…maybe worse. There, I was a woman, but I was still a princess. Here, I am just a foreigner with a strange accent and darker skin." She bit her lower lip. "If I did not have you, it would be impossible for me to blend with a crowd."

Simmas snorted. "I have killed many for the Empire, but no Roman noble would ever offer me a hand in friendship. My only solace is my kin, and those who would die for me."

I gazed curiously at my companion. I never believed the taciturn Hun a philosopher, yet I could find no fault in his words. In a motley empire where thousands of peoples found themselves under the thumb of Greeks and Latins, we outsiders were offered two choices: submit to subjugation, poverty, and suffering, or band together to share the burdens of a dying society. As I looked across Samur, Perenus, and Rosamund, and the others, I knew I had definitively cast my lot with the latter.

"Other than Cephalas, none of us here is Greek or Roman," I said. "That is likely no accident."

Cephalas, hearing his name, joined our conversation. "Roman culture only loves beautiful things. This makes me an outsider"—he gestured grimly at his disfigured face—"in my own way."

From there, our conversation swung between extremes of joy and sorrow, emotions heightened by the river of wine we'd put away over the night. It got to where other patrons glanced in our direction, but only Rosamund seemed even slightly ill at ease until Samur elbowed me.

"One of Solomon's centurions is at the far table," he whispered in the Heruli tongue.

My throat tightened, and I nearly sputtered from an inability to breathe. I dared not stare at the enemy group, taking in only the telltale signs of soldiers' cloaks and fluent Latin voices emanating from their table. Still, I reasoned, they might have been the voices of any of hundreds who had temporarily taken residence inside Constantinople's walls.

"How do you know for sure?" I asked, having spent little time with Solomon's banda.

Samur wrinkled his nose. "I would recognize his thugs anywhere. This one's name is Marcian, and I would bet that others at his table are men of Solomon's banda," he said.

"Goddammit," I muttered. "We need to leave immediately, but without drawing attention."

"Good luck prying the others from their cups." Samur held Marcian at the edge of his vision as he replied.

Ignoring him, I leaned my head toward Mariya with a whisper. "Keep your hood tight. Enemies are near. Make no motions that would beckon their attention."

The warnings were fruitless. For, true to Samur's concern, one of Marcian's men locked eyes with me, his features stern. Though he and I had likely never met, the fierce loyalty all soldiers felt to their commanders meant that he shared Solomon's blood feud with Samur and me. Other members of Marcian's party glanced over at us lazily, only to return to their own cups in short order.

I leaned back over to Samur. Rosamund took notice, her careful gaze following our motions. "Act naturally and don't draw attention to Mariya. They aren't expecting to find a princess in our company, let alone one in a peasant's robes. What they are not expecting to find, they will not see."

"I hope you're right, or our evening is about to get a lot more interesting." Rosamund spoke in terse Heruli, her face set. "This was a bad idea."

"It will be fine," I lied. "But prepare to leave, nonetheless."

Feigning casualness, I motioned that our group should leave, but Perenus balked. "One more round, Varus! We're off to training your Herulians the day after next," he said. "Seize your freedom while you can."

At his words, Mariya fell silent. "Will you be deployed long?" she asked.

I sensed, without her saying as much, that she was asking if we would be in attendance for her wedding.

"It is possible," I said, truly unsure. "We will return to the city for the Emperor's coronation, at least. I believe your marriage is soon after that, isn't it?"

She nodded. "Yes, three days after," Mariya said wistfully.

She tilted her head as her eyes dropped to my neck. Normally hidden underneath cloth and armor, the bronze cross and golden dragon I wore at the end of a steel chain had been pushed to the outside of my tunic. I tucked them away hurriedly, drawing a coy smile from Mariya as her eyes darted back to her cup.

I was outmanned, and my suggestion to leave dissipated in the tavern air. As Perenus sought more libations, Mariya caught Rosamund's attention, asking about life within the Gepid Kingdom. Rosamund brightened at the mention and told stories of her early life beyond the Ister River. She briefly recounted what I already knew of her past as a shaman's granddaughter, spending days collecting herbs and learning the mystical arts of a healer.

"It was a good life," Rosamund said laconically, then added, "though our dirt floors and thatched huts were a far cry from the gilded halls of Arabia."

But Mariya was rapt and all but begged to know more. To my surprise, Rosamund indulged her, and Mariya listened intently as she told tales of the white-haired tribe at the far northwestern edge of the Empire.

Perenus returned, slamming the wineskins onto the table to Sunicas' delight, and pushed Samur out of the way to plant himself between Mariya and me, swaying between our bodies.

Leaning over to Mariya, and interrupting Rosamund, Perenus spoke loudly. "You know, I'm a prince too! Of Lazica!"

Rosamund threw her empty cup at his head. He dodged, then threw one arm around Mariya and one around me.

"We all have so much in common!" Perenus said again. Now Cephalas was glaring alongside Rosamund. Perenus shifted his weight onto me, talking directly into my ear. "Don't ever leave me alone with those Greeks, Varus. I'll be *miserable*," he mock-whispered, slurring his words.

As he made his declaration of brotherly love, his arm around Mariya pulled away her loose-fitting cloak. Her face was plainly exposed to the tavern patrons. I struggled to get out of his grip in a panic, but Perenus laughed and resisted, thinking I wanted to wrestle.

"Give her the cloak!" I hissed. After several heartbeats, he understood and obeyed.

However, it was too late.

"We're going." Samur pulled on my arm. Men from Marcian's table arose, their faces wrought with surprise and anger. I grabbed Mariya's wrist and urged her to the door, catching a glimpse of Sunicas as we moved.

"Take her. I'll slow them down," he uttered. He grabbed a cup and slung it hard toward the nearest soldier from Marcian's group, hitting him square in the chest. Chairs flew back as men stormed to their feet, their voices enraged. The tavern owner called for peace but was drowned out by this small mob of drunken soldiers.

Simmas and Ascum joined Sunicas in the brawl, and I stood briefly frozen.

"Go!" Sunicas yelled, and the rest of our party darted out into the nighttime cold. The wind blew violently, and the walk uphill toward the Imperial Palace was a struggle.

Perenus stumbled and vomited loudly into a gutter, unable to keep our pace. "See him back to the barracks!" I called to Cephalas and Rosamund, who nodded and helped our friend to his feet.

Samur, Mariya, and I ran up the street, wind howling in our ears. My gut heaved as we ran, yet I forced myself onward as I urged Mariya to keep up. She was surprisingly fleet of foot but was hobbled by her ill-fitting boots, which surely chafed her ankles and toes.

As we neared the Forum, I heard hobnailed boots slapping the stoned streets behind me. Panic surged through me just as Mariya's foot landed awkwardly, twisting her ankle.

"We need to go, now!" Samur said over her cry of pain, and urged her to her feet. Mariya grimaced; between her injury and the wine, she could not easily stand.

There was simply no time. Ignoring modesty, I picked her up and threw her over my shoulder.

"I apologize, Lady!" I yelled as I ran. A Greek voice rang out behind us, while ahead, Samur pointed to the palace, guiding us down a dark alley toward a disguised servants' entrance. Looking over my unencumbered shoulder, I spotted Marcian at the far end of the forum, snarling at his men.

Samur found the entrance and opened it just in time for us to spill inside. As he closed the door, I lowered Mariya to her feet only for her to vomit inches from our feet.

"I'm sorry!" she cried, her face ashen with shame. I shook my head and laid a finger over my lips. She was unused to rough treatment, and if anyone should be sorry, it should be me. She nodded, and the only sound was our heavy breathing from the exertion of the run.

In near total darkness, Samur guided us by memory along the maze of passageways that linked all palace halls and rooms.

"Where are they keeping you?" he whispered to Mariya.

"Second level, on a far hallway. Facing the… Hagia Sophia," Mariya slurred. "Horribly drafty."

"Better than the quarters we grew up in," Samur muttered, but kept up his pace through the servants' passages.

We navigated roughly hewn wooden stairs, ascending higher and higher within the palace. Samur led us down another hallway, finally halting at another doorway. He opened the tiny eyeholes, allowing pinpricks of light to flow into our passage.

"Is this your room?" he urged. Peering inside, Mariya nodded. We ducked through the passage door, squinting in the light of the princess' private chambers.

Mariya opened her wine-stained lips to speak, but I cut her off with a gesture to the room's main door. Her Aksumite guards stood outside, unaware that their charge snuck out of the palace long before.

Mariya said nothing. She embraced Samur, who bore her gratitude just long enough to be polite and darted back into the passageway. I moved to follow until a thin hand gripped my arm tightly.

Wincing—for I still nursed an unhealed wound—I turned to Mariya. Her head rose only as high my chest, and her eyes were bright. She wrapped her arms around my body and squeezed tightly.

"Thank you, Varus," she said, her hushed voice full of emotion. "I will never forget this night."

We pulled apart, and I looked into her face one final time. A single tear ran down her cheek, smudging the dark kohl that had thus far remained impeccable. She smiled at me but did not release me fully, and the feel of her hands resting at my elbows was a touch that I desperately wanted to last just a few moments longer. Perhaps, I thought, I might offer to stay.

But no—I shivered at the thought. To do so would be untoward, if not dishonorable. I had surrendered to desire throughout the night, and I would not press my oath to duty any further. Though I was sorely tempted.

"Goodnight, Lady," I said clumsily. Mariya's smile broadened as she released me. As I ducked into the passageway, I waved one final time before shutting the door.

In the corridor, I saw that the thin eyeholes remained open. Samur was peering inside, a thin smile on his face, and he winked at me, dodging my ineffectual punch.

"You want to see this!" he whispered.

I shook my head indignantly and hissed. "It isn't proper, you monkey."

Dishonor be damned—I stole one look inside the room and spied Mariya sitting on the edge of her feather bed. She was smiling sadly to herself, her eyes locked on her hands loosely clasped at her lap.

But we could not stay. After shutting the spyholes, Samur and I snuck toward another hidden servants' entrance and out into the street, then straight to the barracks and our separate rooms. I walked by Perenus' door, which muffled the sounds of violent retching and Rosamund's soft voice murmuring weary reassurances.

I opened my own door and fell inside. Mariya's poor disguise still rested upon my desk, and I smiled. Exhausted, I fell into my bed and was consumed with an urge to sleep.

BALEFUL TIDINGS

THE NEXT MORNING, I woke up alone. My head throbbed as I scrambled to get my clothes together, my mouth a sticky paste. Rosamund had left a pitcher of cool water at my door, which I drank ravenously until my stomach ached. After leaving the barracks, I headed for one of the many palace churches and found Father Petrus.

"Taxing night?" Petrus asked, betraying the slightest hint of amusement.

I pressed my fingers along my throbbing head, attempting to appear vigorous and alert. "Nothing unusual. Went to sleep early."

"Funny. When I was a young man I found sleep restful." Father Petrus grinned. "I had plans for our meeting this morning, but I thought we might discuss the Epistle to the Galatians."

He handed me a calfskin-covered tome, its once-supple exterior worn from heavy use by countless hands. As he carefully lifted the vellum, his bony finger traced a particular line marked in thin Latin script. "Read that."

Nausea threatened to spill into bile, and I cleared my throat and spoke aloud. " 'The acts of the sinful nature are obvious: drunkenness, orgies, and the like. I warn you, as I did before, that those who live like this will not inherit the kingdom of God.'"

"Drunkenness," Father Petrus began, "a habit that our valiant soldiers have frequently turned to. But you are a virtuous influence on your friends' affairs?"

"Unquestioningly," I croaked.

Father Petrus gave a curt nod. He paced to the far edge of his room and procured a small pouch and a small silver cup. It was a crude thing, bent and dulled, matching the priest's plain

69

appearance. After unstopping the pouch, Father Petrus poured a cupful of red wine before drawing a small sip.

"Wine has a sacred place in Christian history, but overconsumption leads to perdition," Petrus went on, "and I know you agree. Perhaps you might share a sip with me?"

The thought made me want to retch, but I feebly grasped the cup. A sour aroma infested my nostrils, and as I brought the cup to my lips, the urge to retch turned to acidic bile. It was no use. Dropping the cup, I rushed for the nearest bucket and vomited before a tutting Father Petrus.

"Go and rest," he said. "But remember how you feel now. All things in moderation."

"I'm never drinking wine again," I choked.

Father Petrus chuckled as I stumbled from the room, wiping my mouth upon a dirty sleeve. At the barracks, I fell back to fevered dreams, sweating into the straw mattress and turning about in half-consciousness. I awoke late into the day, finding others in my banda in a similarly pathetic state.

Even Rosamund looked sickly, her white hair matted against her head. Spending ludicrous sums of silver on a brief sojourn to the market, I fetched her water with a rare cup of shaved ice, as well as a tray of roasted meats and sweet fruits from the marketplace. She slept in one of the empty komes' rooms that I would soon move into, her growing wardrobe stacked neatly across one of the several desks made available to one of my rank.

Rosamund managed a half smile as she ate, one hand holding her forehead. I rubbed her temples as she had so often done for me, and her features slackened in sadness.

"What's wrong?" I asked, worried that she had become truly sick.

Rosamund shook her head out of my grasp. "It is nothing. Just too much wine," she answered in Heruli. I sat at her side, waiting as she slowly revived and took small, frequent sips from my own cup of water. At last, she seemed to be feeling somewhat livelier, and looked at me with the same gloomy eyes.

"Whatever happens, please don't abandon me."

I furrowed my brow. She reminded me of Perenus the night before. "Why would you say that? You are a member of my family...and I need your help with the Herulians."

My weak attempt to reassure her seemed to work. "Never mind," she said, rubbing her eyes with the backs of her hands. "I'll make sure everything is ready for tomorrow morning."

She lowered her head back onto her mat and closed her eyes. I patted her on the shoulder and walked out into the barracks, heading toward the Imperial Palace for my final instructions prior to my departure for the assembling Herulian foederati.

The camp itself was based in Philippi, a mere two days of hard riding to the west of the capital. The city was one of many in the Eastern Empire that suffered a brutal sack by Attila, leaving only bones and ashes for decades after the Huns departed for Germania and Gaul. Emperor Justin had ordered the city rebuilt and populated, with his courtiers positioning several new training camps in the area so that merchants might profit from the Army's expenditures.

Though the uneasy duty to lead atop a horse dominated my thoughts, the duties accompanying a komes of a banda were not insignificant in their own way. I was to be an oath lord, giving coin to those who served the Emperor well and justice to those who broke laws. A komes ensured that his men were fed, watered, and sheltered, replacing fraying tents and ordering broken armor mended. A komes was expected to share in the deprivations and hazards of his men yet remain above the squabbles and hedonism common within the ranks—something that Archelaus never succeeded in. With a stroke of Theodora's quill, I now carried the lives of hundreds of Heruli in my hands, and my own life was to be judged by their collective failures and disappointments in service to Belisarius and Constantinople. All expected of one who, just years prior, had been enslaved to the palace.

My first appointment in the palace was with Narses. Theodora's advisor—who as a eunuch was privileged with easy access to the highborn ladies—had prepared a tally of my inheritance from the Emperor. When I at last found his chambers, he was distinctly impatient.

"I expected you earlier in the morning," he said in a high voice that hardly suited his frame.

I grunted, unwilling to show deference. "Necessary errands," I said curtly, not deigning to elaborate.

"Fine, then," Narses said, waving a hand in the air. He whispered something to a slave boy sitting in a corner of the room, who disappeared out the door.

"This won't take long. I have all of the Emperor's records compiled, and will keep a copy here with the palace records."

Narses recounted the tally of gold and silver in amounts too vast for me to comprehend. What intrigued me most was Justin's estate in Pella, which he'd purchased for members of his extended family decades prior. By now, and by his death, they had all died or moved on, which left a small but profitable collection of farms and buildings near the ancestral home of Alexander the Great.

The income from this estate alone would make me a wealthy man—yielding at least one hundred times more in silver than my pay as a centurion. Narses explained that a steward had managed the estate for several years now, and would continue to do so for me while I marched off to war.

"If you need gold or silver, write and seal a letter to the palace, and we will dispatch it for you," he said matter-of-factly. He handed me a golden ring inlaid with Theodora's name in Latin letters, a cross cut deeply into its center. "This is the seal of Theodora's household, one of three. I have one, and Lady Theodora the other. Anything that you need to requisition while deployed, use this, and the Palace Treasury will reimburse the cost."

Narses finished writing on a scroll and dropped his quill in its inkpot. His eyes rose toward mine. "I don't need to tell you not to lose this, for any reason, correct?"

"I understand," I replied, slipping the ring onto my shield hand. The ring was quite small, fitting snugly upon my smallest finger. As I stood, Narses handed me a heavy leather pouch.

"Some gold and silver for the next month. Lady Theodora would appreciate regular written reports from the field." Narses' eyes turned back to the stack of papers on his desk, lifting his quill once again to scratch comments upon ponderous trade ledgers and reports from provincial governors. Uncertain what was expected of me, I stood at attention, shuffling uncomfortably on my feet as the room's noxious perfumes made my stomach lurch.

Moments later, Narses looked up. "Further, when you are on campaign, you may pass written requests to me through Procopius," he explained. "He keeps all written records for Justinian, and I expect you to aid him if called upon."

I resisted a groan—I became a warrior to escape the duties of a clerk, not to serve one. Nevertheless, I dared not risk offending Theodora's eunuch, particularly if he temporarily controlled my access to Justin's bequest.

"Of course."

"Very good," Narses said, his eyes turning back to his papers. "You'll find that loyalty shall be repaid with advancement, and disloyalty with pain. I do not understand your connection to Theodora, but nevertheless, she expects much from you. Do not be a disappointment."

He dismissed me with a wave, and I departed a great deal wealthier, but substantially more uncertain of my future. Tying the coin pouch to my belt, I ventured toward the palace's atrium and wondered if I had made a mistake. I had sworn an oath to the

Army, and by extension to Belisarius—a season of battle in Tauris entrenched that loyalty. Now I also owed personal fealty to Theodora, who would soon become Empress of us all. What would I do if my oaths came into conflict? Even the more amenable answers like voluntary exile were disconcerting, and I prayed that such a future would be spared of me.

Alas, fate is not only cruel, but also prone to irony. For, heartbeats after leaving Narses' presence, I came upon Belisarius idling just outside the closed doors of the Imperial Hall. Aside from a collection of excubitores guarding the doorway, Belisarius' only companion in the atrium was Antonina—his wife and my onetime classmate in the Imperial Palace.

Though Belisarius and Antonina had been married for over a year, I still found their match curious and ill-fitting. Where Belisarius was ever patient and inviting, Antonina was—as I'd known her—a petulant bully. Though not nearly as unbearable a presence as Solomon, Antonina was somehow crueler, spreading gossip and using her father Basilius' considerable wealth to win the loyalties of her classmates. Even as a girl, bedecked in silks that would have taken a plebeian family a decade's wages to purchase, Antonina knew how to wield influence for her own comfort, usually at the expense of others.

Now, she was the picture not of opulence, but of frustration. Struggling to keep her voice at a whisper, Antonina gestured angrily at the door, balling her soft fingers into a well-manicured fist. Belisarius' normally formal demeanor was forgone in her presence; Belisarius grinned and nodded with each rushed demand from Antonina's tongue, even placing his gloved hand upon hers to calm her. I slid my boots along the marble floor, hoping to stay silent and avoid interrupting, but to no avail; both turned their heads as I drew within twenty paces. Antonina glared, but Belisarius beamed and hailed me over.

"Varus! I was hoping to see you before you left for Philippi," Belisarius called, an uncharacteristically childish grin on his face.

He grasped my wrist in familiar welcome, and I all but jumped in surprise. Though we'd shared several moments in Tauris and during Justin's funeral oration, I would never think to treat my commander and oath-sworn as an equal as he had just done me—even though he was not many years my senior, and even though I had been promoted to the rank of komes.

"I'll wait silently outside the door," Antonina said, rolling her eyes. "There's nothing else I can do, despite everything we've given the Empire."

"Nonsense!" Belisarius cried. "You can speak with good Varus. From what I gather, you both were tutored under Liberius. You have so much in common!"

I stifled a laugh, while Antonina could not help but wrinkle her nose as Belisarius' gaze turned toward me. Though a friendship with Belisarius was a thing to be desired by any soldier, I nevertheless felt awkward, cornered into social courtesy with a woman whom I detested and who loathed me in return. I struggled to find some suitable inroad to conversation.

"Any problems with the Court, Lord?" I asked.

Belisarius shrugged, as if casting off the gravity of the situation. "Procopius' report from our campaign against the Avars is being discussed... and several members of the Court are unhappy that our armies chanted my name as the battle ended."

"After beating back the Avars, they *should* be cheering you!" Antonina scowled.

"Too true," I agreed. "I would be happy to explain that to Theodora."

And so I would have, for whatever small good it might have done. Praise for individual generals had been extinguished in the days of Caesar and Augustus, with emperors fearful that a much-beloved commander might crave full Imperial power and stir insurrection. As the Empire drew closer to oblivion, such worries became all too real. Recognition of formal victory was now reserved for the Emperor's household alone, and it was rumored that Justinian murmured displeasure at Procopius' earlier reports from Cherson.

Belisarius smiled warmly. "Do not fret. I will placate Justinian and his ministers. I think this is mostly Paulus' doing anyway, for he raged against the expense of our campaign in the first place."

I groaned. The courtiers' interference on life-or-death matters exasperated me. Justinian surrounded himself with such men, unpopular though they often were.

Belisarius continued. "Focus your efforts on the Herulian foederati. I will be counting on them come spring when we march against the Persians."

"Any word from Narses' spies—on the invading Persians?" I asked.

Belisarius nodded and told me of multiple reports that arrived in the night and into the early morning. The Persian progress had fully halted; their army in Armenia had even retreated farther east, crippled by an outbreak of flux. The Persians' Mesopotamian Army and Lakhmid allies had been forestalled by Roman units from Alexandria under a general named Domnicus, while another makeshift Roman army from Antioch checked the Persian advance under the leadership of Sittas. Lazica, the least pressured of the three fronts, was only mildly reinforced with mercenaries and Roman gold, leaving the Lazic princes to fight their own war.

Even though Liberius had required I learn the names and locations of foreign lands and armies, my head swam with unfamiliar names and vast quantities of men and horses. I was loath to appear ignorant before Belisarius, but I still held questions about our mission, and could not resist asking.

"Lord, how are we expected to fight so many over a huge expanse of territory?"

"Precisely!" Antonina snarled. "You aren't Herakles. The Court must give you more soldiers."

Belisarius shook his head. "It isn't so easy to bring other units into our expedition. Besides, my role is to defend Armenia and northern Mesopotamia against incursions. Sittas will be able to protect Iberia, and Domnicus the southernmost provinces."

"But that leaves the vast bulk of the Persians as our foes," I pointed out.

"True." Belisarius sighed, slipping a hand through his disheveled hair. "I'd prefer not to worry you with the details, but the situation has gotten worse."

In a voice at times too faint to understand, Belisarius recounted a series of confirmed reports telling of a huge army assembling at Ctesiphon, including sightings of an Indian-trained elephant corps. Led by Spahbad Perozes, the Persian general had dispatched thousands of Zhayedan to reinforce their Armenian front. The legendary Persian Immortals formed the elite core of the Persian army, and famously preferred death over even the slightest of dishonor.

Even wilder rumors were that Kavadh had named an *astabadh*, an overall commander of all Persian forces who reported only to Kavadh himself. The unnamed and mysterious leader was said to be compiling another huge force of Sogdians, Bactrians, Medes, and other wild peoples who populated the Persian Empire's far-flung eastern provinces and borders, riding humped camels and burlier horses into battle.

Little of the news was promising, worse even than Justinian's own public briefing in the aftermath of Justin's funeral. And even if the rumors were only partially valid, it seemed near suicidal to commit a tiny force of a few thousand to engage enormous, richly armed, and better trained men of a thousand nations under the Shahanshah's dominion. My stomach churned to hear the grim news, and I nearly wished he had not shared.

"Lord..." I struggled to gather my thoughts. "This army will be bigger than the one sent to Thermopylae. Ten thousand Immortals, elephants, and a hundred thousand trained warriors..."

"That's why I need you ready to go in a month, Varus. Once Justinian is coronated, we are going to have to face this horde together... and we won't be given enough men or supplies to do the job," Belisarius said wistfully.

I saluted and feigned a smile, feeling little joy and no confidence in my assignment. Before returning to his wife, Belisarius informed me that Justin's former armorer would be meeting with me that evening.

"You're a komes now, Lord Varus. Your men need you to protect yourself," he said.

I thanked him and moved on to my final meeting with Lady Theodora. While Justinian held his court in one of the vast halls of the Imperial Palace, Theodora often met in a more intimate antechamber when the couple worked separately.

As I climbed the marble staircase, I saw that Theodora's rooms were blocked by a number of palace guards, who nodded at me as I walked past their picket lines.

Inside was a relatively simple room, denied the ornate gold foil or Corinthian columns that lined the main Imperial Hall. Instead, Theodora sat in a simple wooden chair set only slightly elevated. For decoration, a huge mosaic of the Empire's provinces spanned the chamber's floors.

Seeing me, Theodora concluded her discussion with a petitioner and ordered the room cleared, leaving only three people: herself, me, and Basilius. As Theodora waved me forward, Basilius observed me from behind her with steely eyes.

"Thank you for attending, Varus," Theodora said as I walked forward. "What we are about to tell you may seem alarming, but I do not intend it to be so. Your mind must be focused on learning to command the Herulians as quickly as possible." Her tone struck the perfect balance of formality and friendliness, so unlike our private conversations where she seemed freer to be frank.

Basilius' voice bore no warmth. "We have finally received word from Liberius," he said. "He is searching for something of great importance to the Empire, and he claims to have found evidence that it resides in Nisibis."

"Nisibis!" I exclaimed. Once a Roman stronghold, Nisibis had been famously lost to the Persians over a century ago. The vast fortress city controlled critical trading roads to the east and gave the Persians ready access into Anatolia, with only the more hastily built Roman fortress of Dara blocking its way.

Basilius nodded. "Liberius intends to enter Nisibis, using unknown means, to obtain the object that he seeks."

I shook my head, wanting to pound the walls in anger. "What could be so important that he would need to cross Persian lines, in the middle of war, into one of the most heavily contested cities in the world?" I puffed.

"That is for Liberius alone to tell you. I can only assume that he will be successful, yet measures must be taken to assist him should aid be required," Basilius said, his eyes narrowing on me. "Lady Theodora, in her wisdom, has decreed that you will be responsible for extracting Liberius from Persia. A tutor in the Persian tongue will attend you to Philippi."

Exasperated, it was all I could do to bow my head to Theodora, angry of this additional charge on top of needing to train to fight atop a galloping horse.

"There is no one else I can trust with this vital mission, Varus. I am sorry, and it again seems that I will be doubly in your debt," Theodora concluded.

I saluted her. "No, Lady, it is my honor to serve you."

Theodora rose from her chair. Embracing me, she whispered into my ear, "God be with you in Philippi, Varus, and come safely back for the coronation."

Saluting again, I marched out of Theodora's Court, leaving Basilius to pore over the mosaic floor as they tracked the movements of armies and supplies across the vast border that extended across forested mountains, fast rivers, and scorching desert. I disguised the foul mood that brooded deep within my gut, spawned from a command I did not want and a charge that I feared impossible. Alone, preparing the Herulian foederati for war was cumbersome but not impossible, for such men had already begun training months prior to my arrival. My charge to discipline a motley bunch of individuals into a cohesive fighting unit was no easy task, yet my greatest concern, privately, was whether I could simply command on horseback at all. Now, looking back, these fears strike me as silly and vainglorious, for only the young could be so bothered by threats to their manhood. Alas, at that time, I was easily overtaxed by worldly cares.

Though the Herulians would prove a personal challenge, Liberius' disappearance was a true test of faith. Why my old teacher would venture into the heart of the Mesopotamian desert was beyond me—even if his search led him to a relic of Jesus Christ himself. I had no idea of how to search for the man, and struggled against fleeting worries that the man had certainly been killed on a bloody and sand-swept frontier. Nevertheless, I was entrusted with seeking Liberius out—alive, or at least with conclusive evidence of his demise. Though I missed Liberius terribly, it was a charge I did not relish.

Moving quickly, I passed by the open doors of Justinian's Court, only briefly meeting Solomon's eyes. My rival, now also a fellow banda commander, glowered at me as he began to approach, yet I ignored his desire to speak as I left the palace.

I walked briskly, making for the barracks as quickly as decorum would allow. Even during the daylight hours, the air across Constantinople grew cold, with hints of frost stretching across the streets and gutters that were stained with muck-strewn rainwater, rotten fruit, and all manners of filth.

The barracks swarmed with soldiers and slaves alike. Men of the Thracian Army received their own orders to return to encampments around Constantinople to assist with the training of hundreds of new recruits, while my own men prepared for tomorrow's departure for Pella. Perenus and Cephalas packed their gear and possessions, including the torn Imperial banner that Cephalas had carried against the Avars. Rosamund carefully wrapped my own equipment and war mementos for travel, including the black Avar battle flag and the white wolf's pelt taken from Shaush, the slain Avar prince.

The others approached me with a wave of excited energy as I arrived in my bare quarters. Rosamund and Perenus hurried me to a desk with wide grins on their faces and thin sheafs of parchment in their hands.

They slammed the parchment onto the wooden table and I gazed down at a crude drawing of a great dragon, coiled and twisted in a way that its mouth gnawed at its tail. It looked suspiciously identical to the charm at my throat, but it also resembled the sword that Justin entrusted to me before I left for Cherson.

"Now that you are a lord, you must carry your own banners alongside those of Belisarius and the Imperial seat," Perenus said, still grinning. "We've been working on this for a few days, and think it fits well with all the Emperor wished for you, and the figure on your sword."

"It is called *ouroboros*," Rosamund blurted out, speaking so quickly that she almost stumbled over her Greek. "An ancient symbol from many peoples, signaling the beginning and end of all things. It is the union of light and dark that comprises the spirits of men who hold the choice in their hands to do good or evil." Beaming, she returned her gaze to her creation, radiating awe and doubtless a measure of pride. Though it was a pagan symbol, the ouroboros seemed fitting with my final conversation with the now-dead Emperor Justin, and I found myself lost for words in appreciation.

"My sigil," I whispered, eyes fixed upon the twisting serpent. "I've seen nothing like it."

My fingers traced the parchment skin, careful not to smudge the delicate lines retraced and scraped clean dozens of times. It was everything that a warrior would desire in battle, both fearsome and unique, easily identifiable amongst a great sea of the Imperial Chi-Rho and the animal banners of hundreds of other minor lords. But somehow it was more, its very creation a gift from those who bled and suffered in their duties alongside me. Father Petrus would not approve of a pagan symbol, but to me, the ouroboros was immaculate.

"How quickly can you have banners and shields painted with this?" I asked the three of them.

Cephalas stepped forward. "I can have a sample banner and shield ready for the morning, and the rest finished when we return."

My fingers found the bronze cross that had been Father Petrus' gift to me, and I stared beyond the parchment, my mind wandering to the Emperor's dreams and Theodora's pronouncement, until at last I nodded.

"Do it, and make sure to have plenty of extras ready," I said, spreading cheers amongst my friends.

When he returned from training with the Huns, Samur approved as well, admiring the smooth lines and contrast between a white serpent upon a black expanse.

"I love it," Samur said, his eyes glinting with mischief. "Although I'm surprised that you do as well. What would Father Petrus say?"

"There's a leviathan in the Bible," I said, thinking. "Punishing the wicked. Perhaps that is now our task?"

A wider grin, mixed with a carefree shrug. "Think whatever you need to ease a troubled conscience. It's a powerful sigil, and will strike a fearsome image on the battlefield."

Our gathering was interrupted by the arrival of Justin's former blacksmith and armorer, along with his several slaves and apprentices. In my emptied rooms, the blacksmith took measurements of my body, barking numbers and notes that were scribbled down with a nervous energy. His callused hands bore the marks of his trade, riddled with burns and cuts from a lifetime before a hellish furnace and an iron anvil.

"I've equipped three emperors, and countless generals and excubitores," the man said proudly. "All will be fit to order, with replacement pieces made available. Any damage will be gladly fixed or replaced, of course."

"And how much will this cost?" I asked hesitantly, still unused to the vast wealth that Justin bestowed to me.

The armorer laughed and casually waved a hand. "The debt is already paid by the palace, don't fret," he said, continuing his measurements. Once finished, the grizzled man promised to have the armor ready upon my return. I thanked the man as he departed, leaving me to organize the last tasks before our morning departure.

After another hour, I bid the others goodnight and sat in my spartan rooms as I stared at the stars that peered through my window. Sleep came slowly, my mind awash with thoughts of Liberius, the Persians, and the knowledge that I would be reintroduced to my people for the first time since childhood.

THE HERULIAN FOEDERATI

T HE NEXT MORNING CAME all too soon, heralded by a rush
of thumps and thuds throughout the wooden barracks walls well
before dawn. Rosamund served me a plate of fruit and hard cheese
as she rushed off to assist with final preparations for departure.
Even after learning of my newfound wealth, Rosamund refused to
allow others to do any work for her, not trusting strangers with my
well-being.

She insisted upon personally testing and serving my meals,
which saw us dine together more often than not. The more
mundane tasks, from the washing of clothes to cleaning the rushes,
she eventually trusted to my new servants, but only after each
passed muster for loyalty and attention to detail. Though I likely
knew more of a servant's duties than Rosamund, I found solace at
her leadership in arranging my caretakers, for even then I found the
task of lord and master as awkward and unnatural. Truthfully, I
still struggle with that to this day—I shall never fully grow from a
youthful slave in the Imperial Palace.

Joined by Perenus, Cephalas, and Rosamund, I gathered my
belongings and readied my horse for travel. Our procession to
Philippi would be divided into two—a smaller cohort under me to
arrive as quickly as possible, and a lagging caravan of supplies.
There was precious little time, for my presence was expected at the
Imperial coronation slightly more than a month later. That I was
expected to bend the Herulians to my will in a matter of mere weeks
defied all reason, yet I maintained no right to question Theodora's
whims, nor the clarity and confidence to suggest an alternative. All
I could do was obey.

Led by Father Petrus, our baggage train had departed the
day before, its teams of oxen straining against their ponderous

loads by road all the way to Philippi. He insisted upon accompanying the slower-moving baggage train, moaning about how an old man's slow pace would only hinder us. He was accompanied by my assigned tutor in Persian, who chatted excitedly with Petrus as the two left the capital for Philippi.

As we departed the barracks, I was met first by Troglita, and then by Samur. Now a komes in his own right, Troglita saluted me, offering up words of encouragement and a promise to share a cup of wine upon my return. With his sharp nose and a freshly shaven jaw, he struck a figure not dissimilar to the earliest years of the Empire, allegedly tracing his lineage to ancient Roman clans. Though Troglita possessed little wealth and only limited power from family connections, I never knew a more trustworthy comrade in battle, or a more steadfast friend.

Still assigned to the Thracian Army, Troglita himself would deploy with Mundus and Germanus to the training camps in the surrounding plains of Thrace, training the hundreds of young men who were recruited to fill the grievous losses that Rome suffered against the Avars.

I stopped and dismounted as I found Samur, who embraced me tightly.

"We're both foederati now!" he said enthusiastically. "Sunicas says the Herulians and the Huns will be working together in next year's campaigns."

"That's correct," I said, my mind drawing anxiously toward the task of learning to become a mounted cavalry commander. "Both units will support Belisarius' army in Armenia and Mesopotamia."

Samur smiled. "One month. I wish I could see the Herulians with you... but I know you'll beat them into shape!"

"Unless they kill me first." I chuckled, masking a dull fear that seemed to churn my guts. "If you were given my duty, would you worry about whether the Heruli would accept you?"

Samur's smile faded, his head bobbing thoughtfully. "Truthfully, yes. Life in Constantinople is utterly unrelatable to the tribes. I can tell the Huns resent it."

"But how would you gain their trust?" I asked. "And how might I earn their loyalty?"

"You can't," Samur said plainly. "They need to convince themselves that you're worth following. And you will succeed—I am sure."

"How are you so certain?"

Samur smiled. "You are fair and honest, which is far better than most Romans I've seen. If you are as protective of them as you are of me, they will come to understand your value. Don't pretend to understand their lives at first, and speak plainly to them. It will be a slow process, but in the end, they will understand that you are not only their kin by blood, but their lord by choosing. And then, they'll follow you into the deepest hell and the darkest night."

Samur's words struck me, not only for his blunt assessment of the Herulians' likely distrust and what was required of me to dispel it, but for the fact that he said them at all. I never knew my brother to be much of a rhetorician, but perhaps his time with Sunicas had invested him with a greater wisdom of the Empire's fringe peoples and foreign warriors than I realized. I wished that he would come with me to Philippi, but I would never deprive him of his continued success with the Huns. Though we both hailed from the Heruli, the task of commanding them was mine alone.

Our route would include one day of riding along the Roman roads, and another by swift boats that would be requisitioned at the Thracian provincial capital of Heraclea. Riding due west from Constantinople, we followed the Via Egnatia, which hugged against the Aegean coastline through southern Thrace and into the hilly provinces of Macedonia. Engulfed by brisk weather, we arrived in the smaller port city of Heraclea, its light ships better suited for our small party than the great hulks and dromons that clogged the harbor at Constantinople.

I presented my travel orders to the wharf master, Theodora's seal marking me as a bearer of Imperial power. It was likely that the captain was unable to follow more than a few words of the Greek and Latin parchment, yet he grinned happily as a bag of silver coins was placed in his gloved hands. We climbed aboard the tiny berths and soon set sail for Amphipolis, a mere half day's lazy ride from Philippi.

Our day at sea was uneventful, save for the rolling waves that brought a green look to Perenus' face. Of the four of us, only Rosamund did not complain, her eyes serene as she gazed into the Aegean and the dangerous freedom of sailing.

To pass the time, we shared tales, with Perenus and Cephalas each asking what I knew of my birth people.

"Little personally, other than what I learned from Justin or Liberius," I admitted. "I've met other Herulians in Constantinople, but they were either slaves or merchants, and never more than gatherings of three or four."

"So why would Justinian and Theodora want their service?" Perenus asked.

I could only guess. "The Herulians were mighty once, before Attila subjugated their clans—a warlike people famous for endurance. And they managed to regain some of that independence after the fall of Attila and his sons. Many even joined Odoacer in the conquest of Italy and helped end the Western Empire. So our generals could only profit from such seasoned warriors, much in the same manner as Constantinople employs Huns."

"I understand why the Empire would want the Heruli as horsemen. What I don't understand is why any of that tribe would oblige," Cephalas put in. "My grandfather hated the Heruli," he added a bit bashfully. "They ravaged Moesia and Macedonia in his youth, though they didn't slay. The Gepids took over their lands."

"It is a matter of survival," I said. "They have always been relatively few in number, and they likely need allies now more than ever, being surrounded by Goths, Franks, Gepids, and Huns. If the Empire needs men to wield a spear, and the Heruli need protectors, then both have every reason to unite."

Though confident in my reasoning, in a practical sense, I had no idea why—or if—such tenacious fighters would accept my command. These Herulian foederati were selected for strength and budding martial skill, which would have come easily to a people acclimated to rapid strikes on foot as well as atop a horse. My charge was to train them to be competent in both: firing arrows and javelins on horseback, and rapidly deploying into formation when Belisarius' shield wall flagged. I held little concern over leading men on foot, but the mere thought of commanding from atop a horse left me greatly worried. There would be no room for failure; Theodora and Belisarius both depended upon mounted fighters in a war that was already grossly lopsided.

I was not a terrible horseman, having spent many hours with Sunicas and Bessas training outside Scythian Neapolis, but my marksmanship from a moving horse was abysmal, and my amateurish aim would earn me no esteem from soldiers who'd spent a lifetime refining the lightning-quick attacks of a cavalryman.

We arrived at the Herulian camp as the sun hid beyond the horizon. The encampment's palisade walls and makeshift wooden barracks were nearly identical to my own training experience in Thrace, though its freshly cut timbers and crisp latrine trenches suggested more recent construction. While the camps and training grounds of more senior or decorated Roman units were dressed in stone and serviced by their own small army of servants, recruits and newer foederati were afforded few luxuries or privileges until they distinguished themselves in battle.

Cephalas announced our presence to the encampment's sentries, allowing us access inside. Guards saluted me as I passed through the palisade gate, some curtly acknowledging my rank and status as the incoming camp commander. All bore crisp Roman uniforms adorned with the Imperial Chi-Rho, and none exhibited any of the stocky bodies or long beards that scholars denoted of Herulian warriors in centuries of written records. I brusquely returned their salutes and made my way to the commander's tent that had been prepared for my arrival.

Rosamund and Cephalas unpacked what few belongings I had taken with us along our sea voyage, and quickly left to find their own lodgings. Sunlight dimmed through the tent's open flaps as the light from a low brazier cast shadows toward its ceiling. I placed my weapons neatly across a low wooden table and sat at the foot of my bed, gazing into the fires as my senses faded. Before falling to rest, however, my tent opened once more, with Rosamund's bright hair catching the brazier's light.

"Something wrong?"

"No," she replied. "I just wanted to say… don't worry so much about impressing the others. They will see you as I do, if you trust in yourself."

I smiled, wondering whether Rosamund and Samur conspired together to raise my spirits. "Thank you, Rosamund. I still do not know how I would live without you."

"Poorly." She grinned. "Take what rest you can, while you can."

Whether from fatigue or a lack of confidence, I did not rush to greet my freshly appointed charges on that first evening. How should I act? What would bring these young men, unacquainted to Roman life, to respect me? There were no easy answers, for the only examples I could draw experience from were Godilas and

Archelaus—the former only taught the sons of patricians, and the latter seemed to crave the pain of others. Still, in some ways, Archelaus' viciousness toward his recruits was sound preparation for the rigor of battle, and I grudgingly acknowledged that some of my former commander's tactics bore sense. But cruelty was something I abhorred, whether toward an enemy or as a means of instruction. Though today many bask in their own wrath and wreak carnage as its own reward, I had been shaped by more traditional lessons of discipline and sobriety, and could only act with violence if there were a justified beginning and a targeted end.

I convinced myself that I could not appear overfamiliar. A measure of aloofness would force the Herulians to see me as an officer, not a mere comrade, I reckoned, and discourage them seeking favors or dispensation for poor behavior or laziness. It was the logic of an underprepared and largely untested young man, and although the commander's persona I crafted was built from some amount of sense, it would prove as ephemeral as it was foolhardy.

The first test of my leadership style arrived quickly as a young Herulian man stumbled into my view, offering a sloppy salute as he introduced himself. Though his body was veiled in shadows from the tent, it was easy enough to tell that he was both young and fit. His body was muscled, but not exceedingly so, and adorned in crude leather, and despite his warrior's physique, his movements showed only the barest hint of Roman discipline, a slackness of attitude that Archelaus or Godilas would have spat upon.

"My name is Fulcaris, Lord, and I wanted to welcome you to camp." His Greek was accented and unsmiling.

I snapped to my feet and walked to the brazier, my eyes forward and deliberately not meeting his.

"Well met, Fulcaris. I do not recall asking for your presence this evening. Is there some emergency that requires you to burst into your commander's tent unannounced?" I asked, stretching my hands over the fire.

"No, Lord. Sorry." There was a distinct note of sarcasm in his voice. "We've just been anxious to meet the Roman officer who will be leading us against the Persians, is all."

Just like the countless lords and ladies who bandied about the Imperial Palace with their pronounced sense of purpose, I kept myself impassive and did not fire retorts back at this stranger. Instead, I waited several heartbeats in silence, listening to the fire crackle as its remaining logs grew black and brittle.

Fulcaris shuffled like an impatient child, although he possessed enough sense to know not to speak up again. At last, once I judged he had stewed long enough, I turned to face him full on and get a fuller measure of this man who shared my Herulian heritage.

Fulcaris could not have seen more than seventeen summers. He wore his long black hair in plaits at his shoulders, and his fair skin was uncommonly clean—perhaps even recently bathed—and unblemished. Though he was neither as tall nor broad as I was, his eyes were nearly level with my own, staring out from a soft, clean-shaven face that belied his status as a warrior of his people.

"I will forgive this breach in decorum, and I recommend that you get rest while you can," I said calmly, yet firmly. "It will be a difficult month ahead. You are dismissed."

Fulcaris blushed and gave another floppy salute before scurrying from the tent. I almost immediately regretted my coldness, but dared not call the man back for fear of appearing indecisive. I was committed to appearing every bit a Roman officer, imbued with skill and confidence that placed me above the undisciplined rabble.

Rosamund left a small tray of food for me at the tent's edge, which I took inside before closing the flap against the cool night breeze. I ate in solitude as the embers burned low and finally extinguished themselves, their final wisps of smoke dancing into the tent rafters. I fell into my bed, my mind awash with plans for how the next week's training would commence.

I began the first morning of training while darkness still ruled the camp. After donning my armor and cloak, I broke bread with Rosamund and Cephalas, who soon hurried to ready the camp for my introduction. As I left the tent, I saw him using his one good arm to raise my banner alongside that of the Empire for the first time. Sentry flames illuminated the black field, made all the darker by the great white dragon at its center, as it danced in the wind.

Perenus soon arrived, appearing uncharacteristically rested and sober in his cleaned and straightened centurion's armor, the plumed helmet at his side. He was grinning. "Well, first day!" he exclaimed. "Any thoughts on our plan?"

It was at that moment I realized: far more thought should have gone into planning the instruction. Several Roman centurions accompanied the Herulians on their journey to Philippi, training them to follow a hodgepodge of Greek and Roman commands and hold the shield wall when fighting on foot. This simple drill was expected to have become second nature to these Herulians; Perenus and I were meant to assign further exercises once we saw what the men could do. Nevertheless, Perenus and I discovered we harbored no notion of what to do. Again, I found myself drawing upon memories as a young recruit in Thrace, learning from a pitiless excubitor.

"Weapon drills today," I said. "Let us see if these Herulians have any skill with combat."

Perenus saluted, beaming with excitement. After hurriedly donning his helmet and securing its straps, he ran off, eager to play his part in the traditional initiation to training camp life where Roman officers wake their men at an unholy hour of the morning.

Soon enough, the sound of clubs thudding into wooden bunk posts echoed through the camp. Bleary-eyed and poorly dressed, men flooded into the central training square, struggling to form straight lines under the guidance of their barking centurions.

The first flickers of light bled across the sky as the ranks stiffened, a nervous energy infecting their discipline. Four hundred Herulians gazed up at their new komes, my armor still bearing dozens of cuts and dents from my time in Tauris.

I paced the ranks, stopping as I found Fulcaris standing next to an older relative, his gaze firmly fixed to the front of the formation. Without breaking my stride, I continued, passing through each of the eight lines that made up the oversized foederati banda.

After making a circuit through the ranks, I returned to the front of the formation and addressed my new banda.

I cleared my throat before sounding across the massed group of men. Rather than reveal my heritage, I addressed the foederati in Greek, the most common language of the Eastern Empire and the required tongue of any who would serve in her armies. "Welcome to the Roman Army. I understand that most of you will have undertaken several weeks of training. That is excellent, for the Empire and General Belisarius are relying upon you in the war ahead. I promise you, though, that you are not nearly prepared to serve in my army."

A low muffled grunt leaked from the third rank of the Herulians, followed by a thinly disguised chuckle. A centurion ran into the ranks, screaming into the guilty man's face. I raised my hand, and the centurion ceased his screaming and nodded in my direction.

"Bring the offender to me," I said, feigning nonchalance. After some shuffling in the ranks, a younger Herulian man emerged before me. He appeared younger than I was, and wore the impetuous look of one totally ignorant of the hardships that all Roman veterans knew by heart.

I asked the man his name, once again addressing him in Greek.

"Alaric, Lord," the man said, his voice full of near-boyish defiance.

"Alaric." I took care to speak the name with an exaggerated Greek accent. "The Empire thanks you for volunteering for service. But you would be a fool to think you could survive in battle. I've seen men like you piss themselves with the first clash of shields, screaming for their mothers and running away. My task is to burn from your mind any hint of fear, and turn this banda into a singular force of death."

I was poised to continue when Alaric spat and mumbled in Heruli.

"I could fuck you bloody with any weapon, Roman."

I grinned.

"Is that so?" I cried in clear, booming Heruli. The shock of the moment was palpable, and I relished it. "Perhaps your centurions speak little of the Heruli tongue," I went on, "but you shall find no such deficiency in me. I hail from the Herulian people, just as you."

The murmurs and rustling of the ranks grew louder and more restless. Seizing the opportunity, I motioned for a nearby centurion to bring wooden training blades. The man hustled as he placed them in my outstretched hands, and he saluted sharply before returning to the ranks.

"Let us strike a bargain," I said slowly to Alaric, emphasizing each word in the Heruli tongue. "If you can defeat me in single combat, I will pack my things and leave the foederati to its own leadership. I will even recommend you to be its komes!"

I tossed the wooden blade to Alaric's feet. He did not move for it, merely stood at attention with his eyes locked on mine.

"Is there a problem, Alaric?" I asked, letting derision seep into my tone. "Perhaps you would like more of an advantage?"

Immediately, I called for a steel blade to be brought forward. It was a simple thing, forged with a skill that ensured that it would not shear or break in the stress of battle. Once again, I flipped the weapon toward Alaric, who narrowed his eyes further.

"Pick it up. On my honor, if you manage to kill me, no man here will harm you," I said, careful to show no outward signs of concern at the prospect. "Do my officers agree?"

At that, each of the centurions saluted and hailed their komes. I nodded and motioned for Alaric to begin.

The man bent over and raised the metal blade, testing its heft and balance with wide, unmeasured slashes. A flicker of worry sparked within me: had I challenged a veteran swordsman, then goaded him to kill me? But no, the fear vanished as Alaric rushed at me, swinging his weapon with vigor, but the clumsiness of a green recruit.

I sidestepped his blows, barely deigning to move my head or arms as his blade whirred over my head or at my sides. Instead, I watched his eyes, which betrayed his every move, bright with eagerness to defeat a Roman commander.

After dodging a dozen or so of the wide and unfocused slashes, I ducked under Alaric's blade and used the flat of my own wooden sword to slap at the man's ankles. Alaric tripped, falling flat in a cloud of disturbed grass and dirt as he scrambled to return to his feet.

"There is no substitute for skill, and skill only comes from the endless training that you will do in this army. Train hard, and you may survive the wars to come," I declared, my voice carrying over the ranks. "I am not the best swordsman in the army — far from it. If you cannot defeat me, you have much to learn about fighting against a more determined enemy whose survival depends upon them killing you as quickly as possible."

Alaric rolled to his feet and charged again. He lunged forward, the point of his blade aiming for my torso. I parried lazily, knocking the blade cleanly from Alaric's hands and onto the grass.

"Fight honorably and loyally for your officers, and I promise that we will do the same for you. No man of mine will go hungry, or suffer poverty, or fear for their loved ones should he fall in battle," I lectured to the unit, ignoring Alaric's grunts as he struggled to retrieve his blade.

Led by Perenus, my centurions began pounding their spear butts into the ground, the rough tempo filling our ears. The Herulians remained silent, observing every move of the bout before them.

Alaric charged one final time, feinting toward my sword hand as he twirled toward my unshielded left. Dodging the blow, I stepped past the man and blindly swung the flat of my sword against his back. Alaric crumpled again to the ground and made no attempts to continue the fight any further.

"I only want volunteers in my foederati. If you have no desire to be here, I will provide you with food and a horse, and you may return to your lands. But if you stay, I will teach you how to fight against any enemy that this world has to offer," I said, tossing the wooden blade down to the ground.

I paced across the front rank, taking stock of the men once again. Alaric slinked back to his place in the third rank, leaving his sword on the ground in a sign of submission.

"I am a Roman officer, but my blood is Herulian. It is an honor to command you in battle, and I will not take your trust for granted," I barked, finally yielding a measure of assent from the ranks as several nodded their heads.

Finished with my inspection, I nodded to Perenus, who barked orders for the men to file into groups for weapons instruction. Before returning to my tent, I spied Alaric running energetically toward the training ground, while Fulcaris shadowed his centurion as spears, bows, blades, and a variety of blunted objects were distributed to the men.

With the centurions giving the daily instruction, I spent my time planning for a more rigorous exercise on the morrow, and reporting to Theodora regarding our safe arrival to Philippi. The few couriers available to me were quickly put to work, and it soon became evident that a far greater number of attendants would be required to serve the needs of the foederati. Though this request would not be fulfilled until returning to Constantinople, I made a note to bring additional servants into my household to execute the thousands of tasks expected of a banda leader, from baking and washing to those willing to clean the camp stables and attend the endless needs of a mounted unit. I knew Rosamund would protest at additional servants, but they were inarguably necessary; I was well beyond my days as a *dekarchos*.

My clerical tasks complete, I summoned Perenus to my tent and asked for a discreet favor.

"Your life as a chariot racer… did it give you any skill with fighting on horseback?" I asked.

Perenus grinned. "That's one of the main reasons I wanted this assignment. My feet were starting to get sore from all the marching the Romans love so much."

While the bulk of the Herulians trained under their centurions and the watchful eye of Cephalas, I asked Perenus if he might instruct me privately on horsemanship. Perenus, only too happy to exercise his favorite talent, agreed, and we mounted horses near the camp stables and trotted off to a good-sized plain veiled by a nearby hill and well beyond earshot of camp.

For several hours, I followed Perenus' instruction. Each circuit increased in pace as he goaded me onward, resting effortlessly in the saddle as he barked instructions.

"You can ride well enough," he called. "Your body is as stiff as a wooden log, but you have good sense in guiding the horse."

With a sigh, I rubbed at sore knees and all manner of chafed skin. "It's not the riding that worries me. It's the fighting. I feel like I'd topple over if I plucked a bow or thrust a lance."

"Aye, well, that's why we practice." Perenus grinned. "For once, you won't be the most naturally skilled fighter in the training yard. You have no idea how I would have loved to send you toppling onto your arse when we were recruits. Archelaus would have kissed me on the mouth."

Though I grumbled, Perenus' enthusiasm only multiplied as he arranged wooden targets that had been crudely painted to resemble an armored and bearded Persian spearman. He guided me fifty paces distant, then ordered me to exchange my spear and shield for a bow tied against my mount's saddle. No riding—only firing from a stationary position.

"We were all trained with a bow until our fingers became as tough as a cow's backside," Perenus said. "The only difference is that your feet aren't on the ground to stabilize your body. That's what the stirrups are for. Get a sense of the horse's body, rise in the stirrups, and fire."

It seemed so simple. Indeed, I'd witnessed the Huns under Sunicas and Simmas execute the same maneuvers countless times. I suddenly wished for Samur, who had somehow so easily learned to emulate his Hunnic warlord mentors; perhaps he could share with me some secret. With a deep breath, I wrapped my shield behind my back and tossed the spear to the ground. I reached down to the saddle, where my fingers fumbled at the knot securing the bow. After several moments of struggle, I unfastened the bow from its restraint, yet it dropped to the dirt with an inglorious thump.

Perenus burst into laughter, nearly falling from his horse as the beast lurched forward from the sudden noise. "The Persians will piss themselves in fear when they see you coming."

"Not helping," I said, resisting the urge to gallop to the nearest dock and sail for Constantinople. Instead, I dropped from the horse to reclaim my soiled weapon before leaping onto the saddle once more. As I did so, however, my momentum nearly carried me from my perch, bringing a fresh wave of laughter as Perenus trotted forward to correct my error.

"Don't be so quick to anger, Varus," Perenus replied. "I know this is foreign to you. Take failure with humility, and you will master horsemanship."

Still flushed, I grunted in agreement, unhooked my quiver, and nocked an arrow against my bowstring. These exercises were familiar enough; the horseman's bow required less draw strength, allowing for greater ease of movement atop a horse. With my mount at a halt, my boots dug into the stirrups as I surged upright. It was a single, fluid motion, and one that felt both natural and gratifying. Perenus did not chortle as my arrow missed its target by a full dozen paces, only nodded at my progress.

"You have all the strength of an ox," he remarked. "Control your breathing, and your aim will follow. Breathe in on the draw, and out on the release."

His painfully simple directions required far more concentration than I anticipated. In many ways, it reminded me of the countless hours of footwork drills spent with Godilas, who claimed that a warrior's survival depended as much upon his balance and movement as much as it did his skill with a blade. After a dozen wild shots, my first arrow thumped hard into the roughly hewn chest of my wooden Persian foe, its feathers fluttering from the raw force of impact.

"See? With the raw power of your arm, that poor fellow would be dead before his body hit the ground!" Perenus exclaimed, his leather gloves slamming noisily together in applause.

Another dozen shots yielded eight strikes, with only one miss sailing far from its target. Before I could celebrate, however, Perenus ordered me into a slow trot, sending my next six shots in every direction except my wooden foe. As I exchanged my empty quiver for a replacement, I mumbled something to Perenus to the effect of such skills being beyond my ability.

"Patience!" he said. "The day is still young, and we have many days before you'll need to ride and shoot with the foederati. Your complaints only waste precious time."

Ashamed — for he was right—I nodded and continued the drill. With each draw and release of the bow, Perenus cried out for me to stay upright and steady my breathing, which left me no time to ruminate between the failures of each shot. I guided my horse to a circular trot around our target, and another twelve arrows found only dirt and grass as their victims, although each attempt grew steadier and more comfortable. At my first hit, Perenus whooped with glee, drawing his own bow and sending an arrow clean into the spherical nob that was the Persian's head.

We practiced for hours. While I would be a liar to claim that even my best efforts that day would have been suitable to the battlefield—my stiff movement and cumbersome drawing motion made me an easy target for an enemy archer—I did find that, as my pace quickened and successes began to add up, my apprehension over my training duties mellowed, even if only slightly.

Though not intended to be as deft in mounted archery as the Hunnic foederati, the Herulians were expected to reliably hit a rider or spearman from at least one hundred paces at full gallop. From his days as a charioteer, Perenus rode as if a centaur, man and beast flying across a low plain in synchrony as he calmly guided his bow toward its intended target. By the end of the day, I managed similar success at full gallop, but only at thirty paces, and only after ten dismal failures.

Perenus cheered, though this did little to raise my spirits as I grew anxious at the prospect of embarrassing myself before my countrymen. These Herulians came to the army with inherent skill as mounted warriors, and would need little instruction in horse archery that would be demanded of us in the coming battles against Persia.

"Excellent progress." Perenus grinned. "Truly. You were born to do this."

"I couldn't scare a Persian child with my horsemanship, let alone a column of Immortals," I said, my shoulder screaming from overexertion and legs raw from riding.

"A few weeks, and you will be serviceable," he insisted, trying but failing to turn my mood. We returned to camp filled with the stink of sour sweat and excrement from another day's labors. With the sun hanging low, cold air from the sea drove many to shiver, although they dared not retreat to the comforts of warm food and snug bunks until their centurions granted permission. I gave that happy signal for the day to end, unleashing groans of relief from the Herulian ranks.

Leaving the others to share their meal in the training yard, I chose to eat silently with Rosamund in the privacy of my tent. It was simple camp fare—little more than a handful of twice-baked biscuits and the sprats that the poorest Greek fisherman could haul from the sea for a desperate meal. Barely better than slop if one were accustomed to the soft cheeses and shaved ice of the Imperial Palace, but for slaves and soldiers, it was rich, ample nourishment, and I devoured it with glee.

Rosamund opened her mouth several times as if to speak but did not act upon that impulse, and she kept her eyes down toward her food. As she removed our empty trays, Rosamund moved toward the tent's exit, halting only upon my request. She gazed at me quizzically.

"Is there something you need, Lord?" she asked with concern.

I shook my head, letting a smile break through my melancholy. "I have told you that you do not need to call me that, especially when we are alone or amongst friends."

"Roman customs." Rosamund gave a dismissive wave. "A thousand rules for a thousand peoples, all of which change on a whim."

"The Gepids have no use for titles, then?"

"None," Rosamund said. "My people would address a village chief in the same manner they would a captured slave. No confusing conventions, no false modesty, and no honeyed words. I have no patience to remember which should be which and when, so I can call you *Lord* at all times or never at all. And I doubt the latter would be acceptable."

"Such familiarity would never be tolerated in Constantinople." I laughed and handed her a leather pouch, its contents clinking. "Regardless, this is for you. While we are gone tomorrow, go into town and buy something. These wages are painfully and unacceptably late in reaching you."

Though Philippi had only recently begun to rebuild after the destruction left by invaders, a good number of traders established warehouses and bartering posts to accommodate the recurring presence of the Roman Army. Many nurtured connections in Constantinople, where for a fee, virtually anything could be imported after a brief sea voyage.

"What shall I buy, Varus?" she asked in Greek, emphasizing both syllables in my name. "Something the camp needs?"

"No," I said. "Something that you desire. Whatever it may be."

Her eyes widened, a thin smile spreading across her lips. "Anything at all?"

"Whatever the traders of Philippi may have is yours for the choosing," I said. "Take the coins and spend them all before returning, that is all I ask. If you need more, you shall have it. These wages belong to none other than you."

Bemused, Rosamund left my tent, my dagger belted to her waist. The coins were but a tiny portion of the wealth Narses

103

entrusted to me, yet it was an amount nearly equal to a year's pay for a lower-ranking officer in the army. I thought of Rosamund as I extinguished the tent's brazier and lay out in the darkness, concerned whether our new life afforded her any sense of true happiness. I did not expect gold to rectify the horrors and hardship she suffered before and during my service, but material comfort was at least within my power to provide. Though she was of my household, I did not wish Rosamund to think of herself as a servant—she had earned far greater trust and status than that, in my eyes if in no one else's.

I awoke early with the centurions the following morning. A small mountain of leather packs had been stacked in a pyramid near one edge of the training grounds. The centurions rounded up the Herulian men even earlier than normal, the sky pitch black from heavy clouds and a lingering night. It was predawn of a day that seemed little different than any other that preceded it, and my sleepy foederati appeared confused but not particularly perturbed about what may follow.

They were wrong. For that was the day that I intended to push the men to their limits, just as Archelaus had tested Perenus and me two years prior. Where Archelaus dispatched three hundred recruits upon a near-suicidal march without any warning or preparation, I intended for the Herulians to fully comprehend the toils laid before them. More, I intended to suffer alongside the men with each bone-cracking lash of the oar.

In full armor, the Herulians stood at attention, though many struggled to keep their eyes open. Outside of the camp's palisade walls, the sound of hooves thundered toward the south, drawing curious glances from many. Taking my place at the front of the formation, I saluted the Herulians, who did their best to snap to.

"Soldiers, a crucial lesson that will determine our survival as a unit is whether we can trust one another at the point of exhaustion and beyond. My men in Tauris stood against thousands of howling Avar spearmen, and none ran in the face of death," I bellowed, my voice washing over the lines. Though I was confident in my words, my role as komes still seemed utterly foreign in the training yard. Most of all, I remained uncomfortable with hundreds of eyes following my every move, although I forced myself to appear at ease, with my head upright and back straightened with each step. I thought of the late General Godilas and did my best to emulate the his comportment.

At my cue, camp servants rushed across the lines, distributing heavy packs to each of the Herulian men and their Roman officers.

I roared my final instructions. "Your centurions will guide you to the coast, where you will be given further instructions. I expect all of you to return to the camp this evening."

Led by Perenus, the Herulians filed out of the camp and mounted horses. I took my place next to Perenus and led a long winding column of Herulian horsemen on our road to where the next stage of my plan awaited us.

A coarse winter gale blew from the sea as we approached the coast. The earliest hints of dawn rose in the sky, with violet streaks breaking through the black veil of night. Centurions reformed the mounted Herulians into lines along the Macedonian shore, greeted by rows of ten long wooden boats–one per centurion within the foederati. Though a far cry from the great dromons that served as warships of the Roman navy, these boats still required an immense amount of energy to operate and were usually oared by galley slaves who lived and died under the toil of sea travel.

Each centurion lit two torches, which threw glinting light onto the mailed armor of the Herulian riders. Perenus stood close as he held a torch high over my head, ensuring each of the ranks could see their commander. I saluted again and explained the exercise.

"The island of Thasos lies about seven miles from this beach. Your centurions will guide you there and back on one of the boats you see before you... and I expect each man here to return to our camp at Philippi this evening," I declared. At that, many faces grew pale and slack with fear. The Herulians were not a seafaring people, and I doubted if more than a few dozen could swim long enough to be pulled from the rough winter sea waves.

My final words were of encouragement. "In battle, as with the sea, your life depends upon the men to your left, and the men on your right. Stand firm as one single body, and no enemy will defeat us."

There were no shouts of brotherhood. No stomping of feet or clattering of spears. No appreciation or respect for the task at hand whatsoever, as if the Herulians simply did not care that it would harden their bodies and toughen their resolve for the suffering that awaited us in Mesopotamia. But they did not balk, nor complain aloud. And in that moment, I began to believe they might be worthy to join Belisarius' army.

Centurions barked commands, breaking the lines into separate units within each boat. I clasped Perenus' hand as he left to command his own men and then moved amongst the ranks to determine which boat I would join on the exercise. At first, I found a boat with Alaric, the man scowling behind a face still bruised from my prior encounter. Rather than join in that unhappy boat, I instead sought the more cheery Fulcaris, who alone seemed to seek my approval despite my occasional remarks about his poor discipline or skill. I found him standing near a man who I recently discovered was his cousin, a man named Irilar, and threw up a hand in welcome. The experience would allow me to test Fulcaris' worthiness to serve as a junior officer of the foederati. I instructed the group's centurion that I would join their boat.

"Glad to have you, Komes," the centurion replied in Greek. "My name is Opilio, and I'll make sure the lads keep to your requirements. They're brash but uncommonly loyal once you gain their trust."

"Excellent, but change nothing on my behalf," I answered. "Discipline or praise, command of the boat is yours."

Impassive, Opilio stroked a dense cropped beard before tugging his helmet over a prematurely balding head. Though little older than me, Opilio could have passed for a man nearing forty, his face scarred from pox and marked by deep crevasses. From all that I read as a boy, Opilio struck a figure common amongst the legions of old—stocky, tall, and yielding absolute obedience to his commander. Though I'd encountered such men in Belisarius' army, I discovered perilously few hardened warriors in my time with the Thracians.

"Listen!" Opilio yelled to the dozens under his command. "The komes will be joining our boat. But if you piles of sheep shit think I won't drive a boot in your arse for sloth, you're absolutely wrong! This is an army of foul language and murderous intent, lads, and I intend to keep it that way!"

Again, no response. Fulcaris and Irilar stole a glance at one another, brows furrowed and eyes wide. Others muttered to one another, their words lost in swirling coastal winds that left a frigid wet kiss against unguarded skin. Opilio, however, snarled in anger.

"Do I have a herd of mutes under my command? Tell me— am I not dealing with men?"

The Herulians roared with defiance. Instinctively, I wanted to join them, almost forgetting that my role was to be an impassive and unconquerable komes. Privately, the group's initial shouts left me giddy, temporarily displacing concern over the arduous task ahead. Satisfied, Opilio ordered the men to the boats, allowing our exercise to begin.

We shoved the boat into the water, its shallow keel scraping along pebbles and sand before finding the sea. I took my place near the front of the formation, and at the centurion's signal, we rushed into the freezing water, low waves reaching first to our calves and then to our hips. As the boat began to float beyond the breakpoint of the waves, men jumped aboard, shivering as they took their seats at its many benches.

Each bench sat two men, with a long wooden oar resting at their feet. The centurion ordered the oars to be locked into place and took a seat before a small drum at the bow. The dekarchos of the ship pounded a steady beat, yelling for the men to row with each thump and creating a rhythm as the oars rose and fell into the sea.

The initial efforts of the men were pitiful. Despite the regular thrumming of the drum, their oars slapped and tangled, spraying frigid seawater onto the decks. Men cursed as they pulled the oars, their faces paradoxically drenched in sweat as their bodies quivered from their wet clothing. Waves rolled our boat ever so slightly, with some weightier waves yielding involuntary shouts of fear and concern. Archelaus would have scoffed, but I said nothing. I would never begrudge a land-dweller his fear of drowning — of all within the Imperial Army, there were few who despised boats more than I — but neither would I allow fear or even nausea impeach this exercise.

Slowly, the boats pulled apart from one another as we left the shore of Macedonia behind. While never flawless, the rowers fell into enough of a pattern where the sound of cracking wood grew rarer, replaced instead by the light breeze and few jibes that the heartier of the Herulian ranks managed to shout at one another. Again, shouts of camaraderie left me nigh on elated — perhaps these men could train to serve Belisarius with honor and determination. More than that, they would serve as *my men*, molded in the vision of Justin and the teachings of Liberius. They would always be horrible behind an oar, but for horsemen in the Imperial Army, these abilities mattered little.

Even after the sun fully pierced the horizon, the day promised to be brumal. One of the rowers on the boat's starboard hissed as he drew his hand to his mouth, showing raw and cracked skin. Blood trickled through his open wound, yet the man quickly gripped his oar and attempted to regain control, clenching his teeth against the pain. I did not wish to coddle my men, but I did not want to seem cruel, either. I stood, my head swimming from seasickness and my legs unsteady on the rolling deck. The injured Herulian rowed all the harder as I drew closer, his hand bleeding copiously and his eyes upon his oar, and stopped only when I tapped him on the shoulder.

"Take rest," I said. Fulcaris, I realized, was sitting behind him, and had been speaking low words of encouragement.

I lifted the man to his feet and took his place at the oar.

"Lord?" he said.

"The life of a warrior is one of suffering," I explained. "But not useless suffering. Your job is to maim the enemy, not yourself. Find something to bind your hand, and once you are ready, replace another in need of respite."

His confused stare soon softened. "Absolutely, komes," he shouted, shuffling onto the central walkway.

I took a seat on the vacant bench and grasped the oar, its wooden handgrips stained by blood and warm to the touch. The bench sagged under my weight but held firm as I pulled with my neighbor along the drum's percussion.

Despite the strain and rigor of hauling the boat forward, the men visibly relaxed after this exchange. The man I replaced soon offered a moment of rest to another who grew weary under the oar, and others did the same, until nearly half of the boat had taken a turn to sit at rest. As the sound of waves diminished as the boat ventured farther out into the open Aegean Sea, a rower on the port side of the boat farted noisily, drawing noises of disgust from his neighbors and hoots of laughter from those farther away. I could not stop myself from joining the mirth, sensing then that my actions gained at least a small note of approval amongst my fellow rowers.

"Ridiculous, Miekislas," Irilar moaned in Greek. "You'll make all the fish in this fucking ocean go belly up."

"Apologies, comrades." The offender grinned. "But it's the fish these Romans make me eat. Maybe a few dead swimmers will convince them to find other fare."

More laughter, broken up after several heartbeats by Opilio. "Row, you whoresons! I don't care if your stomach slips from your rectum and onto your feet, you will row this boat to Thasos."

And so we did. Grunting and sweating, shivering and spitting, we pushed the boat ever farther out into the Aegean. As the rhythm of the oars grew steadier and the labor predictable, several of the men began to ask questions of my own time in the army. I did not expect familiarity on this early outing, and so I secretly rejoiced at their interest, to the point of restraining myself from pouring out every last scrap of wisdom I learned in the training yard and behind the shield.

"Opilio told us of your battles with the Gepids and the Avars, Lord," Fulcaris began. "They say your army surrounded an Avar horde twice the size of your own."

"That's moronic, Fulcaris," another rower called out. "And impossible."

I grinned. "Not impossible. The Avars attacked in far greater numbers than that, but we encircled them all the same."

None of the rowers yielded a rejoinder. Instead, all turned in my direction, seemingly awaiting the tale. Irilar cocked his head thoughtfully while Fulcaris nodded, and thus encouraged, I continued.

"The Avars were fierce warriors, and brave. Even so, they were undisciplined and unimaginative. General Belisarius exploited this mistake to their doom."

"But Lord, how did you hold your line against such unfavorable numbers?" Fulcaris asked, others leaning toward me with similar interest. "I believe you, but such a thing *does* seem impossible."

I sighed. I had not taken even a small measure of pride from our efforts since leaving the blood-soaked plains of Tauris. Normally, those memories earned me nothing more than nightmares. Before the Herulians, the Thracian Army's great stand against the ravenous charges of Shaush and Tzul—our insane encirclement against a vast and confident foe—was something I yearned to recount in full. As I began the tale, the pain in my hands and ache in my shoulders dulled, and none of the Herulians let slip so much as a sneeze to interrupt.

"We held against multiple charges because we did not have another choice. Breaking meant death, and what few men I led feared letting down their friends in the shield wall more than dying at the edge of an Avar blade," I said grimly. "And we did break... after nearly all of my men took terrible wounds, or died. Even then, hurt and weaponless, many of my men fought with their bare hands against the Avar warlord, giving Belisarius just enough time to utterly destroy the ragged Avar lines with his cataphracts. For a morning and the better part of an afternoon, we cut the Avar host to pieces, and nearly all died as a result. That's what war means, and that's what we face if we're unprepared for the foes we have ahead of us."

There came no response. Perhaps my honesty was excessive; I did not intend to frighten the foederati with images of their own potential annihilation. Had Mundus voiced such raw truths to me when I was a recruit, I certainly would have envisioned some grisly death in a far-flung province, my form speared bloodily by any number of tribesmen that stalked the Empire's borders. Still, if any here imagined such a fate, none

111

appeared shaken by it. After perhaps twenty strokes of the oar, it was Fulcaris who broke the silence.

"For our people, there is no greater honor than standing in a great battle, particularly one that would be talked about for generations," he said. "Victory or defeat, it makes no difference. The gods honor the brave. I hope that I accomplish something that men will sing with pride about one day."

Though Fulcaris' words struck me with how closely they aligned with my boyhood yearnings, I had no time to respond. A half dozen questions rose around me, asking about what cataphracts were like, whether the Avars ate human flesh, and whether the Persians were equally ferocious. Though the questions were too numerous to answer, I did my best, and basked in the men's attention.

"You know, a few generations ago, the Romans might have wondered the same about the Herulians when they fought alongside Attila." I chuckled. "The Persians are disciplined where the Avars were chaotic, but are just as numerous as those black-shielded barbarians."

Irilar scowled. "But they have weaknesses, these Persians?"

Channeling a memory of Godilas, I nodded. "All men have weaknesses. I know little enough of Persian customs, but if any Roman can discover and exploit them, it is Belisarius. He commands Greeks and Latins, Armenians and Huns, Sclaveni, Alans, and Arabs, and soon he will include the Heruli in his force. Belisarius told me personally that this foederati will be the weapon that shall tip the struggle of battle into Roman favor, and will be something that no army in this world is prepared to face."

As soon as I spoke the words, I cringed. Surely this was too weighty, too boastful for the moment. But the compliment seemed to inspire the Herulians to redouble their efforts. Chests puffed and backs straightening, many all but beamed at this foretaste of

Belisarius' attentions, their lust for glory and honor sated by the difficult assignment ahead.

Though conversation lagged from the exertion of rowing, light questions still found their way to me regarding the army, the capital, and the palace. Many wondered about the tastes and attitudes of Roman women, while others grew curious of tales of the monstrously huge stone buildings that lined the Imperial capital. I indulged their fantasies with a chuckle, resisting the faint image of Mariya that followed me even into the edges of the wintry Aegean Sea.

As the sun's rays rose to offer some weak measure of warmth, the island of Thasos came into view. First a dim line on the horizon, its forests and hills began to rise into the sky. Opilio's drum inadvertently quickened from excitement of nearing the end of our journey, with the rowers shoring up their reserves of strength in a final push to the finish.

With the shore in sight, Opilio's drum finally slowed, and we drifted onto the rock-strewn sands. The shallow keel slid atop the soft grains, and men jumped overboard into the shallow waters to push the boat farther uphill. Once everyone reached dry land, a ragged cheer arose from the ranks, and I, too, could not help but smile at their accomplishment. I nodded to Opilio, who saluted and fought to retain a stoic gaze.

Packs were drawn from the boats, their leather straps torn open with raw and bloodied hands. Men uncapped waterskins and groaned in pleasure as the cool liquid fell down their parched throats, followed soon thereafter by strips of salted mutton and twice-cooked bread. Many from my boat lay on the beaches of Thasos, watching other boats pull onto the shore and sunning themselves with what little warmth the day could offer.

Some grumbled, yet nearly all joined me in good spirits as the weather remained cool but thankfully devoid of rain. I allowed the men time to rest, forbidding any from wandering too far from the beaches in search of a nearby town.

As the sun rose high into the heavens, Perenus bellowed for the men to return to their boats. Grudgingly, each of the units gathered around their temporary homes and guided the vessel from the sands and into the sea. Thoroughly wet, men boarded and fell into their benches as Opilio began the slow rhythm of his drums, its cadence setting the pace of our oars back to the coasts near Philippi. We were all thoroughly exhausted, but none were defeated.

"I don't know about you lot, but I'll never complain about bitter food or a hard bed again," groaned the flatulent Miekislas. "I'd happily give up a day's meals if one of you would take this oar from me."

Irilar chuckled. "Unfair trade. I'll never be so happy when we leave all these bony fish behind. I don't know how meat can be greasy and dry at the same time."

While less frigid, the voyage back to Philippi was far more arduous. Few men bantered or jibed with one another as their bodies were pushed beyond their limits, their hands and feet blistered from the friction of the oar. Breaks were taken more longingly, the temporarily reprieved rower lying prostrate at the stern of the boat's walkway as he gathered the strength for another half day's exertion.

"Keep up the pace!" Opilio roared. "I'll toss any laggards overboard. With the flab on you lot, I'd be justified in awarding more exercise."

Of course, these words were empty threats, and none of the men appeared to shirk their duty. Freezing spray began to splash onto the deck, and men wrapped sodden cloaks over exposed skin in a desperate attempt to keep warm. The back and forth of rowing soon pushed their cloaks from their shoulders, creating a constant battle between increasing discomfort and the need to keep the boat moving forward.

Our boat did not return to the Macedonian mainland until the edge of dusk. Many of the Herulians were pale and shivering and were quick to abandon their seaward vessel for the horses guarded for our eventual return. As other boats filled in behind our own, Opilio bellowed for our formation to move out, and we made the short journey back to our camp in Philippi.

As we filed into the camp, men paraded into the training grounds and were dismissed by Opilio. Servants handed out roasted meats and mulled wine, which the Herulians gulped greedily to restore their constitutions from the winter air. A small number cleaned and bound open wounds on their hands and feet before a roaring campfire, but most simply retired to their bunks, too tired to care for their other ails and pains. I waited until the last man disappeared into the barracks before seeking my own respite, both pleased and fulfilled at the Herulians' progress. After such a successful exercise, I was blind not only to the danger that lurked ahead, but also the disaster that would soon follow.

ERRARE HUMANUM EST

HAVING RETURNED EARLIER from the market, Rosamund had prepared a meal for the two of us and awaited my return bedecked in her purchases, which she proceeded to describe in enthusiastic detail as soon as I arrived.

"Onyx shirt and trousers from Egyptian linen." She beamed. "Feel how soft! The merchant claimed that the dark hues were difficult to produce, but even if he lied, I loved their look."

She thrust an arm toward my face and waited for me to run a finger along the shirt's cuffs. She was correct—compared to the coarse fabrics of inland Greece, the garment was practically liquid, flowing over her form without any of the itching and chafing most of the common Romans suffered through.

"Lovely," I said. "But why all black?"

"It's what my grandfather wore," she explained. "A marriage of color, unstained by anything it confronts."

I did not fully grasp her meaning, but my compliment had been honest. In the brazier light of my tent, the pitch-colored garments made her already pale skin appear bone white, more vulnerable but somehow still as fierce and vital as ever. Her hair was bound with a black bone comb, and her feet covered with soft black leather boots far suppler and more elegant than the standard-issue hobnails of Roman soldiers. It was only clothing, though in eschewing her usual faded, threadbare linen, Rosamund had transformed herself into an imposing figure.

"It's wonderful, Varus. Thank you." Rosamund smiled. "But that's not even all. I now own a proper collection of medicines!"

She led me to a separate tent to show me a freshly lacquered box, compact but weighty, replete with multiple compartments that could be moved and rearranged for storage.

"Bandages, needles, thread, all the obvious items that an Army physician would possess," she narrated, placing them one at a time into my hands. "But also the roots and powders of a wealthier apothecary. For example…"

Rosamund placed an herb with verdant roots into my hand.

"Some sort of weed?" I joked.

She paid my teasing no mind. "That's ippomarathron, wonderful for problems with urine. And this"—she exchanged the first root for a white powder in a long tube—"is glukoriza, for painful stomachs. I used to grind this plant for hours with my father. Useful material!"

I smiled at her excitement, though I could not have been more confused. I knew nothing of the healer's arts—the palace's physicians saw to ailments—yet peering into Rosamund's box, I spied an item that I did recognize, a plant as thick as a thumb and laced with spines.

"Aloe?"

"Very good!" She beamed. "A wonderful herb to heal wounds or burns. This would certainly be used by a Roman healer, but there are others I possess that would not."

I frowned. "No?"

"Greek and Roman medicine neglects the body and the spirit," Rosamund declared. "Gepid shamans have collected bark sap, willowleaf, ergot, beeswax, burdock, bilberry, and nettle. Hundreds of others we borrowed from the mystics of other tribes who have long since passed to dust."

Rosamund laughed as she saw my concern. "Don't panic, Varus. They won't turn you into a pagan. But I do promise, they will save many limbs and lives in the months ahead."

I held no grounds to object beyond a general discomfort at pagan rituals meldling with Roman medicine, and besides, I could not deprive Rosamund of unabashed contentment. So I merely smiled and encouraged her work. Ministers within the Imperial government might disapprove of a pagan medic, but no Roman soldier bleeding in a trench would refuse an experienced healer, no matter her creed. More, the Herulians under my command, being mostly pagan themselves, would likely find nothing but reassurance from her presence.

Our supply train arrived late the next day and was quickly unpacked by several servants who carried wooden barrels and crates into the camp. Rosamund handled my belongings with particular care and was accompanied by Father Petrus back to my tent. Petrus looked upon me with relief in his eyes, happy that his bumpy journey along the Via Egnatia was finally complete. Father Petrus embraced me and nodded approvingly at the state of the foederati camp but frowned at the news that few of my Herulians followed Christ.

"I will never scold you for demonstrating the virtues of our faith to pagans, but I occasionally worry about those you swear into your service," he said, whispering in Latin to prevent eavesdropping.

"My faith is unshakeable, Father," I said. "I promise you. And all here will loyally serve."

He nodded, still frowning. "I have little doubt. But tread carefully, Varus." He laid a finger upon the bronze cross at my throat. "The Lord tells us that unvirtuous company stains good morals like ink upon parchment. See that they change to your will, and not the other way around."

My Persian tutor followed closely behind. I was to study for several hours each day, but the lessons were slow going; the Persian tongue was nothing like the languages of my childhood. Still, the tutor emphasized words or phrases that might be most useful in battle, and after several weeks, I built a small vocabulary of a few dozen phrases, despite frequent interruptions from Perenus.

"*Dušmen dūraiy arštiš,*" the translator recited.

I listened closely to each syllable, and at his nod, attempted translation. "Enemy spears in the distance."

"*Ima hašiyam naiy duruxtam!*" he replied. "Truth, not falsehood. Excellent, komes. In a few months, you will be passably conversant, if not fluent, though we'll need to improve that accent."

"No need," Perenus interrupted, shaking his head. "We don't intend to have *conversations* with these bastards. Now, if I can call an Immortal's mother a hairy goat, that will garner us a measure of success, but..."

The interpreter shot me an exasperated look.

"Perhaps another time," I said. "For now, Belisarius needs me to train with these foreign words, with no distractions. If you would like to study with me, I shall enjoy your company."

At the suggestion of days of rigorous study, Perenus dismissed himself, as I suspected he would. I never truly enjoyed the additional obligation, burdened as I was with my duties to the banda, but regular study of the Persian tongue did give me a certain feeling of accomplishment. Though many Roman soldiers would have scoffed at language lessons as a task for clerks and eunuchs, I knew that if I wanted to both survive in a Mesopotamian war and search for Liberius, building skill in the Persian tongue was far from busywork.

The remainder of that first week was filled with weapons practice and an endless list of drills to build stamina and harden muscle. Rosamund attended to the more serious bruises and injuries that inevitably arose in a Roman camp, while Perenus and I tirelessly trained for horse archery and general husbandry. As the second week started, more of my arrows hit their mark while galloping at a fast pace, yet I was still woefully insufficient in comparison to what was expected of the Herulian foederati in our upcoming war.

It was exhausting, endless toil. But I grew more confident in both the Herulians' discipline and my own ability to command, and ended each evening with a sense of progress. As the foederati drilled, I either expanded my Persian vocabulary or built up my endurance in the saddle. I earned particular praise for improving my still-limited accuracy at a gallop, and I even managed to assuage Father Petrus' fears for my soul through daily lessons with the Gospels, although I made few attempts at encouraging others to join.

I had not been required to demonstrate riding skill before the full foederati, but after nearly two weeks of daylong lessons with Perenus, this obligation was no longer possible to delay.

"You're more than ready for this," Perenus whispered as the Herulians donned their patchwork armor. "Keep calm in the saddle, and don't let emotion overtake you. With that clarity, you will ride through the hills like Alexander."

"Indeed." I was not so certain. Though I felt flashes of confidence at the end of each private lesson with Perenus, I felt only anxiety boiling in my guts as my banda saddled their mounts. I was even tempted to cancel the exercise, thinking up some excuse to delay another week, but I knew a last-minute delay would make me seem indecisive at best, if not weak or downright cowardly. So, with a silent prayer, I committed myself to the riding drill, begging God to keep me from humiliation before my kinsmen.

Four hundred Herulian riders and their centurions mounted horses and readied themselves in rows along the camp's training grounds. While the Herulians had been middling swordsmen or spearmen upon my arrival, they were effortless riders, maneuvering their horses with frightening ease. Each rider held a bow, two short spears, and a long spatha, which is a top-heavy blade useful for the heavy-impact slash that comes from a charging horseman. Despite considerable time spent scouring and cleaning, each of their weapons and armor bore signs of overuse and even rust, although no Herulian complained. These steel instruments would have been cherished amongst the tribes, passed from father to son regardless of any imperfections in the metal or overworn leather in the saddle.

I mounted a horse that had been saddled for me and nodded to Perenus, who bellowed an order to fall out of the camp and proceed toward the plains beyond. Though small, Philippi was chosen expressly as an ideal location to train horsemen for its multiple types of terrain, from flat grasslands that hugged the Aegean coast to hillier and craggier country that typified the more inland regions of the Macedonian Provinces, offering the necessary variety. Many centuries prior, the region had been a training ground for many of Alexander's Companions, which famously fought in desert and jungle, mountain and plain, all throughout the east. Even I, unaccustomed to fighting in the saddle, understood Philippi's value as a cradle for horsemen.

Soon we arrived at our designated training location—a rolling grassland that gave ample space to train riders in tight formations as well as mounted group archery. I gave Perenus position as lead centurion of the foederati and the direct commander of half of the men, with me leading the rest. Together, I reasoned, we would form twin pincers that could move fluidly around a set target. Servants erected dozens of wooden posts and sand-filled sacks in the center of our formation, an army of dummy Persian spearman and cavalry.

Nervous, I signaled for the exercise to begin, and a rush of horses poured forth and quickly rose to a full gallop. I kept a strong pace at the front of my two hundred riders, fighting to keep proper form atop the horse as wind whipped around us and made my plume wave about. Thundering in a broad circle, we soon closed the loop with Perenus' formation, with no man having fallen or lagged behind in the process.

We spent much of that morning pushing the horses onward, riding hard in the worn saddles allocated to us from Constantinople. Few griped over such a rigorous drill, with most of the Herulian men having spent much of their childhoods riding horses in the lands north of Dalmatia. After a short rest, the men were equipped with bows and a sheaf each of blunted arrows, and the true test began.

The exercise started at half speed, with the horses barely nudged into a fast trot. I drew my bow and nocked an arrow, picking a target at the center. Mouthing another prayer, I simultaneously recalled Perenus' insistence upon proper breathing, regulating the rise and fall of my chest as I gave the first order to strike.

"Draw!" I yelled, with my two hundred Herulians swiftly obeying as they pulled bowstrings back to their ears.

There was only the briefest pause. Unlike foot archers, horsemen preferred to launch their missiles in one fluid motion, with the strain of holding back a taut bowstring doubly taxing when staying balanced atop stirrups. Having practiced hundreds of attempts with Perenus, I understood such concerns well. More, however, I worried about overthinking the effort and choking my own success, sending an arrow sailing wildly off target to a chorus of laughter. Instead, I followed each of Perenus' instructions, desperate to prove to the foederati that I had earned the right to lead these men into war.

"Loose!" I called again, and a volley of arrows rang out fifty paces from the still targets. From the far end of the field, Perenus' horse archers followed suit, leading a hail of blunted wood to fall.

Euphoric relief flooded over me as my arrow sailed true, landing near the center of the formation at a taller target. Most of the Herulian arrows had similar measures of success, the force of the blow lodging even the wood-tipped shafts deep into their intended targets. Splinters rained from each mock Persian, causing many to waver from the sheer force of repeated impact. The Herulian arrows were like rain, their honed steel arrowheads covering the ground so thick and fast that even Sunicas and the Huns would have approved.

We went for another round, kicking our horses into a faster gallop with Perenus mirroring our movements on the opposite side of the circle. I plucked another arrow from a loose cloth sheaf and called again for the men to draw back the nocked arrows into their bowstrings. Even at that fast speed, nearly all arrows again found their mark at the center of the formation, popping sand-packed bags that spilled onto the ground below.

My arrow was not among those which found their proper target. Its feathered edge easily noticeable in the grasses outside of the massed wooden targets, my arrow fell five paces short of an acceptable mark. I stole a glance back at the ranks, checking to see if any deigned to laugh or criticize their commander, but I was met by stony glances as the men awaited their next orders. Shuddering, I plucked another arrow from my quiver, snarling for the men to follow close behind.

I guided my horse farther away, widening the loop of our training circle to eighty paces and close to the radius of what our foederati would be expected to execute in the midst of battle. Flecks of spittle flew from my horse's mouth as I sped to a fast gallop, and as I drew another arrow, I picked a target—no thoughts on my breathing or the instincts of my mount. I gritted my teeth and roared my orders, shot through with lust for a sure strike on the Persian.

The call to draw and loose our volley came and went, and again nearly all my Herulian riders hit their targets. Once again, my arrow fell well short of its mark, joining my earlier arrow as a monument to my failure. I wanted to scream, to drive a fist into the crude wood, to insist that I made splinters of such targets just a day prior. Only, when none were watching, save Perenus.

"Fucking hell," I grunted.

"Lord?" called some Herulian behind me.

I did not answer. A burning sensation rose from my chest and toward my face, yet I refused to look back or stop the drill. I kicked my horse forward again into a murderous gallop. Men rushed behind me, their horses' hooves rumbling into the dirt like mallets atop a massive drum. I called for another volley, prompting another compact volley of shafts that would have skewered a massed Persian line.

My arrow sailed far overhead, driving itself into the soft soil beyond the center targets. The gallop continued as I refused to break, my face flush with shame I could not fight back.

But further disaster struck. I paid no attention to the ground head of my speeding horse. One of its hooves grazed a rounded stone, and my mount buckled with a jerk that sent me sailing from the saddle. I landed several paces away; soft grasses broke my fall, yet I struggled to breathe. Gasping, I raised my arms over my head, afraid I might be trampled.

That wave of hooves never came, with my men smoothly halting their progress before my crumpled body. Concerned and confused voices called out from the formation, with several men dismounting around me. Fulcaris appeared from the corner of my eye, his eyes wide with fear as he called for help.

Other voices grunted in disdain, however. I heard two men muttering to each other in Herulian, their voices not ten paces from my prostrate body. There was no laughter, nor any noises of concern. Only disappointment and anger. And to me, drawing jagged breaths with sore ribs and stifling moans, their response could not have been worse.

"A man who cannot shoot from horseback is no warrior," I heard one sneer. Through the low din of voices that worried over my body, I recognized the next one.

"A man who is thrown from his horse is not a man." Alaric swore and spit onto the grass. At that, Fulcaris popped upright, and men flooded forth in a scuffle. I fought to sit up, my chest pounding, cursing God for allowing me to live through such an accident; if my neck snapped or head was smashed open, I would not have had to hear to the derision of my men, or my own thoughts as they repeated my deepest fear—that I was incompetent, little more than an upjumped dekarchos, a soft Imperial favorite with no real right to command.

"He whipped you easily, Alaric. If he is no warrior, what does that make you?" Fulcaris growled.

Another of Fulcaris' friends moved closely behind. "Since the Commander arrived, I've been fed regularly and treated fairly. That's more than I can say of any of those other perfumed Romans."

Others voiced their approval, although Alaric and his contingent stepped forward impetuously. "Yes, he fights well on foot. In battle, however, a leader who cannot ride or shoot will lead us all to our deaths. I joined the Roman Army to pursue a better life and to protect my people... not to be massacred on some desert border against a foe I have no quarrel with," Alaric said, raising the anger of the massed men.

"Back up! I said back into lines!" Perenus called in Greek. At Perenus' command, several centurions began to enforce order as they directed the men to remount their horses.

"Gently now, pick him up and carry him back to the camp," Perenus said to the other officers. "His servant can see to his injuries and pray to her gods that his lung is not punctured."

"Stop blaspheming," I said, and coughed.

Perenus only laughed. "Stop speaking," he said, and I obliged as riders slowly carried me back to camp and into my tent.

The camp medic was pale as he assessed my condition, but was soon flushed with indignation as Rosamund arrived.

"Lord, this Gepid woman has no right to practice the healing arts in a military camp," he sputtered. "She is more like to kill you than to offer any relief!"

I coughed a response. "Leave us," I rasped. The guards saluted and departed, but the medic stood still. "Leave me with Rosamund," I clarified.

The medic's face pinched like he'd eaten something sour, but he left without argument.

Finally alone, Rosamund hurried to my side, her hands running over my arms and torso as she collected an understanding of my injuries. Gingerly, she removed my armor, its rents still showing damage from our battles in the Tauric Peninsula. I used my failing strength to prop myself up and survey my bare chest.

Though still young, my body already held multiple scars and wounds from my time with the Roman Army. One forearm held a thin white line that served as a reminder from my raid into the Gepid Kingdom, while a puckered circle on my shoulder as well as a dozen smaller gashes lined my body from my battles against the Avars. Perhaps most shocking was a ragged and angry scar on my left hip, a more grievous injury taken from single combat with my former commander, Archelaus.

Rosamund frowned as she examined my body. "I don't feel any breaks, although I can't be sure," she said in low, soft Herulian. "You will feel stiff and sore for several days, though."

She set to pulling jars from her box of herbs and medicines and ground together several ingredients into a sticky white paste, which she lightly applied to my flanks and back. It soothed some of the pulsing pain that radiated up through my spine.

Rosamund also concocted an elixir and urged me to drink it. "It will help you sleep, and your body to mend itself," she said.

I nodded and drank with her help. After several minutes, my eyes grew heavy despite the sunlight that still flooded into the tent, and I fell asleep as Rosamund sat at the foot of my bed.

I awoke late in the following afternoon, finding Rosamund napping in a far corner of the tent. Always a light sleeper, Rosamund shook awake at the sound of my rustling and brought a pitcher of cool water and simple food. She fetched Father Petrus, who blessed my good fortune having been not seriously injured from the fall. Under his arm was a stack of scrolls and documents, all sealed and unread.

A flurry of dispatches had arrived from the Capitol, detailing dramatic shifts in the Empire's fortunes at multiple points of the ongoing war. Each of the scrolls bore the seal of Theodora, and emphasized, in the small, prim handwriting of her advisor Narses, the importance of the Herulian foederati in the coming year.

Our provinces along the Ister had been raided by a loose alliance of Gepids, Sclaveni, and Langobards, which found their greatest successes in the Roman province of Scythia Minor. There, a war band of Sclaveni routed the local *limitanei* and ruthlessly sacked the provincial capital of Tomis, scattering its people and making off with vast herds of sheep and cattle. The still undermanned and untrained Thracian Army had been called to beat back the three-pronged attack, with Germanus, Mundus, and Troglita leading separate wings against each of the three barbarian tribes.

Meanwhile, Justinian had been largely unsuccessful in recruiting allies for war against the Persians. Kavadh had bribed the Hephthalites to attack the vast Göktürk Khaganate, leaving the distant northern Empire uninterested in sending soldiers to attack the Persians farther south. Likewise, none of the rich principalities of India were interested in such a military venture, preferring instead to profit from the continued trade with the warring Roman and Persian Empires. One sliver of positive news came from the Aksumite Kingdom, which pledged itself and its warriors to the Roman cause. The Aksumites threatened the Persian hold over southern Arabia, and even a limited invasion of Himyar might weaken the forces that Kavadh and his astabadh could deploy across their extensive border with Rome.

But such good news was hardly enough to outweigh the rest. Worst of all were the grim tidings of Persian movements in Mesopotamia. Though still limited in their effect in midwinter, the Persians launched raids from their positions near Nisibis and Tigranocerta, enveloping a number of Roman towns and driving a wedge between the armies of Sittas in the north and Domnicus to the south. Within that salient, several critical Roman fortress cities had been nearly cut off from resupply, including Martyropolis, Amida, and Dara. The loss of this region meant losing Mesopotamia, and likely the wealthier lands of Syria beyond that. Strategically, it was a massive blow, but I feared more personally for Liberius. This left him in even greater danger, for even if he safely arrived in Persian Nisibis, the effective border back into safe Roman territory had moved dozens of miles westward.

The last message was of a more personal note. Whereas Narses' wrote in neat Greek letters, this message was in Latin, with bulkier script that was written exclusively for my eyes.

The letter was addressed from Theodora herself, and thanked me again for my sacrifices in training the Herulians for battle.

For your services to the Empire, Theodora wrote, *I have secured for you a marriage contract with Hilda, the natural daughter of the late Vandal King Thrasamund and a half brother to their current King Hilderic. The marriage will take place at the spring equinox, one month before the Roman armies will deploy against our enemy in Persia.*

Had the letter not been signed in Theodora's name and sealed with red wax, I would have hardly believed it was the truth.

As I took in this last message, Perenus entered the tent, expressing gratitude for my recovery that I barely perceived. Instead, I reread Theodora's final message aloud.

"Who is she?" I asked Father Petrus. "This..." I was too stunned to speak aloud the name of my bride-to-be.

"Hilda," Father Petrus said, "is approximately thirty years old. And she is reputed to favor the true faith," he added piously.

A woman nearly a decade my senior, whom I had never met. My hopes dropped. "But what of her nature?" I asked. "What is she like?"

Petrus sighed. "Hilda is also thought to be prone to... fits of madness," he said reluctantly.

"That would explain why she hasn't married," Perenus said dryly. "You're sure of this, Father?"

"From what Basilius has told me, yes," Father Petrus replied.

I glared at him. "You knew of this already?" I asked.

Father Petrus shrugged. "Only that it was a possibility. It seems the new Vandal king, Hilderic, has a marked interest in our faith against that apostate Arian, and may abandon the heresies that plague the Vandals and their African subjects."

"So, I'm to marry a half-mad bastard, then," I said, and immediately regretted my harshness. This was hardly the decorum expected of a Roman officer, though I could not ignore a nagging resentment. How many times would I see my life's course twisted with no regard for my own wishes? The Vandals were a longstanding enemy of the Roman people, having seized our rich African provinces and brutally subjugated their considerable Roman population a century prior. Though long ago a pagan people, many Vandals had since converted to a heretical sect of Christianity, and retained their noted savagery in battle in their ceaseless wars with their neighbors. It was rumored that much of the age-old Roman treasuries had been stored in Carthage, the converted Vandal capital, including hundreds of priceless artifacts from past Roman conquests in the age of the Caesars

"You can always leave for the north. You've sacrificed enough to these Romans," Rosamund said, fixing her healing supplies for another salve to aid with my aches.

The usually genial Father Petrus shot her an uncharacteristically venomous look. Only Perenus broke the tension with laughter.

"What do you expect *but* sacrifice?" he said. "Our job is to stay alive as long as we can, and *maybe* snag our own piece of happiness along the way. Other than that, we are just pawns in the grand plans of kings and emperors."

I raised an eyebrow. "You're a prince in Lazica," I pointed out. "Hardly a pawn like the rest of us."

Perenus chuckled again. "Yes, but where I am from, any man can call himself a prince so long as he's got a hundred spearmen and a hilltop fortress. Until someone takes issue with that claim and fights him for it, at least."

Perenus' words made me laugh—painfully—prompting Rosamund to apply more cooling salve with a tut. Father Petrus looked on, seeming pressed to offer a defense of Lady Theodora.

"Be that as it may, this is a chance to move up in the world, Varus. Hilda is descended from Vandal royalty, even if illegitimately. Her status will elevate your own in the eyes of the Empire, and may even help bring the stubborn Vandals to ally with Rome, or even return the African provinces to the Empire." His voice was strained but carried a note of conviction.

I considered. In this, I saw the wisdom of Perenus' own words. Though I have no doubt that Theodora cared deeply for me, she was also shrewd enough to ensure that her gifts always brought larger benefits to the Empire than onto her intended recipient. A marriage between a Roman officer and a Vandal princess, even a bastard one, might calm the recurring conflicts that flared with the

Vandals and heal the deep mistrust there. For me, the match would provide an elevation in status I could hardly dream of otherwise. In my soul, I still felt that this marriage was not of my desires. Those, I knew, burned elsewhere.

Perhaps, in the grand plans of greater men and women, even senior officers of the army must be thwarted in their heart's desires, but at that moment, I possessed no inclination to think on the matter further. Instead, I solicited an update on the men from Perenus and spoke at length with Petrus for nothing else than comfort, then slowly returned to a rest that my body sorely required.

From my bed, I could now see that Rosamund had unpacked my belongings and hung them up. A great Avar banner spanned one of my walls, its torn cloth serving as a reminder of the tribe's defeat in Tauris. Next to it hung the snow-white wolf's pelt, as well as a number of maps and weapons that I accrued in service to Rome.

Rosamund offered another elixir to help me sleep and insisted that she sleep at the far corner of the tent in case that she was needed in the night. As I drank, her hand rested upon my own as she looked into my eyes.

"I would follow you anywhere, even if it meant leaving all the power and gold behind," she said firmly. "You, me, and Samur… all we need is each other."

The lids of my eyes grew heavy as I nodded, a weak smile on my lips. Rosamund helped position my stiff body into a more comfortable position, and I fell into another dreamless sleep.

UNBROKEN

AGAINST ROSAMUND'S WISHES, I returned to training on the morning of the next day, eager to make use of what limited time I had to prepare the foederati for its spring deployment. Cephalas and Rosamund helped me don my armor and helmet and strapped my sword and dagger onto my sides. I winced as I cinched my belt tightly, relieving the weight of the dangling armor that otherwise worsened the pain upon my bruised shoulders and back.

I saw the men off to their drills with their centurions before leaving with Perenus. I knew I could not avoid our lesson in horse archery, especially now. Perenus, it seemed, had tapped Fulcaris to join us, and the young Herulian trotted behind excitedly as we made for our private training ground.

From early dawn until well after dusk, we rode hard along the sloped grasslands. Several spare horses were brought along, allowing us to swap out spent mounts rather than slow the pace of our training throughout the day. Fulcaris shadowed my every move as Perenus watched from a distance, shouting commands to increase our pace or to fire at posts dug into the ground.

Fulcaris offered several suggestions to improve my form, arguing that my stiff movements made for inaccurate marksmanship at any distance beyond fifty paces. I watched as he demonstrated a fluid, more effective motion that relied upon instinct and speed rather than a careful aiming of the bow. I was skeptical, but Fulcaris' arrows hit their marks nine times out of ten, even from a hundred paces.

My body strained at the labors of practice, and I could barely ignore how the thick bruises across my back made every twist and gesture painful. Between Perenus' riding skill and Fulcaris' horse archery, my confidence grew in the saddle. By the end of the first day, I was able to hit my first target from one hundred paces at a full gallop, yet whether this was from luck or skill, I could not tell. Fulcaris and Perenus hooted and cheered at the sign of progress, trotting toward my position with wide grins on their faces.

Constant, painful training continued for another week. While the Herulian ranks drilled with their centurions, the three of us spent our days in relative isolation. I could soon sit longer and steadier in the saddle without tiring, and thick calluses grew on my hands as I grew more proficient with the bow. Fulcaris gradually added new challenges: hitting a moving or uncertain target, firing from a greater distance or into a heavy wind. My first attempts were usually laughable, arrows falling or flying drunkenly to the side, yet Fulcaris was patient with the bow, and Perenus astute in correcting my every minor mistake atop my mount.

At last, toward the end of the week, I gathered the courage to ask Fulcaris what the men thought of their commander.

"Most of the men know you as a skilled fighter, and a fair leader," he said. "They just haven't seen you fight or lead atop a horse. You just need to show them how far you have come."

"Most of the men," I repeated. "What of the others, then? Like Alaric?"

Fulcaris shrugged. "Alaric has always been disagreeable. I don't mean him necessarily." He avoided my eyes, and when I did not prompt him further, continued. "Many of our tribe worry that Rome is not strong enough to protect our people—the women and children in the Illyrian and Moesian provinces, I mean. And if Rome cannot fulfill that half of the promise, then why should we serve in the foederati?"

"But why wouldn't Rome hold true to the promise?" I prodded.

Fulcaris sighed. "We see in the Eastern remnants of the Empire those same sicknesses that brought the Western Empire,

Rome and Ravenna, to its knees. Our tribe has been whittled away by battle and famine, and our chieftains told us Constantinople might be the shield that protects us from being swallowed whole by the Goths, or the Franks, or the Lombards, or whoever. We know we are weak compared to what we once were. But many in the foederati are not so sure that Rome's armies could withstand an assault either."

I considered. "And they see me as proof," I said in low voice. "That Rome is unable to fight."

Fulcaris smiled weakly but did not contradict my assessment. "You will show them what you can do, Lord," he said. "Alaric, and the rest of them. Once you gain their trust on horseback, they will follow you anywhere."

We finished the remainder of our week together with vigor, but I could not match Fulcaris' satisfaction at my progress.

"All that I need to do is to perform in a group, in harsher conditions, and against live soldiers," I muttered.

In truth, I still dreaded the day I returned to the head of the Herulian riders, and that day came soon enough. Centurions rattled the men awake, and after practically inhaling their thin porridge, the Herulians dressed and mounted for the day's exercises. We left again for the vast clearing that comfortably fit all four hundred riders and were met by a number of servants who'd built targets and established obstacles and markers that would guide our training.

We strapped heavy circular shields to our backs and grabbed bows and sheaves of arrows. Dividing again into two pincers, the ranks trotted to opposite sides of our training circle. A stiff breeze flitted down from the mountains and into our plain, which would influence the flight of any arrows that would be launched. Hundreds of eyes fell upon their komes, and I raised a hand to begin the exercise.

Thunder echoed from the hooves of our horses, kicking grass and dirt high into the air. I pushed our pace to a gallop, with Perenus mimicking our motions at the opposite end of the circle. Quickly glancing back, I found Alaric's face fixed upon mine, a light smirk on his face despite the jerking motions of the horse beneath him. We reached fifty paces from our targets, which was the first marker of the day's exercises.

I shook the image of his face from my mind and fought to focus upon the task at hand. Drawing my bow, I picked a raised target at the center of the massed wooden stakes, many of which had been decorated with mock Persian armor and wicker shields. Taking a deep breath, I began the cadence that would guide the foederati toward their attack.

"Nock, and draw!" I yelled, the command echoed by the centurions at my back. My eyes focused forward as I tried to relax my torso, Fulcaris' lessons reverberating through my mind. After a heartbeat, my thoughts cleared, and I turned my body to face the target toward the right of our slowly arcing gallop.

"Loose!" I called, spurring hundreds of arrows toward their center targets. Instinct took. I *knew*, the moment it released from my bowstring, that my arrow would strike true, and I followed its path as it stuck fast.

I waved a mailed hand for the formation to widen and took the foederati out to eighty paces from the center target. By this time, our horses had dashed through a complete circuit around the training circle but showed no signs of flagging. I called again for my men to nock and draw their arrows, then yelled for a volley to hail down upon the mock Persian ranks.

The breeze pushed harder as we loosed our arrows, yet mine dropped in a beautiful arc and punctured a thick sack of sand right in the heart of the massed targets. Others suffered worse luck, their arrows blown off course or falling short, but I did not stop to identify the culprits and instead signaled that the circle of riders should expand further.

Soon enough, we reached a marker that indicated one hundred paces out, a point where the targets shrank so small that we were forced to squint in the sunlight to discern their outlines.

Breathing deeply, I drew an arrow and called for my men to do the same. We drew, the bowstring falling farther back to accommodate the greater force needed to ensure the arrow would reach its target without falling harmlessly to the ground. At my signal, the men once again let their arrows fly, and my eyes fixed upon our volley as it rained down from the sky.

Fulcaris cheered behind me, generating further howls from the men as my arrow struck home. I grinned and shouted to press on, our pace quickening as fast as our horses and formation allowed.

We released nine more arrows at that distance, and seven of mine sailed true. As the formation slowed to a canter, even Alaric yelled in victory, seeing our mock Persian ranks thickly quilled with hundreds of blunted arrows. Perenus pumped a fist in my direction, and I laughed as I dismissed the men for a brief respite.

After a time, the men grabbed arrows and mounted fresh horses. We continued further, firing volley after volley at a faster pace than before. As exhaustion set in, many arrows fell outside of their intended target, yet no fewer than half had connected solidly with shields, helmets, and other massed objects at the circle's center. Even when extending the circle a further twenty paces, our men retained enough killing force to eviscerate a massed Persian rank, drawing panting men to place bets with one another regarding who could hit more enemies from increasingly ridiculous distances. By the end of the second cycle of training, the top half of one central post slid cleanly off of its moorings, having been cut in half by dozens of arrows over the course of the afternoon. The men cheered at the sight and chanted Herulian war cries as the two pincers gathered together in a great victory circle.

I would never come close to the effortless skill of the Hunnic horse archers, nor could I ever replace a Herulian foederatus atop a horse, even after months of determined practice. But I grew confident and capable enough to be dependable in combat, and I left the training field with my chest held high.

For several days thereafter, the foederati drilled incessantly on horseback, with new formations and challenges added into the drills to better simulate the chaos that comes with battle. I instructed the centurions to select dekarchos within each of their units and was pleased to find Fulcaris awarded the officer's plume. He chatted excitedly with Alaric and Irilar, both of whom had also been given the honor of a command of ten men.

By the third week of our accelerated training in Philippi, the Herulians had mastered formations as mounted archers and dismounted spearmen alike. Groups of fifty were ordered to ride from before dawn until well after dusk, carrying a full array of weapons and armor, with minimal rest. Though caked in salty sweat, no man abandoned their task, and all sat high in the saddle as they returned to our outpost, crisply saluting the attendant officer before being dismissed to rest.

On other days, the foederati brawled in groups of two to ten, taking turns with blunted swords and blunted spears in toppling their enemies to the ground. With each passing day, the mock battles grew both more vicious and more cunning, yet even those colored with a latticework of bruises or who spoke through bloodied mouths begged to return to the fray. It was nothing short of manic, but I approved each measure of progress that each man made in their Roman training.

Satisfied with their progress, I shifted our training regimen to emphasize our dual role as rapid reserves for Belisarius' spearmen. Specifically, the foederati was expected to be able to quickly ride to growing weaknesses in our shield wall, dismount, and form our own wall to shore up any gaps in the line.

Where mounted archery had been a grueling challenge, the shield wall was a welcome task, and I led the Herulian foederati into the exercises with zeal to foster their discipline. Only a handful of men at Philippi had ever fought in a shield wall, with most relying upon Perenus or myself for orders. I even ordered Cephalas, despite his half-crippled arm, to don armor and assist, and his face brightened as he hustled along to Perenus.

The first attempt at the wall was atrocious and slow. Herulians struggled to unsling the shields from their backs and stumbled into lines while Perenus screamed in indignation at the numerous gaps where the shields did not sufficiently overlap.

"The Avars would have pissed themselves laughing if they would have seen you lot," Perenus cried. "All it takes is one gap in the line, and we are dead. An ant should struggle to find any holes to crawl through. High and tight!"

Cephalas barked similar orders and instructed the men how to hold their shields tightly together in a thick line of wood and iron that could repulse even the hardest charge or fiercest blow. We remounted and prepared to drill again.

Progress was slow, yet after hundreds of trials over the course of the week, the Herulians improved to the point where their wall was passable as a measure of reinforcement for the heavy infantry from Belisarius' front lines. By the end of the week, Perenus grunted in approval as he found no weaknesses in the Herulian lines, causing the confidence of the men to soar as a result.

In our final week in Philippi, I organized a mock battle between two halves of the foederati and equipped them with wooden swords and blunted spears for the exercise. Perenus took command of one wing, and I another, and we rapidly dismounted to form opposing walls at one another. In the space of five heartbeats, all four hundred men dismounted, drew their weapons, and formed a wall that would have made Baduarius sing in delight. The ranks crashed into one another, the deafening boom of wooden shields a foretaste of what the foederati would expect in live combat.

Pushing at one another, the walls struggled for the better part of an hour. The exercise concluded as I signaled Cephalas, who blew a shrill whistle that broke the lines apart. I walked in the narrow gap between the lines, remarking on my pride in their strength and their readiness for the fighting ahead of us. The men grinned and knocked shields with one another playfully, their energy palpable as their time in Philippi came to a close.

By our final evening in the encampment, much of the camp had been packed and readied for its journey to the outskirts of Constantinople. As the winter sun dimmed, I had torches lit across the camp's training grounds and ordered the men back into ranks for one final gathering as recruits.

They quickly assembled, and I mounted a horse to better see over the massed ranks. Perenus called for order, snapping four hundred Herulian men to attention.

"Men," I called out over the ranks, my voice echoing across the wooden barracks that lined the yard, "you have taken the rigors of training in stride. Rome will proudly count you amongst its soldiers."

The centurions growled in assent, their voices a booming thunder that filled the yard. Confidence rippled throughout the ranks as men grinned, keeping their bodies stock still.

"Roman soldiers, no matter where they hail from, all swear the same oath," I called out. "I, Varus, and Herulian by birth and blood, am honored to administer this sacred creed to you. When our enemies are numerous, and the odds against our favor, remember these words, and they will see you through your greatest darkness."

My voice triggered a smattering of cheers, which were quickly silenced by the officers. All eyes stared forward as I guided my horse to walk along the ranks, taking stock of the armored foederati.

"I swear to faithfully execute the Emperor's commands, to never desert my service, nor shrink from Death in pursuit of the glory of Rome," I said, drawing a resounding echo from the Herulians.

"I swear to defend the weak, to protect the innocent, and serve as the shield to the poor and the mighty alike," I called out again. As the men responded in turn, many began to pound their spear butts into the earth, a rough rhythm that reverberated into the town of Philippi. Others joined in, and soon enough nearly all men added their spears into the show of brotherhood.

"I swear to honor and love my God, to seek justice, and glorify those dreams that are greater than myself," I recited again.

The pounding grew quicker, making the ground beneath us rumble from the force of the spear blows. I caught Fulcaris and Alaric, their dekarchos plumes rising above the ranks to signify their newfound status. Fulcaris' eyes grew wide with frenetic energy, while Alaric grinned wolfishly, his body moving in rhythm with the pounding of his spear.

"I swear this oath before God and of the Roman people, who shall never falter," I said, finishing the oath.

The men followed and exploded into a great cheer, a cacophony that filled our ears and drowned out all other sound. As the din died down, it gave way to singing in the Heruli tongue as a few men struck up a war chant from their time as great conquerors on the plains. Dozens of others picked up the tune, and soon the melody of hundreds of voices swelled into the jubilant night of the induction of the foederati. Torches cast shadows in the darkness as our only source of light, and illuminated my figure as I saluted the new soldiers of the Roman Army.

We departed Philippi before dawn the next day, emptying the camp while still gripped in the clutches of night. The centurions were directed to follow the Via Egnatia to the outskirts of Constantinople, where a larger outlying fort had been prepared for our arrival. Behind us remained only the small number of servants who would maintain the camp for its future occupants.

Nearly all were mounted, promising a much faster pace back to the capital than would have been expected from a massed formation of spearmen on foot. I made sure that Rosamund and Cephalas were granted their own mounts, while our supplies and belongings had been carefully packed in a number of lighter carts that brought up the column's rear. Father Petrus was granted the rare honor of riding in a carriage, preferring its mild comforts to the jerking rigors of long-distance travel atop a horse.

Despite the nagging cold, relatively fair weather ensured good progress along the road. After two days of leisurely riding, we reached the outskirts of Traianopolis, and a further two days saw us to outside the town of Heraclea. Each evening we made camp, digging shallow ditches for our latrines and establishing a secure perimeter that was thoroughly patrolled by appointed sentries. At makeshift camps, our evenings were far less comfortable than was experienced at Philippi, although there was always enough food to go around, and the tents kept out the worst of the evening winter frosts. Father Petrus began each morning with a prayer to the largely pagan Herulians, while my tutor in the Persian language hounded my steps as we drilled in that poetic yet utterly foreign tongue.

By the end of the week, we arrived at our appointed fort. The foederati entered and were quickly set to task to establish their temporary home, which was intended to house men and horses for the remaining months of poor weather. Unlike most of the foederati, I was to return to the Imperial Barracks to conduct business as a more senior officer. I was also expected to attend the coronation of Justinian and Theodora. Cephalas and Rosamund collected our belongings and prepared for the final stretch of our journey back through the immense stone walls of Constantinople, and Perenus joined us. I tapped Fulcaris to shadow my small party, quietly advising that he speak only Greek while in the capital.

"You have demonstrated your prowess and willingness to fight on Rome's behalf," I told him, "but Roman society scarcely tolerates outsiders. To them, Herulians are little better than one of the roving bands encamped outside the city."

When I arrived at the outer walls, I passed my orders to the guard, showing Theodora's seal as proof of my business in Constantinople. The iron gates creaked open to allow us passage through both the inner and outer walls, and I noticed Fulcaris all but gaping at the dozens of archers and ballistae that lined the battlements of both.

We arrived at the barracks, which was nearly deserted except for a small number of senior officers who had also been invited to the Imperial coronation. Troglita greeted us upon arrival and shared the news of his own nuptials to a princess of the Mauri people. Vassals to the Vandals, the Mauri retained a mixed Roman and Moorish heritage and frequently rebelled against their overlords.

"It seems like all of the officers are being married off," I said darkly.

Troglita chuckled. He seemed generally pleased with his predicament, boasting that his intended bride was known for her quick wit and knowledge of Roman culture. "Auria, daughter of Masuna," Troglita said, allowing her name to roll exotically from his tongue. I wished my friend well, pleased for his happiness yet morose from my own predicament.

"Germanus and Mundus should be here in the next few days," Troglita added. "Their units took heavier blows than mine, but the Thracian Army was able to repel most of the war bands back across the Ister."

I nodded at the relatively good fortune. "Will the Thracians be ready for battle?" I asked, as there were few healthy veterans who returned from Tauris.

Troglita shrugged. "We've gained thousands of recruits, and most will have seen a small taste of battle," he said pensively. "Whether they hold against a mass of disciplined Persian Immortals... I'm not so sure."

We spent the evening reconnecting with friends. Samur rushed me with a wide hug of surprising strength given his sinewy arms and slim frame.

"It seems like you didn't crack your skull falling from a saddle," he said gleefully. "Still want to get footsore fighting with the infantry?"

I rolled my eyes. "If Belisarius asked me to abandon the foederati and scrape dung from Baduarius' night bucket, I'd be sorely tempted."

"Our kinsmen can't be so bad as that!" Samur laughed. "Sunicas and Simmas lead the Huns on a ten-mile ride each morning, and I wouldn't trade such freedom for anything. Each man of the Hun foederati is as a brother... I only wish you had joined me."

Samur's enthusiasm made me smile. Though I saw him as the same mischievous boy, Samur had grown physically into a man thanks to his time with Sunicas: leaner, yet with all the contours of muscle to pluck a bow two hundred times without tiring. With a sunburnt face and a curiously grizzled jaw, Samur seemed to stand taller as he spoke of his time with Sunicas—even wearing the telltale Hunnic furs in place of a traditional Roman cloak.

"The Herulians are every bit as stubborn as the Huns, you'll see," I said. "Do the Huns treat you well?"

"I'm not sure I'll ever be able to lead any Huns," Samur conceded, "but they share all their food and correct every mistake that I might make. Sunicas most of all, for even as a tribune, he allows me to ride at his side. With my Huns and your Heruli, the flatfooted Persians will have no chance!"

Soon thereafter, Samur led me to Sunicas and Simmas, who were drinking with a vengeance at a nearby tavern with a group of Belisarius' officers. Ascum teased me for the news of my marriage, which had apparently spread throughout Belisarius' officer corps, while Bessas offered to help me steal the fastest horse in the Imperial stables and run fast for the northern border.

Most notable within their happy gathering was Baduarius, the Gothic officer who lost his brother in the war against the Avars. A vast beast of a man, Baduarius grasped me in a tight embrace, his fists pounding my back with aggressive affection. Baduarius' province was a lone area of peace throughout the Empire, and many of the farms and estates sacked by the Avars had been slowly repopulated. Baduarius gave a hearty welcome to Fulcaris, hugged Rosamund, and left us to drain a heavy wineskin with Perenus and Ascum.

Our burgeoning group was soon joined by John and Belisarius, the latter in a simple freeman's cloak and tunic. John greeted me and sat by Sunicas, who had been deep into his wine cups by that point in the evening.

Belisarius smiled warmly at Troglita and me. "Congratulations to you both on your impending marriages," he said jovially.

Troglita beamed at the compliment, while I dutifully returned his congratulations with all the joy of a flea-ridden ox. Seeing my expression, Belisarius quickly changed the subject to share his own fortunes.

"It is still early, but... Antonina is pregnant." Belisarius, normally impassive, broke into a wide and unashamed smile.

"That is wonderful news, Lord!" I exclaimed, clapping him happily on the shoulder.

Belisarius shone with pride, yet all too soon turned the conversation to preparations of war. I remarked at the considerable progress of the Herulian foederati, which would fight within Belisarius' army.

"We will need each of them," Belisarius remarked grimly. "Kavadh's armies are dormant for now, but come spring, we will lack the force to stop any of his blows."

"And what of Dara? Any word of its inhabitants?" I asked. My concern for Liberius was doubtless written on my face, but I could not bear to ask.

Belisarius' face grew melancholy. "We are occasionally able to run supplies into Dara and the other cities, but such mercies are becoming difficult. The Persians are moving carefully through Mesopotamia, and it is said that a young Zhayedan general leads an army of Immortals into each engagement."

I shivered at that image. The Zhayedan haunted the dreams of many Romans. For nearly a thousand years, the Persian Immortals had slain thousands upon thousands of Greek and Roman soldiers, including multiple kings and emperors along the way. It was said that each Zhayedan was picked from an early age from the most gifted Persian families and trained in nothing but combat and service to the Shahanshah for the rest of their lives. The Zhayedan general, Belisarius told me, was a young man called Xerxes, the namesake of the Achaemenid emperor who nearly destroyed Greece in his lust for control over the world.

Belisarius next introduced me to one of his traveling companions. An Arab man, his darker skin stood out amongst Belisarius' officers, made all the more noticeable by the crimson-and-gold robes that adorned his skin. His dark hair was cropped short, and he sported a bushy beard. Most striking of all were his dark amber eyes, which seemed oddly familiar even in the dim

146

lighting of the Roman tavern. Belisarius introduced him as al-Harith, eldest son of Jabalah, King of the Ghassanids.

Al-Harith took my arm into his own with a formal greeting. "My father could not be here for the coronation but will arrive for the wedding. As soon as it is over, I'm heading back to Arabia for the spring fighting against the Persians and the Lakhmids." The Arab prince spat as he said the tribal name of his bitter enemy, which had allied itself with the Persians as the Ghassanids had pledged themselves to Justinian's cause.

The prince and I spoke of differences in battle and of culture. Al-Harith was jovial enough in the company of his Roman hosts, except that he seemed puzzled at the esteem granted upon his future brother-in-law.

"Does Solomon have many military honors or successes of his own?" al-Harith asked me. "My father was happy enough with the match, especially once Solomon was given command of many men in the campaign against the Avars."

As I thought of how to answer, he added further, "We haven't heard much of Solomon's exploits in Tauris, however."

I was taken aback by the prince's brazen assessment of Solomon's character. It made little sense for al-Harith to question the honor of his soon-to-be brother-in-law. Roman patricians would never resort to honesty if flattery was an option, and if I were to agree with him and be found out as embarrassing my betters before our Ghassanid guests, I would have doubtless had my throat slit by Senator Nepotian's cronies and my corpse dumped into the Golden Horn as food for fishes with the rest of the decaying waste.

Yet I was torn: sorely tempted to denigrate my rival though unwilling to offend Prince al-Harith, let alone endanger Rome's alliance with this critical partner in Arabia—an alliance that was, according to Mariya, of considerable importance. The tug of my conscience pulled me back from petty rivalry, and I did my best to assuage al-Harith's concerns.

"In Roman custom, it is a great honor to be descended from a noble bloodline... and Solomon is of that class. Justinian and Theodora intend to show their friendship with the Ghassanids by marrying Solomon to your princess," I said, equivocating as best I could.

Al-Harith grunted. "Curious," he said, with just a hint of danger in his voice. We changed to a happier subject as we shared cups of wine, engaging Belisarius in the conversation.

After a time, several members of our party slipped away, unwilling to enjoin the aggressive drinking that typically followed such a gathering. Perenus and Rosamund tried to force me to stay, yet I, too, left for the barracks alone, wishing my friends well as I brooded over my fate. My mind raced with questions about how a person could be simultaneously blessed and cursed, and convinced me that I would trade all of the gold in the Imperial treasury for just a chance to pursue my soul's greatest desire.

THE DARK RIDER

AWAKING AT DAWN the next morning, I chuckled at the sound of Perenus' moans of pain as he vomited into a bucket. Fulcaris lay prostrate in the hallway, having struggled to find his bunk in the dark hours of the night. I kicked his leg, and though he stirred in indignation, he refused to rise into a more comfortable position.

Rosamund was faring just as poorly, so I fetched her chilled water and soft bread to ease her nausea. Unable to lift her head, she raised a hand in thanks, and I closed her door to offer a modicum of privacy.

As I strode into the barracks hall, a bronze-collared slave waved me down.

"You are Varus, of the Herulian foederati?"

I nodded. Upon closer inspection, he appeared to be a boy of some thirteen years, though it was difficult to tell with the layers of soot and prominent lines by his mouth and eyes that belonged on a man three times his age. His fingers were mottled with painful-looking sores, and beneath the grime, slivers of bone white shone from his unevenly cropped hair. Was this boy enslaved after the raid in the Gepid Kingdom? I shuddered—the assault had been as brutal as it was unnecessary.

"The Imperial armorer is waiting for you. He is very busy, so I would not tarry for long."

I paid him two copper coins, gathered my attire, and strode from the barracks' confines. Half running to the armorer, I found his servants sweeping the front of the shop. One beckoned me inside, unlocking the door to the blacksmith beyond.

A wave of heat surrounded me as air from the furnaces filled the room. I found the armorer hammering a greave plate at an anvil, to which he arrived at a stopping point and waved.

"Ah, Varus. Good to see you. You'll be pleased with my work, I have no doubt," he said pridefully, putting down his tools and guiding me to a private office. White cloths covering their hands, servants carried my new armor inside and positioned it upon wooden stands. The smith carefully fixed the helmet and plume and unwrinkled the red cloak that hung down to the planks of the floor.

Light from flickering tapers mirrored off of the polished metal as I stood speechless. The smith was correct—the armor was as much a work of art as it was a collection of leather and steel.

The chest piece was layered with thick steel scales, each cut into teardrops and backed with a soft mahogany leather that would withstand all but the most vicious arrows at one hundred paces. This pattern hung below the beltline and was cut in several separate strips to improve the wearer's range of motion. A matching layer of mahogany leather rested underneath to protect the lower thigh. The chest piece was cross-latched with leather bands that slung diagonally over the collarbone, bearing four small silver symbols of the Imperial Eagle and Constantine's Chi-Rho. At the center of the chest was a larger silver medallion that bore my sigil, the ouroboros.

A set of matching iron lamellar greaves and armguards lined its limbs, while thick layered shoulder guards rose nearly to ear level. The shoulders bore images of snarling dragons, in keeping with the armorer's insistence on faithfully portraying my newfound foederati's sigil. The costume was topped with a flanged skullcap, its back covered with a thick layer of cow's leather and its front marked by two hinged cheekpieces and a nose guard. A tall black plume rose far above the helmet, making the wearer seem far taller.

It was a rich set, reserved for only the wealthiest or most senior commanders in the Empire. I gaped at its clean lines, raising an eyebrow in skepticism at its weight. Surely such a piece was far too heavy for a cavalryman, let alone a spearman fighting in the suffocating press of the shield wall.

"Try it on, Lord. Feel how it moves," the smith said.

With the help of two servants, the armor was buckled and strapped onto my body. I inadvertently gasped; it was as light as any simple mail hauberk and did not restrict any of the movements necessary in battle.

The smith laughed. "I loathe parade armor and will never spend my time making it. Everything you see in this shop is meant to be carried into war." He invited me back into one of his storerooms to view the remainder of my purchases, which contained a sea of onyx cloth and wood.

Hundreds of blackened iron-rimmed shields were stacked neatly from hooks, hanging upright to show their thickness and length. Above them hung dozens of black banners of varying sizes, which momentarily brought an image of the Avar army to my mind. One banner was far larger than the others and was meant to be mounted high above a city's walls to show the presence of a lord of the Roman Empire.

At the center of each shield and banner rested the white ouroboros, its scaled body framed by the black field upon which it rested. I ran a hand along the cloth of one of the banners, nodding in approval at the substantial progress made here. There were enough banners and shields for a foederati of at least twice the size of my Herulians, meaning that we would have no trouble with spare equipment on our march.

"Whenever you need more, just send a dispatch, and I will repair any damage in your armor at cost," the smith said, pleased with his work.

As I shook his hand, he ordered the shields and banners carried to the barracks on a series of carts. Before leaving, I paid for the immediate transport of the shields and banners to my foederati outside of the capital and levied purchases for additional armor for my men, as well as a similar custom set for Perenus.

"That large an order will take considerable time... or will require many more hands," the smith said, and paused.

Whether genuine concern or bargaining tactic, I brushed the remark aside. "Pay for all the help that is required, and I will reimburse the expense. I intend to armor all my men, and want these finished before I leave for the campaign."

Grinning at his newfound fortune, the smith agreed to rush the order and sat back at his anvil. It was hardly extravagance: Aside from a few custom pieces, most of the armor would be hammered into a design that, while not necessarily beautiful, was more than sufficient to stop a blade from slicing Herulian flesh.

Back at the barracks, Perenus and Fulcaris gawked at the armor and grew all the more excited at the prospect of their own high-quality steel as the smith's servants, who accompanied me, set to taking measurements. Most of the foederati originated from barbarian tribes, and the Imperial quartermasters rarely afforded them decent weapons or armor, preferring to reserve the hardiest equipment for established Roman citizens. Outfitting my own units would cost a small fortune, but Justin's generous inheritance let me easily shoulder the cost. As Perenus squawked excitedly, insisting the smith's apprentices add extra space below his belt for "personal reasons," Rosamund approached me from her quarters.

"Varus, do you think they'll have time to make something for me?"

It was an odd question, one I would never have anticipated. No Roman woman would ever adorn herself with boiled leather or coarse mail when elegant, enviable silks could be purchased for the same price. Then again, Rosamund was neither Roman nor ruled by the social mores of Constantinople. I was dumbstruck, yet her steady, even gaze demanded a response, and a sincere one.

"I am not sure. I do not think they receive many women," I said truthfully. "Why do you think you will need armor as well?"

"I don't think it; I know it. A komes is required to be in constant contact with the other commanders, though you have only Cephalas to serve as your messenger. I am fast and loyal as any, but a woman running through the army would draw attention. Few would notice another figure dressed in armor."

I began to protest, concerned for her safety, but she cut me off.

"Besides," she said, eyes gleaming, "I'm tired of waiting behind to hear whether it's victory or defeat. I want to help you fight."

I considered her request. "An army's march is rarely safe, and never comfortable," I warned her. "Our food is often poor, and we will be exposed to the rain, the heat, the wind—"

"I can handle it. I always have." Rosamund waved off the concerns. Her expression darkened. "What else do I have to do to prove my worth to you?"

"Rosamund—"

"I know what my name is," she snapped. Then she softened. "What I mean to say, Varus, is that just as you swore me an oath of loyalty and honor, I swore to serve you in all things. But I cannot fulfill that oath if you treat me like a child."

She was correct, of course. Still, the thought of Rosamund trailing Belisarius' army left me distinctly uneasy, but I knew that if her mind was made up, my only option was to acquiesce and accustom myself to the idea. I summoned one of the armorer's servants and told him to include Rosamund in the list for new armor. He gawked, then tittered, then fell silent. I reiterated my demand.

"And spare no expense—whatever she wants," I added. "Send a manifest for the armor's cost to this man, Empress Theodora's courtier." On a thin scrap of paper, I wrote quickly to Narses, asking to pay the expense against my holdings, and sealed the message with a stamp of Theodora's seal into hot red wax. The servant bowed, taking first the proof of payment and then Rosamund's hand to lead her for measurements. Her voice rose with exhilaration as she detailed her desires.

"I expect it to be as expertly crafted as my own," I called after him, and left Rosamund to her happiness.

The next three days were filled with frequent meetings as war leaders plotted the movements of armies for the upcoming spring. Huge maps of Lazica, Iberian Armenia, and Mesopotamia were dotted with positions of Roman and Ghassanid armies currently in the field, as well as a rough outline of Persian movements based upon the latest available information. The frontier held a notable gash along the Euphrates River, where holdout Roman cities had become virtually surrounded by Persian and Lakhmid soldiers. Roman positions in Lazica generally held strong, although the same could not be said of Iberia, where General Sittas had been continually harassed by lightning-quick attacks from Xerxes and his Zhayedan-led forces.

Belisarius listened carefully to reports and suggestions from his senior officers, speaking mainly to ask questions about the terrain, enemy capabilities, and the ability for resupply and reinforcement at strategically important points along the projected marches. He jotted notes at key intervals and seemed particularly curious regarding descriptions of the various Persian units and their generals.

Spies procured a wealth of knowledge on the key Persian commanders. The two active generals were Perozes and Xerxes, both of whom claimed heritage with the vast Persian royal family. Perozes was the head of the House of Mihran, one of the Seven

Great Houses of the Persian Empire. He had spent considerable time expanding Persian influence in Arabia, leading armies as far as the distant shores of Himyar. Xerxes was a Persian prince, a younger nephew of Shahanshah Kavadh. Though only about twenty years of age, he had been given to the Zhayedan before he could even walk, a move which, while hindering any potential challenge to Kavadh's sons for the Persian throne, also trained a powerful leader of the Persian armies.

The Persian astabadh was discovered to be a man named Azarethes, a seasoned veteran who gained his fortune fighting against the Indians as well as certain tribes of the Huns that stalked the far eastern borders of the Persian Empire. Known to be an exceptionally capable commander, Azarethes had been awarded overall control of all Persian armies facing Rome and its allies, and was the leader responsible for the strategy that brought Persian forces deep into Roman Mesopotamia and Osroene.

Justinian occasionally joined the sessions, passionately arguing for the protection of key cities and rich provinces ravaged by the Persian offensive. The heir to the Empire berated his generals for losing vast swathes of Mesopotamian territory, a forfeit that threatened to cut the Empire in half and separate Constantinople from the vital grain supply of Egypt. At last, it came to pass that Justinian, taking command of one strategic alliance, ordered Roman ships within the Red Sea to ferry Aksumite spearmen into Himyar, destabilizing the Persian hold over the southernmost reaches of Arabia.

At this declaration, all but Belisarius avoided Justinian's gaze, and the room grew noticeably less tense only when the Emperor departed and took his baleful moods with him. Calmly, Belisarius mapped out the path that his men would take, including a preliminary voyage along the Anatolian coast toward Trapezous, and then southward through Armenia and toward the line of Roman fortresses near Dara. It was a bold plan, requiring the army to skirt mountain passes and march nearly two hundred miles through enemy territory, yielding the greatest opportunity to break the Persian encirclement of Roman Mesopotamia and draw the Persian generals into battle.

"How are we going to resupply across the mountains?" Germanus asked, his finger tracing the Pontic interior.

"The main army will haul a baggage train from Trapezous, while the bulk of our spare weapons and food will sail from Constantinople to Antioch," John answered. "It'll be a rough march through Armenia—hilly—but we won't go hungry. I've sent missives to a half dozen cities in northern Mesopotamia to prepare for our arrival."

I attended each meeting but spoke little other than to answer questions about the Herulian foederati or offer opinions about how a mounted force might traverse poor terrain. Not that I minded—John appeared to anticipate and resolve all problems well before others could even consider them. He was unlike any officer under Belisarius' command, with unmatched wits and a mind for even the most monotonous of army logistics. Belisarius heeded even the smallest suggestions that John had to offer, and I took every opportunity to learn from his planning sessions.

Though the announcement would not become official until after their coronation, Justinian and Theodora created a high command to rival that of the Persians led by Azarethes. That title, Magister Militum of the East, was conferred upon Belisarius, who would have the overall strategic leadership against the Persians and would exercise direct control in Mesopotamia. The Lazic and Armenian armies would be nominally independent, while Belisarius' own forces would be joined by the Thracians under Germanus and Mundus, the Egyptians under Domnicus, and the allied forces of the Ghassanids under King Jabalah.

Though large by Roman standards, the combined force would be only half the size of a single Persian army. The Persian troops were manned and reinforced by the vast multitudes of men and horses that Kavadh could call upon, and though he was not even thirty years of age, it was Belisarius who had been entrusted with the duty to hold these massed enemies at bay.

Belisarius, in turn, tapped each of his senior officers to share the burden of this heightened command, and it was not uncommon to spy John working late into the night over dozens of candles, or Bessas and Ascum bickering with merchants and smiths for spare weapons and supplies. Others, like Baduarius and Sunicas, spent their days training with their men, preparing them for the many hard marches that the Persian war had condemned us to. My task— to prepare the new Herulian foederati—was largely accomplished, but my work had not ended; I frequently found myself laboring with Belisarius and John, agonizing over how we could keep the thousands of Roman soldiers fed and protected over hundreds of miles of harsh and dangerous terrain.

These tasks busied my mind and left me with plenty to fill my days with in the week leading up to the Imperial coronation. Perhaps most important of all was my ability to ferry messages from Belisarius to Theodora, who had otherwise been surrounded by dozens of courtiers fighting for a moment of her attention. Theodora smiled and embraced me when we first reunited, hungering for details about her new Herulian foederati as soon as privacy was assured.

"Tell me, will the Herulians be ready for war?" Theodora demanded. "Did you have trouble?"

"Yes, on both accounts," I replied. "They will perform their duties. But it was often both taxing and… humiliating, Highness."

Theodora scowled. "Humiliating?"

"Have you ever been thrown from a horse in front of hundreds of people judging your every move?"

"No," Theodora said. "But I am intimately familiar with jealous and prying attentions. I know well that this was not your

157

preferred assignment, Varus, but if you've succeeded, your sacrifice will be repaid a thousandfold."

"I hope so, Highness."

Theodora's sternness slipped back into a smile. "I know so. Though I have worked tirelessly to swell Belisarius' numbers, few Greeks and Latins are willing to do more than join the limitanei. Your Herulians, and the Huns, and others from a dozen tribes might be the best defense our people have against our enemies. And believe me Varus, our enemies are many."

I lowered my head. "Apologies, Highness, I do not mean to offend. But regarding enemies, have we discovered more of Liberius?"

"Yes, but very little. Narses' spies search each day. I want you to take rest and refreshment while you can, because your time in Mesopotamia will be little marked by rest."

I chuckled. "It certainly seems so. But I have work with John and Belisarius to continue, Highness."

"Of course. See it done." Theodora nodded. "But please enjoy the coronation. And," she added, "the wedding of the Ghassanid princess. You'll be an honored guest as a komes of a new foederati."

Her words were well-meaning, but they struck like a spear to the gut. "I'm not so sure my presence would be appropriate," I demurred. "Nepotian's family has no love of me, and none will appreciate a Herulian in their midst."

"Nonsense!" Theodora smiled. She knew nothing of my hatred for Solomon and my resentment of his betrothal. "Learn to enjoy yourself amongst these expensively dressed peacocks. I'll even share cups of wine with you, smiling to the crowd while whispering all manner of gossip."

"Of course, Highness," I muttered, unable to decline.

Admittedly, despite the endless labor, I longed for sessions in the Imperial Palace. Not because of any time spent with

Theodora, although she was a loyal friend who helped me rise high in life. No, I craved those visits for the chance to catch even a glimpse of Mariya, who still kept residence in the palace until the day of her wedding.

Each day that I entered the palace, Mariya was absent from any gathering. Sembrouthes, the leader of her Aksumite guards, could be seen walking the palace grounds, yet neither Mariya nor her female attendants made any appearances in Court or in the city marketplace.

On one occasion, I found Marcellus, the chief excubitor and one of Justin's old pupils. The grizzled commander smiled and waved heartily, asking about my time as a new commander. The excubitores would be joining Belisarius' army in battle, he told me. Then he asked about any news of the front, and of our joint mentor Liberius.

We shared what rumors and information were available and chatted about how fights with the Persians would occur differently than other enemies of the Roman Empire. Marcellus had fought against the armored elephants that the Persians transported into several battles and sieges in their wars against Emperor Anastasius. Few knew definitively if they would marshal the beasts against us now, however, though Justinian was particularly worried that elephant riders might easily scale the walls of his new desert fortifications.

After our discussion, I changed subjects and gathered the courage to ask whether Marcellus had witnessed any sign of the Ghassanid princess.

"She's been isolated in her rooms with her maids, served only by a small number of servants and her Aksumite guardsmen," Marcellus said, referring to Mariya. "It must have been at least a month since I've seen her in public."

My heart sank at the news. Having free rein to roam the palace, and even to carry a weapon in the Emperor's presence,

Marcellus had the best chance of anyone outside Mariya's personal retinue to come across her.

My mind raced with all manner of dark thoughts. Did Mariya regret meeting with me? Was she trying to put her escapades in the past in preparation for her new life with Solomon? All the better for Mariya, I supposed, to enjoy a clean start to her life as Roman nobility. I dared not seek out her rooms to gain answers, and instead tortured myself with the realization that I had been a fool.

I tried to bring myself to hate Mariya. In rare moments, I even convinced myself that I did not desire her, and never did in the first place. Indeed, what purpose would such desire serve? Her father was the king of a wealthy nation, while mine was unknown, one of thousands of farmers who tilled the soil and died young. The Romans took Samur and me when we were very young, lone survivors from an unnamed raid, leaving nothing to prove their significance to the world.

In the heart of the night, as I sat in my bed and stared at my unsheathed sword, my anger teetered on the verge of despair. I wanted nothing more than to ask my old master all of the questions that lingered in my mind—to ask why he showed kindness to me. The ignorance was its own form of cruelty, for I would never know why I was allowed to grow up with the trappings of Rome's elite families, yet also doomed to sweep the palace floors and clean night soil from discarded basins. I had been given more gifts than most could ever dream of, but I was still condemned to a life of servitude and toil.

The dark Avar banner caught my gaze, and I swept to an empty room, fuming. Rage overcame me. I seized my sword and held it high over my head and cut down frantically at the wooden bed frame. Yelling hysterically, the blade chopped easily into the mat and its supporting beams, showering splinters around my head. One blow sent the frame clattering onto the floor, and I screamed again as my enemy fell before slaking my bloodlust. My heavy panting soon turned to thick sobs, which grew heavier as my door drew open.

From the hallway, someone peered in—Perenus, who caught my gaze and called for help. Rosamund hurried inside and ordered Perenus and the others away.

"Leave us," her hollow voice rattled, forcing Perenus to comply. Rosamund closed my door and asked me to lower my blade, which was still clenched firmly in my fist. My eyes dropped to its runed and whorled blade, and I dropped it to the floor with a clamor.

My tears grew thicker as I looked back up at Rosamund. She took me in a tight embrace, her hand running through my hair as I sank to the wooden floor. Rosamund beckoned for me to sit as she departed for a few moments, returning with the large wooden box of her many healing remedies.

She lifted a slat within the box to reveal a hidden compartment, from which she withdrew several powders that she mixed together in a clay cup. A few drops from a small glass container of a dark amber liquid created a puff of smoke as it hit the powders and congealed.

My sobbing slowed as I caught sight of her experiment. "What is all of that?" I asked, leveling Rosamund's eyes with mine.

"Ancient magic learned from my grandfather. That is all you need to know," she said in a hushed voice.

I lacked the will to note my concern at the pagan ritual she performed before me, recoiling in fear all the same.

Rosamund's free hand grasped mine. "Take this." The order only worried me further, which Rosamund must have seen on my face. "It will help you to sleep, and let go of all of these worries that plague your mind," she added.

In my weakness, I accepted the raised clay cup and tipped the foul substance toward my mouth.

All I felt initially was a low burn in my chest, not even enough to warrant minor discomfort. As moments passed, the burn grew into a flame as my vision clouded and the walls of the room grew far away. Taking my arm, Rosamund lifted me to my feet and carried me to her chambers.

I tried calling out in fear, but my own voice sounded distant. When I reached out, my hands grasped nothing. Rosamund's voice echoed in my ear as she lay me down.

"Sleep, Varus. Everything will be okay," she said.

My eyes grew heavy as I obliged, unable to move beyond the simple task of breathing. Visions danced in my head. I felt elsewhere, far away from the press of Constantinople, yet somewhere nevertheless familiar. My soul floated away from my body as I soared high in the air, glancing down at a great mass of people moving along rolling hills and snowcapped mountains. At their head was a dark figure, a person who walked alone while leading the swirling mass. None dared approach, leaving a gap of ten paces within which no living creature walked. A tattered black cloak hung well beyond the figure's horse, dragging along the ground and tearing at the earth behind it.

I took stock of the environment: a mixture of growth and destruction whipped up from the leader at the head of the great crowd. Descending, I crept slowly behind the figure, gliding next to the figure's dragging cloak, and at last stood alongside its horse as my nose flooded with the scent of burning flesh. Apprehensive yet unable to halt, I moved a pace forward, and the figure turned toward me. Angry, unblinking red eyes met my gaze as the figure reached out and grabbed my arm, the gloved hand burning my skin.

I pulled away, and as I did, found my sigil etched clearly in a circle of burned and puckered skin. The figure laughed in an impossibly deep voice as it drew its bloodied sword and swung down toward my neck.

Gasping, I awoke in a sweat. The room was filled with light. Rosamund shot upright, having slept on the floor at the far side of the tiny room. She rushed to my side with water, peering into my eyes.

"What did you see?" she asked. "You slept nearly into midday."

Rubbing my eyes, I slowly rose from the stupor and gulped the sorely needed water. I told Rosamund of my dream, of the great mass of people, of tumultuous change, and of the figure in black that was the cause of it all.

"That was the figure that my grandfather saw. It is clearly a sign," Rosamund said, her face bright with wonder. She tore on excitedly about the brand until I interrupted.

"Why would you give that... drink to me?" I asked. "I trusted you with my care—why would you tend to me with something that would yield such dreams?"

Rosamund shook her head, her voice a soft coo. "You were in pain, Varus, and I took that away from you, if even for one night. But the dreams are a good thing. They clearly show that this world is dying and will be replaced by something new, and stronger."

"If you had explained its purpose beforehand, you know I would not have approved," I said. "It's not something Romans use. What if it had poisoned me?"

"I have prepared it hundreds of times," Rosamund countered. "The ingredients are well-known to me. You were in no danger of anything except a vivid dream. If you cannot trust what you do not understand, then trust me, Varus. The quacks of your Empire would only question your resolve as a man, while I understood the true pain in your heart."

I said nothing, for I had nothing further to say. After gathering my clothing, I left Rosamund behind to meet with Father Petrus, and then spent an extensive day in the training yard. I told no one else what had happened, and even Perenus said nothing of it when we sparred together later in the day. I had enough on my mind without talking of frightening omens and restless dreams, let alone thinking further on Rosamund's wish to gallop hard to the ends of the Empire and beyond. Instead, I trained my thoughts on the Imperial coronation, and the wedding that would soon follow.

THE MAJESTY OF FLAVIUS PETRUS SABBATIUS JUSTINIANUS, IMPERATOR

JUSTINIAN'S CORONATION WAS HELD the following day. Though somber and rich in ceremony, Justinian had already served as the functional monarch of the Roman Empire for months, and well before Justin's death. I woke early, donned my armor, and led my retinue toward the Imperial Palace.

Early hints of spring filled the air as crisp winds blew along the stone-lined streets of the capital. Masses of city residents thronged before the palace, eager for a glance of Roman nobles who were attending the first coronation in nearly a decade. Several voices mumbled complaints within the excited mass, although violence and destruction of property had been kept to a minimum by the reinforced rows of palace guards that stood before and around the palace steps.

I passed through a small clearing in the crowd and presented my sealed documents granting me entry to the coronation, and led Perenus, Fulcaris, Rosamund, and Cephalas over the steps and through the entryway. Rosamund and Fulcaris gaped at the vast interior decorated with gilded panels and frescoes amidst a small sea of Corinthian columns. We found Troglita standing near the palace entrance, and he guided us to the mass of officers and dignitaries that formed Belisarius' party.

Belisarius had shunned the simple clothing he usually wore for all the finery of a leading commander of Roman armies. Belisarius' armor had been polished to reflect all light, while his helmet bore the extensive goose feather plume of a magister militum. He smiled as I approached and clapped me on the shoulder.

"Beautiful armor, Varus," Belisarius said. "The smith is a master craftsman. I source my own armor from no one else." Belisarius' core officers had already arrived and had even taken the trouble to wash their bodies and comb the more stubborn lice from their beards. Baduarius, John, and Bessas were similarly armored as their commander, while Sunicas, Simmas, and Ascum preferred the heavy furs that made their figures all the more striking to a less warlike Roman aristocracy. Samur stood next to Sunicas and greeted me with a broad hug as Perenus introduced himself to the dozens of senior officers that were now his comrades.

Next to Belisarius' officers stood Germanus and Mundus, who led a smaller contingent of commanders of the Thracian Army. Mundus, who looked much haler since we'd parted last, commended my rise in status as a commander of the Herulian foederati and asked about preparations for the upcoming Persian war.

"My new recruits are all blooded now, but it was a hell of a time fighting back the Sclaveni," he said gruffly, referring to the Thracian Army's fight against the joint barbarian invasion along the Ister River. "We had to strip the Anastasian Wall nearly bare to compensate for our wounded, but at least we now have enough men to form a complete army to complement Belisarius."

Troglita had offered similar comments days prior, although he'd painted a darker picture of the status of the Thracian Army. New recruits had to be gathered from provinces as distant as Epirus and Thessaly and left the Empire's European provinces nearly empty of soldiers.

"Aside from the limitanei, there are maybe two thousand trained Roman soldiers in all of Europe," Troglita mentioned. "Now that the northern invasions are quelled, everything is being thrown against Persia... and even then, I am not sure it will be enough."

Despite the unsettling rumors that had spread regarding the sheer size and skill of the Persian armies, the tenor of the gathering was one of optimism and splendor. Justinian spent lavishly on his ceremony, including tens of thousands of fragrant flowers that blocked out the horrifying stench of the city beyond. The palace guards were bedecked in gold-gilt armor, while singers filled the arching halls with the glories of Christ the Savior of the World. Lining a violet walkway were the excubitores, with Marcellus at the front, just before the vacant Imperial throne.

Procopius sat at a wooden desk in the corner of the room, tasked with the need to record the proceedings of Justinian's reign for posterity. John nodded in the clerk's direction, and I could not help but mark his disdain.

"Justinian is ordering Procopius to accompany our campaign. Him and some government official named Hermogenes," John said. He sneered at Procopius, whose quill moved in rapid motions as more Roman dignitaries took their places in the audience.

Justinian's advisors flooded into the hall, with the more senior individuals taking places along the dais and just below the throne. Paulus, the Imperial treasurer, moved first into the position of honor, drawing rumblings of disdain from the crowd that Paulus pretended not to hear, though he did not complain when additional palace guards were placed before him. Following him was Tribonian, Justinian's master of laws, who proved to be only slightly less unpopular than his colleague before him.

Other senior courtiers followed, including Cassiodorus, Justinian's chief official on Imperial religion, and a representative of the elderly patriarch, Epiphanius. Alongside Epiphanius stood Basilius, the late Emperor Justin's longtime friend and colleague in the administration of the Empire. Most curious of all was Father

Petrus, who leaned against his weather-worn cane as he took his place next to Basilius.

Though not as honored as the senior courtiers, Solomon and his father, Senator Nepotian, stood at the front row of the onlookers. Solomon's armor shone brightly as he carried his arm in a sling, delighting in comments of concern by ladies from the Imperial Court. Solomon's hair had been oiled flat, and his skin seemed to shimmer against the light of the morning. Beside him stood the recently arrived King Jabalah of the Ghassanids, who spoke animatedly with Nepotian, as well as the more austere figure of his son, Prince al-Harith.

Narses stood nearby, aloof, his eyes near unblinking as he seemed to record in his mind all that he saw. He was perfectly still save the slight twitching of his supple fingers as they twirled his golden ring in tight circles.

With the ceremony moments away, the hall had grown hot from the hundreds of bodies that filled it, though the din of the palace had diminished somewhat. Among the last to arrive was a small delegation of crimson-dressed Ghassanid ladies and their Aksumite guards, who bore yellow robes that shone brightly against their dark skin. Last among them was Princess Mariya, who carried herself with cold dignity as she walked forward, eyes fixed upon the throne.

My heart quickened. I tried to catch Mariya's eye without drawing attention to myself. She passed within a handsbreadth of where I stood, her perfume washing into my lungs and long silken dress nearly brushing my feet, though she neither slowed nor made any sign of recognition. Mariya took her place near Solomon, who grinned wolfishly at her before his attentions were drawn to the chief excubitor.

Marcellus rapped his spear butt onto the stone floor, wordlessly commanding silence in the room as Cassiodorus drew a scroll from the folds of his robes.

Cassiodorus prayed for blessings upon all gathered, and for Justinian, who claimed the majestic throne of the Romans. His long white beard reached to his belt, yet his pace of speech seemed to irk many in the audience. Basilius rolled his eyes at the doddering man, remaining silent as he called for God's favor upon Justinian, who would restore old glories to the Empire and purge it of all the unclean and uncouth elements that infested it.

As Cassiodorus finished, a chorus of singers chanted hymns, their melodies echoing from the marble stone that lined the floors and walls. This cued Justinian to appear, and he meandered down the violet carpet. His body was lined with gold cloth and jewels, and a long purple cloak hung three paces behind his steps. Justinian halted before the empty throne and bowed, and much of the audience followed his lead.

It was Basilius' turn to speak. Where Cassiodorus had rambled almost incoherently, Basilius called out with a clear, almost sweet resonance that held all rapt.

"You, who comes before the vacant throne of Caesar, what is your name?"

"Flavius Petrus Sabbatius, known as Justinian," came the response as Justinian rose slowly from his bow.

"And do you, Flavius Petrus Sabbatius, come to the throne of Caesar Augustus of your free will, with a mind toward selfless service of the Senate and People of Rome?"

Justinian cleared his throat before responding, as though trying to match Basilius' grandeur. "Yes, I do."

Basilius' eyes rose to the audience beyond. "What say you, People of Rome? Do you accept this man's claim to the unfilled throne of Caesar?"

The excubitores pounded their spears onto the marble in a careful, exact rhythm, and a few cries of support sounded across the ranks. The rich baritone of Belisarius cut through the din as he cheered, and his officers, too, joined in. Samur and Rosamund did not cheer, but looked on skeptically, while Fulcaris laughed and added his own voice to the cacophony.

Basilius raised a hand to silence the crowd. "You have the People's love and support, Flavius Petrus Sabbatius, called Justinian. Behold the great mantle of Rome, and tremble at its power."

Basilius signaled toward the other senior courtiers. Paulus came forward first, depositing a loaf of bread and a golden *solidus* at the foot of the throne. Tribonian came next, placing a scroll of Roman laws and a scale of justice near Paulus' offerings. Marcellus turned and placed his naked sword upon bare stone and quickly snapped back into place at the head of his men. Last came Cassiodorus, who deposited an ornate golden cross above the rest.

Gesturing to the offerings, Basilius continued his scripted lecture to Justinian. "Claimant to the heritage of the Caesars, do you intend to provide for the wealth and sustenance of your people, to execute justice fairly, to defend to your dying breath the sanctity of the Empire, and to honor God?"

Justinian nodded. "I do," he called out, far more confidently than before. Basilius bade him kneel, and was handed an Imperial diadem from Father Petrus. It was a simple enough thing, a golden circlet dressed in light pearls, yet Justinian eyed the ornament with a hunger bordering on lust.

"Almighty God and the People of Rome find you worthy to claim the purple. On behalf of their sacred power, I, Basilius Venantius, a onetime consul, crown you as Caesar Augustus, Emperor of Rome." Basilius lowered the diadem onto Justinian's head. After fixing it snugly into the new emperor's hair, Basilius fell back into line and bowed to Emperor Justinian.

All followed Basilius' example as Justinian rose. The crowd bowed again as he took his seat at the Imperial throne, waiting several heartbeats before signaling his subjects to stand upright once again.

From the throne, Justinian raised a jeweled hand, two fingers stretched outward. "For my first act, I call for the Lady Theodora. Come forth and greet the Roman people."

Marcellus stamped his spear again as servants relayed Justinian's command. A low rustling filled the hall as bodies jockeyed for position, eyeing a low door that was swung open to reveal Justinian's young wife.

Where Justinian wore the trappings of a grand monarch, Theodora approached the throne in a simple and unadorned silken dress. Her black hair tied back into a veil, Theodora held her head high as attendants straightened the trail of her gown, which had been sewn with the dark-olive-green thread that the Lady favored. Antonina was one of that number, her pregnancy hardly visible as she followed her mistress toward Justinian. Theodora gave a brief smile and a wink as she passed by and continued forward until reaching the Imperial dais.

A similar diadem, heavy with pearls and polished gold, was yielded to Justinian's outstretched hand. With little pomp, Justinian rose from his throne and stepped down toward Theodora. She kneeled and remained motionless as Justinian placed the crown upon her head, naming her Empress of the Romans.

At this, much of the crowd cheered, their voices only swelling as a second throne was placed alongside the Emperor's seat. Basilius beamed, while Paulus and Cassiodorus scowled. Amidst the applause, I caught the briefest glimpse of Mariya, who clapped excitedly for the new Empress.

The two monarchs took their seats, formally surveying their collective Court for the first time. Justinian leaned toward Theodora and muttered something inaudible that drew a graceful laugh from the Empress. Justinian smiled and sat back in his chair as though drinking in every detail of the moment, then dismissed the collected courtiers back into the audience so he might address the Court.

"As our first act in joint rule, we call Strategos Flavius Belisarius before the thrones," he said, his voice carrying to our far corner. Belisarius smiled and walked forward, allowed to pass by the palace guards as he approached the Emperor and Empress.

Belisarius fell to both knees, prostrating himself before Rome's rulers. His helmet rested on the floor at his side, allowing Belisarius to offer his bare head and cropped hair to the audience around him. Justinian bade him to rise, and Belisarius gave a crisp salute before standing at attention.

"Flavius Belisarius, we name you Magister Militum of the East, the High Commander of Rome's frontier with Persia. Our security, and the safety of the Roman People, is solely within your hands. Protect our people from this ancient foe," Justinian said formally.

Theodora rose and passed Belisarius an ivory baton that was crowned with a golden eagle. "In the waning days of the Republic, the Roman People granted their generals with the command of imperium. Symbolized by a baton topped by the Roman Eagle, its bearer held supreme power in all military matters of the Empire and spoke with the collective voice of the Senate and of the People."

Where Justinian's voice rose and fell with his emotions, Theodora's stayed fair and even, all the way to her final call to action. "Lord Belisarius, take your imperium east, and lead your men to victory against our enemy. You are our great hope in this war to preserve the Empire, and the heritage of Caesar."

The excubitores pounded their spears again, and nearly all of the soldiers gave a riotous cheer; I did catch Solomon smirking, but most all others were caught in the joy of the moment. Belisarius saluted the thrones, accepting the immense charge lain across his shoulders.

The Court soon concluded after Belisarius returned to our ranks. Men jostled for his attention, slapping him on the back and grabbing each of his arms. Belisarius grinned and laughed, graciously accepting their attentions, yet saved his time for his longstanding friends. Belisarius grasped Sunicas and Simmas fondly around the neck, then embraced Ascum, Baduarius, and Bessas. He patted me on the shoulders before giving an embrace, offering words of thanks at my sacrifice.

"As you see, I'll need you once again in the days to come." His eyes were twinkling, yet his voice was serious.

"Always, Lord. Without question," I said, and he gave me a nod of respect. Most of all, Belisarius embraced John, whom I discovered had grown with Belisarius since the two had been boys together in the hills of interior Thrace.

As they filed away from the palace hall, seeking respite from the oppressive heat, many nevertheless paused to offer their blessings and words of support to the new General of the East. Others stayed behind to meet with the new Emperor and Empress, and I snuck through the press to join their number. While most of the older courtiers and officials crowded around Justinian, I easily found Theodora, who smiled widely. Ignoring decorum, she hugged me briefly and half yelled so that her voice would carry through the chaos.

"I've waited for this for some time, and I have you to thank for much! I promise you, it is not forgotten," she said. "It is unfair for me to ask another favor, but I hope that you will be my eyes on the frontier with Persia, and update me with all that you hear."

"Of course, Empress." I saluted, which drew a heavy laugh from Theodora that only ebbed when she caught sight of my perplexed expression.

"I am sorry, Varus. You are the first to call me by that title… and it will certainly take getting used to," she said, gathering her breath. "But promise me that you will always provide wise counsel and push me toward what is right for the people, even if it may go against my wishes at the time."

"I promise, Empress," I said, grinning.

Sensing Theodora's need to speak with others, I bowed and shuffled away as I was dismissed from the Imperial dais. My eyes searched wildly for signs of the crimson-dressed Arab princess, but I only caught a glimpse of her attendants as they hurried out of the room. I tried to push my way forward, only to be blocked by a sea of silken nobles and marble columns.

I turned around, but something heavy collided with my groin, and sharp pain radiated through my body. Solomon withdrew his knee, his face coming close to my ear.

"Sorry, friend. It is difficult to see where one is going in all of this madness," he said sardonically. "It often does help to know one's place. I've found that sage advice helps me from injuring myself, or others."

"Is that how you received that injury to your arm?" I muffled, holding back tears from the pain between my legs. "Or did you prick your hand on a splinter?"

Solomon's face grew pinched, his nostrils flaring. "Never you mind. We will continue this conversation again at my wedding, of which I expect to deeply enjoy your company," he said, his voice staying low over the din of the crowd around us.

"I wouldn't miss it," I said firmly, though I wished I had the wit for a sharper retort.

Solomon pushed off of me as he trotted away, finding one of his father's old friends as they shared stories of their service in Rome's armies.

In truth, it was a day that I dreaded. I spent the next few days training in the Imperial Barracks while Rosamund and Cephalas filled orders that the foederati would require on the march. Belisarius occasionally joined me, providing rare opportunities to meet with the general without the distractions of his retinue. Belisarius shared his visions and concerns for the expedition ahead, occasionally broken by giddy talk of Antonina and the coming of their first child.

One training session was held with Samur, who'd developed whiplike reflexes in his extensive time with the Huns, and now wore thin mail and furs. When I offered to purchase him armor for the campaign ahead, he demurred.

"Maybe later," he said. "The Huns prize speed over protection, and I need to be able to fit in with Sunicas' riders." Samur took particular relish in his bowmanship, and regularly challenged Fulcaris to marksmanship contests atop a horse.

However, these distractions did little to alleviate the dread and exhaustion brought on by the impending wedding. Bile welled in my throat whenever my imagination contrived images of a triumphant Solomon, shining in his successes. Worse, I would have to go alone, for I had no right to bring a retinue as a mere komes amongst a wide body of landed nobles and wealthy commanders.

It was a waking nightmare, and I was expected to smile and clap. These were the moments when I shamefully questioned the will of my Creator—why did the wicked prosper so? And worse, why could I not do anything to change their fate?

THE MESSAGE

SOON ENOUGH, THE morning of the wedding arrived. Rosamund helped me prepare for the event, trading my armor for less martial wear. Rosamund's newfound tastes came through in her selections, which included a black linen shirt paired with light-gray trousers. The shirt was generally comfortable, hanging somewhat loosely from my frame, though as my body had grown used to layers of hardened leather and metal, it left me feeling naked. The bronze cross and golden dragon rested below my throat, while Theodora's sigil ring served as the only other trappings of wealth and success that I deigned to bring to the event.

The wedding was to be held in the palace in the Emperor's private chapel. Highborn nuptials would usually occur in one of Constantinople's grander churches, but as the Hagia Sophia had just recently been rebuilt, it lacked the rich ornamentation that Solomon's father demanded for his eldest son. While a wide and deep room within the palace, the chapel quickly filled up with attendees in the early hours of the morning, all of which jostled for a seat rather than having to stand for hours for the Orthodox Christian ceremony.

I arrived early and stood outside with Belisarius and John, preferring the cooler air in the drafty hallways than the balmy interior of the church. I nodded along, paying only scant attention, and scanned the attendants who made their way inside. King Jabalah and Prince al-Harith were in attendance, of course, dressed in all of the considerable finery the Ghassanids could offer, and much of the senior nobility who attended Justinian's coronation was now here to make an appearance at perhaps the second-most prominent social gathering of the winter season.

Chief among those was Senator Nepotian, who was flanked by two personal slaves and a handful of highborn friends who gossiped in his ear. The senator held his chin high as he spoke, acknowledging compliments of his son and taking every opportunity to mention his various businesses in the trades of grain, silk, and slaves. Justinian and Theodora arrived and greeted the senator, offering formal blessings upon the marriage and its conferred benefits onto the Empire.

Soon enough, all were ushered into the room, taking up the remaining available space in the packed hall. The ceremony began with an Orthodox service, with Solomon standing before an altar. Though I proscribed to the Latin rites of Catholicism, I followed along near Belisarius, who diligently prayed as the attending priest continued the service. All seemed normal, except for one crucial detail.

There was no sign of Mariya near the front of the hall, nor anywhere in the crowd. Several of her ladies were standing near the front of the procession, yet the princess was not among them.

Another ploy, I assumed, to draw attention to Solomon's family. When Solomon glanced back at the audience, however, his furrowed brow and stricken expression made me reconsider. Amidst the harmonious song of the church service, Nepotian gestured for Solomon to face forward once more, which he did, a deep scarlet spreading across his face. Faint whispers hissed along the walls, and even Belisarius was scanning the area as though seeking an answer. At last, he leaned over to me, but my attention was diverted by a hand at my shoulder.

A tiny scroll was thrust into my hand, and a crimson-clad figure flew away in a blur. Squinting, I unfurled the scroll and barely made out the faint writing within.

Third floor, far hall, facing the sea. Go now.

I crumpled the scroll in my hand, heart racing. Belisarius furrowed his brow and tilted his head at me, a question in his eyes, but I hastily shook my head and returned my attention to the service.

With the song echoing off the high walls, I considered ignoring the request. It could be many things—an idle joke from Samur, or even an ambush set by Solomon's friends, who would be able to corner me while the rest of the Court was occupied. I had entered the ceremony with a determination to see it through without incident and resented anything that might make the difficult day more torturous.

My curiosity got the better of me. I rose to exit, only to feel Belisarius' eyes upon me. I gestured at my gut.

Bladder, I mouthed. Belisarius chuckled, and I snaked my way to the rear of the crowd until I could finally slip from the sanctuary. I closed the heavy door behind me, immediately muffling the noise from the ceremony; the only noises were echoes from my boots as they slapped heavily against the marble.

Other than the rare servant, the palace was remarkably empty of bodies, reminding me of the long-ago night of Emperor Anastasius' death. I walked across a hall of ornate statues and decorated columns, arriving at a flight of stairs that led upward to the highest reaches of the palace. The third floor had been reserved for distinguished guests of the Emperor, and I quickened my pace as I neared that richly carpeted and gilded area.

On the landing of the aforementioned floor, I turned in the direction of the sea and hustled down the long hallway with its dozens of offices and apartments. My thoughts turned to Liberius, who often kept quarters in this area, and would surely go back to them upon his return from Persia. My heart rose at the thought of seeing him again, and my pace quickened to a trot as I closed upon the end of the hall.

I was greeted with nothing. A high window flooded light into the hall, yet silence prevailed upon those privileged halls. No Liberius, nor any reason for rising hopes on a day of misery. I had been foolish enough to follow an unsigned and unwanted letter, and had run around the palace like a fool in pursuit of some childish wish.

Fear rose in my gut as I heard footsteps sneak up behind me. I spun around to face my attackers, certain now that Solomon's men had lured me into a trap. I clenched my hand into a fist, determined to rush through the ambush and flee to the streets beyond, but as I turned, I caught sight of the crimson blur who'd delivered the note in the church below. A young woman flinched and raised her hands, and I dropped my stance.

"This way," she said urgently, her voice hushed despite the otherwise deserted hallway. Skeptical, I followed her through an unmarked door, which was quickly closed and bolted behind me. With the curtains drawn, the room was nearly pitch black, and I raised a hand to get my bearings. I called out to my guide, but my eyes burned as she threw open the curtains, revealing a rush of sunlight that reflected from the sea beyond.

And on a couch at the side of the room sat Mariya. The princess was adorned with the lavish crimson-and-gold gown that was to be her wedding dress, with rubies decorating her hair and ears. A particularly large garnet hung at her chest, sparkling as it caught light from the windows.

"Lady?"

I could speak no more as my voice caught in my throat. Two thick tears ran down Mariya's face, running slight streaks through the kohl around her eyes. She rose to face me, her hands clasped around her waist.

"Varus, I need you to take me away. Right now, before the others notice that I am gone." Her voice was taut, urgent.

I stammered as Mariya drew closer. "Lady, I don't understand, the Court is waiting for you downstairs—"

Mariya threw herself close, her lips closing on mine in a delicate yet passionate kiss. The warmth of her body flushed over me as her perfume buried itself in my clothing. Balancing on her toes, she wrapped her hands around my neck, holding me in a trance.

At last—too soon—Mariya pulled back a handsbreadth. Her amber eyes stared into mine, resolved. "I'm going with you. But we need to leave now."

Out of instinct, I nodded, stunned and reeling. My mind raced through the dozens of routes out of the palace, most of which required a daring, foolish rush out of the doors and into the gargantuan city beyond.

"What about your guards? Where are they?" I asked of the Aksumites who had never left her side.

Mariya smiled weakly. "They think I am still getting ready in my apartment, and I locked the door and snuck here using the same passageways that Samur showed me."

I took a deep breath and considered. Then I crafted the outline of a plan.

"You need to change clothes," I said. "This dress would stand out anywhere in the city."

Mariya wiped a lingering tear from her cheek and nodded. "I can switch with Alia," she said, referring to the other young woman in the room. "I can trust her in this."

I nodded my head. "Then we must move now."

Alia opened the bedroom door, peering into the hallway beyond. I gestured for her to follow, and we crept several doors down, shuffling our feet to limit any echo.

We arrived at one of the dozens of nondescript servants' doors that lined the palace. Alia cracked the entrance open, and Mariya and I followed behind, ducking low to descend to the second floor and Mariya's private apartments.

With what limited light was available to us, Alia picked her way to the princess' room, opening its hidden door in a way that masked noise from its hinges. Mariya bade me to wait as she disappeared inside, leaving me with nothing but the sounds of rustling silk and metal as she changed her ensemble.

A heavy banging sounded from the apartment doors, followed by the accented voice I recognized as one of the Aksumite guardsmen. Eyes wide, I jumped, nearly crashing into a nearby table. Mariya instantly poked her head out from behind the door, scowling, and placed a finger atop her lips.

"Princess, they are nearly ready for you, you must come down now," the voice said, deferential yet firm.

"Nearly ready!" Mariya sang cheerily, her voice tinged with a sweetness that nearly fooled even me. "Just a bit more time. These things *cannot* be rushed!"

"Understood, Princess, but many are becoming quite… angry," the voice continued. "Shall I send more for attendants to aid you?"

No. The very thought almost made me vomit onto Mariya's priceless silken carpets. I must have grunted, for Mariya glared again and violently gestured once more for silence. "That will not be necessary!" she called, her cheerfulness only slightly strained. "Ten minutes, I promise!"

With muttered assent, the Aksumite dismissed himself. Mariya, however, paused.

"For someone who lived amongst nobility, you are terrible at holding your tongue," she whispered. "I'll be ready in moments, but watch the door."

I nodded, the painful knot in my throat refusing to depart. My ears attuned to even the faintest creaking that echoed from the outer hallway, believing that a frustrated Imperial attendant or courtier would burst through the doorway and discover me inside. There would be nary a trial, for Solomon's men would be within their rights to butcher me in that very room like a common thief. In a way, I suppose that I was.

After several moments, the door to the servants' hallway opened, and Mariya shuffled inside. She donned Alia's simpler gown, but still wore the elaborate jewels that could only betray her status.

I opened my mouth to protest, but Mariya shook her head.

"I know they are conspicuous, but I will not leave them. They were my mother's, and they are all I have of her," she said firmly. Against my better judgment, I nodded, and we scurried down toward one of the hidden alleys that would lead us toward the barracks.

As we emerged from the gloomy hallway onto the stone streets, I motioned for Mariya to stay close, and we weaved our way through the tiny alleys that led away from the palace, a twisting path that sidestepped any exposure to the palace or the mass of well-wishers that gathered at its steps. Though my mind was wrought with anxiety, Mariya beamed with unadulterated delight as she skipped along the stone-hewn streets. We gained entry to the barracks and ran toward my rooms, seeking out the small retinue that accompanied me to Constantinople.

At the commotion, Cephalas ran to my door with a blade drawn in his lone good hand. I raised my hand to stay him, and confusion contorted his face.

"No time to explain. Go gather the others and prepare horses to leave immediately," I said. "And make sure you find my brother too."

Cephalas jumped to action, and he darted away to a cacophony of belongings being hurriedly packed away. Samur arrived soon thereafter, equally confused at why I'd returned so soon.

"Jesus Christ," Samur blasphemed as he made eye contact with Mariya. A mischievous look spread across my brother's face as he smirked. "Looks like we're leaving after all," he said, shutting the door and barking orders to the others.

Exhaling hard, I gathered the few possessions I held in my room and made ready to leave. To save space, I began putting on my armor, struggling as I lifted the scaled chest piece over my shoulders. Mariya helped secure the scaled armor, which I belted at the waist before securing its greaves. Saving the helmet for last, I secured it over my head and secured its cheekpieces, finally ready to go. Mariya, though, paused, her light fingers atop the scales, and stole another soft kiss, speaking low in her slightly accented Greek.

"I don't want there to be fighting, or for anyone to be hurt because of me," she said.

"There won't be," I answered, "but we do need to leave soon, before orders come to close the city gates."

With my weapons secure at my waist, I took Mariya's hand and left the room. Rosamund burst inside soon after, saying nothing as she grabbed the remaining decorations along the walls and carried them to Cephalas and Fulcaris. Within moments, my retinue was ready to depart, with Samur leading a horse for each person at the barracks gates.

As we left, I slipped two silver coins to the spearman on duty. "You saw nothing." The young man gave a hurried nod, and I helped Mariya onto her horse, then vaulted onto my own. With Cephalas, Fulcaris, Rosamund, and Perenus in tow, we followed Samur to the Gate of Melantias, which led us away from the forum and the bazaar where we were most likely to run into trouble despite the indirect route required to get there.

Commotion rang out from the direction of the palace, and Samur urged us onward, and faster. Soon enough, the city bells rang in alarm—the signal for the city watch to stand ready to execute the Emperor's orders.

Unlike many of the other gates through Constantinople's immense walls, the Melantias Gate primarily serviced merchants and tradesmen who resided in small settlements just beyond the city's boundaries. For years, Paulus and Tribonian attempted to

184

demolish these makeshift towns, decrying them as illegal tax havens and security hazards, yet the shanties would continue to crop up all the same. A press of carts and men jammed the gates, which had begun to swing closed, drawing the ire of the massed crowd.

Guiding my horse forward, I cleaved through the masses and found the centurion of the gate standing idly as a dozen spearmen responded to the city bells. The centurion saluted, seeing my plume, and I returned the gesture with an indifferent grunt.

"Soldier," I said, "I am a komes of the Roman Army, and I am on urgent Imperial business. I demand that you allow my party passage," I said, lowering my voice for effect.

The man shook his head. "Lord, with apologies, but I have orders to close and hold these gates until receiving direct orders from the palace otherwise," he said, speaking respectfully and with a tinge of fear.

I dismounted and approached the centurion, drawing close so that only he could hear my next comments. "What is your name, centurion?" I asked.

"Alcander, Lord," he responded, his eyes widening in fear as he saw the anger doubtlessly growing on my face.

I drew a golden solidus from my belt and raised it to chest level, careful that only Alcander should see.

"Alcander, I am prepared to forget this altercation. Allow my party to pass forward, and this will be my gift to compensate for your troubles," I said, moving the coin closer. "Refuse, however, and I will have to consider a less friendly response."

Alcander darted his eyes in all directions, blinking rapidly. Seeing no other option, he nodded and snatched the solidus from my hand.

"Good lad," I said, turning and remounting my horse. I led the others through the inner wall, and then the outer, and hurried along the road toward the Herulian encampment that lay less than a half day away.

Samur took the lead, yet kept the pace leisurely to accommodate Mariya, who had far less experience as a rider. Before the sun moved lower along the horizon, the Herulian camp arose in the distance, framed by black-and-white dragon banners that flapped vigorously in the wind.

The sentries saluted as I approached, opening the palisade gates to allow my party entry. We filed inside as Rosamund and Cephalas hurried to unpack my belongings in the empty tent reserved for a foederati commander, eliciting whispers of interest from the Herulian ranks.

I directed Mariya into my tent and called Perenus before following her inside.

"Inform the men of our predicament. Only Imperial legates may enter the encampment until further notice," I said.

Perenus saluted formally and trotted off to the other centurions, barking orders to return to their daily routine.

Inside the tent, Mariya stood near a lit brazier as Rosamund and Cephalas continued their business. Dirt had smudged the hem of her borrowed dress, which lacked the golden threads and decorations of the one that she'd traded to Alia. Still, in such finery, she shone out against the roughshod camp, marked by its dirt floors, open cookfires, and hundreds of stinking and swearing warriors.

Mariya did not complain. Far from it—joy and eagerness sparkled in her eyes, though I sensed fear also; she could not know what to do next, or what might befall her.

Rosamund and Cephalas soon departed to prepare an evening meal, leaving me alone with the princess. I gestured to a low wooden table, and we sat near the rising fire to finally share a respite from the chaos of the day. As I gazed into her amber eyes, she flashed a smile, which left me uneasy despite her beauty.

"Lady, I—"

Mariya interrupted. "I love you, Varus. I have been told that Rome is a country where a woman cannot be forced into a marriage that is not of her will, and I rejected the match that my father prepared for me," Mariya said, her face now serious. "Instead I choose you... if you will have me."

I let Mariya's words wash over me, the thrill of them greater than destroying an enemy's shield wall. Though poets and singers tell of such moments, I scoffed at such talk as foolish prattle for sheltered children. My scorn had carried me through the past months, where I dared not hope for even the slightest recognition of my heart's desire. Even so, Mariya's words nearly lifted me from my seat as I fought for composure, mind racing. When I saw she was frowning, I fell out of my reverie.

"Lady, you offer me my deepest desire, yet you hardly know me. Worse, I fear that you do not understand the hardship that you will put yourself through with me. My life is a far cry from the palace, even doing all that I could to provide for your happiness." I instantly regretted my honesty, but there was nothing to be done.

Mariya's eyes narrowed as she drew closer to me. "I will be no man's possession," she said in Greek, "and I do not require others to make my way through the world. I choose you, Varus, because it is my will to do so."

I could say nothing in response, too enraptured by Mariya's gaze. Her aura bound me like a spell, made all the more alluring by the music of her voice.

"Whether in a palace or in the wild under the stars, all I need is someone who will offer me love and respect. And I want that person to be you," she said.

My hand shot out and grabbed her own. Mariya squeezed, the golden bands along her slim fingers digging into my skin, and as she smiled again, the spell broke, giving me the courage to speak.

"I love you too," I blurted out. "I've loved you since I first saw you in the palace. Whatever comes, that will never change."

Mariya leaned forward, a hand running through my hair as she kissed me again. "So be it," she whispered. We sat for a time by the fire, our solace broken only by a light meal that was served as the sun fell from the sky.

Just before nightfall, our peace was disrupted by Perenus, requesting entry to the tent for a formal report.

"Riders from the capital approaching," he said nervously. "Shall I seal the gates and deny entry?"

Sighing, I shook my head. "No. I'll join you on the rampart and see for myself," I said.

A look of concern flooded across Mariya's face. "Varus, what will happen now?" she asked fearfully, coming to terms with the enormity of her decision.

"The palace will try to send you back to Solomon, with the hopes that he will accept you with forgiveness for this indiscretion. Is that what you want?" I could not ask her the real question: Do you choose to return to your life of privilege, even if it binds you?

To my surprise, she responded with a question of her own. "Will anyone be hurt because of me? No one else deserves to be punished, especially you, Varus."

"Probably not," I lied, feigning confidence. "If you wish to return, I will not think less of you," I added.

"Never," she said adamantly. "My decision is final—unless you would rather I leave."

Nodding, I followed Perenus out of the tent, ordering Fulcaris to stand guard over Mariya. After climbing a small wooden ladder, I stepped atop the sentry post above the palisade wall and glanced at the Imperial flags that trailed behind a small retinue.

Leading them was a darker figure that I made out as al-Harith, Mariya's brother. He was followed closely by a number of yellow-clad Aksumites, as well as a half dozen Romans who likely came from the Palace Guard.

As they neared, a Herulian sentry turned to me for orders, his eager expression plainly ready for a fight.

"Let them pass inside," I said, and descended the post to return to my tent.

After a cacophony of creaking gates and slowing horses, Prince al-Harith was directed into the tent, followed by the sole figure of Sembrouthes, leader of Mariya's Aksumite guards. The two men ducked through the hanging tent flaps and ambled inside, quickly making eye contact with Mariya and me. She squeezed my hand as her brother drew close, her breathing noticeably rising as he sat down with us. Sembrouthes remained standing near the brazier, using the fire to warm his hands from the cold journey from Constantinople.

Al-Harith greeted her in Arabic, but Mariya shook her head. "In Greek," she said. Her brother rolled his eyes but complied.

"Our father commands you to return to Constantinople at once," al-Harith began, his voice cold and eyes unblinking as he stared at his sister. "He was fuming as I left, and could not bring himself to meet Solomon's father from the shame you placed on us all."

Mariya snapped at her brother in anger. "If Father loves Solomon that much, then *he* can marry him in my place," Mariya said, her voice tipped with venom. "He has been lacking a spouse for several years, after all."

Al-Harith raised a hand. "This is not a personal alliance, Mariya. It is a political necessity. You understand—we must protect all the Ghassanids by binding ourselves firmly to the noble families of Rome. Solomon would not be my choice for you—I realized this after speaking with the man you have absconded with. But while Solomon is both cruel and a braggart, his father is powerful and his

189

family close with the Roman Emperor. That is what is important to our people."

Mariya glowered. "You would condemn me to a life as some foreigner's broodmare? Solomon is a brute, brother!"

The prince drew closer, his eyes wide, almost as if hurt. "Mariya, you are my only sister, and I have always loved you. Father adores you, despite your impetuousness. It pains me that this is your fate, but it *is* Father's will."

Mariya was undeterred. Her jeweled hand again reached for mine as her eyes burned into the Ghassanid prince's. "This is my choice. I have learned much of Theodora's laws these past months. In Rome, no woman can be married against her will, nor forced to be the property of any man, high or low. Father will have to be satisfied with that."

Al-Harith sighed. "Mariya, you are not Roman," he said dismissively. "Not yet, anyway."

The prince's gaze left Mariya and looked into my own. Al-Harith's eyes were ringed with deep black circles, his energy sapped from an unpredictably long and arduous day.

"I remember you, one of Belisarius' officers. You seem like a good man, but I do not think that you can provide my father with his desires," al-Harith said, his words cutting into me. "My sister has no experience with life in a camp and will face incredible scorn from Solomon's family for the injuries done to them this day. You can end this madness now and demand that she return to Constantinople by forcing her from your encampment."

Mariya's brow furrowed as she drew back in anger, yet I addressed the prince with respect all the same. "I can command the princess to do nothing. If she wishes to leave, I will provide her with a horse and wish you both well. But if she does not..." I said, trailing off. My words fell upon silence as al-Harith's unblinking eyes focused upon mine, offering me one final chance to defend the princess' choice.

"Yes, it is madness, but I love your sister," I said. "I am lowborn, and a soldier, and many other things that make this arrangement more difficult, even improbable. But I would treat her with the respect that she is due, and will honor your house with the wealth that I possess to ensure her comfort and safety."

Al-Harith rubbed his bare hands before his face, rubbing his eyes. "So I cannot convince either of you to end this now, while it is still relatively easy to do so?" he asked, noticeably unhopeful of an ideal ending.

"Never," Mariya said curtly. "If Father allows you and our other brothers to have their dalliances and skirt around his wishes, then so can I," she added cryptically.

I suppressed a chuckle and attempted to calm the situation. "I am sorry, Lord, but no. If Mariya wishes to stay with me, I do not wish for her to leave," I said more respectfully.

Al-Harith nodded sadly and stood as if to leave. "Very well. I will tell Father of your decision. I cannot guarantee your safety after I leave here, Mariya," he said with concern. "Nor for any of the men who provide you shelter."

Mariya gave me a nervous look, yet I stood to meet the prince's words. "I welcome any into this camp, but fear no threat. We will be safe," I said with false bravado.

In truth, my mind wandered to a vast Imperial Army that could easily encircle my small palisade fort, killing all inside within a matter of moments. However, al-Harith nodded. "Sembrouthes wishes to remain in the encampment for the time being," he said.

"Why?" Mariya asked. Al-Harith simply shrugged as he left, leaving it to the burly Aksumite commander to explain.

"Princess, I have served as your personal guard for five years... my oath is to you, and no one else," he said in heavily accented Greek. His usually stony face contorted with real pain as his eyes fell to the floor. "Why wouldn't you trust me with this secret? Do you have no faith in me?"

At that, Mariya's resistance broke, and she rose to bring her longtime friend into a warm embrace. Sembrouthes could not have been past his late twenties, yet his arms had been checked with dozens of minor scars that bore evidence of his martial history. Sembrouthes swore to protect his princess as she buried her face in his robes and quickly departed to organize the other Aksumite spearmen to set a watch over our tent. I found later that Sembrouthes had taken half of Mariya's personal guard, with another six Aksumites taking residence in the Herulian encampment as the last slivers of light disappeared in the sky.

The three of us spoke late into the night, broken up intermittently by visits from other camp occupants. Though all offered updates of the camp and the foederati, many seemed to merely be interested in the drama of the day, desirous of a view of the fort's latest inhabitants. Outside the tent, many of the Herulians could be heard drinking and singing around a fire, gossiping and taking guesses at what their commander had gotten himself wrapped up in.

Fatigue soon set in, and I made for an empty officer's tent on the opposite side of the encampment. I was sorely tempted to stay with Mariya, but I did not want to bring her any dishonor, and instead provided her with my own quarters for the evening. Sembrouthes set a watch rotation amongst his men, and Mariya stole another kiss as I departed into the blackness of the night.

Rosamund passed by as she ducked into my tent. Never in her life had Mariya slept far from one of her maids, so Rosamund volunteered to stay with her. Though the situation made her visibly anxious in her quick movements and darting eyes, Rosamund nevertheless presented an air of courtesy to the princess, doing all she could to acquaint her with the deprivations of camp life.

As I walked to my assigned tent, I passed Perenus, who hooted as he raised a fist in the air. Fulcaris and the small number of other Herulians who remained awake followed his example, and all I could do was shake my head and chuckle. I ducked inside the diminutive quarters and closed off its makeshift door, awash with a flurry of emotion from the day.

The following morning began like any other within a foederati encampment, save the presence of an Arab princess. Al-Harith departed well before dawn, occupying a private tent rather than gallop back to the capital in the dead of night. In a measure of mercy, the prince left behind a small trunk of the princess' wardrobe, affording her fresh clothing for the days ahead.

While Rosamund and Mariya chatted in my tent, I joined Perenus and the other officers for a much-needed day of training with my Herulian soldiers.

That idyll was broken in the late afternoon as Imperial banners were spotted again on the horizon. However, whereas al-Harith's retinue had been marked with smaller flags and a small handful of men, a full banda of Imperial spearmen lined the road, with richly decorated banners flapping in the wind.

Looking more closely, I spied Belisarius' wolf alongside the Imperial Eagle, and found Belisarius at the head of the column. Beside him rode the Empress Theodora, dressed in all the raiment of her newfound office. The banda had been laden down with heavy gear and dressed in a full panoply for war.

I shuddered. I knew that al-Harith would not be the last envoy seeking to retrieve Mariya, but the Empress herself—that I had not anticipated. As the holder of my oath to the Empire, Theodora could command me to return the princess to Solomon, and I would have little recourse but to obey.

"Open the gates, immediately!" I called to the sentries, who saluted and drew the wooden doors slowly open.

Perenus appeared at my side, taking in the army facing us. "Think we'll have to fight Romans today?" he asked, putting on a brave face.

I grunted. "It won't come to that," I said. "Form the men into lines in the training square."

With Perenus sent to his task, I descended to the dirt below and walked alone through the open gate. I paced forward as the banda approached, meeting Theodora and Belisarius a full twenty paces from the camp's entrance.

I greeted the Empress and Belisarius with a formal salute, yielding my command of the camp to their judgment. Theodora slid from her horse and walked over, her face stony and stoic. As she approached, she raised a hand and slapped me hard across the face, my exposed skin stinging from the blow. The surprise rattled me, although I dared not shy away from Theodora's gaze.

Instead, I kneeled at her feet, remaining still for several heartbeats. Theodora said nothing at first, allowing the late winter air to blow lightly through the grass. My eyes remained fixed toward the ground as I awaited her command, struggling to find the words that could answer her anger.

"Rise and escort me into your camp," Theodora said in a low voice. I obeyed and rose, bowing again, and allowed the Empress to remain a half pace ahead as she walked through the open gate. Belisarius remained outside with the banda, which formed into four long lines as they lazed informally along the low hills, leaning on spears to offset the weight of their armor.

Theodora glanced quickly at the foederati that had been organized in the yard, led by Perenus in his centurion's armor. With nary a further direct command, she continued into the commander's tent, leaving me to hustle behind. I closed the tent flap behind us.

The interior had been uncommonly well lit, allowing the Empress to take stock of her surroundings. Mariya rose to her feet out of respect, while Rosamund bowed deeply at my signal, still unfamiliar with the Imperial customs.

Theodora turned her head toward Rosamund, her eyes narrowing as she inspected the young Gepid woman.

"What is your name?" Theodora asked in Latin. When Rosamund's brows knit, the Empress repeated the question in Greek.

"Rosamund, Highness," Rosamund answered in thickly accented Greek.

Theodora gave her a thin smile. "Rosamund. That is a Gepid name? And you serve Lord Varus?"

Rosamund nodded. "Yes, Highness. I have served Lord Varus for over a year now, since I was taken from the Gepid Kingdom."

Theodora raised a well-manicured eyebrow, intrigued. "Varus took you as a captive?" she asked, her tone light with curiosity.

Rosamund rose to meet the Empress' gaze, shaking her head. "No, Empress. Varus saved me from those who would enslave me… or worse," she said, and my mind flooded with memories of the fateful day that Rosamund's childhood village had been put to the torch.

Theodora nodded in approval. "Thank you, Rosamund of the Gepids. If you would be so kind, please bring a pitcher of wine… I have much to discuss with your master."

Rosamund bowed again and hurried outside. Theodora's regal figure was left alone with Mariya and me, and we waited in silence as Rosamund closed the tent flap to the outside world. Theodora's nose flared as her stern gaze moved throughout the tent once again, eyeing the Avar flag, my weapons, and finally Princess Mariya. I wished desperately to break the tension, remaining still and silent as I stood at Theodora's back, unable to reach Mariya's side.

Once the tent was secured, Theodora began to shudder lightly. I worried that she was having some sort of convulsion, but as I rushed to her side, I heard the sound of laughter, which only grew louder as Mariya and I looked on, perplexed.

"Empress?" I asked tentatively. When Theodora turned to me, the iciness of her initial greeting had completely melted.

"I admit," she said, stifling her mirth, "I am rarely surprised, but this current arrangement caught me unawares."

Theodora began pacing the room, examining the few possessions that I held to my name. She laid a long finger across the Avar banner, teasing at a jagged tear in the blackened cloth.

"Nepotian is furious, of course, but I am not of a mind to appease him. My husband disagrees, although not enough to rise in the senator's defense," Theodora said again, her eyes fixed along the walls.

"Empress, I..." I stammered, yet I was interrupted again by Theodora.

"Varus, I cannot say that I am pleased," Theodora said firmly. "A year of planning spoiled like week-old soup. We still may salvage the broth, however many bones must be broken in the process."

Mariya moved forward. "Empress, I humbly apologize for disrupting your plans, but I will not marry Solomon." Her voice was even as she addressed the most powerful woman in the Empire. Mariya added, "The laws of the Roman Empire protect a woman from marrying against her will, and the only way that I would marry Solomon is by force."

Theodora's eyes narrowed. "Yes, I know. I was the one who crafted that decree." Theodora turned and sat at a rough-hewn chair before the brazier, flattening the emerald gown she so often favored.

Sitting calmly by the fire, Theodora stared into the flames, allowing their warmth to flood over her exposed face and hands before claiming a bench adjacent to a low wooden table. After several moments, she removed the crown and veil that denoted her high status and placed them gently upon a nearby table without leaving her perch. Theodora gathered her long black hair in her hands and smoothed over the deep impressions that the veil and crown had left, massaging her temples as she did so.

"I am less disappointed by the disrupted marriage, and more that you did not trust me enough to discuss your plans, Varus. This position is a dangerous one, and I cannot suffer a lack of confidence from my closest advisors in the future. Is that understood?" Theodora asked, filling me with a deep shame at not fulfilling my oath.

"Yes, Empress. It will not happen again," I said deferentially.

Theodora smiled weakly once more. "Good. Now kindly allow me to speak with Princess Mariya in private... We have matters to discuss."

Mariya looked at me with concern, nodding all the same. I saluted the Empress and left the tent, finding Rosamund standing just outside with Theodora's wine. As we waited, several Herulians passed curious glances toward my tent, excitement lighting their faces as they clamored for another glance of the Roman Empress. Perenus barked at the men to return to their training and to not gossip like a bunch of girls, although that feigned attempt at discipline did little to stop several soldiers from pretending to run errands that just so happened to be near their komes' tent.

Sembrouthes also stood guard with two other Aksumite spearmen, his face stony as he judged the martial character and combat prowess of his Herulian hosts. I invited the Aksumites to train alongside my men, but Sembrouthes politely declined. "Maybe another time, when things are less... uncertain," he said gruffly.

By this, I could only assume he referred to whether Mariya would remain in my camp for much longer, and I did not press the matter.

Our wait ended as Mariya opened the tent, summoning us inside. I ducked inside, and Rosamund followed, pouring wine in a simple wooden cup and placing it beside the Empress.

Theodora looked upon me with a bemused look. "Well, Varus, the princess has convinced me that this escapade was her idea, and that otherwise you have behaved gallantly. For that, at least, I thank you," she said, taking a sip of the red wine. Camp wine was poor quality even when fresh, and this batch had surely gone sour, but Theodora drank it as easily as if seated at a palace banquet.

"King Jabalah will need to be placated, although I think he will not balk when he understands that you are the effective heir to the old Emperor's estate and do not require a dowry. He will demand a wedding soon, and before the armies leave for Mesopotamia, and I would like to oblige him," Theodora said, her eyes narrowing as they slowly moved from me onto Mariya.

"This is more than agreeable, Empress, and thank you," Mariya said, a broad grin on her face. I echoed Mariya's words, and with that, the matter was resolved.

Theodora clapped her hands. "Good. Just have it done within two weeks." The proclamation sent a flurry of questions through my mind, unsure as I was of how such an affair could be organized in so little time. It became apparent later that Theodora did not intend for a large affair, which would only draw attention to Solomon's shame, but a more modest one that was just enough to satisfy her Ghassanid allies without being showy.

Theodora returned her gaze to mine. Her deep-green eyes shone with raw intelligence, betraying nothing of her larger strategy, giving the Empress a calculating but inscrutable look.

"I will deal with Nepotian, although it would be wise of you to avoid his son in the future. At any rate, the senator has made himself far too familiar with my husband's advisors, and a bit of forced humility will be good for him," Theodora said stoically.

"However, I do expect complete loyalty in the future, Varus. Even if the knowledge you have to share with me is unpleasant."

"Yes, Empress. Absolutely."

Theodora finished her cup and nodded at Rosamund, who dutifully refilled the wine to a polite smile from the Empress.

"Excellent. Now that the unpleasantness is behind us, it is far too late in the day to return to Constantinople. Varus, if you would be so kind as to provide me with sleeping quarters, it would be very informative to observe the foederati training alongside Belisarius' spearmen." Theodora spoke as though making an idle suggestion rather than a command. "Oh, and be sure to prepare a feast to celebrate your betrothal... enough to include Belisarius' men as well."

I nodded, my stomach fluttering at the complicated logistics that had been thrust upon me late into the day. Rosamund snapped to attention, bowing deeply yet clumsily to the Empress before disappearing from the tent. Following Rosamund's example, I bowed and left the tent, stealing one final glance at Mariya. She winked at me slyly, remaining with Theodora as I returned to my men.

Perenus ordered the Herulians armored and mounted, and they hurried into lines as I followed their example. Cephalas helped me into my armor, and I took my place at the front of the ranks as Fulcaris led a horse to my makeshift quarters. Outside of the fort, camp servants had already begun ferrying hundreds of heavy packs that Belisarius' banda had hauled from Constantinople. A messenger relayed Theodora's orders to Belisarius, and the banda hummed like a buzzing hive as the men formed mock battle lines.

I ordered wooden training swords to be carried to Belisarius' men, with the camp stores possessing just enough to ensure that the Roman ranks could participate in the mock battle. Soon after, Theodora and Mariya emerged from the commander's tent and were guided atop the sentry platform to gain a heightened vantage point to observe the exercise below.

After scanning the escort that brought her from Constantinople, Theodora turned to review the mounted foederati. At last, she nodded, and I nudged my horse forward as she summoned me with a light wave of her hand.

"You may begin, Lord Varus," Theodora said nonchalantly.

Rosamund ascended the viewing platform, offering the Empress a chair while she and Mariya stood patiently behind.

I saluted and bellowed for the foederati to follow me through the gate. A great roar echoed through the yard and over its palisade walls, yet the lines moved in an orderly fashion, continuing their great cheer as they went. After leaving the gate at a trot, they sped to a gallop as they fanned out before the walls, leaving a gap of one hundred paces between our riders and Belisarius' men. Samur followed close behind me, taking part in the exercises as an experienced horse archer with Sunicas' Huns.

As the last rider emerged from the camp gate, I caught Perenus' attention and called out our next order.

"Pincer!" I yelled in Heruli, a word that even the Greek-speaking Roman centurions in the foederati had become intimately familiar with.

Another booming howl rose through the ranks as the two halves of the foederati quickly separated, forcing their mounts into a rapid gallop. Perenus, leading half of the men, cut diagonally in front of me to confuse our target, and I led my own men in the opposite direction. Hoofbeats thundered across the plains as the howling grew more frantic, with Fulcaris and Alaric goading their men into louder taunts against the enemy.

Belisarius' spearmen looked on as the Herulian foederati circled their positions three times. Each circuit took but a short time due to the condensed nature of the Roman spearmen. As I passed near Perenus at the end of the third tour, I signaled for the men to form opposing shield walls, effectively outflanking the Roman soldiers and forcing them to fight back to back. As I put the plan into action, I stole one last glance back onto the fort's ramparts, where I found Theodora rising from her chair in rapt attention.

The maneuver was executed beautifully, with the shield walls forming in a fluid manner as men quickly dismounted and fell into lines not twenty paces from Belisarius' spears. Belisarius attempted to organize his men into opposing wedges, hoping to predict the maneuver, and I felt his eyes following my every move as he shouted his orders.

Perenus raised his banner, ready, and I gave the signal. In good order, our dragon-painted shields surged forward, crashing into the Roman wedge that faced either side. I instantly saw the logic of Belisarius' maneuver: the formation broke some of the ferocity of our advance, though the Roman lines ultimately lacked the strength to withstand the Herulian foederati.

Even with wooden swords and blunted spears, the men fought like demons under the watchful eye of the Empress. One of Belisarius' centurions hacked at my plume, seeking to steal the honor from the field, so I gutted him with a mock stab through a tiny gap in the Roman shield wall. Belisarius kept ordering his men about until, seeing the desperate state of his forces, he drew his sword and threw his own weight against my lines.

The shoving match of the wall continued for a few more moments until a deep horn sounded from the camp, bringing the exercise to a close. Lines separated amidst the curious sound of laughter, which rarely accompanied the press of men, iron, and leather that would have dominated a real battle. With sweat streaming from his face, Belisarius approached me with a wide smile on his face, laughing with the rest of his men.

"My God, but what a maneuver that was! I'm glad that your foederati are fighting on our side in the war!" he exclaimed. Belisarius' praise was not totally earned, for he would not have been caught so easily off guard for a mounted unit to surround him, although the compliment brought a note of pride to my officers all the same. Belisarius ordered the twin bandae to form into normal training lines and accompanied me back to my camp.

"I guess that means that congratulations are in order," Belisarius said amiably as we walked up the low hill toward the gates.

"Lord?"

Seeing my confusion, he laughed. "You and the Ghassanid princess! Well done, by the way," he added. "Love is so rarely found in the Roman government. The two of us seem to be the lucky exceptions."

I offered heartfelt thanks and inquired after Antonina's well-being. At the mention of his own wife, Belisarius beamed.

"She's doing well, although she's become somewhat particular about her food as of late. Basilius chides her to take more rest, yet Antonina insists on accompanying me to Court." Belisarius' voice was warm with pride, though what he said was something of an understatement. Antonina had done more than simply follow her husband in support; she railed against his tendency to modesty. Belisarius argued that he cared little for the typical politicking of Rome's noble families, yet Antonina hounded him all the same to claim the recognition he was justly due.

Theodora, having reached the gate, grinned down from the sentry's battlement. "Riveting!" she called down, abandoning the aloof decorum expected of a Roman Empress. We walked inside as Theodora applauded us and was helped down a short wooden ladder by Rosamund.

"Truly exhilarating to watch. I knew you could form the foederati into fighting shape," Theodora said generously. Theodora took Belisarius' arm as they walked back into the commander's tent, with Mariya and I following closely behind.

"Is that what it's like in battle?" Mariya asked, her voice light but with a note of true concern.

"At the beginning. Then it gets messier, and bloodier," I said, teasing her innocence.

In truth, my limited experience in the shield wall had taught that only discipline held together an army grown ragged from fatigue and gashed with enemy arrows, where men were fed by the competing urges to run from the field and kill their enemies.

Mariya gave my hand a playful slap as we followed the Empress. "However it goes, you do not have my permission to get yourself hurt." Her voice was lighthearted, although her face remained grave. Her worry was not unfounded, and I said whatever words I thought would ease her mind, achieving little success for my labors.

As the men trained and servants readied what thin feast our camp was able to offer, our small group sat and indulged Theodora's excitement. Even surrounded by the trappings of soldiery, it was tempting to forget the looming war that was only weeks away. Theodora's exhilaration and energy echoed the words of Justin, who held a grand vision of reclaiming the lost provinces that had defined the Roman Empire. Theodora spoke of grand cathedrals and vast infrastructure projects, but most of all, she spoke of peace throughout the land—an impossible dream from centuries ago, when the darkness was held at bay and Romans did not have to scratch what meager living they could from decaying soil. In those moments, when I could forget the human cost of mad hopes, I believed in that dream too.

The foederati and Belisarius' Romans filed into the camp in the early evening, met by long benches and tables that lined the training yard. Piled high were cuts of roast chicken and salted beef, further adorned by several barrels of wine that I kept stored in my tent. Space was limited, yet there was room enough for all to squeeze in.

Cephalas offered Theodora a private table, but she politely refused and sat amongst her soldiers. Belisarius sat to her right, while the Empress gestured that Mariya and I should take our places across from her. Samur jockeyed for position at my left, growling at a Herulian man to make space for the commander's brother. I invited Rosamund to join the rest of us, and though she did, she remained aloof, carefully monitoring the dinner for any disruption or unhappiness.

There was little fanfare at first, with hungry and exhausted soldiers pawing at slabs of greasy meat and hard bread to slake their hunger. Perenus made himself into a nuisance with Sembrouthes' Aksumite spearmen, goading them into swig after swig of wine despite the long, sober night watches ahead. More than one of the Aksumites snuck a drink when Sembrouthes' back was turned, eliciting howls of laughter from Perenus and Fulcaris as they proceeded to make themselves drunk.

Though I would have been plenty happy continuing onward with Mariya leaning gently against my side and my friends all around, the Empress insisted that any good betrothal required a toast. Seizing the opportunity, Belisarius rose to his feet, shouting in Greek for the assembled men to raise their cups in celebration of the impending marriage.

Belisarius first greeted the Empress, and then the gathered men who would comprise no small part of his future army. The Romans roared for their commander, echoed swiftly by my Herulians. Belisarius kept his words brief, recalling my rise in the army and the friends that I gathered in that time.

"All of us here can appreciate that it is one thing to be born high, and yet another still to carve out our own success from the toil of our labors. No man present knows that lesson more than Varus, a man of impeccable character and truth," Belisarius bellowed, prompting further noise and thudding from the Herulians as he mentioned my name. Mariya leaned over and planted a kiss on my cheek, which made Samur and Theodora alike laugh merrily, and I felt myself blush—happy, embarrassed, unused to the weight of so much attention.

Belisarius concluded with a cup in the air. "My friend, never let anyone deny you the happiness you have earned!" With that, he led hundreds of others in a toast to our welfare. Theodora insisted that the cups be refilled, raising further cheers from the benches as she led the soldiers in gulping their wine.

Belisarius leaned forward as Mariya spoke of her home in Arabia, complimenting her and taking in knowledge of his future Ghassanid allies. Theodora used that opportunity to grab my attention, the wine inspiring her sense of mischief.

"And *another* thing I must do is to cancel your betrothal to Hilda," she said. Her words were playful, yet they drove a startling sense of shame deep into my chest, for I had not thought of my intended Vandal bride even once since absconding with Mariya.

As I mouthed further apologies for my disruption to the Empire's plans, Theodora raised a hand to assure that all was well. "It is likely a blessing in disguise, for we've heard rumors that the Vandal King Hilderic has grown unpopular with his people."

I failed to suppress a shudder. The Vandals, Theodora explained, disliked Hilderic's softness toward the Romans, and many of the Vandal warlords along the African coast hungered for war against their neighbors.

With the conversation swelling further still, torches and braziers soon blazed along the camp, offering light for our party and warmth against the cool night breeze. Cephalas dutifully carried cuts of meat to the sentries unlucky enough to draw the watch assignment on such a boisterous evening, while Rosamund finally surrendered her cares and took a seat at our table.

To my surprise, the Empress continued to drink heavily, matching many of the burlier soldiers in their ardor for celebration. This was a rare reminder that Theodora was still a young woman, not much older than me, who rarely had the freedom to behave in a manner similar to most of her subjects. Her sheer vitality drew Perenus and Fulcaris to the table, who proceeded to tease their Empress with a torrent of games, riddles, and lewd jokes. I gaped in horror as Perenus slurred a particularly ripe abomination, yet Theodora guffawed at his words and urged him to continue.

Other than the Aksumites, Samur alone stayed relatively sober, drinking small sips from his cup as he jibed at the gathered guests and egged Perenus on further. As the evening wore on, he threw an arm around me and squeezed tightly, and was met with a wide hug from my betrothed.

As the stars above grew bright in the sky, the last of our food was snagged with greedy fingers. Several men began to sneak off for a well-deserved rest, and many of Belisarius' banda exited the camp toward the rows of erected tents one hundred paces from the camp entrance.

It was not until several of the torches began to burn out that the makeshift feast was finally called to an end. Perenus and Fulcaris engaged in a rigorous wrestling match at the behest of a giddy Theodora, who chortled at the sight of the men having stripped to the waist and attempting to knock one another over. Samur teased them further, offering increasingly impossible suggestions for the drunken men to individually claim victory.

Belisarius laughed at the futility before dismissing himself, congratulating Mariya and me again before he left with his men sleeping outside the camp. Mariya and I each helped Theodora walk back to the commander's tent, masking her swaying steps as she struggled to keep upright. Rosamund followed closely behind, eyes darting around as she took measure of the potential hazards that could befall my oath-keeper.

Sembrouthes held the tent flaps open as we helped the Empress inside, laying her flat on a low bed that Rosamund did her best to cushion for our Imperial guest. Theodora lay back, patting me on the cheek as she struggled to get comfortable, her silken dress stained with wine and dirt. Rosamund sat at the Empress' side, agreeing to help ready her for the evening once I had departed.

Mariya took up residence in another small cot at the opposite side of the tent. As a distracted Rosamund gave Theodora small sips of cool water, Mariya glided over to me and wrapped her jeweled arms around my neck. She indulged in one intimate kiss, then bid me goodnight as she closed the tent to all potential interlopers. I backed away, offering a respectful nod to Sembrouthes as I walked to the opposite side of the camp. Other than the sentries, only Perenus and Fulcaris remained awake, singing bawdily to one another of the various tales they learned in the taverns and wine-houses of Constantinople.

Theodora departed the next day at the head of Belisarius' banda. She embraced Mariya before leaving, noting that our foederati should arrive in the Imperial Barracks in six days' time. Belisarius nodded and led the Empress back to the capital, leaving me with less than a week of relatively blissful training and rest as the last vestiges of winter faded into spring.

In that time, Mariya was eager to help with the management of the camp, with Cephalas refusing to allow her any labor that he felt was beneath her station. The princess did have a way with organizing the camp servants in a more efficient manner, and promised to procure additional household servants from her retinue to assist with the camp's needs. Privately, Rosamund fumed at this development, arguing that it was thoroughly unnecessary, although I held firm and overruled her, reasoning that it would make her tasks easier and grant her much deserved authority in my household.

While messengers flitted continuously from Constantinople to our outpost, two deliveries were of note in that time of blessed peace. The first was a series of large wagons that bore the first tranche of armor that I had ordered, prompting another series of cheers from the Herulians as they fought for the most comfortable fit. Perenus strutted in his customized mail, while even Rosamund brightened as she armored her body, striking an image of one of the Amazons last seen in Alexander's long-ago foray into the Sogdian wastes along the Jaxartes River.

A day before departing the camp, the second included a message from the palace, carried in a scroll marked with the personal seal of the Emperor. Inside was a formal blessing from King Jabalah, who wished for his daughter's happiness in her marriage that was to take place a mere two days after our arrival in the Capitol. Mariya beamed at the message, which served as an equal measure of relief that Theodora managed to smooth over any perceived insults that the Ghassanid king may have felt.

However, our only knowledge of Solomon came from a briefly written note from Troglita, who congratulated my good fortune yet warned me of potential danger to come.

Stay clear of Solomon's banda, Troglita wrote, *for he's unlikely to ever forgive Mariya leaving him, and he has few distractions to keep him from thoughts of revenge.*

Silently thanking Troglita for his warning, I placed the letter over a lit taper, watching as the paper coiled and blackened into ash. Though on edge, I kept the warning to myself, preferring to spare Mariya and my household the worry that comes from a determined and spiteful enemy on the horizon.

The foederati's inevitable departure for Constantinople was a relatively grand affair compared with its earlier experience at Philippi. Where the men had been clad in ragged clothing and rusted armor, they now bore shining mail that was resilient enough to resist all but the most determined sword slashes, but light enough to not overburden their mounts. Black banners swirled high above the Herulians as they vacated the camp, the white ouroboros snarling at the center of each flag. As with Philippi, a token force of servants was left behind to tend the upkeep of the palisade walls and wooden buildings, their labors made lighter from the departure of the hundreds of Herulian riders.

Mariya rode alongside me at the head of our column, the sun catching the deep-crimson-and-gold linen that framed her dress. She did not balk at the dawn departure from the camp, offering compliments and words of encouragement to each of the men she passed by. The princess smiled as she took in the morning sun, followed closely behind by Sembrouthes and his thin line of Aksumite spearmen.

Toward the southern end of the walls, we arrived at Constantinople's Rhegian Gate, our banners acknowledged by the gate's centurion. Perenus and I directed the Herulians toward the barracks while Sembrouthes escorted Mariya back to the palace, where we would be separated for a few days until the wedding. Mariya's attendants had already begun planning the ceremony, which seemed a Herculean task based upon what details Mariya shared with me.

As we parted near the barracks entry, the princess blew one final kiss. "Soon," she said. I watched her ride away, captivated by the same allure I'd felt when I first saw her over half a year ago.

The Herulians were guided to the Imperial stables, leaving their horses as they walked the remaining short distance to the barracks that housed many of Belisarius' men. Our foederati was one of the final units to arrive, with Sunicas and Simmas' Huns finally granted entry the day prior. Though little space could be found as the men jostled for the most comfortable bunks, enough room remained in that great hall as well as several warehouses near the docks to accommodate thousands of Roman soldiers.

Upon my arrival to my private quarters, I was met by an angry Father Petrus, who rapped me with his cane as I approached for his blessing.

"You go off and find a bride without telling me? Justin would be mortified!" Petrus croaked, with real pain straining his voice.

Shaking off the shock of seeing my faithful priest—and the surprising pain from the wooden stick—I dropped to my knees and touched the hem of his black cloak, begging forgiveness. Petrus laid a bony hand on the crown of my head, ordering me to rise. He met my face with joy in his eyes, offering an unceremonious hug as he did so.

"Just think of all that has happened in two years," Petrus marveled. "I just hope to live and see what fruit this all bears."

In our time together, I discovered that Father Petrus was indeed old by Roman standards, but looked far more aged and decrepit than his years should have shown. I gathered the foolish courage to ask what the man had seen, but he gave me nothing more than an idle wave of the hand.

"Sixty years? Sixty-five? Or thereabouts." Father Petrus always seemed ancient, far older than even Liberius, although they were likely close in age.

Brief training sessions filled my few days until the wedding, when I would be joined with Mariya again. Many of the men joked and ribbed me for my predicament—all in good humor, but never in the presence of Solomon's men, who arrived in the Capitol with the rest of the Thracian Army. Germanus and Mundus each gave their hearty congratulations, too, yet as Belisarius' grand army congealed into a complementary mass of Roman might and experience, I saw no sign of Solomon.

The wedding day arrived, and with it came spring. The harsh winter gales from the Sea of Marmara gradually stilled, and the city air grew more temperate while staying refreshingly cool.

Troglita, with his more noble background, was indispensable in helping me prepare for the wedding. Though my time as a palace slave had trained my manners to a respectable level, I knew little of proper conduct as a bridegroom, having witnessed few weddings due to Justin's advanced age. Troglita gamely instructed me on what to wear and how to carry myself in the presence of such austere guests, and I appreciated the assistance in my hours of anxious excitement. The wedding was held on a quiet afternoon, and I was escorted by my friends and companions as we made our way to the designated church.

Rather than consuming a vast Imperial hall or gold-trimmed church, the wedding would be joined in one of the few Catholic chapels that a century of emperors maintained out of respect to their colleagues in the western half of the Empire. Small windows and wooden benches made up its décor, forcing all observers to squeeze together in order to find a seat.

Inside, I found Father Petrus standing at the altar, his weathered face offering a warm smile as he waved and told of his responsibility to officiate the wedding. Eager to make himself useful, Cephalas followed close behind, taking instructions from Petrus as he scurried about.

Few of the aristocrats from the prior affair were in attendance, yet Belisarius and Antonina were seated prominently in the forward rows, while Belisarius' officers lined the hall. Baduarius hooted as I walked past, earning an icy stare from Father Petrus and a wave of angry mumbling from others. Perenus, Fulcaris, and Rosamund took places near Sunicas and Simmas, the latter three pagans clearly confused by the ritual while Perenus offered muffled jibes to lighten the mood. John sat to Belisarius' left, whispering in the general's ear while Bessas and Ascum leaned against the church wall in their own private conversation.

Mariya was represented by her brother, Prince al-Harith, as well as the full contingent of Aksumites. Several maids and ladies attended her as she prepared for the wedding, although Mariya's father was conspicuously absent from the event. The most surprising attendant was Basilius, who found Antonina in the press

211

of bodies and loomed over the occupant to her right until the young man moved away.

The place of honor was reserved for Empress Theodora, who had been escorted by the excubitor Marcellus to her seat in the front row of the church. Theodora sat regally, beaming as she caught my attention, then whispered to Marcellus in the moments prior to the event. The Emperor Justinian was absent, yet few in attendance seemed to miss his presence.

Nearly all my lifelong friends and companions lined the hall, and Father Petrus could only try in vain to restore a sense of decorum to the holy building. Among those still living, the only person whose presence was sorely missed was that of Liberius, who remained missing in the Persian frontier near Nisibis.

Taking the old teacher's place was Samur, who grinned wildly as the event began. "Still plenty of time to steal a swift horse and gallop far away," he murmured, cocking an eyebrow. I laughed, though given my brother's disdain for Roman customs, the suggestion might not have been a joke. Samur, though, laughed as well, and we shared a rare moment as brothers as we waited for the ceremony to begin.

Even with an overstuffed building, the wedding was a simple affair. Young women left garlands and flowers along the church floor, while Sembrouthes filed stiffly to the altar, his presence serving as a warning to any who would harm his mistress. All eyes quickly turned toward the entry to the tiny hall, competing for a view of the princess who had stolen so many hearts in the Roman Capitol.

Several moments after Sembrouthes took a seat, there was still no sign of the Ghassanid princess. A lump rose in my throat. Anxious shuffling gave way to mutters of disquiet, and even I began to consider whether I would share Solomon's unhappy fate. I caught myself swaying from one leg to another, forcing my body still as I imagined the cold and humiliating possibility of leaving the church alone.

At last I heard gasps that could only come from the first glimpses of the bride. Indeed, Mariya was simply radiant. She wore her mother's extensive collection of rubies—those jewels I had balked at her taking during her escape—which gleamed against the rich material of the wedding dress that she intended to wear in the weeks prior. Her hair was tied in high knots, bedecked with pearls and crowned with a tiny golden circlet that told of her status as a member of an Arab royal family. All the gilded finery must have hung heavily upon her slim frame, yet as she slowly glided through the benches and toward the altar, she moved with a grace that seemed to bear all the wealth and stature of the entire Ghassanid nation. At last, she reached my side, and her kohl-lined amber eyes met mine. She gave me a wink, though a tear threatened her makeup, and she gave a nervous laugh too faint for anyone but me to hear.

It was difficult to comprehend all that had come to pass. Even now, so many decades later, it seems impossible that my burning desire would come to pass, that a foreign princess would bind herself to me in the presence of the Roman Empress. It was, I have no doubt, madness, for Mariya and I shared little beyond our yearnings to live beyond our rigid societies, to discard the opinions of those with little patience for those who are different. Madness, yes, but the most pleasing madness I ever encountered. For those brief, beautiful moments, flanked by my brother and a gathering of my beloved friends, I felt whole.

Father Petrus conducted the marriage ritual in Latin, and though few besides Belisarius and the high nobility could easily follow, all stood respectfully as Petrus spoke the ancient words that would join Mariya and me as one flesh in the eyes of God. I swore that I saw a tear welling in Petrus' eye, yet Petrus muttered gruffly that it was just the rheum of old age.

Theodora arranged for a private reception to be held in a smaller palace facing the Golden Horn. With lavish food and drink, well-wishers toasted us throughout the night. Mariya charmed the guests to the last, even when I grew utterly exhausted and she resorted to a sly, playful pinch to my leg to keep me alert.

Belisarius and John waited to speak with me until the line of friends shortened, partaking in the rich wine and foods arrayed on long tables across a far palace wall. Fulcaris and Simmas quickly stole away, gorging on rich fruit that had been an unaffordable luxury in any military camp. Theodora had even procured blocks of ice that had been shaved and mixed with honey for a frozen delicacy that few possessed the wealth to enjoy. Perenus consumed no fewer than four, complaining to Rosamund each time that the icy sweetness gave him a thunderous pain in his head. Antonina wrinkled her nose and looked only more sour as Samur, stuffing his face alongside his Lazic friend, offered her a cup of her own.

Belisarius and John, meanwhile, drew me aside. "The officers wanted to offer a gift," Belisarius said formally, "and you'll receive it tomorrow."

John laughed. "You had better like it, or I will take it for myself!"

I tried to push the two men for answers, although they refused playfully and escaped to indulge the Empress with dozens of ideas for building a new Rome.

Most stayed throughout the night and into the few hours before the morning sun, when the sky turns a deep shade of blue. We thanked each guest individually, accepting warm wishes or a friendly embrace from nearly all. Baduarius nearly crushed Mariya as he lifted the princess into the air, swearing oaths of undying affection.

"Just bring my husband back alive!" Mariya cried, to the laughter of the remaining officers.

Other than Sembrouthes, Theodora and Marcellus were the last to leave, giving the Empress an intimate opportunity for her own embrace and words of friendship. She smiled at the golden ring that I carried on my hand, her fingers running through the grooves that bore her sigil. Theodora offered her final congratulations and informed us that a private apartment overlooking the Forum of Constantine had been prepared for our use. Mariya and I bowed as the Empress left, taking our own leave soon thereafter. We walked together from the palace door, hand in hand down the empty streets of Constantinople.

Immortal

THE DESOLATION OF ARMENIA

My TIME WITH MARIYA was short, for Belisarius' initial expedition to Trapezous was intended to depart four days after the wedding. Mariya begged to accompany me, but I adamantly refused.

"We're heading through rough terrain—mountains, forests, and all manner of great beasts—all of which has been sacked and burned by the Persians," I told her. "The risk is too great."

Mariya, though firm in her desire, could not argue the geography, and soon dropped her petition in a flurry of tears. At long last, her sobs quieting, she sat in silence, and I found my resolve breaking.

"Perhaps you could sail for Antioch," I said, by way of compromise. "It won't be too far from the expedition's end point, and your brother will be leaving on a dromon for that city as well."

Mariya brightened. "Will Belisarius refuse? I don't want to jeopardize your position with your soldiers."

I shook my head. "If anything, he will likely appreciate it. Antonina demanded to go too, and she will be accompanied by a hundred Roman spearmen. I doubt she will have many other women to talk to."

"Pregnant and taking a monthlong journey at sea." Mariya frowned. "I'm not certain that is wise. But it is Antonina's choice."

Appeased—at least somewhat—Mariya agreed and gave me an affectionate kiss. As I prepared to leave for the barracks, where I would in turn prepare the Herulian foederati for departure, her hand grazed the twin pendants at my neck and gave me leave with a final request.

"I mean it, Varus. Keep yourself safe. Don't leave me a widow after offering so much happiness."

We embraced, and I darted into the city streets, thoughts wandering toward the distant frontier that had already seen so much desolation.

Upon returning to the barracks, I found John waiting impatiently outside of my rooms. After inquiring to his visit, the Armenian grinned and led me to the training yard, revealing the gift that a dozen officers had acquired.

John gestured toward a massive palomino stallion that cropped at a rich mixture of oats and hay. "A Nisean, and a damned fine one too. A smuggler managed to bring a small herd in from Media a year ago, when this one was just a babe."

Agape, I approached the stallion, which eyed me with an animal's instinctive suspicion. According to John, despite its considerable size, a Nisean horse was known to be just as quick as the Herulian ponies of my foederati, but far stronger, capable of bearing armor at full gallop.

My fingers ran across the Nisean's mane, and he whipped his head toward me. His eyes bored into my own, his nostrils flaring as he judged me.

"What is his name?" I asked.

"Ignis," John said. "After his temperament."

The Latin rushed over me. "Fire," I whispered in the stallion's ear. "Let's see if it is well-deserved."

After the handler prepared a saddle and handed over the reins, John and I walked the horse through the city streets to the Hippodrome, where the plumes on our heads and the Empress' ring on my hand granted us unquestioned entry. As I walked Ignis through the gates, the horse reared his head, attempting to steal the reins from my hands. I fought him for control and did not yield, and after arduously guiding the horse onto the thin layer of sand that lined the racing course, I secured the saddle's straps to ride.

With a nod at John, I vaulted onto the saddle and was almost immediately bucked from my seat. John only laughed. "Get him to run, and you'll see why the Niseans are beloved!" he cried over the snorts and stamps of the angry stallion.

With gloved hands wrapped tightly around the horse's reins, I competed with Ignis in a battle of wills. His bucking grew all the more violent and nearly threw me off, but I tightened my knees around his muscled body, using the saddle's stirrups for support. Gradually, his anger began to wane—or his limbs began to grow weary—and I urged him forward.

Ignis bolted, clearing huge distances of the Hippodrome track with minimal effort. Wind whipped into the gaps of my cheekpieces as we cleared multiple circuits around the track, the horse only beginning to flag after a great distance. As he slowed, I directed Ignis toward John, who clapped in appreciation of the effort.

"You see!" John yelled. "A magnificent breed, worth every ounce of silver."

Straightening my armor, I agreed, offering thanks once more. I patted Ignis' neck as his nostrils flared for air, and John offered a bucket of water from a nearby Hippodrome stall, which Ignis drank greedily as he recovered his energy. We walked the Nisean stallion to the Imperial stables, and I took considerable pains to guarantee his care on our sea voyage east.

Our remaining time in the city passed with a blur. Long, exhausting days were spent equipping and preparing the Herulians, most of whom had never sailed at sea, and my few free night hours were spent with Mariya. She did all she could to alleviate my worries, primarily by insisting that I have more help to manage the foederati, although even the addition of several of Mariya's household servants did little to reduce the burden of my office. Rosamund helped coordinate my burgeoning staff, while Cephalas ensured the quality of the food and additional weapons and armor that would accompany the collective armies for the campaign ahead.

Belisarius frequently called gatherings of his officers to address new information from the front and offer instructions to the existing armies already in the field. From where he led our battered Roman forces deployed in Mesopotamia, Domnicus sent increasingly frantic messages begging for reinforcements, certain that the isolated Roman fortresses in places like Dara and Amida would not be able to withstand renewed Persian attacks.

Justinian's participation in these meetings grew as our departure date neared. Though Belisarius was anointed with overall command of the expedition, our Emperor commissioned an Imperial legatus to speak on his behalf in any negotiations that would take place between the Persians and Romans between battles. Justinian's appointment was an older man named Hermogenes, who bobbed his head and frequently complimented the Emperor for his extensive wisdom and assured Justinian's core advisors that their collective will would be executed prudently and vigorously. John rolled his eyes at the pronouncement and leaned over to explain the ill news.

"The legate will bind and restrict our army, just you wait. This is Tribonian's doing, or that rat Paulus."

Hermogenes threw us a glare, annoyed at the disturbance of his speech, and John raised a hand in contrition. "Apologies. I shall keep my sneezes to a minimum."

Other administrative posts were attached to Belisarius' army, many of which were likely assigned months in advance. This included a small force of priests that, while theoretically appointed by the elderly patriarch, were more likely hand selected by Cassiodorus, who nodded in approval as their names were called out for service. Another position included the post of Justinian's official historian and clerk to the army, which was awarded to the diminutive Procopius. The man wet his lips and beamed in excitement, while Narses, as well as several of Belisarius' own officers, glowered with wordless ire.

Aside from these meetings, final orders of the Herulian men were filled by delegated centurions, who ventured into the maze of market stalls to acquire a number of trinkets, food, and wine that would distract the men from the labors and boredom of long marches and uncomfortable nights. Hundreds of servants carried the bulk of the foederati's equipment onto the ships the day prior to departure, yet the men worried over deprivation and even starvation on the march. To quell such fears, Belisarius had personally purchased additional stores of grain, salted meat, nails, rope, and dozens of other items that were always in demand by a marching army, and the men of the barracks were informed that the supply depot would be sent by ship to Antioch along with Belisarius' pregnant wife.

Though the dromon sailing to Antioch would not leave for another week after our own voyage, Belisarius meticulously planned to ensure Antonina's safety, placing a hundred veteran spearmen and two healers as her personal retinue. They were led by a centurion named Sergius, who had a reputation for brutal efficiency with his weapons on the battlefield, as well as Prince al-Harith, who would quickly join the Ghassanid armies forming under King Jabalah. Belisarius was particularly grateful that Mariya was to join that voyage, giving Antonina a rare friend who would share not only her social standing but also the travails of extended travel.

As Belisarius explained the centurion's duties, Sergius spoke with assurance. "Don't worry, Lord. I'll make sure they arrive in Antioch safely."

Belisarius handed Sergius a thick pouch of gold and silver coins to cover any bribes or equipment that the unit should need, either for the comfort of the two ladies or as Sergius' men departed Antioch to meet Belisarius' army in Mesopotamia. Sergius stoically accepted the bag, tossing it lightly in the air as he tested its heft.

Departure day came all too quickly, and I awoke with my chest soaked with Mariya's tears. Her long nails dug into my skin as she held me close, as if her strength alone could keep me safe in Constantinople.

"Just a month, and we will see each other again," I said, attempting to cheer her up.

"Are you sure of that?" she asked, her voice weary and eyes rimmed red.

"Certainly," I lied.

That timeline was ambitious and hoped for, yet even Belisarius acknowledged that a thousand obstacles could bog his collective army in Pontus or Armenia, let alone have the freedom to leave the war in Mesopotamia. I considered qualms about whether to force Mariya to remain in the Capitol, although I doubt she would have listened at that point. I did what I could to raise her spirits, while secretly harboring my own dread that after this day, there was a good chance we would never meet again.

Though Rosamund and Cephalas packed my gear and belongings, I insisted on checking on the foederati as we departed. The Herulians fidgeted as they watched their horses and equipment carried away by ox carts, yet did nothing to disturb our looming expedition. Even bold Alaric was noticeably skittish, his hands slightly quivering as I found him alone in his rooms. I patted him on the shoulder, and he nodded, returning to his ten men to assuage their own fears.

Having gone through this exercise once before, I anticipated a busy yet tedious morning, my mind torn between the impatient desire to get on with the sea voyage, while also dreading the passage of time that would take me away from everything that I knew as home. Turning to the remnants of my komes' quarters, however, I arrived at a surprise that I had not foreseen.

Sembrouthes leaned softly against the wooden paneling outside of my rooms, speaking softly to nine other yellow-vested

Aksumite warriors in their indecipherable language. Alarm coursed through me, wondering if they spoke of Mariya, and if something had happened. But Sembrouthes soon saw me and explained his presence.

"The princess commands me to join you on your campaign, and to see you safely back to Constantinople," he said, backed by firm looks and resigned grunts from his men.

"But your oath is to protect Mariya!" I cried. "Return to her quickly, before she walks into the city on her own!"

Sembrouthes raised a hand, calling for calm. "I agree with you, although the princess says that you are in her household now, and it is our holy oath to protect you when she commands. And she does so now," he said. "I did make sure to leave a half dozen men to protect her until we return."

Despite many protests, Sembrouthes insisted that his men would prove invaluable in battle. They did look fearsome enough, and the Aksumite armies had proven their worth on the desert battlefield of Himyar, having wrested control of the region from a Persian satrap and their mercenary Arab armies. For my part, I argued that the Herulian foederati would fight on horseback and on foot, depending upon what Belisarius required, but Sembrouthes only shrugged: he would follow orders and engage the enemy when necessary and helpful, and that was that.

Seeing no other recourse, I ordered Perenus to prepare additional bunks for the Aksumite men and a private berth for Sembrouthes. Galley slaves carried the Aksumites' clothing and weapons onto the ships, and most of the Aksumite men marched neatly down the streets of Constantinople to the curious looks of Romans who rarely saw such dark skin. Sembrouthes accompanied me everywhere, carrying his colorful shield covered in a buffalo hide that bore the Orthodox Christian cross favored by the King of Aksum and a weapon that was part spear, part axe, a long wooden shaft topped with a vicious metal blade. In our training bouts,

Sembrouthes later showed the ease with which he moved the heavy spear, as well as the curved sword that hung at the Aksumite commander's waist.

After breakfast, the Herulians were ordered to file into a thick column and marched into the city streets as we headed for the ship that would carry us to Trapezous. A few citizens lined the streets out of curiosity, though most eyed the Herulian foederati with suspicion, presumably seeing them as barely removed from the reavers who savaged the Eastern Empire a few generations prior. Many possessed gaunt faces and bleeding gums, the early signs of poor nutrition and too little food. Though the worst of the city riots had been quelled in the months prior, I was glad that Mariya would soon escape the Imperial Capitol and the current of resentment and desperation that bubbled below its surface.

By mid-morning, we finally reached the docks, where we were directed to one of a vast array of transport ships that would carry us the distance to Trapezous, in Roman Pontus. I left it to Perenus to see the men aboard and walked with Sembrouthes as I found the Imperial delegation that observed the departure of the army. Theodora stood in front of a number of Justinian's advisors, including a half dozen priests who prayed for the safety of Rome's men.

"Varus!" Mariya broke through the crowd, her guards struggling to keep pace with her amidst the sea of onlookers. Mariya unceremoniously threw her arms around my chest and squeezed, her face buried in my shirt.

"Come back to me safely," she said. "Don't leave me here alone."

Gathering Mariya in my arms, I did my best to console her, promising again to see her near Antioch in the coming months. I delayed as long as I could, yet our final moments together were cut short by the ship's captain, barking of the needed to set sail while the tide was in our favor.

With Sembrouthes in tow, I left Mariya for the ship, frequently stealing glances over my shoulder as my chest tightened in pain and regret. I remained on the ship's deck as we pulled away from its moorings, heading toward the Euxine Sea and eastward to Trapezous. Theodora's retinue waved in support of their army, yet my eyes rested firmly on Mariya, who collapsed in a heap as our ship pulled farther into the sea.

Tightly hugging the coast of Bithynia and Paphlagonia, the fleet of Roman ships arrived in Trapezous several days later. Our ship was one of the last to dock in the city ports, which despite not being nearly as large as Constantinople's, were able to offload all passengers and supplies within a half day's work.

Although Belisarius gave the men two days to recover from the sea voyage before departing on campaign, he insisted that the armies camp outside of the city, and that any theft or brutality on behalf of his soldiers would be harshly dealt with. The few complainants from Trapezous who reported poor behavior or destruction of property were quickly compensated half again the full value of their loss, though Belisarius left the details of sifting truth from opportunistic dishonesty to John and a local prefect.

After a quick recovery, Belisarius ordered the men south, and I vaulted into Ignis' saddle to lead the Herulian foederati away from our camp in a column measuring eight riders across. We were joined by the Huns, who bore less armor and rode on swifter ponies than those of the Herulians. Several of the Huns bore stunted and malformed calves, bearing witness of their preference to ride in a saddle over walking on land. Samur appeared nearly a son to Sunicas, their black hair and dark furs shifting in the light breeze of the Pontic morning. I nodded to my brother, who yielded a wide grin as he relished his time riding with the Hunnic leaders.

"This is real adventure, Varus!" Samir beamed. "No skulking in mists, waiting to be butchered by the Avars. Only a horse to ride and the wind at my face, and a thousand miles of journey ahead."

"Until we meet the Persians," I said.

Samur bobbed his head affirmatively. "Sunicas says that a mounted Hun is worth ten Persians, so I'll be sure to thin their ranks for you!"

Rosamund rode alongside Perenus and Sembrouthes, her own light mail reflecting in the sunlight. While some of the Romans looked askance at an armored woman, none of the Herulian riders dared insult Rosamund, whose blackened visage blended easily with my sigil and banners. She let her white hair fly freely behind, offering the only sign of her sex as she rode stiffly forward.

Seeing the other units form into their own columns, I gave Perenus command of the Herulian foederati and nudged Ignis toward the small group of senior officers at the front of the formation. Sembrouthes followed close behind as I galloped past Belisarius' vanguard, which comprised the near totality of excubitores currently under arms for Rome. As Justinian's hardened elite, they wore thick well-forged armor and carried a diversity of keen weapons. Whereas the foederati and other Roman units joked and sang as they marched inland, the excubitores rode silently, their officers scanning the road ahead for any sign of ambush or attack.

Baduarius and Ascum shouting greetings to Sembrouthes and me as we approached. Nearly all of Belisarius' senior officers had gathered, as well as Marcellus on behalf of the excubitores and several from Germanus' staff within the Thracian Army. I introduced Sembrouthes to Mundus and Troglita, who each bade him welcome as our horses kept the forward pace. Dozens of banners flew proudly in the air, many on behalf of Justinian and a select few for Theodora, while others bore the personal sigils of two dozen senior commanders that populated the Roman Army.

A notable absence from the gathering was Solomon. Indeed, Solomon had hardly been spotted during our preparations for departure, and his subordinate Marcian carried messages to the expedition leadership in Trapezous. Troglita assured me that Solomon accompanied the armies, keeping his baleful presence isolated from the other Thracian officers in virtually all meetings. Normally, I would have been grateful to be rid of Solomon, yet his relative absence in Armenia left me uneasy. As a man who'd give a slave a broken bone merely to show his own power, Solomon would not have forgiven Mariya's slight to his household with graciousness. I held little doubt that, without Sembrouthes' unblinking guard and Belisarius' patronage, a cutthroat's dagger would have found itself lodged between my ribs in Armenia's smothering nights.

The Roman command shared the singular state of simultaneous excitement and boredom as the armies moved away from the temperate coastline and into the hills. Belisarius' early route was uneventful, following an old Roman road due south from Trapezous toward Roman Armenia. Along the way, Belisarius ordered Procopius to dispatch messages to Roman forces in Lazica, noting the relative position of the main army as well as which messenger posts would most easily reach his officers. Wary of written orders being intercepted by marauding Persian war bands, Procopius wrote in code, assuring the officers that his counterpart in the Lazic capitol of Phasis would be able to decipher his words.

Despite the ever-present need to move forward, I still began each morning with a visit to Father Petrus, who accompanied one of the many carts assigned to Belisarius' army. Petrus' spirits seemed high despite the deprivation his body felt; it was, he claimed, the fresh mountain air and the excitement of youth surrounding him that kept him vigorous. After our sessions, I spent time with my Persian tutor, who tutted at my many mistakes despite the functional progress made toward phrasing simple sentences. As I worked with the language teacher, Father Petrus did his best to proselytize to Fulcaris and some of the more polite Herulian riders, yet made little progress, as they preferred the strength and character of the many gods of their people.

Rosamund and Cephalas still kept order in my household, with Rosamund in particular directing the additional foederati servants that Mariya offered to us. When not in her armor, Rosamund wore black, again an unusual choice, and one that piqued the interest of several of the pagan elements in Belisarius' army.

Though a devout Christian, Belisarius never chastised any man or woman for their religious beliefs, allowing the dozens of tribes who comprised Belisarius' soldiers or even his household *bucellarii* to worship their gods in relative peace and with only minor interruption from less-understanding Roman officials. Hermogenes particularly disapproved of Rosamund's presence, summoning me into his tent upon the first evening after departing the Pontic coastline.

"Komes, I have never approved of women joining a military campaign, even as camp followers," he began, "but Gepids?"

Bowing my head, I was careful to speak slowly so as not to anger the all-powerful legate with an angry outburst. "Legate, I, too, hail from the Heruli, a people not dissimilar of the Gepids. They are both loyal and competent, as is Rosamund."

"I do not question your honor, komes," Hermogenes countered. "But you are a Christian. My slaves tell me that your Gepid attendant worships fire, and entices other pagans to join her."

"Legate..."

"I will not deprive you of a servant in wartime," Hermogenes warned, offering no opening for rebuttal. "But keep her under control, and eliminate these incredibly superstitious practices. Our Emperor would build a world free from that darkness."

By the third day of the march, John announced that our vanguard had reached the dividing line between Pontus and Armenia, a land marked by snowcapped mountains and deep fertile valleys, and Bessas agreed. The rest of us could not help but wonder how the two Armenians could tell that they had entered into their ancestral homeland.

"The roads have started to break up," John explained. "The result of centuries of war over this region."

Bessas gave a swift nod. "Keep your eyes open... We are effectively in hostile territory now."

Belisarius ordered outriders to circle the Roman forces along a five-mile ring and to make regular reports on any signs of life, be it Roman, Persian, or Armenian. Spring thaw began to send small rivulets snaking down the sides of several mountains, yet there was hardly any wildlife in the area, let alone any residents.

After two days in Armenia, Belisarius directed the armies slightly westward, eager to avoid the smaller cities that lined the Persian border. Another day passed uneventfully, yet I commanded my foederati to keep their noise to a minimum, wary of how sound traveled in the low passes of the Armenian mountain ranges.

The following morning, Roman scouts rushed to Belisarius, their faces flush from exertion as they gibbered with nervous excitement. One carried a charred wooden plank in his hand, and another a warped copper cross, burned and partially melted in whatever desecration befell its previous home. Belisarius ordered his officers together, and we rode hurriedly forward to the site of discovery.

All that remained was a ruined town, its few standing stone walls lacking roofs and living areas disturbed. What once had been a sizeable pen for cattle and sheep had been torn to pieces, its occupants long slaughtered as sustenance for the Persians. The only stimuli that greeted us were blowing winds and trails of long-dried blood that tracked and pooled suggestively along pathways.

Belisarius dismounted, navigating the dirt paths that had likely been the town's main thoroughfare. His officers followed closely behind, trailing Belisarius as he found the town church, its high cross having buckled from flames that licked and weakened the wooden roof.

Curiously, the church walls remained standing, and its thick doors were sealed with a heavy iron lock on the exterior. Belisarius called for assistance, and Sembrouthes hefted his spear to break the metal barrier. Belisarius and Sembrouthes hooked the curved edge of Sembrouthes' spear against the lock's chain and pulled hard against the wooden shaft, the metal straining under the force of the two warriors.

Whether decayed from exposure to the elements or made brittle by fire, the chain soon snapped, and Sembrouthes pulled its remnants away from the door and tossed them aside. Belisarius tried to respectfully prop the door open, although it still refused to budge as if propped against a heavy counterweight.

"Varus, lend your shoulder to us," Belisarius asked.

I dismounted from Ignis and stood alongside the other two men, and we heaved forward with our collective weight. The thick wooden doors splintered and finally tore open, revealing the horror enclosed within.

The doors pushed aside dozens of shriveled corpses piled against the doors and poured limited light into the chapel beyond. Even more bodies lay stacked in a great heap at the center of the church's stone floor, including several smaller figures that were wrapped carefully in the arms of larger Romans.

"Just children..." Belisarius said in fury as he stepped inside.

Many of the bodies had been mummified by the heat of the blaze that consumed them, their skin stretched tight over bones and the fat effectively melted away and onto the floor. There were dozens of them, maybe even a few hundred, yet had all been taken from this world no longer than one month prior.

I remember most clearly the sight of broken fingernails in the wooden paneling. The townspeople had literally tried to claw their way out like animals.

I was not the only one horrified by the gore, though I concealed my shock. One of the newer Thracian officers vomited, only to apologize in profuse embarrassment.

"There's no shame in this kind of disgust, lad," Mundus said, patting the man on the back and directing him out into the fresh air. Troglita gagged at the lingering smell of death, while Sembrouthes backed away from the desolation with others, all averting their gaze from the miserable remnants of so many lost souls.

Belisarius alone walked the church grounds, emerging from that blackened horror with a look of violence upon his face. His eyes darted wildly across his officers before composing himself.

"What knowledge can we gather from this?" Belisarius asked, his voice dangerous despite the more stoic look on his face.

"No Persian did this," Bessas spat. "Nor could they."

Baduarius grunted. "How can you be so sure?"

Bessas walked over to a burned-out stone building, pointing to a small glyph that had been sketched with a dark mahogany paint. He reached out a finger and scraped lightly at the edge of the symbol, which appeared a roughly hewn X, with a small blotch in the top gap that mimicked a human head.

"Hephthalites," Bessas said, as if the name itself were a curse. John and the other Armenians spat and crossed themselves, while Sunicas' face grew firm.

Germanus appeared equally apprehensive. "How are they this far west?"

Though Kavadh had recruited thousands of Hephthalite mercenaries to shore up his power on the Persian throne, the assumption by Narses' spies was that the Hephthalites had been procured to fight against the Göktürks Khaganate and the Indian princedoms on the northern and eastern borders of the Persian Empire, but Bessas assured us that such a distinctive symbol meant that the fierce warriors had invaded Roman Armenia.

Scholars called the Hephthalites "White Huns," although Sunicas vocally assured us that he knew of no ties between his people and our enemies in the Persian army. The Hephthalites did not behave as nomads like the Huns did, yet did organize themselves into wide bands of horse archers and light infantry to raid their neighbors. Reports told that the Hephthalites were ruled by a council of their seven fiercest warlords, where an opening to such leadership only arose upon the death of a sitting member. Liberius once lectured that few within the Hephthalite leadership died peacefully in their old age, painting an image of a people constantly at war, and constantly in flux.

The Hypohalites' purpose was to sow terror in Persia's neighboring provinces. As pagans, the Hephthalites had no qualms with the full-scale massacre of women and children, and had been rumored to sacrifice war captives to appease their dark gods. They reminded me strongly of Avars, except that the Hephthalites retained superior organization and a shrewd thirst for gold where the Avars roamed the steppes for the sheer prospect of death and domination.

Eyes turned to Belisarius for orders. Belisarius visibly struggled with his anger but managed at last to propose a reasonable conclusion to move forward.

"We will camp outside of this town. Pick detachments to bury the dead, and send outriders far in every direction. We need to see how far the Hephthalites rode into Roman territory... or if there are any survivors."

Following Belisarius' wishes, John levied more detailed orders, kicking the officers into a frenzy of activity as we set to what small tasks we could undertake to improve our situation. Belisarius cautioned his officers to tell our soldiers only what was strictly necessary regarding the Hephthalites; we hoped, in so doing, to avoid demoralizing the men at the thought of such gruesome foes.

In the sanctified ground of the church burial yard, I found Sembrouthes and a half dozen Aksumites digging graves despite their overall exemption from manual labor in Belisarius' army. Curious at the sight, I asked Sembrouthes why they did not leave such arduous tasks for others in the army.

"The dead deserve to be treated with respect and care," Sembrouthes said. "And if a similar fate befell me and my men, I would want others to pay me the honor of a Christian burial."

Nodding, I picked up a shovel and joined the Aksumites. Amidst issuing orders to my foederati, we caught the gaze of Marcellus, who joined our toil and engaged several dozen excubitores in the effort. With our collective labor, we were able to dig enough burial plots for each of the bodies found inside of the church, as well as a small number of others that had been found under the rubble of other ruined and abandoned buildings. Marcellus led us into an assembly as Father Petrus led prayers over the lost souls in the heart of Armenia, in hopes that they may be rejoined with the Father and Son and granted salvation and a chance at paradise.

Afterward, Procopius complained that a Catholic priest had no business offering these prayers in Roman Armenia, where these dead men and women had followed their own, different Christian practice. Indignant, I huffed in Father Petrus' defense, but Petrus calmed me and looked Procopius in the eye.

"These are our brothers and sisters in Christ, and deserve heartfelt prayers to ease their passing into the afterlife. If an Orthodox priest were to lead a prayer, I would be among the first to follow and pray with him. For does not the Epistle teach us that in Christ, there is neither Jew nor Greek, male nor female, slave nor free man?" Petrus spoke reverently, a touch of awe in his voice.

Procopius nodded and mumbled some agreement, not deigning to mention the many Orthodox priests who had indeed been deployed on our expedition at Justinian's order. Later, the writ of Saint Paul notwithstanding, he grumbled further at the indignity of Catholic prayers in an East Roman Army, yet only Hermogenes cared to hear out his complaints.

Belisarius, however, expressed his approval at the efficient burial of the Roman dead, and kneeled alone within the field of graves. Belisarius clenched his hands together, mouthing words of prayer as his officers solemnly looked on. His devotions concluded, Belisarius overheard the deployment orders for our outriding expeditions and gave his permission to commence.

John offered one such command to the Herulian foederati. I called up Centurion Opilio and tasked him with taking two detachments of ten under Alaric and Fulcaris to sweep east in the direction of the Persian border, with explicit instructions to keep clear of major settlements or war bands that doubtlessly roamed the Armenian countryside. Opilio saluted at the honor and gathered his men for a deployment that afternoon.

Our first outriders, led by Thracians under Troglita, returned the morning of the third day after their departure, having scouted the safer western routes toward the interior of Asia Minor. They reported a relative peace in the region, though they found only small groups of Roman citizens—refugees, it seemed, loading belongings on heavy carts and heading due west from the conflagration along our Persian border. Other detachments told a similar story, yet still reported no indication of a current Persian presence beyond trace evidence: discarded equipment, forests stripped by heavy foraging.

Another detachment of Sunicas' Huns returned from the south, offering a more gruesome account of the path that awaited us. Led by a man named Sinnion, the Huns told of a half dozen other towns pillaged and sacked in a similar manner.

"Any signs of Persian forces?" Simmas asked, his face sharp and intent.

Sinnion nodded. "A few Kassite scouts riding ponies from the Persian far east," he said casually, adding, "They will not offer any further trouble."

The Hunnic officer noted greater concern at signs his men detected within the abandoned villages. Sinnion pulled a charred wooden plank from his pack and offered it to Simmas, who took it and traced the faint outline of another glyph.

"They were definitely here then, the Hephthalites," Sunicas said. Bessas, too, nodded, and all attention settled on Belisarius.

Belisarius first ordered a Hunnic rider to lead small Roman detachments to each town, given the duty of burying Roman dead. Ascum brought up, respectfully, that such labors would delay our progress, at which Belisarius nodded, but he did not relent. The deployments would begin immediately while the army awaited the return of our final scouting parties, after which time the armies would move briskly toward Martyropolis and Amida.

Within two days after the departure of our burial detachments, our final scouting parties returned for a report. One of Bessas' Armenians offered a lone bit of good news in the form of a dispatch written on a scraped lambskin bearing the seal of General Sittas, the commander of Rome's smaller Armenian forces.

The message greeted Belisarius and provided some long-awaited intelligence on our Persian enemies. Sittas confirmed that not only Hephthalites, but also a half dozen other mercenary bands, were indeed roaming the Armenian countryside. Sittas had moved

Rome's Armenian forces eastward into Iberia near Manzikert, pressuring the northern Persian flank that encircled a wide swath of territory from Tigranocerta to Melitene. Interestingly, Sittas reported that the Hephthalite bands had departed around a week prior and had been replaced with Persian units led by Xerxes. Scouts reported that the Hephthalite bands had merged with a second army under Perozes, which massed in Persian Assyria.

Xerxes' forces were capped by a huge mass of Zhayedan Immortals, the bulk of which slowly navigated south to the west of Dara and Nisibis. By all appearances, Xerxes had ceased raids into Roman towns in the region, holding Roman fortresses at the old Persian border under siege. At this, John groaned; it went directly against Justinian's orders to not only protect such front cities, but to build further fortifications due west of the Tigris River. Belisarius, for his part, thanked the messenger and ordered Procopius to submit a detailed response, and then stood over a vast map of the region as John and Baduarius repositioned symbols of armies based upon Sittas' information.

The Herulians were the last to arrive, galloping into camp red faced and visibly exhausted. Nevertheless, Opilio dismounted sharply and saluted Belisarius and me, and would not rest until officers foisted refreshment on him. After giving the men time to recover, I ordered the scouting leaders to deliver their report, cautioning them to keep critical information private until told otherwise by Belisarius.

Opilio gave an overview of their route, noting conditions of the terrain and what dirt paths and roadways were found that may not be on any Roman map. Belisarius listened carefully, only pressing the men for information on signs of Romans after their overall report concluded.

"Any survivors had been taken as captives or fled. The whole region is essentially emptied of people," Fulcaris said.

Alaric and Opilio grunted their agreement.

"And the Persians?" I asked. "The Hephthalites?"

Opilio shook his head. "Some large force marched through the area within the past few weeks, although we saw no one," Opilio said. Alaric nudged him, as if reminding his centurion of their last piece of information, and Opilio added, "We did run into those symbols that you mentioned. Is that proof of the Hephthalites in the area?"

"Yes," I said reluctantly, "but we've received a report that they vacated the area for Assyria not long ago."

Burial dispatches departed later that day, while the bulk of the army moved slowly forward. After another week, Belisarius' forces passed through the more forbidding mountain passes of Asia Minor, which slowly gave way to the rolling hills of the upper Euphrates River. Outriders reported our first sightings of Persian scouts, and thus Belisarius summoned his war council.

Belisarius was determined to push forward and break the Persian stranglehold upon Roman Mesopotamia, and declared we would continue the army's march southward. To pressure the Persians into flight, he ordered the Herulian and Hunnic foederati to sally forth ahead of the army and harass smaller Persian bands.

"Do not engage any large force and avoid pitched battle, but let the Persians know that they are not welcome here," Belisarius said. John drafted orders for supplies to be levied to each of the foederati units, and within another day I found myself at the head of our armed and armored men. I waved toward Samur and the Hunnic commanders as we parted, with my Herulian foederati and Aksumite guards tailing close behind.

Riding at a brisk trot, my foederati reached tributaries to the Tigris River within another three days. Ignis rose high above the other Herulian horses, yet had no trouble enduring alongside the lighter ponies of my men. We traced the rivers south and then east, reaching within a mere twenty miles from Martyropolis as the Persian presence became ever clearer.

Ever vigilant, Perenus rotated a series of scouts that rode ahead of our position, regularly reporting of their findings. By the fifth day, scouts reported activity at five miles distant, setting off a low rustling of talk as the foederati anticipated this first mission that would at last break the tedium of the march.

Our scouts reported that a small Persian band, maybe fifty strong, traversed a nearby ford in a tributary to the Tigris. Only a small number were mounted; the majority, carrying thickly woven wicker shields and iron-tipped pikes, followed close behind. I called Perenus and the centurions together to discuss our next move.

"What say you?" I asked the gathered officers. "Attack, or leave them be?"

Perenus grinned with all his teeth. "Definitely attack. It's time to bring death onto the Persians' heads for a change."

The other officers grunted and muttered sounds of approval.

"Very well," I said. "Attack we shall."

We drew up our plan. Per Belisarius' orders, I forbade any officer from allowing their men to dismount. "Distance attacks only!" I called to the men as they strung their bows.

"Lord, why not test our spears?" Alaric said. "I could cut through their ranks like chaff."

"Undoubtedly you could," I said. "But time for the shield wall will come. For now, easy kills are Belisarius' desire. That, and to leave no scout alive to tell of our movement."

Alaric grunted. "They won't escape, Lord."

Divided into our two columns, I signaled the foederati forward, our pace quickening as we crested one hill after another. After a time, we rose over a final wide hill, with Ignis' hooves splashing in a thin stream that cut into a shallow valley. Beyond were the Persian masses, who scrambled into a ring of shields and spears in defense of the attack.

All I saw were dead men. Eighty paces distant, I unslung my bow and nocked an arrow, calling for my men to follow in a cloud of iron and feathers. My arrow flew a heartbeat ahead of the foederati, whistling in the wind, until it struck a mounted Persian officer high in his helmet. One moment, the man screamed in pain as the arrow drove its iron point through his helmet and into his soft jaw. The next, a dozen other bolts hailed down and pushed man and horse into the dirt.

The Persians valiantly clung to their circle in a show of discipline, yet slowly crumbled under the continuous pressure of Herulian archery. More than one Persian burst from the circle, javelin in hand, only to fall, quilled with shafts, as soon as he left the protection of the shield wall. It was over within moments, leaving a circle of writhing and bleeding flesh on the thin Mesopotamian grasslands.

Fulcaris approached, laughing at the easy success of the morning. "Should we take any prisoners?" he asked lightly.

I surveyed the massed Persians for any survivors who might survive for more than a few moments. Finding none, I shook my head. "Dispatch them quickly, and without malice," I lectured the young Herulian, who saluted and took a dozen men to conclude the day's butchery.

With the final sword stroke, the Herulians cheered at their first success, boasting of strength and prowess under arms. Privately, I confided in Perenus that such a display may make them too cocksure of themselves in a real battle against a well-informed and much larger foe. He only shook his head.

"This was good for the men," Perenus said. "They're plenty afraid of a massed enemy, but now they know that you have good judgment and can lead them to victory."

He was right. Thanking my friend for his counsel, I gave permission for the bodies to be looted and spoils taken. Despite the small number of our enemy against our four hundred riders, the

Persians held a surprising amount of gold and silver on their bodies, as well as a number of well-forged swords and daggers. Alaric and Fulcaris both presented me with twin blades from the Persian officers, but I merely patted the dragon-headed sword at my side and declined.

"Keep it for yourselves—that's fine steel, or an expensive trophy back home."

The two Herulians grinned as they tucked the blades into makeshift scabbards and hooked them onto their leather belts.

Persian supplies were divided amongst each of our dekarchos, which gave us enough sustenance to avoid foraging for several days. I ordered the bodies buried respectfully but in haste, concerned that the smoke plume from any fire would signal other Persian enemies. With that task accomplished in a few hours, we topped off our waterskins in the nearby stream and remounted our horses to continue east for another half day.

The rest of our raid into Persian-controlled territory was less eventful, with small contingents of the foederati trapping and slaying two Persian scouting patrols over the next five days. We passed through several burned-out villages, nearly all possessing crosses and other Christian symbols. Each location was strewn with maggot-riddled bodies, and we did what we could to honor Belisarius' wish that Rome's citizens be given the honor of burial where possible.

As our supplies grew thin and sightings of Persians diminished, I called for the foederati to return to Belisarius' army. John had given the estimated progress of the army each day, and I peered at a crude calfskin map provided to the Roman raiding parties. We followed the route of the Tigris west and then north, following noted landmarks as we traced our path back to friendly forces. Our scouts stole glimpses of Amida on the route back, spying the Persian forces that lazily besieged the Roman fortress city.

After another week, we caught our first signs of the main army, which surpassed John's estimates. Roman scouts hailed the foederati as we grew closer and guided us toward the numerous Roman columns that spiraled along the Mesopotamian lowlands.

Mounted atop his own horse, Samur galloped in greeting as the Herulians and Aksumites reentered the Roman camp and were dismissed.

"Find any Persians?" Samur asked, his eyes glancing over our ranks.

"One small war band and a few scouting parties. All dead," I reported. "What about the Huns?"

Samur grinned wickedly. "Two war bands, about fifty each. Sunicas made sure that they won't bother us anymore," he said, teasing me for my relative lack of success.

I leaned from my horse and punched his shoulder playfully, and we trotted toward my camp.

Father Petrus smiled warmly as I entered the camp, while Cephalas grabbed Ignis' bridle and promised to treat the horse gently. Against my protestations that I needed to find Belisarius, Rosamund forced me to sit and eat, closely inspecting my body for any scratches or wounds as I groaned in complaint.

After satisfying Rosamund's examination, I wandered to Belisarius' improvised quarters, eager to offer my report alongside that of Sunicas and Simmas. Belisarius' guards acknowledged me and threw Belisarius' tent open, and I entered an ongoing meeting of several men. Their faces were gaunt and serious, and several frowned as they met my gaze.

"Ah, Varus, it is good to see you safely returned," Belisarius said cordially. "Please take a seat."

Confused at the mood of the room and Belisarius' unfamiliar tone, I sat at a circular table, my eyes moving across the officers for signs of friendship. Troglita gave a weak smile, and

241

even Baduarius shook his head. I looked to Belisarius with fear in my eyes.

"Varus, I need you to remain calm," Belisarius began. A lump swelled in my throat. "We have some unfortunate news, and some of it directly concerns you."

Belisarius gestured to three scrolls that littered the center of the table. Two were rolled crisply around a wooden pommel, the fine sheet so near translucent as to betray the writings in black ink. The third was more ragged, and more of a crumpled piece of cleaned animal hide than a formal dispatch. Belisarius grabbed the first two and unfurled them as he handed them to me.

"This came the day after you departed. Messages from the Capitol, carried here by galloping riders through rain and darkness," Belisarius said. "The first states Hilderic, King of the Vandals, has been deposed in an uprising led by Gelimer, a lord and military leader of that people. Gelimer executed Emperor Justinian's priests allowed to preach by King Hilderic, and expelled all Romans from Vandal territory as he reinstated a heretical form of Christianity as the state religion."

"Looks like you escaped a trap with that Vandal princess," Ascum muttered to me, drawing angry looks from his companions.

Belisarius paused, allowing the information to settle in my mind before proceeding. "Gelimer has also launched raids from Leptis Magna into Roman Libya, putting a half dozen towns outside Ptolemais to the torch."

"Good lord," I said, to a chorus of grunts of agreement across the table.

Belisarius explained that the scroll ordered General Domnicus to retreat with his army back to Alexandria and provide a bulwark against possible Vandal attacks into the provinces of Egypt.

At that, I groaned. Even with the Egyptian forces, Belisarius had been sorely outnumbered by multiple Persian armies. In response to Domnicus' departure, the Ghassanid forces under King Jabalah and the newly arrived Prince al-Harith would move north and follow the Euphrates River to Belisarius' position.

"No word from Antonina or Mariya," Belisarius added quickly, "except that they arrived safely in Antioch with al-Harith."

Amidst these waves of disastrous tidings, news of Mariya's safety poured relief over my entire being. I burned to ride directly for Antioch but likely would not have the freedom to do so for some time.

"The second letter," Belisarius began, "is a command from the Emperor to move with all haste to Thannuris, where the Emperor's treasurer has designated that a new border fortress will be built to defend against Persian attacks. Our role is to protect the builders as they engage their work."

"Bastards," John said.

Others agreed despite Belisarius' pleas for calm and decorum, and it was easy to see why. Thannuris lay on the other side of the Persian salient into Roman territory, although Belisarius noted that raids by the Hunnic and Herulian foederati drove Xerxes to withdraw the westernmost of his forces to consolidate near the Tigris River. Large walls and towers would take considerable time to construct, and would disable Belisarius' ability to maneuver in the relative flatlands of Mesopotamia. Such a shackle would give the Persians, already far larger in numbers and supplies, the added advantage of being able to strike and maneuver at their convenience and absent any threat of a counterattack.

Making matters worse, Hermogenes was present to enforce the Emperor's wishes. Though the Emperor could not see the impossibility of our position in real time, the Imperial legate retained the full authority to demand compliance with the letter, and Belisarius was not apt to rebel against such a command. Instead, respecting Justinian's wishes, the Army would march at double pace to reach Thannuris in a week's time, with hopeful reinforcements from the Ghassanid Arabs arriving soon thereafter.

Though the first two scrolls held terrible news, it was the third that I most feared. Belisarius snatched the ragged animal skin from the table and unfurled its roughly scribbled text. Unable to speak the words aloud, Belisarius placed the document in my hands.

"This came yesterday, carried by blockade runners from Dara." Belisarius' voice was hoarse.

Almost trembling, I held the missive closer and read.

Petrus Marcellinus Felix Liberius, a lord of the Roman Emperor's Council, was seen captured by Persian forces in Nisibis. His current whereabouts are unknown.

Unknown. I banged my fist on the table and shot to my feet, wanting to scream and smash the wooden table into splinters. Incredulous, I reread the scroll, teeth clenched and tears welling in my eyes, until all I could do was rock back and forth.

Marcellus stood with me, his neck pulsing in anger. "Is there anything we can do to help Liberius, or at least make sense of where he may have been taken?"

Belisarius nodded sadly. "Liberius is one of the most honored statesmen the Empire has produced since Agrippa, and it is the solemn oath of Roman soldiers to reclaim such leaders from enemy hands," he said. Belisarius nodded to John, who cleared the wooden table and laid a map of Mesopotamia flat on its surface.

John placed a small wooden figure near Edessa. "This is indefensible terrain for our army," John said, placing five additional pieces to the east. "And these are our scouts' estimations of the Persian forces under Xerxes and Perozes." The smaller forces under Xerxes were positioned between Amida and Dara, while the larger collection under Perozes remained further east in Assyria.

Belisarius traced his finger southward, taking in the geography of Thannuris. "Our army needs to reach this point in

244

seven days," Belisarius said. He traced his finger slightly northward, adding, "Which is a further day's ride from Dara and Nisibis."

The twin fortresses sat closely together, serving as the critical barrier between Persia and Rome in times of peace. Dara remained heavily cloaked in Persian forces but still flew the Roman Eagle over its stone walls and high towers.

John continued. "Our information on Nisibis is that it is a vast city despite its heavy fortifications. This makes it nearly impossible for an army to capture, but relatively easy for a dozen men to sneak in unnoticed if they are able to reach its walls without incident."

"That is a serious *if,*"' Ascum put in. "The Persians will be looking for Roman spies, and they won't hesitate to hang anyone they suspect of sending messages to their enemies."

Belisarius nodded hesitantly. "I will not obligate any man to take up such a charge, for this is well beyond the oath you swore to the Empire. But if Liberius is alive, it is likely because he did not leave Nisibis, and this is our only chance to bring him back."

With no hesitation, I spoke. "I'll go. I can identify Liberius better than any man in this army."

"I will go as well," called Sembrouthes.

Bessas would not hear of it. "Aksum is at war with Persia, and your skin betrays you there," he said. "Varus can pass as a Hephthalite, especially with his heavily accented Persian, but you would not fool even the most untested of city guards."

Troglita and Mundus both offered to accompany me, but their western features would be too easily noticed. Marcellus nearly insisted that he go, but Belisarius overruled him, correctly citing his crucial role in commanding the excubitores against Xerxes' elite Immortals.

At last, Bessas turned to me. "If you are determined to go, Varus, take my man Barzanes with you. He speaks Persian, and spent time as a boy in Nisibis."

I nodded gratefully, my heart still racing and vision blurring. What would be my next move? I jumped as Belisarius laid a hand upon my shoulder, only half hearing his queries as to whether I was sure I was prepared. When I nodded, he embraced me.

"I would go with you in a heartbeat if I could," Belisarius said, a hint of guilt in his voice.

"I know it," I replied. Belisarius dismissed me to prepare for my journey, which had to begin as soon as possible to give Liberius his best chance at survival.

"I am ready now," I said, but Belisarius shook his head.

"You must promise to wait until the morning, Varus," he said. "Give your body as much time to heal from your previous excursion as you can. It may end up your only weapon."

Grudgingly, I nodded and left the tent to a chorus of murmured well wishes before the remaining officers settled in to plan the Army's route to Thannuris.

Bessas followed close behind so he might introduce me to his man. Barzanes, a fellow Armenian, was an officer in Belisarius' cataphracts who, thanks to a Persian mother, could pass easily in the ranks of our hated enemy. He agreed to accompany me to Nisibis, and we agreed that we needed to leave well before dawn on the coming morning.

Rosamund shrieked when I told her the news.

"These Romans care nothing for you!" She slammed a fist into my shoulder, eyes livid. "Their Emperor is happy to send us barbarians to die in some faraway land without a care so long as his friends and pet projects are safe!"

For once, my decision was totally unmoved by her anger. "No one is sending me. I volunteered, Rosamund. Liberius is like a father to me. I cannot leave him to rot in a Persian dungeon."

Rosamund balled her thin fingers into fists. "No *father* would want you to commit suicide on his behalf! Stay here, Varus, or take me north and we can leave these Romans behind for good."

I shook my head, biting back the anger that I felt rising in my chest. Rosamund had not spoken aloud of her dream to leave and seek the freedom of the northern steppe in quite some time, but her simmering distaste for Roman patricians argued for it all the same, and I had quite simply had enough. I regarded her: her reddening face, the translucent skin of her neck pulsing with anger, her mouth open as if searching for words.

"You're selfish," she snapped at last.

"*What?*" I could hardly believe her. "What did you call me?"

"Selfish!" she cried. "You're selfish, Varus. Why else would you charge off on some adventure that will more than likely kill you? How else could you disregard all of us you'd leave behind? Your young wife, your brother, the dozens of people who depend on you?"

"Rosamund, you know that's not my intent."

"Then explain to me," she said, each word vicious. "Explain!"

An Aksumite ducked into my tent, scowling at the uproar, but I subtly waved off his spear, and he retreated, allowing Rosamund and me to continue in relative privacy.

"If it were you who was held captive, and Liberius were here insisting that I stay behind, I would still go," I said, keeping my voice even. "You know that I would."

"I do." The fury in her voice ebbed a bit, if only in volume. "I know. In a way, you did, with Archelaus."

I nodded. "This is not about duty. Nor is it about the Romans or the Emperor, even. Liberius is my friend, and I will bring him back to safety as I would any friend. Even at the risk to my own life."

Unclenching her fists, Rosamund lifted her eyes to meet mine. Mere heartbeats after lashing out, she became cool and calm, somehow both serene and stern at once. Those eyes bore into me, seeking any untruth, and though I dearly loved Rosamund, and would not lie—had not lied—to her, my skin prickled as she drew close. There was a part of her that would always leave me uneasy, I suspected.

Raising a finger, she traced the silver ouroboros that decorated a thin plate upon my armor, her long nail brushing against the engraving.

"Belisarius' men will see me safely into Nisibis," I went on tentatively. "It will be a simple assignment. Over within a few days."

"No, it won't." Rosamund dropped her hand. "But I shall say prayers for you all the same. Your work is not finished, nor is mine."

Fulcaris and Perenus were curious to hear of Rosamund's anger, and both grew stern as I told of the evil omens discussed in Belisarius' tent.

"I'm coming with you," Perenus stated flatly.

I shook my head. "No. If I am away, I need you to command the foederati," I said. "You'll need a helmet of a komes."

Perenus laughed weakly, agreeing with my logic. "I'm giving it back as soon as you return. For the Herulians' sake, return quickly."

Fulcaris, though, had no such obligation to impeach his going. "I'm not a high officer," he said, "and I can blend in with the Persians' mercenary men."

"It's far too dangerous," I told him. "And you owe no fealty to Liberius. I could not ask this of you."

"To Liberius, no. But I swore an oath, the same as you," Fulcaris said. "And perhaps this is beyond my required service, but I want to do my part to help Rome... and my people." His voice was firm, final.

Perhaps it was the disagreement with Rosamund, or perhaps the Herulian's sense of duty disarmed my better judgment, but after some time, I nodded, agreeing to take him with us on the morrow. We ate our final meal in silence, gathered supplies for the morning, and stole what little rest was possible on the hard Mesopotamian ground.

Immortal

CURSE OF THE MAGUS

CEPHALAS WOKE ME well before dawn. After a light breakfast, I met with Fulcaris and Barzanes at the edge of camp, and we vaulted onto light ponies that would guide us through the Persian lines and into Nisibis.

All signs of our Roman allegiance were left with the army. My armor, clothes, and weapons were exchanged for Persian equipment that had been taken on the raids of our foederati, and I was forced to leave Ignis behind for a separate horse. The Persian garb felt oddly heavy against my skin, but I did not doubt its authenticity, especially when Barzanes remarked on our resemblance to Persian armies and mercenary forces.

Last of all, I tucked Theodora's ring, as well as the chain that bore Mariya's golden dragon and my bronze cross, into a soft leather pouch, possessions I dared not risk falling into Persian hands. Tying the bag shut, I kissed it, then handed the lot to Father Petrus, who promised their return upon my safe arrival back into Belisarius' forces.

Under the cover of profound darkness, we removed ourselves from camp and pushed our horses hard to the northeast, seeking a strip of unguarded territory along the extensive Roman–Persian border by which we could sneak into Nisibis unnoticed. Fulcaris chatted excitedly about how we would present ourselves to Persian city guards, and whether pretending that we were slaves to Barzanes would provide sufficient cover.

"The Persians don't keep slaves," Barzanes corrected. "They feel it is an affront to their God, the Ahura Mazda."

Fulcaris snorted, seeming to believe it a joke.

"Fine, then," I replied. "Fulcaris, you're a mute. Keep your mouth shut and pretend that you cannot speak a word."

"Well, that's going to be impossible." Fulcaris snickered, and Barzanes rolled his eyes insisting upon the urgency of the ruse. I was reluctant to chastise my young Herulian volunteer but did my best to impress upon him the gravity of our mission, which needed utter seriousness of purpose to succeed and survive. Fulcaris nodded, his usually joyful face marred by a light frown.

"That means now, both of you," Barzanes snapped. "From now on, we speak only Persian. Any scout within a mile of our position would know that Roman spies were heading eastward by now."

Visibly nervous, Fulcaris obeyed Barzanes' commands, keeping silent as we galloped along the southern bank of the Euphrates. We kept as vigorous a pace as possible, traveling by night and resting during the heat of midday, taking care to ensure that our horses would not collapse from exhaustion or injury as we proceeded toward the Tigris just south of Amida.

That night, low fires in the evening horizon betrayed the presence of Xerxes' army nearby, which appeared to be moving in force at a heavy pace. Torches danced in the distance atop the heads of walking and mounted men, with the din from their movements carrying well across the flat plains.

"The army is on the move south, with some haste," Barzanes remarked in Persian, choosing his words carefully. Ignoring Fulcaris' looks of confusion, I nodded in recognition, my mind turning to Belisarius in hopes that the general would be able to anticipate whatever Xerxes' latest maneuver toward Thannuris might entail.

By the fourth day, we definitely crossed into formal Persian territory some forty miles north of Nisibis. Barzanes altered our course in an arcing southeasterly direction, slowly closing our distance to the fortress city in a meandering arch. We passed by several small contingents of Persian soldiers who hailed Barzanes as we passed by, yet otherwise had few concerns outside of the rare outbursts from an exhausted Fulcaris.

The following morning, we reached the mouth of the Saokoros River, a distant tributary to the Euphrates. We followed the meandering waters south and then slowly west, making our way slowly toward the ring of outlying fortifications around Nisibis. After another day, we arrived at Sisauranon, the northern strongpoint around the Persian fortress that guarded the major roadways that connected Mesopotamia and Assyria.

Though walled with stone and encompassing a larger area, Sisauranon was laid out congruous to our army encampments. Sentry towers and fighting platforms were positioned every twenty paces, while reinforced gates allowed approved visitors entry into the town from all sides. With Xerxes' army to the immediate west, Sisauranon showed few signs of the smoldering war that had consumed dozens of towns and thousands of lives across Armenia and Mesopotamia, with several of its watch towers noticeably vacant.

From Sisauranon, it was possible to see the outline of Nisibis far in the distance on a clear day. The town guards paid us no mind as we walked into the town center, which had its own bustling bazaar despite the relatively small size of the settlement. Sweeping his Persian robes over his shoulders, Barzanes dismounted and walked toward several stalls, finding one whose sign bore the sigil of a horse trader. Fulcaris' eyes grew wide with curiosity at the sight of the foreign fruits and exotic goods that flooded into Sisauranon.

"Keep silent," I whispered to him. "And touch nothing."

Fulcaris wandered toward a particularly expensive set of display armor reserved for a Persian Zhayedan, recoiling in shock as I slapped him hard on the hand for such insolence. An old Median woman minding the stall laughed at this display, her mouth bearing several missing teeth over sun-weathered skin.

With Fulcaris in tow, we followed Barzanes into the horse trading stall, finding our comrade already engaged in a spirited debate over the value of our exhausted ponies that, unbeknownst to the merchant, had carried three Roman soldiers into Persian lines at a breakneck pace.

Though I had significantly improved with my command of the Persian tongue over several months of daily training, Barzanes and the merchant spoke far too quickly and far too angrily to follow. Still, I was able to discern the overall gist of the spirited attempt at barter, but looked around nervously in fear of attracting attention. If any in Sisauranon's bazaar thought our arguments out of character, it did not show, for most carried on with their mornings or even engaged in similar behavior with other potential customers.

After what seemed an eternity, Barzanes and the merchant came to an accord, with the Persian smiling broadly at the result.

"I sold him our horses for an ox and a cart, and enough gold to fill it with grain," Barzanes explained in Persian, adding that the merchant had likely cheated them by a significant margin.

"Why?" I asked. Barzanes' strategy to see us discreetly into Nisibis was beginning to make me wary.

"You'll see soon enough," was his explanation. "Just keep the Herulian from doing anything stupid."

Eager to oblige, we followed Barzanes toward a far stall. He struck a faster bargain with a grain seller, vastly overpaying good silver for heavy bags of cut wheat even despite the ongoing war. The grain peddler snapped orders at younger boys that were likely his sons, who carried the bag to Barzanes' newly acquired ox cart.

Satisfied, Barzanes signaled our readiness to depart Sisauranon, heading first toward a wide road that connected Nisibis with the more easterly provinces of the Persian Empire. Barzanes ordered us to place our small Persian daggers onto the cart but leave our swords swinging freely at our hips. The

Armenian man cut open several of the bags of wheat, allowing the long stalks to sift freely onto the flat bed of the cart. A heavy press hid the thin blades, making it so that only a determined investigator would be able to discover their whereabouts.

Our ox moved slowly until reaching that stone-dressed pathway, despite Barzanes' constant prods to the beast's flank. When at last we reached the road, we merged into a busier line of traffic that comprised the bulk of supplies and trade leading into Nisibis. Barzanes laid a careful finger over his lips, signaling for quiet as our cart blended in with hundreds of others eager to sell their goods to the massed forces in Nisibis.

Where Sisauranon resembled a more heavily guarded military camp, Nisibis rose high along the horizon. Its stone walls were built five times the height of a grown man, making it impossible even for those riding along the backs of armored elephants to easily crest Nisibis' battlements. Small companies of archers peered lazily at the procession of merchants and visitors to the city, while a separate detachment of Persians inspected each new arrival.

Barzanes urged our ox forward as we moved slowly toward the inspection point. As the line shortened and our turn arose, a city guard waved at Barzanes to approach. The guard looked over our cart with a near glassy look on his face.

"Purpose for entering?" he asked formally.

"We wish to sell this wheat to the army," Barzanes replied in flawless Persian.

The guard nodded. "You'll need to surrender your blades, which will be numbered and returned to you as you depart," he said, signaling for two attendants to grab our swords. We surrendered the coarse, dented blades without incident, pretending to show a deal of concern about how we could retrieve such possessions later on.

Pacing along the cart, the first guard leisurely lowered his spear and stabbed lightly into the bundled grains. The wheat shuffled around, and for a moment I feared the man had found something of interest. Indeed, he paused in his attack, yet at last he simply withdrew the spear and brushed away residue from the wheat stalks. Finding no hidden spies, the guard waved us forward, his eyes already focused upon the men and women who stood next in line.

Safely inside, our cart rolled into a hive of activity, with dozens of tribes and peoples that comprised the Persian Empire milling about in service to the army or to the city market. Colossal limestone fortified the city's expanse, and I could count no fewer than a thousand bowmen patrolling the crenellated walls and towers.

Curiously, where Constantinople or Singidunum had been riddled with miasma and filth, Nisibis' gutters appeared swept of detritus and purged of human and animal waste, leaving only the not exceedingly unpleasant mixture of urine and straw assailing the nostrils. Armed men seemed to pack every open space and corner, although vast teams of blacksmiths and tanners hauled their wares into the choked throng of Nisibis' streets. Streaks of colorful fabrics and stacks of incense lined the distant walls, crowned by banners of nations far beyond even where Alexander had trod. Their voices, lilted and clipped in the Persian of the foreign-born, called out their wares.

"The bitter vegetable!" one voice called. "Embolden the mind and heal the stomach with a fragrant cup!"

Another young woman pointed to me, beckoning with a smile. "You desire tastier food, yes? Come to my stall, and I will sell you powders from India that you will weep over."

Others offered all manner of spears, blades, and armor, meeting the budget of a wealthy Immortal to the lowliest peasant spearman. Both organized and rife with chaos, the press of bodies yielded an uncomfortable heat and a nagging fear of pickpockets. Barzanes appeared unperturbed, however, acknowledging none and driving ever forward. Flustered, I nevertheless followed Barzanes' example, drawn aback only by the sound of Greek voices laughing amidst a sea of Persian warriors and subjects. Voices arose from the throats of three gray-haired men, their linen garb far more acceptable in Constantinople than in any eastern expanse.

"Greeks?" I whispered.

"Justinian banned pagan philosophers from the schools of Athens," Barzanes hissed. "Kavadh welcomes them without condition. Doubtless there are hundreds in Ctesiphon."

"And they stay, even with the war?"

"Persecution from the Emperor, or suspicion from the Shahanshah." Barzanes shrugged. "Which would you prefer, if your life was exchanged for their own? I hold no grudges against such men, but neither do I feel any responsibility."

Goading our ox forward, we followed the city streets in the direction of the market, our progress soon swarmed by men and animals that pushed and ran in various directions. More than one angry merchant screamed at Barzanes to move our cart from the road, yet none seriously threatened our group as we struggled toward the marketplace.

A deep trumpeting noise bellowed over the press of men and animals. Fulcaris jumped, and I saw his mouth droop open as he hunched defensively. Following his gaze, I looked down a side street that led to the city stables and gasped at the sight.

Clad in glistening bronze plates, a huge Persian elephant roared in protest at treatment given by his handlers. Standing three times as tall as a man, the elephant swung its head violently, forcing its attendants to dive away from the long ivory tusks that protruded well beyond the elephant's trunk. Another elephant trumpeted at this display, stomping a foot that quaked the ground underneath.

The piercing, sonorous bleats of the elephants faded as we continued forward. Fulcaris and I gaped at each other, still struck with shock and fear. Though the presence of such beasts in the Persian army had been legendary, and rumors abounded in Belisarius' army that the Persian Astabadh Azarethes deployed several within his armies, tales of the elephants seemed outrageous and unbelievable. My stomach turned at the unanswered thought of how Romans were supposed to fight against such raw strength and size, let alone kill them.

The bustle of men and carts grounded to a halt near the city's administrative center, just before its marketplace. Barzanes sought out alternate routes to continue our progress but was stymied at each turn by an equally perturbed mob of confused Persians. I pushed my way in between shifting gaps in the crowd to catch a glimpse of our impediment and found myself witness to a ceremony with all the formal dignity of any triumph in Constantinople.

A slow procession of Persian priests walked in a small column along the street, with city guards blocking the road with their long ash spears. Several of their number began to disappear into a looming structure that seemed to be the palace of some satrap or governor, unfazed by the clamor of city noise. A hush fell across the crowd as a lone man shuffled toward the rear of the column, his tall physique and wild beard initially disguising his advanced age.

Individual shouts rose above the crowd, transforming tension into adulation. "Hakhamanish! Hakhamanish!" several shouted, the cries quickly picking up within the mob.

Fulcaris looked upon me with a concerned gaze, yet I motioned for the Herulian to keep calm as I used my height and strength to jockey into a better viewing angle of the man who garnered the awe of so many Persians in the midst of war.

The man bore the standing of a Zoroastrian magus, with a tight white cloth bound atop his head and a spotless white cloak and mantle that covered the length of his body. An orange sash swayed from the man's waist as he strode forward, helped by a thin onyx walking staff. Per the crowd's rising cheers, I assumed the man's name was Hakhamanish, but if he cared for cries that flooded the streets, his face showed nothing. Nor did he balk at calls to share a vision of the future that made me shudder with the thought of such heresy.

Though I had little exposure to the Zoroastrian religion as a slave in Constantinople, I'd pieced together lessons from Liberius as well as from planning sessions with Belisarius that the Zoroastrians held old beliefs that centered around the worship of a deity named Ahura Mazda, with its priests using fire as a primary symbol of the god. Beyond that, I knew little else, for the teachings of the Persian faith were heresy in the eyes of nearly all Christian priests, including Father Petrus, and not something to be studied and discussed.

Hakhamanish's thick beard was interrupted by a thickset mouth and a heavy brow that gave the magus a permanent look of anger. A jagged scar forced his left eye permanently shut, yet his dark right eye scanned the crowd as he moved slowly forward. Persian guardsmen struggled to hold back the adoring crowd, and more than one used a gloved fist to knock back the especially zealous. I followed along with the crowd's energy, using the weight of my body to firmly secure a place in the front rank as Fulcaris and Barzanes pulled at my back. Hakhamanish shuffled ever forward until, a mere ten paces from my position, he stopped.

The magus' pause was brief, and those in attendance that day may not have even noticed. However, as Hakhamanish scanned over my position and met my eyes, his gait slowed and his staff stood upright for a heartbeat. The angry right eye came level with my own, and I froze in shock.

A foreboding sense of doom washed over me as the magus' eye washed over me, seemingly boring into my soul. Out of instinct, my hand reached for my belt but grasped at air where my sword would have normally been. Barzanes' hidden daggers remained shrouded by wheat in our cart, and I was left with nothing to defend myself from the Zoroastrian priest.

As abruptly as my encounter with the magus began, so, too, did the man break his hold over me and proceed. After rising onto the steps of the palace, Hakhamanish disappeared with his attendants, leaving Persian guards to swing shut the massive wooden doors that barred entry to the fortified building to the remainder of Nisibis.

Barzanes tugged violently on my cloak, pulling me back from the crowd.

"What are you doing?" Barzanes hissed in Persian as he half carried me back toward our cart and away from the masses.

The passing of Hakhamanish helped alleviate enough congestion to push our ox forward, the wooden wheels grinding atop rounded stones, dripping mud, and a swill of unmentionable horror that many households dumped onto the streets each morning and night.

"No more problems, understand?" Barzanes scowled again. Fulcaris frowned, confused. "We could have already started looking for the man we are supposed to find, but you insist on a scenic tour of the city."

I nodded, although my mind remained fixed on Hakhamanish, the outline of his dark eye burning in my mind. My body grew weak with a chill despite the heat of the Mesopotamian city and the thick press of unwashed bodies, and I quivered until my teeth chattered from that brief memory.

Undeterred, Barzanes eventually led us to the market square of Nisibis and dragged the ox cart toward a half-disguised corner that was covered with a cloth awning and heavy shade from the position of the sun. The Armenian searched blindly for the daggers and distributed one to each of us, instructing us to hide the blade well within our robes and draw no attention to their whereabouts.

"We need to find a way into that palace," Barzanes said in hushed Greek, temporarily breaking his own rule so that Fulcaris could understand our next actions. "If Liberius is still here, he'd be held in that building. If not... we'll at least be able to find out what happened to him."

Fulcaris and I both bobbed our heads, yet I still held concerns.

"How will we be allowed to roam the halls? Let alone locate Liberius in there." The palace was large—vast, even.

Barzanes took a more confident view of our situation. "Liberius is most likely in the city dungeon," he said. "Now, we cannot be sure exactly where that is, but Roman buildings typically hold captives underground or several stories in the air to prevent escapes."

"But this is a Persian city," Fulcaris put in.

"Yes, but it was constructed as a Roman city toward the end of the Empire," I said, following Barzanes' logic.

"Precisely," Barzanes said. "And I doubt the Persians changed much. Saves on construction costs."

So there was our choice: underground or high in the air. The administrative palace was certainly built high enough to support either theory, meaning that both would need to be explored.

"Couldn't we just ask where the prisoners are kept, and if a man matching Liberius' description was seen there recently?" Fulcaris asked innocently, struggling to be helpful.

Barzanes lashed a hand out, nearly striking the Herulian on the head. "Fool, do you want to draw attention to yourself? Those types of questions will just raise eyebrows. If you want to leave here alive, we need to be as discreet as possible."

Face reddening, Fulcaris nodded and fell silent. Barzanes broke our meeting, leading the cart back toward the open market.

Finding a grain merchant, Barzanes hailed the older man and struck up a conversation as the prelude to selling our wares. The merchant greeted Barzanes warmly, showering hopes of blessings from Ahura Mazda as he bobbed his head at the Armenian man. The merchant scanned Fulcaris and me, his brow furrowed and eyes pinched as he reviewed our figures. I offered a light smile and nod to the merchant, while Fulcaris tied his cloak and robes tighter around his body.

Barzanes briskly sold the wheat stalks for a small leather pouch of silver, undoubtedly far below a competitive price. The Persian grain peddler flashed crooked and stained teeth as the deal was struck, guiding our ox to an enclosed expanse behind his stall. He wished us a blessing upon our day as he walked along, handing the ox's lead to an older Persian woman and disappearing into the hive of the market.

Barzanes tucked the pouch into his belt, securing it with a thick leather thong. He motioned for us to follow as he paced through the market, eyeing the stone palace that rose within the city center well into the sky. Barzanes stopped at certain intervals, judging that great building, until after some time he smiled in victory.

"I know how we are getting in," Barzanes said slyly as we moved closer. He looked upon the building, an arm lightly outstretched so as to draw our eyes toward a side door of the palace without striking an unduly suspicious pose. "There," he said, and moved closer to lay out the details of his plan.

However, as he did so, an airy horn blew atop the marketplace, spurring a flurry of activity as men and women alike scrambled for side alleys and stalls to escape or hide. Barzanes' eyes grew wide as he looked for relative safety or shelter, unsure of what threat would disrupt the day's commerce. He pivoted toward multiple alleys, yet was rejected by other angry and frightened merchants or was chased out by hired thugs paid to protect the private property of wealthier Persians in Nisibis.

As the horn sounded for a second time, Barzanes ran back in the direction of the city gates, frantically beckoning for us to follow. Our sandals slid along the wet stones as we chased the Armenian, and more than once I lost my footing on the slick coating along the street. Though I did not fall into the muck, I still conducted a terrible pace as Barzanes sprinted ahead of us.

Nearly at the gate, the Armenian suddenly turned back, darting again toward the center of the market. "Run!" he growled at us, and we blindly ran back from whence we came. Echoes from nailed boots flitted along Nisibis' stone walls rang out behind us, and I picked up my pace in a desperate search for freedom from the impending threat behind us.

Horns rang out for a third and final time, and despite our exertions, we were doomed. Another troop of Persian spearmen flooded into the market forum, their helmeted faces angry as they searched through several stalls for their intended target. I caught a glimpse of our grain merchant speaking with one detachment of the spearmen, an aged hand pointing in our direction.

"You three, halt!" the leader of the spearmen shouted. Ignoring him, Barzanes dashed toward an alley, ducking between other Persians that hid from the invading soldiers. As soon as he disappeared, Barzanes reemerged back into the square, desperately searching for an escape.

One of the soldiers lowered his spear and motioned toward Barzanes, the features of his face overshadowed by a tall iron skullcap and a mail coif that sat snugly beneath his chin. Barzanes spat in defiance and drew his dagger, charging past the man's spear as he lunged forward.

A handsbreadth from the Persian spearman's neck, Barzanes' body jerked violently as he was impaled on a spear thrown by another of the Persian guardsman. The spearhead cut easily through Barzanes' unarmored body, the wooden shaft driven well into the man's body just below the ribs. Blood bubbled from his mouth, and the strength gave out from his legs, only the angle of the spear preventing his total collapse upon the ground.

"Who sent you?" the leader of the Persian guards yelled at Barzanes. When Barzanes said nothing, the leader twisted on the spear shaft, loosening a small piece of Barzanes' intestines out onto his robes. With a shaking hand, Barzanes tried to shove his own exposed viscera back into his body, wincing in his failure.

I struggled forward to help Barzanes but was hit across my back with the wooden end of a spear that sent me sprawling to the ground. Fulcaris soon followed suit, with the two of us staring onward at our guide.

"Tell me, now!" the Persian ordered.

He grew closer to Barzanes, whose mouth began to move amidst waves of pain that coursed through his injured body. With the guard a few feet away, Barzanes spat a thick gob of phlegm and blood into the Persian's face. At such an insult, the leader bared his teeth, drew his sword, and swung violently for Barzanes' exposed neck.

Blood sprayed across a nearby stall. I could see Barzanes' exposed veins and bones as the head lolled atop the now-still corpse, a single jet of dark crimson pooling beneath our friend's body.

"Motherless bastards," Fulcaris cursed in Herulian between clenched teeth. Our captors signaled to the Persian leader, pointing to our prostrate bodies.

"Take them to the cells. We'll question them soon," the leader responded. Fulcaris and I were jerked painfully to our feet, our hands roped behind our backs. One spearman patted our legs and torsos, easily finding Barzanes' hidden blades within the folds of our robes. They were handed to the Persian leader, who scoffed in anger before we were taken away.

With spears digging into our backs, Fulcaris and I were led into the palace and forced up multiple flights of spiraling stone stairs. The spearmen called out to guards atop each floor that prisoners were on their way, ensuring that we would have no respite with any attempt to escape. Beams of light flooded through exposed windows, yet such kindnesses were repaid with an intense heat that grew with each flight of stairs we ascended.

Several floors up, Fulcaris and I were led into a small stone room whose only light source included a pair of torches and a thin square window cut into the outer palace wall. The dungeon's lone attendant unhooked a rusty iron key from his belt and used it to open a damp barred cell, the hinges screaming as the door swung outward. Spearheads dug further into our backs, forcing us forward and onto our knees. As we crept away from the malice of our captors, the cell door swung shut and its lock was secured, leaving Fulcaris and me standing against dank stone walls with our jailor sitting lazily outside.

Eyes wide with fear, Fulcaris made to speak until I covered his mouth with my hand. Shaking my head, I motioned for the Herulian to keep quiet and listened to the muffled discussion of the Persian guardsmen on the other side of the dungeon wall. A deep, craggy voice interjected amongst the gathered Persian spearmen, followed by a burst of activity as the men moved away from the jail and out of earshot.

Given a moment of respite, I took stock of my surroundings, searching for a route of escape or some measure of solace. The cell bars were well worn and rusted, seeming far too sturdy to break against sandals, and made considerable noise when moved. Likewise, the cell floor and walls were dressed stone caked in dirt and filth, and offered no tools or options to craft a weapon. My mind raced as I thought of other strategies, disrupted only when Fulcaris laughed aloud. The Herulian's eyes were frantic and full of fear, yet he cackled sardonically all the same.

I tried and failed to motion Fulcaris into silence. "What *is* it?" I whispered in Herulian.

"There's no one else here!" Fulcaris' laughter gave way to heavy tears, and he kneeled down, his face close to his knees.

It took a few moments for Fulcaris' words to take effect.

"Liberius is not here," I said aloud, my spirits sinking. Thoughts spiraled into an abyss of anger and hopelessness. According to both Belisarius and Barzanes, our best chance at recovering Liberius was within Nisibis. If Liberius was not here, he must have been moved toward the distant provinces of Persia's interior, or, more likely, executed as a Roman interloper and spy. Barzanes' sacrifice, which would soon be shared by Fulcaris and myself, was for naught.

Enraged, I kicked on the cell's bars, startling our jailor to his feet. He swung a thin club against the iron bars, rattling Fulcaris, who scurried out of reach.

"Be silent, or next time I'll crack your skulls," the jailor grunted crudely, his Persian barely decipherable. He glared at me until I sat down, then lowered the club.

"Ah, obedient whelps!" he said cheerily, and left the cells for the fresher air immediately outside of the dungeon door.

Fulcaris and I sat alone in the cells, sweating amidst the sweltering heat of our cage. I quickly trained my body to breathe through my mouth alone, wary of the horrid stench that formed a miasma around our bodies. The only other object in our room was a lonely wooden bucket stained with all manner of foul substances, and I initially avoided it out of pride. As daylight faded into evening, pride gave way to the basest of human necessities.

It was later in the evening that our first visitors arrived. Though not yet starved, our bodies rumbled in hunger, and my head grew light as I fought to show an impassive face against my enemies.

A dozen men filtered into the room, many of whom carried thick woolen cloths over their mouths and noses. One man's face was completely covered with a dark-gold cloth, broken only by a thick black beard plaited into a long strip. He stood at the rear of the party, his eyes silently scanning the room and analyzing the two men before him who disturbed the peace of Nisibis.

Servants arranged chairs for several of the men, while one of their number approached the iron bars of our cage. His face was marked by a wispy black beard and heavyset eyes, while his hands and arms bore gold bracelets and rings that could have paid the wages of my banda for half a year.

Pressing an embroidered cloth to his nose, the man adopted an angry look as he made eye contact with me.

"On your feet, heathen!" he growled in Persian, his voice a higher tone than his body would suggest.

Defiant, I stared back at him, unmoving. The interrogator took pains to hoist his dark-gold robes above the filth-strewn stone floor, exposing soft crimson slippers underneath. The man nodded to our jailor, who raised his club and jabbed its blunted point into my ribs. I made a deliberate show of standing slowly, unbreaking my gaze with the interrogator as I did so.

The questioner began again. "Do you understand my words?" he barked again in Persian, his nose wrinkling as he momentarily removed the cloth from his face.

"Yes," I responded curtly.

"Good. Then tell me, who sent you to Nisibis?"

I scowled. "No one sent me. I came to trade."

The interrogator laughed haughtily. "You are no merchant—or not a good one, anyway. Robbed blind by an old man," he said. "And your body is not the soft flesh of any trader. Nor was your dead friend's."

My eyes dropped to the floor as I fought my own anger. "He was an innocent man, a man you killed for no reason."

The Persian interrogator was unfazed. "Who sent you to Nisibis? Tell me, and this will go much easier for you."

"Your mother," I grunted.

My jailor whipped his club between the bars, cracking me along the shoulder before I could defend myself. Pain shot through my body as I inadvertently recoiled, sheltering myself from another blow.

The interrogator grew closer, fury lining his visage. His nostrils flared as he gathered the words to continue, his chest rising and falling rapidly.

"Did Perozes send you? Azarethes? Tell me now, Hephthalite, or things will go very badly for you and your remaining friend," he said.

I shot back in confusion, uncertain of the line of questioning. The interrogator's fury gave way to a look of smug triumph, and he only dug further in his inquiry.

"No Hephthalite is supposed to be in Nisibis, yet here you are. So, I ask again. Were you sent by Perozes, and did the spahbad instruct you to harm Prince Xerxes?"

"I don't know what you are talking about," I said through clenched teeth.

My eyes shot quickly to the jailer, who raised his club for another attack. The skin on my hand stung viciously as I caught the wooden weapon in my hand, dragging the jailor headfirst into the iron bars. A sick cracking rang out as the man's skull collided with the bars, leading others in the room to rise to their feet in concern. Knowing the fruitlessness of further resistance, I tossed the club at the interrogator's feet.

"You are a fool, and I *will* pull answers from you," the interrogator said acidly as he turned away for the door. Robes swishing above the dungeon floor, their retinue hurried from the room, with many voicing sighs of relief as they escaped to a cooler atmosphere that was not riddled with filth.

Fulcaris and I were left in relative peace as the darkness of night set in, mercifully cooling the room down to a less oppressive level. I pondered the inquisitor's assertions as two tin plates were brought in and slid under our bars.

"Eat," the jailor commanded.

Even a starving dog would have been skeptical of the meal, which was a thick gruel laced with what seemed to be rotten vegetables. My mouth watered at the sight, and Fulcaris and I devoured the meal with filthy hands. We did not even bother to wait for the meal to cool, and it burned our mouths and throats, making my tongue swell throughout the remainder of that night and into the next day.

Four guards arrived mid-morning on the following day, unarmored but clad in heavy scaled armor. Our jailor opened the iron door and allowed the guards inside, who proceeded to bash their fists into our arms and torsos. The men were careful not to strike our heads, forcing Fulcaris and I to take turns watching as they beat us one after the other.

Soon thereafter, the inquisitor returned alone and asked his same questions with a look of conviction and superiority. Groaning, I still managed to spit defiance at the man, who shook his head and retreated from the room. Fulcaris and I were subjected to another round of beatings, and I called out as a sickening crack thudded deep within my friend's rib cage.

We muttered words of encouragement to one another in the night, having few other opportunities to raise each other's spirits. Though Fulcaris continued to show anger at his captors, his resistance grew weaker as their blows sank in. I voiced concern at the man's wheezing, which grew worse throughout the second night and left him with troubled and interrupted sleep.

On the third morning of our captivity, the guards changed their tactics. While the same four men entered the cell, one chained me to the bars of the cell while the other three cornered Fulcaris.

Their blows rained heavily upon my friend, whose eyes eventually slid into the back of his head, and he crumpled to the ground. My eyes widened as I feared that they had killed Fulcaris, but my fears were assuaged at the sight of the man's labored breathing on the floor of the cell.

The inquisitor arrived soon thereafter, offering a cup of red wine and a heavy plate of seasoned roasted meats. Another silk-robed Persian followed close behind, his bearded face masked with thick folds of golden cloth. The man said nothing as the inquisitor goaded me with insincere questions of my well-being, assuring me that all of this pain could quickly come to an end. I lusted after the food but growled at the questioner instead, earning me nothing more than a hearty laugh.

"Your friend seems in need of a doctor. Tell me of Perozes' plans, and I can see to that immediately," he offered, his voice tender with mock concern.

Fulcaris stirred weakly on the floor yet remained in a daze, semiconscious in his pain. The inquisitor offered the food again, which I snagged from his grasp and carried to the rear of the cell.

"Perozes will kill you for this," I said. My threat yielded only further laughter.

The inquisitor repeated his line of questioning, but I remained mute until he shrugged in frustration. "We can continue this for some time, you know. I am in no hurry," the man said. "Months, even."

As the man left, I stirred Fulcaris awake, feeding him with the rich food left for my consumption. Fulcaris smiled weakly and gnawed at the meat, eating several chunks. He heaved and vomited later, his body having grown unused to rich food, yet he tried again soon after.

Days and nights blended together as time passed. While our guards never fully relented on me, and inflicted a number of ugly bruises along my body, their fury was largely reserved for Fulcaris.

The Herulian man slipped into unconsciousness more easily each day, his body jerking loosely as the guards delivered metal fists or leather boots into his filthy, ragged clothing and exposed skin. Fulcaris grew increasingly delirious at night and occasionally began to cry incoherently, calling out in Herulian for his mother and wishing to go home. I cradled Fulcaris to help him sleep, rocking him against the stone floor.

After an eternity of beatings and inquisition, our schedule was interrupted by a new figure. His retinue urged him to keep away, that such work was beneath him, but the figure simply growled and ordered that he be allowed to see the prisoners. A hurried attempt to clean the dungeon was made, and a richly embroidered carpet sprawled out before our cell that was topped with a cushioned chair, the servants frowning when the chair legs left unsightly creases in the soft fabric.

The rooms marginally cleaner and its visiting area decorated with rushed grandeur, the door swung open as the burly figure stepped inside.

"Leave us!" Hakhamanish commanded. He glowered at one lingering, simpering servant, who promptly scurried out into the hallways. Hakhamanish limped into the room, leaning on his cane until reaching the low chair facing my cell. Its wooden legs creaked as they absorbed the magus' weight, and Hakhamanish turned his single eye upon me.

The magus' gaze seemed to burn into my skin with a power that conjured images of thousands of insects crawling over flesh in my mind's eye.

"What is your name, Roman?" Hakhamanish asked, his voice rumbling against his chest.

I turned my head in surprise, furrowing my brow, then shook my head.

Hakhamanish face contorted as he cackled aloud. "Don't worry, Roman. Despite all the shows of piety by Persia's well-dressed courtiers, they tend to ignore the wisdom of their priests. Your secret is safe with me," he said.

I kept my silence as the magus' eyes fell upon the low fire that burned by a torch mounted along the stone wall. Hakhamanish stood slowly and walked over to that open flame, its tendrils shining against the magus' single eye as he passively absorbed its warmth.

"Your friend," Hakhamanish said, breaking the silence, "he is Herulian, yes?"

"No."

"A lie," Hakhamanish snapped, "and a poor one. Your young friend is Herulian, and his health is fading. But what does that make you, then?" he demanded, his eye turning from the flames and back onto me.

"A Roman, like you said."

"Another lie! Even if it is one you tell yourself. What people do you hail from, really?" the magus asked, his eye narrowing as he took stock of my condition.

"Herulian," I admitted. The magus smiled weakly, yet his face offered a more sardonic look than one of warmth or friendship.

"You Romans chirp about your beloved culture, as if that elevates you in the eyes of your God. However, you whore, and steal, and subjugate others less fortunate under your boots," Hakhamanish said. "And where has this gotten you? Greek remnants of a dying people, your fingers clutching anxiously at what few riches remain in your grasp."

I snorted. "Then what does that make you, or the whole of Persia's empire? Brutalizing innocents in Armenia... surely *that* is the sign of a civilized people."

Hakhamanish croaked in amusement. "You mistake me, Roman-with-no-name. The whole world is dying, and we, too, are following in your example. The great battle for the world began four generations ago, and the enemy is winning."

"The enemy?" I did not follow.

The magus' eye narrowed at my question. He grabbed the torch from the wall and carried it toward my cell. Its flames cast long shadows across the walls that made Fulcaris stir and moan in protest.

"The God of Truth, or what we call the Ahura Mazda, and the God of Lies, who I shall not name in this dark place," the magus said, shivering at the thought of his great enemy. "For thousands of years, our God of Light and Truth reigned supreme, and the world's peoples rose each year into something greater than themselves."

Hakhamanish paced along the cell's expanse, shining light onto Fulcaris and gaining a better view of the man's injuries. A disgusted look grew on the magus' face as he shook his head.

"The next time a man or woman uses dishonesty to achieve their means, ask yourself why they do so. Such efforts are the offspring of the Father of All Lies and are never without consequence," Hakhamanish said, a cold fury in his voice. His gaze weakened for a moment before he added, "And they have cost us everything."

I rose to my feet, feeling a growing urge to defy the man's heresies and condemnation of my people. Hakhamanish ignored such movements initially, but then slowly turned to meet my gaze.

"Perhaps in Persia, but Rome remains a light to the world, and we are building for our own better future," I bragged, standing straight despite the sores that had formed across my back.

Hakhamanish cackled in a low wheezing tone at my display. "Perhaps once, but no longer. You are condemned to fall, the same as the thousands of other lands and peoples that scratch at the earth."

The magus moved toward me suddenly, his eye full and wild as he moved with speed uncharacteristic of a man of so many years. Hakhamanish held the torch just a handsbreadth from my face, so close its flames blinded me.

"This was Rome once, and Persia before her," he said. Pulling the torch back, Hakhamanish drew a thick triangular dagger from his belt, laying its iron blade across the metal ring that supported the torch's lit end. Orange and yellow flames diminished, yet a dimmed light continued to emit from its remaining opening.

"Rome fell victim to the great darkness of the Evil One and lost its heritage. What remains is a dimmer imitation of itself," Hakhamanish said. The magus slid the blade closer to the center of the lit torch, the flames dying as they licked against the metal.

"And each year that passes sends you further down the inevitable path of destruction," Hakhamanish said, his voice adopting songlike qualities. The flames grew lower until all that remained were glowing embers that escaped from the edges of the knife.

With a swift motion, Hakhamanish covered the torch with a thick cloth, allowing darkness to fill the room. "I have seen the fate of men, and this is it," the magus bellowed, his voice echoing across the stones. "The light of our nations may dance for a time and grow brighter from our exertions, but our fates are written in blood. The enemy has come, and we are too late to turn his unstoppable blade from our world."

Icy air blew through the dungeon despite the swelter of summer, and I shivered as my eyes adjusted to the darkness. Still, I could see nothing in that abyss, only hear the low moans that wheezed from Fulcaris' chest.

"No man can see the future," I said with a deliberateness and confidence I did not really feel. The magus' laughter rumbled in the darkness, carrying into the hallways and out onto the streets below our prison.

"Oh no? Don't be so sure of yourself, my boy. Your God has no power here."

My eyes stretched wide as I peered into the darkness, making out the barest of outlines of the older man. Silence, laced only with the faintest wheezing of the magus, was at once distant and uncomfortably close. Gripping the bars, I felt my heart pound as I mouthed a prayer, unwilling to blink lest I miss any sign of an attack.

Then, as if by a crash of a thunderbolt, the room was filled with blinding light.

Hakhamanish ran his hand over the torch, stoking the flames far higher than they had before. Eyes stinging, I recoiled in shock and drew my arm over my face. Rings of light flooded my mind as I rubbed my eyes, listening to the magus' words.

"When I look at you, all I see is death. We would be good to snuff out your life here and now and sever the tree of the Evil One forever," the magus threatened.

Forcing my eyes open, I saw Hakhamanish's outline swim into view. "I—" I choked, taken aback again as I struggled to stand and face my attacker. "I have no fear of you. Conjurer's tricks, nothing more!" I yelled.

Veins pulsed in the magus' neck as he seethed at me, his lone eye frantic and dancing with the flames. He threw a white powder into the flames, making them dance higher as he edged his face into the smoke.

His eye's dark center rolled into the back of Hakhamanish's head. The magus clenched his crooked teeth, emitting a foul grinding sound as spittle formed at the corner of his mouth.

"I see the last of the Romans. A bride of darkness, an uncrowned king, a soiled monarch, and a windblown son will meet in the ruins of the world, and from their unholy union will be borne the damnation of the Greeks," the magus growled, his voice hollow yet impossibly heavy.

Then he screamed.

The sound led to a flurry of banging at the prison door that went unanswered. "All you are, my boy, is a creeping death that will cloak the world in blackness."

Dropping the torch to the floor, the magus gasped for air, dropping his head between his knees. Servants finally unlocked and opened the dungeon door, yet they were met only with growls of disapproval.

"Out!" Hakhamanish bellowed, and the servants and jailor rushed back out into the hallway. He panted and rose to his feet, his face drenched with moisture. Gathering his cane, Hakhamanish clicked weakly across the stone floor, shuffling slowly to the exit.

"Heed my words, Roman, and be wary. The Great Lie is already upon you, the scion of sin."

He coughed violently into his hand and opened the door, disappearing into the hallway beyond. Our jailor entered and gazed angrily in our direction, but he did not add to our torment. He returned the torch to its holster along the wall and exited, leaving Fulcaris and me alone in the flickering light of our cage.

Though the passage of time was difficult to track in the Persian dungeon, I attempted to keep count of the rise and fall of the sun, whose light flooded into our thin window each day. Violence from the guards substantially diminished after Hakhamanish's visit, although Fulcaris remained weak from his existing injuries and general lack of nourishment. Our food remained thin gruel and stale bread, but we sopped up each morsel greedily, often licking the copper-tasting plates clean.

With Fulcaris slowly healing, our daily tedium was broken only by twice-daily visits from the inquisitor. The man continued with his same line of questioning and was met only with angry silence or even outright defiance. The Persian threatened to restart our torture and even went so far as to bring the armored guards into one of his sessions. In the aftermath of my discussion with

Hakhamanish, the Persians did little other than prepare grist-ridden starvation rations as our days passed in the sweltering heat.

This routine continued unbroken for at least another week. In that time, Fulcaris had begun to sit unassisted, and even made light of his predicament as he vividly discussed the hundreds of ways that he would butcher his Persian captors as soon as he found a way to break out. In the night, as Fulcaris slept, he mumbled and jerked in his sleep, frequently rising with a shout as his eyes peered through the darkness.

Our monotony was to be broken on a most curious day. It began unremarkably, with sunlight filtering through clouds and our narrow window and a low hum of activity rising from the streets of Nisibis. A rising cheer from the surrounding area seemed odd enough, for the volume and tenor of such joy seemed uncommon in a city within Persian Mesopotamia. Horns blared in the streets, while mid-morning was marked by the staccato of sandals and boots that paraded across the cobbled streets just outside of the palace.

Fulfilling his morning schedule, our inquisitor came and went, hardly deigning to make a serious attempt at answers but threatening to cut off what remaining food was allocated to us each morning. I merely grunted and spat toward the man, who jerked back from his chair and stormed off indignantly. A similar ritual came in the late afternoon, with the inquisitor throwing what passed for our daily meal onto the stones near our cages. Fulcaris and I eyed the Persian angrily as he left the room, yet scrambled to scoop up any chunks of bread or vegetables that could be found, using our soot-covered fingers as vessels for the lukewarm brown liquid.

Fulcaris and I talked idly as darkness began to set in, pretending not to notice one another when relieving ourselves in the near-overflowing bucket that our jailor rarely stooped to exchange for another. My mind raced whenever I thought of

Mariya, wondering how she would take the news of my capture and likely execution at the hands of the Persians. I fought to form an image of her face in my mind, dulling my senses and perception of the damp stone room that I found myself in. It was in that semiconscious state that our door swung open, allowing a visitor inside at a time where none entered since our first evening in captivity.

A man with a thick covering over his face entered, and I recognized him as the thickly bearded Persian who previously visited our cell on at least two other occasions. Dropping a heavy bag to the floor, he muttered to the jailor in a voice that was muffled by the cloth that guarded his mouth and nose from the stench that permeated the room, but whatever words he spoke caused our warden to slam the outer dungeon door securely shut and scurry inside.

"Check the lock. I am concerned that it is weak from rust," the man mumbled in Persian.

The jailor walked over and inspected the lock where it hung from a loop in the iron cell bars, then shook his head. "*I* don't see anything wrong," he said, shrugging heavily for effect.

"There's rust, you fool. Look closely this time," the masked figure said.

Nodding, the jailor leaned forward, his eyes narrowing on the crude iron. He mumbled about some tiny imperfections in the metal and drew closer, squinting. As he did, the masked figure drew a thin dagger from the folds of his robes and sliced it across the jailor's exposed throat.

Blood spurted onto the stones as the jailor fought to right himself, but quickly collapsed. His eyes stared up at me, his mouth opened as if in a scream, half pleading for help that would never come.

Fulcaris and I backed away from the attacker, our hands running across the stone walls of our captivity as we edged as far as possible from the murderous Persian. He wiped the blade on the jailor's ragged tunic and placed it securely within a hidden sheath, turning as he faced us.

"He was a vile creature," the man said in muffled Persian. Aged hands rose to the man's face as he removed the cloth before his nose and mouth. "Do you not know me?"

I shook my head. In the flickering gloom of the dungeon, I could still make out the thick black beard that hung in plaits. The man's face appeared dark, although even then it was clear that heavy creams had been applied to his skin. Short black hair was cut into curls in highborn Persian fashion, making the man seem exotic yet unremarkable against the number of other Persian faces that paraded through Nisibis' palace.

"No? Well, neither did the men who manage this decaying slum. Still, I expected more from you." His Persian was sarcastic, and his voice deeper than would be expected given his slim build.

"I am sorry, stranger, but no, I do not know you," I replied. Wary of the man's intentions, I kept my back against the wall and my eyes trained on the blade he carefully disguised in the folds of his robes. In a further show of defiance, I added, "And you are fooling yourself if you think that you will escape unnoticed from the palace."

The man covered his mouth as he laughed, stifling the sound despite the sealed door that blocked all but the brashest of noises. "Now that truly hurts, Varus. I have spent far too much of my life for you to be rude to me, let alone permitting yourself to be so easily trapped in a Persian cage," he said in flawless Heruli.

Fulcaris jumped at a language he could finally recognize. No longer in gruff Persian, the man's voice became instantly recognizable. Awestruck, I shot toward the bars, ignoring the pool of blood that streamed between the lining of our stone floor. He concealed himself well, with a combed and dyed hair and beard that looked nothing like his famously unkempt appearance. The heavy creams bronzed his skin for a more youthful glow, yet his eyes sparked with the same hint of mischief that filled my childhood.

"Lord!" I exclaimed in Heruli, so loud that Liberius raised a hand in caution. "I thought the Persians killed you after taking you prisoner!"

Liberius furrowed his brow, feigning offense. "Prisoner? Dead? Old and decrepit that I am, I have much better sense than to find myself in such a predicament." After a brief pat-down search, he procured the cell key from the jailor's corpse, dragged the body away from the cell, and pried open the door's lock.

Stepping over the thicker puddles of blood, I rushed Liberius, throwing my arms around the older man.

"There's no time for that now, and you smell like the bowels of Hades." Liberius reached for the bag that he'd carried into the room and produced two sets of Persian trousers and robes that he handed over to us.

As we dressed, Liberius explained his plan for escape. "It has taken me two weeks to figure out the guard schedule, and we have a few hours of relative calm. We need to sneak down three flights of stairs and into the stables for horses, all the while avoiding the scrutiny of any servants or spearmen," Liberius spoke lazily in Herulian, seemingly unconcerned over the difficulty ahead of us.

After an explanation to Fulcaris of our good fortune in finding Liberius as well as our need to make haste out of Nisibis, the Herulian man scoffed.

"Even if we make it out of the palace, the city gates are closed until morning. Our dead jailor will be discovered by then," he said, glancing at the cooling corpse a few paces away.

Liberius grinned at the challenge. "Leave the gates to me. However, we cannot leave until I complete my reason for coming to this city in the first place."

Fulcaris and I looked at each other nervously, eager to leave the room and put Persia well behind us. However, supremely confident, Liberius assured us that his work would take but an hour of our time, and we would be safely out of Nisibis before dawn broke for a new day.

"There is a scroll that I have been searching for years to find. I heard rumors that it was in Dara a bit over a year ago," Liberius said. "When I arrived there, more compelling information pointed to Nisibis, which made far more sense to begin with. Perhaps I am the dull halfwit that you claim, Varus!"

"Certainly not, Lord," I said. Liberius rolled his eyes. "But we received word weeks ago that you were captured and taken prisoner."

"Fools," Liberius grunted in Heruli. Believing the insult directed at us, Fulcaris quickly took offense, his face lined and angry until Liberius clarified with an explanation.

Taking a breath, Liberius told his tale. "In an effort to be a polite guest, I told the governor of Dara that I would be leaving his fine city for Nisibis. Despite my insistence upon discretion, the man demanded that a guard follow me into the desert, unaware that I had already concocted a plan to blend in with the Persian lines. I led the fellow, who was innocent enough, until darkness fell on our first night together. As he retired into a small tent for rest, I let him know that I would range outward to scout the area but would remain close. Atop a horse, I rode out for a ways and changed into this disguise that I'd been preparing for months, and left my Roman cloak and bag on the ground. The guard must have found them hours later and reported that I had been taken by the Persians."

I rubbed my temples, a flurry of questions storming my mind. "What scroll?" I asked, confused why Liberius would take considerable risks upon himself for a piece of paper.

"Never you mind about that, and other questions can wait until later," Liberius said. He pulled a sealed document from his robes and pointed to a strange script that I deduced was some form of Persian.

"A convincing forgery—this took months of work. It has seen me safely into Nisibis... and will get us safely out," Liberius said. "Once I have my scroll, that is."

I sighed. "Lord, why do you need our help for that? Why not retrieve the scroll weeks ago, like you said?"

Liberius shook his head. "Varus, your continuing commitment to my stupidity is truly disheartening. If the solution were that easy, it would already be manifest. Yet here we are, so listen to what I need both of you to do."

Details were sparse, although Liberius explained that the scroll in question was located in Nisibis' library, yet guarded each day and night as one of a number of precious and restricted items. Though silent on its contents, Liberius did reveal that the scroll was perhaps the last of its kind remaining in the world, and he could not leave Nisibis without it.

"I need the two of you to create a distraction that won't raise an alarm for the guards, but *will* grab the librarians' attention," Liberius said, "which will give me enough time to search their records for what I need. So no killing," he lectured, pointing at me, "and no foolishness or idle curiosity," he said to Fulcaris.

"How will we know you are ready to leave?" Fulcaris asked.

"Ah, at least one of you still is polite enough to ask about my well-being. I will whistle loudly, which should carry easily across the library. So don't wander far, and be vigilant of my signal," Liberius concluded.

Liberius inspected our clothing and gave our disguises a nod of approval. "It will have to do, despite the stink. Just keep your mouths shut and follow me closely." After carefully inspecting his own robes for signs of blood, Liberius opened the jail door and guided us into the hallway, then locked its horrors safely behind us.

My teacher adopted a brisk pace as we ascended another flight of stairs. Fulcaris limped along, and he quickly grew winded. I was surprised at my own fatigue at climbing the spiraling staircase. Muscles in my legs cramped at the effort while I grew dizzy, fighting forward as we hung close to Liberius. Though still hot and cramped, the air in the hallways stung my nostrils as my body adjusted outside of my filthy confinement.

At the top of the landing, Liberius led us toward a vast enclosure that housed thousands of scrolls and tomes. Securely harnessed torches lined the walls, illuminating manuscripts with dozens of writing styles, including several that were chipped and faded with the passage of decades or even centuries. Liberius showed his forged seal to the guard, who allowed the three of us passage into the rooms. He then nodded to the librarians in a show of familiarity and led us far out of eyeshot as he initiated his plan. As we moved away, I caught a better glance of what lay behind those men. Black iron gates enclosed a smaller subset of works, which undoubtedly was the housing place of Liberius' desire.

"Remember, nothing suspicious, and nothing violent," he whispered in Herulian. Fulcaris and I nodded and watched Liberius slip away.

Fulcaris and I looked around nervously, making sense of our newfound surroundings. "Well, what do you think we should do?" I asked.

Fulcaris shrugged at first but soon developed a low smile as he sized up the hundreds of shelves that lined Nisibis' library in a maze of columns and rows. After gathering a better understanding of the library's layout, Fulcaris backed up two paces, and then vaulted forward with all the force he could muster.

His shoulder collided with the center of one of the bookcases, sending several scrolls and a few bound tomes hurtling toward the floor. As it fell away from Fulcaris, the wooden bookcase toppled toward the floor, nearly pushing the next case over under its weight.

The crash drew the attention of the librarians, whose slippered footsteps slid against the stone floors as they bounded in the direction of their disturbance. Fulcaris led me away, careful to mask the sounds of our own movements, and we shuffled toward another line of bookshelves and spied the two other men.

The librarians voiced heavy anger at the sight of the downed case, with one man lamenting a torn calfskin that contained the words of a famous Persian poet. Heavy boots followed soon thereafter, finding the librarians staring over the wreckage.

"Any trouble?" a gruff voice inquired in Persian.

"No," one of the librarians answered. "Unfortunately, this happens from time to time. It cannot be helped."

The guard grunted and thudded out of the room, back to his post. Alone, the two librarians gathered up the delicate parchment and then set to the task of resetting the heavy bookcase, cursing as they lifted it from the floor. In the middle of their labor, Fulcaris reared back and toppled another bookcase, the force of which knocked over two others positioned just beyond. Once again, we slunk well beyond eyeshot, hiding between several other repositories as I listened to the librarians' complaints. Thankfully, the soldier did not venture out of his post at this new development, leaving the two men to address the growing destruction that spread across their room.

One of the librarians yelled in anger and rushed to survey the damage. As the two men sorted texts, a low whistle hummed at the far entrance to the room. Fulcaris and I snapped to attention, hurrying toward Liberius' location and finding the older man near the room's exit.

"Did you find it?" I asked, nearly out of breath from the effort.

Liberius laid a finger over his lips and nodded, patting a section of his robes. Nodding, we followed the man out of the library and down the stone steps that led to the entrance of the palace. Lines of torches flickered along the halls as we moved ever downward, my legs complaining of fatigue as Liberius led us to freedom.

When we finally reached the ground floor, Liberius nodded familiarly to the guards, who rushed to their feet to open the palace doors to the streets of Nisibis. "Lord Mithridates!" one guard called to Liberius, offering to shield him on his business outside of the palace.

Liberius answered to the name with no hesitation. "No need, my friend," he said, pointing toward Fulcaris and me. "Besides, the streets are empty at night. May the war come to a beneficial end soon."

The guard nodded again, echoing Liberius' wish for an end to the conflict, and held the heavy door as we ventured outside, touching open air for the first time in weeks.

Moving swiftly, Liberius guided us to the stables, showing sealed documents that told of the need to appease Kavadh's messenger at all times, and for all purposes. A street guard merely confirmed our right to move freely throughout the cobbled passages of Nisibis, while the guard of the stables nearly balked at Liberius' request of three saddled and provisioned horses. Liberius snarled at the man, who threw up his hands and prepared our requested mounts.

Though we spent only moments in the stables, their high ceilings differed from those of Constantinople, which tended to be built half again as tall as a man in order to better retain heat in the midst of winter. Pacing through the rows of hundreds of mounts, we arrived at a barred and secured enclosure of the great gray elephants that had nearly rampaged into Nisibis' trading forum on the day of our arrival. Their stench was foul, but Fulcaris and I still gaped at their massive size as we waited for the stable master to return.

Soon enough, horses were led to Liberius, who snatched the bridles in anger. Mounting, he beckoned for Fulcaris and me to follow suit, and we wordlessly left the stable master behind as we ventured toward Nisibis' southernmost gate.

We could have cleared the distance in a much shorter time, but Liberius ordered that we take a leisurely pace, so as to not attract unnecessary attention from warier sentries and city guards. As we passed by the palace again, we could hear distant shouts of alarm calling out high in the air, but Liberius kept his measured pace.

Upon our arrival at the gateway, we were stopped by a Persian spearman who demanded to know our business. Identifying himself with his sealed parchment and status as a Persian noble, Liberius made some mild remark about wishing to exit Nisibis in the cooler hours of night, yet still drew resistance from the guard.

"Lord, Astabadh Azarethes issued strict orders that the gates of Nisibis remain shut each night until the conclusion of the war," the spearman said nervously, eyeing the disdainful anger that hardened Liberius' face.

Liberius spat in indignation. "Soldier, I am on the business of Shahanshah Kavadh, light of the Persians, may he be immortal and lead us to prosperity. But you, a slip of a man with no grace of the Ahura Mazda, would question the judgment of our Padishah?" Liberius growled in formal Persian.

The guard shifted, fidgeting with his spear as he struggled for words at the well-spoken and aristocratic man that defied what authority was given to the guard of Nisibis' southern gate. Yet, before the man could offer a response, Liberius dug a hand into his robes, procuring shining coins that clinked in his hands.

"But of course you would not do that. And as a token of our dear Lord Kavadh's blessings upon you, his devoted servant, I will reward your faith in the Shahanshah with gold that bears his own holy image," Liberius said, emphasizing the Persian ruler's name and title at each instance.

Grabbing the guard's free hand, Liberius tucked away several gold coins, offering the man several years' wages. The man's eyes grew wide at the sum and slowly nodded.

"Glory to the Padishah, may he reign forever," the guard said as if in a trance. He signaled to his comrades to open the gate and allowed us to ride out into the flat expanse to the south of Nisibis.

With the gates open, Liberius at last quickened his pace, seemingly eager to put significant distance between our party and the Persian fortress behind us. Our horses trotted along throughout the night and well past dawn, turning west as Nisibis faded along the horizon. We came to a stop only as the sun came into full view along the eastern horizon, indicating another sweltering day of unforgiving heat.

"Dara is only a short ride away," Liberius informed us. "We'll rest for a bit, but we must reach its gates before nightfall."

"How will we get in?" I asked. "Isn't Dara besieged?"

Liberius shook his head. "The siege was lifted weeks ago. Xerxes' men marched south, although I cannot be sure why they would abandon such a prize."

My mind raced back to Belisarius, who had been commanded to the south of Dara to facilitate the construction of another Roman fortress city. I shook such worries from my mind, thinking again of Mariya and my own household receiving the news of my capture in Nisibis.

Undeterred, Fulcaris quickly obeyed Liberius' order, tying a horse against a thin Mesopotamian tree and throwing a blanket under its shade. The Herulian man began snoring within moments, his body spent from a long evening of exertion.

Even as my own body screamed with fatigue, I remained eager for answers from Liberius. "Lord," I began, "why didn't you tell us your plans?"

Liberius frowned, showing his first signs of sadness in the half day of our time together. "I didn't mean for this to trouble you, Varus. For that, I am sorry," he said, offering no other explanation.

I thought to prod further but shied away when I saw Liberius' obvious discomfort with the question. Instead, I asked how he knew that the guard would allow us to leave Nisibis rather than placing us under arrest.

"Men see what they wish to see, Varus. That guard was a weak man and wanted to believe that my gold was a sign of my authority under his master," Liberius lectured. "It cleared his conscience to accept my money and think no further of it."

Liberius allowed me a few other questions that dogged my mind, offering brief explanations in turn.

"How did you know that we were in the palace dungeon, Lord?" I asked Liberius, one of hundreds of questions that swirled in my mind.

"With my disguise and forged documents from Kavadh's palace, it was easy enough to convince the city guard and local leadership of my right to inspect their preparations for war. The Persians never suspected a Roman man in their midst, and they tend to believe that Romans cannot speak fluent Persian," Liberius said. With a wicked smile, he added, "And frankly, they are usually correct."

"But how did you find us?" I asked again, suspicious that Liberius withheld a significant portion of his tale.

"I am now quite concerned about what the army is doing to your manners, Varus. Really, interrupting a man as he is telling his story, that is beneath you," Liberius chided me. After a few moments of silence, he offered a brief explanation.

"My curiosity was piqued when guards yelled to cordon off the market, and I had an easy view into the market square when your friend was decapitated," Liberius said matter-of-factly. "I thought it may be a Roman spy mission and joined in the delegation to question you. I recognized you right away, although those fools thought that you and Fulcaris were Hephthalites sent by a rival Persian noble to assassinate Xerxes."

"But why, Lord? Is there some mistrust amongst the Persian commanders?"

Liberius sighed. "I do not have the full understanding of the situation, although it seems that there was a significant disagreement between the younger Prince Xerxes and the other Persian commanders. Xerxes sent his Zhayedan and armies south and commanded the Persian mercenaries to return to Assyria with Perozes' massing forces. Beyond that, I truly do not know."

My next question was halted unspoken by Liberius. "Sleep now, while you can. You are no use to me if you fall in exhaustion along the road," Liberius said.

Reluctantly, I agreed, and collapsed alongside Fulcaris as I breathed in the clean Mesopotamian air.

A thud rocked me awake not long later, with the sun well into the sky. I moaned as my body demanded further rest, yet slowly forced myself awake at Liberius' command.

I found Fulcaris sitting by my teacher, who'd unplaited his beard and cleaned his face of the powders and creams that gave him a more Persian look. The dyed blackened beard and hair would be able to grow out soon enough, although Liberius had already taken on a more natural look.

Liberius threw me a waterskin and a crust of bread, which I gnawed at hungrily as I followed Fulcaris' example. Slowly becoming aware of the filth crusted over my body, I threw off my robes and upended the waterskin over my bare head and torso. I watched layers of grime and muck flowed in rivulets down my body and used the blanket to wipe away the more stubborn patches of dirt, blood, and other foul substances. Interested, Fulcaris followed suit, sucking in quick spurts of air as his hands rubbed against sickly yellow bruises that lined his body.

Laughing, Liberius threw over his own waterskin. "Better use another," he joked, but I made sure to leave a reserve as I finished my makeshift bathing session.

After giving me a few moments to stretch and digest my food, we mounted again and headed west toward Dara. Sweat beaded against my brow as the sun's heat exacted its toll, yet Liberius assured us that our journey's end would not be long in coming. We continued on as the sun began to lower from its perch, though plenty of daylight remained to reach our destination.

"By the way, Varus, I never did congratulate you on capturing an Arab princess! I doubt Solomon's father is pleased at that one, his simpering son bested twice by a former slave." Liberius cackled.

"Gratitude, Lord," I replied sheepishly. "But how did you learn of this here?"

"Nisibis exists at the crux of trade, even amidst this war," Liberius replied. "And the Persian nobility find hilarity in a Roman vassal being humiliated. You would be amazed at what you might overhear in a bazaar, if only you would open your ears to listen."

As we crested over a low hill, we gained a view of the city of Dara. Its walls were just as massive of those of Nisibis, but these bore blackened scorch marks that hinted at previous attacks by the Persians. What captured my attention was not the city itself, but a long plume of dust that trailed across the city's far western expanse.

My eyes widened and heart sank as I realized what I was looking at.

"What's that?" asked Fulcaris, pointing toward the same plume.

"A defeated army in retreat," Liberius said formally, his face showing no sign of emotion.

A battered Roman army snaked into Dara, its banners torn and hanging low. In their midst I spotted the Roman Eagle as well as those I'd grown familiar with in our march through Armenia. Belisarius' bear could be seen alongside the eagle, and I soon saw my own ouroboros trailing a few paces behind.

Our party had escaped Nisibis but stumbled upon a far worse situation at Dara. For Belisarius' army had been defeated and lay at the mercy of the innumerable Persians that circled just beyond.

Immortal

BOUND BY DUTY

I GALLOPED TO THE SECTION of the army that waited to enter Dara, hurrying toward the banners bearing my sigil. Liberius called for caution, although I ignored such concerns as I urged my horse forward. Liberius and Fulcaris followed close behind, leaning forward in the saddle to keep balance over the rock-strewn terrain.

The first face I recognized was Perenus, who shone in his new armor as he rode toward us on his gelding. Drawing his sword, Perenus whooped for a detachment of Herulians to follow him, his face lined with bitterness and concern. As I drew closer, the Lazic prince recognized me and ordered the men of the Herulian foederati to stand down.

He raised a hand in friendly greeting. "Varus! We heard that you'd been captured by the Persians... and then nothing," he said, flashing his teeth as he beamed. Perenus then warmly greeted Fulcaris and nodded to the third figure that remained unfamiliar to the Herulian foederati. "Who is this?"

I nodded. "We were, and then we escaped. I'll tell you the whole story later," I said. "This is Liberius, who needs to get to Belisarius immediately. What happened to the army?"

Perenus hung his head, eyes falling to the dirt that churned under the feet and hooves of an army on the march. "Hermogenes wouldn't let us abandon Thannuris, and Xerxes was able to trap us between the town and the river," he said reluctantly. "Belisarius had no chance."

"What of our Herulian foederati?" I asked with concern. "And Samur? Rosamund? Cephalas? Father Petrus and Belisarius' staff?" A thousand grim scenarios flooded my mind as I imagined the brutal slayings of my loved ones, my chest pounding as I hung on Perenus' every word.

293

Perenus raised a hand and motioned his horse forward, seeking to calm me. "They're all right, all of them. All foederati were only engaged from a distance, and the core of the Roman Army is intact," Perenus said stoically.

"Then what happened?" I asked. "Why the retreat?"

Perenus sighed and offered a brief recount of the details. He told of the Persian army's abandonment of the siege of Dara and how the army fell upon the joint forces of Rome and the Ghassanids, who reached Thannuris at about the same time.

"I went to Belisarius' officers meeting on your behalf, and it was chaos," Perenus remarked. "John insisted that the army abandon Thannuris altogether, while Ascum argued that we should flee east to defend the larger walls of Antioch and Odessa."

"Was Thannuris really in that bad of a condition?" I asked.

Perenus nodded sadly. "The stone walls barely rose to our knees, and not solidly built at that. It would have taken another year to properly fortify the place, even with the Emperor's insistence and adequate resources. But Hermogenes would not listen to sense and threatened to arrest and hang Belisarius for cowardice and desertion if Thannuris was not defended."

I hissed. "That bastard!"

Perenus scowled. "I thought there was going to be a riot. Baduarius threatened to hand deliver the Imperial legate to Xerxes personally, which only triggered Hermogenes to order Marcellus and the excubitores to place Baduarius in chains. Before it could get further out of hand, Belisarius demanded silence and said that he would obey the will of the Emperor."

I ran my hands through my freshly washed hair, massaging my scalp in frustration as though I could push forth a solution to my commander's situation. "So Belisarius fought at Thannuris?" I asked, already knowing the answer.

"Yes," Perenus replied. "Xerxes arrived in a matter of days, and Belisarius drew up the best lines that we could."

Perenus paused, sniffing and cuffing his eyes before continuing further. "At least thirty thousand Persians streamed over the hill, all armored and well-disciplined. We held well at first, with the Thracians on the left, Belisarius' core army at the center, the Ghassanids on the right, and Marcellus with the foederati in reserve. The Persians came first with their own cataphracts, but our spears held well against the false charges. Thankfully, we saw no Hephthalites or any war elephants. Small blessings, eh?"

I did not answer, letting my friend's dark humor carry in the midst of our gathering. Sensing tension, Fulcaris took his leave, trotting toward his Herulian brethren, while Liberius prodded for further details.

"Did Xerxes bring the Zhayedan, the Immortals?" Liberius asked, his face lined with uncharacteristic concern.

Perenus nodded again. "Three thousand of them. All smothered in iron scales and bedecked with all manner of weapons. They came atop giant horses that belched heat, crashing into our lines. Many stayed on horseback, yet others dismounted to join the Persian shield wall," he said, shivering as he spoke.

"And they broke our lines?" I asked impatiently, gaining a measure of our foe.

Perenus shook his head. "A young Immortal commanded them to charge us, again, and again, and again. We must have killed scores of them, even the Immortals. They did not stop until they found our weakness."

"The Ghassanids," Liberius said, as if he already knew the answer.

"The Ghassanids," Perenus confirmed. "They fought well for a time, until their leader was slain."

Perenus turned to me, a baleful look in his face. "I'm sorry Varus, but King Jabalah, your father-in-law, was killed outside of Thannuris. The Ghassanid lines broke hard at his death, and Prince al-Harith is still struggling to instill order in the Arab ranks."

Though I'd never personally met King Jabalah, I lowered my head in respect. "Were messengers sent to Antioch?" I asked, thinking of Mariya.

"A day ago," Perenus replied. "They should reach the city in a few days, with good weather. No word from Antioch since we heard that Mariya and Antonina arrived safely."

I acknowledged the mixed tidings and followed Perenus into Dara. Blooded and torn cloth lined the bodies of many men, while dented and cracked wooden shields were carried by others. More than a few were helped into Dara, their faces and bodies covered in soiled cloth bandages that covered the horror of their wounds.

As I entered the city, hands grabbed at my legs, nearly throwing me from the saddle.

"Varus!" the voice called. Dismounting, I turned my head to find Rosamund, who threw her arms around me. Her white hair bounced against the light mail and leather that lined her body, disguising a more feminine figure that would not have been entirely safe in an army of thousands.

"Gods, you stink!" she exclaimed, wrinkling her nose as she pulled away slightly. "What have you been doing all this time that makes you smell this bad?"

"You probably don't want to know." Samur grinned as he appeared behind Rosamund. "I knew you would come back—those Persians don't know how to kill you."

"Kill me?" I said, a bit taken aback.

"That was the rumor, anyway," Samur said. Catching sight of Liberius, he bobbed his head and made a formal welcome in immaculate Latin.

Liberius beamed, eyes twinkling. "It warms my heart to see you remember your lessons, Samur. And manners! You should have seen your brother insulting my age and intelligence our entire ride from Nisibis," he said. Liberius turned in greeting to

Rosamund, impassive at the sight of a metal-clad Gepid woman, and drew her into a private conversation.

"So, how bad was it?" I asked Samur. "Thannuris?"

"It could have been worse, but the Ghassanids are essentially out of the war for at least a half year," Samur said, snorting and spitting a gob of phlegm onto the ground. "If Xerxes attacked us now, we'd be hard-pressed to hold this city, even with the thousands of men we still have to man the walls."

I nodded, surveying the other soldiers as they passed through Dara's gates. The last lines of my own foederati soon followed, buzzing as they recognized the underfed yet still-living body of their commander. Alaric led the men in a cheer—a sound that startled many of the other Roman ranks that remained mired in the shock of defeat. With Liberius and Rosamund in tow, I followed the men before seeking out Belisarius, finding a half-empty storage building containing rows of makeshift bunks had been erected for the Herulians.

Father Petrus directed the organization of the building, chastising dozens of uncouth Herulians in a futile attempt of assuring a regimented amount of space was kept between each bunk. Father Petrus smiled warmly as he caught my gaze, calling out in joy as he came across Liberius.

My teacher towered over Petrus, his frayed hair slowly abandoning its Persian curls in favor of his natural look. Liberius grinned at the sight of Petrus, and for once made no quips about his situation.

"My friend, how long it has been," Liberius said. He took the old priest in his embrace and parted soon thereafter.

"Did you find it?" Father Petrus asked, his voice cracked and wheezing where Liberius' had been firm.

"Yes, with help from our pupil," Liberius said, waving lightly in my direction.

"One moment…" I took a moment to understand. "How long have you known one another?"

Father Petrus laughed, and for once actually answered one of my nagging questions. "Nearly all my life," he admitted, taking Liberius' arm in his own as they slowly walked away.

Rosamund shot me a confused look that I shrugged off, my mind wandering toward the dozens of responsibilities that resumed their place in my role as komes of the Herulian foederati. Finding Cephalas, I began issuing orders for the tallying of men's injuries and sullied armor, eager to bring the foederati back to fighting condition as soon as possible.

"Later, Varus," Samur interrupted. "Belisarius will want to see you as soon as possible. Sunicas said that they've taken residence in the governor's palace."

I agreed and handed my responsibilities to Cephalas and Rosamund as I followed my brother into the streets of Dara. Though I had not noticed it before, the public thoroughfares were rife with chaos, and many citizens ran hurriedly from one building to the next. Centurions from Belisarius' household had placed detachments at the larger gathering places in the city, and Samur and I passed multiple groups of four spearmen that hustled along the stone-lined streets. As we passed Dara's main forum, we found two Romans dangling from a high post, tongues bloated and lolling from their blue and lifeless faces.

"The first groups of the army arrived yesterday, with the fresher and healthier soldiers taking up the rear that you saw entering today," Samur said. "Belisarius issued strict orders that the locals were not to be harassed, but some refused to listen."

Though we had become no stranger to death, the sight of men executed for crimes deemed unforgiveable under Roman law chilled my nerve. One of the men bore a sign that told of their status as rapists, separating them from the Church and preventing any hope of their forgiveness in the eyes of God or men.

Samur guided me to the city governor's palace, leaving me at its door as he returned to the Hunnic foederati that established had its quarters in a vast city storage building. Confused by my Persian garb and disheveled look, two Roman spearmen blocked my passage into the palace until Mundus arrived at the palace gates soon after and vouched for me.

"Glad to see you've returned, although you look awful," Mundus said gruffly, slapping me on the shoulder. "There were wild rumors that you had been captured by the Persians."

"I was," I said. "I'll tell you about it once we find Belisarius. How is he taking Thannuris?"

"Badly," Mundus answered frankly. "Hermogenes cut Belisarius' legs from under him but still demanded victory. How is a heavily outnumbered army supposed to win a battle when it is not allowed to maneuver, and its decisions are made by office clerks?"

"Maybe this is why Rome has always suffered such ill luck against Persia," I said.

Mundus grunted. "Worse news yesterday," he said. "A detachment of reinforcements from southern Armenia was ambushed by another army of Persians near Mindoros, and the Armenian tribune Stutias was captured. Spies say that the Persians impaled him, yet he died slowly as his skin cracked under the sun."

"Is this open knowledge?" I asked.

Mundus shook his head. "The men are already frightened. They're outnumbered, under supplied, and fettered by their own government. More bad news and we'll start having desertions on our hands, and more than in ones and twos," he said, his expression taut with resignation.

Mundus' frustration took me by surprise, for the man had always been coolheaded even in the most desperate of situations against the Gepids or the Avars. I followed my old centurion toward the hall commandeered for Belisarius' war planning, my eyes flitting across the palace halls. Though not nearly as grand as the Imperial Palace in Constantinople, Dara's buildings were surprisingly elegant in their construction, with white columns lining high windows so that cool air could filter inside and drown the acrid Mesopotamian heat.

With Mundus throwing open the doors to reveal the other senior officers, I was greeted with a barrage of well wishes and excited questions. Sembrouthes rushed at me with an irritated look on his face yet flashed a rare smile as he determined that I had returned in relatively good health. A lone exception to this was Solomon, who I had seen little of since our initial disembarkation in Trapezous. Standing aloof from Belisarius' officers, Solomon smoldered as he saw me, his nostrils flaring as he directed his gaze elsewhere.

Belisarius offered warm greetings, wincing slightly as he moved his body to face me. A thick bandage wrapped Belisarius' arm tight against his body, throwing him off balance as he moved around the room.

"A Persian lance took me high in the shoulder," Belisarius explained. "My armor caught the iron head, but the force of the blow threw me from Xanthos." Like Ignis, Xanthos was a Nisean stallion that Belisarius had ridden since before his campaign against the Avars and stood higher than a man, capable of galloping half a day with horse and rider in full armor.

I explained my predicament to Belisarius, and all that had happened in the weeks since we parted. Belisarius and Marcellus both brightened at the note that Liberius had been found and returned to Roman territory, looking disappointed when the old statesman was nowhere to be found.

"And Barzanes?" Bessas asked, his face downcast as he likely guessed his friend's painful outcome.

Wordless, I shook my head. Bessas nodded and sighed deeply. "He was a brave man," Bessas said. Baduarius and John muttered their agreement, pouring glasses of wine in celebration of their fallen friend.

"Incomparably," I said. "We had no chance of getting into Nisibis without him." Even those who did not know Barzanes raised their clay cups at his memory, all eyes on Belisarius as he cleared his throat.

"To Barzanes, a centurion of Armenia, who sacrificed his life in service of the Roman people. He will not be forgotten, and we shall not look upon another like him again," Belisarius said somberly, with others echoing his final words.

As the other officers scanned maps, I pulled Belisarius aside and asked about his experience at Thannuris. Though his mood darkened, Belisarius was surprisingly forthright in his assessment of the battle.

"I've had ministers and clerks complicate my battle plans before, but Thannuris was the first time that it was truly crippling. Men died because I could not overcome my own limitations, and Thannuris is now a smoking ruin as a result," Belisarius brooded, keeping his voice low.

"Lord, not one person I have spoken with blames you. Quite the opposite. It was Hermogenes' fault, none other," I argued in return.

Belisarius shook his head. "Hermogenes certainly did not make things easier, and Procopius has further complicated my standing with the Emperor with his incessant letter writing, but the army is inevitably my responsibility," Belisarius asserted. He added, his voice barely greater than a whisper, "And I'm concerned that Thannuris was our only realistic chance to defeat the Persians. There are simply too many of them, and our numbers dwindle with the Arabs retreating and regrouping in Syria."

"Did you see King Jabalah fall?" I asked, changing the subject.

Belisarius nodded. "He died bravely in the front lines but fell from a stray arrow. The Arab flank collapsed almost immediately in shock."

Belisarius attempted to break the gravity of the moment with lighter news. "Dispatches from the Capitol included a letter from Theodora. She wishes a report from you soon," Belisarius said, gesturing to a servant to retrieve the Empress' words for me. "Her clerk, Narses, seems to be under the impression that your reports since Trapezous have not been frequent enough."

"For good reason," I muttered, although I knew I would take care to meet the Empress' demands later that day. My eyes turned back to Belisarius, who smiled as he continued.

"And another report from Antioch that was addressed to both of us," Belisarius replied, his voice lightened with mischief.

"Words from Mariya?" I asked hopefully.

Belisarius nodded. "Written in Antonina's hand. We received these days ago, although I kept its words private while waiting for your return. All is well, but Sergius decided to keep his detachment in Antioch to preserve the Ladies' and clerks' safety."

"But what of the letter?" I asked. At that, Belisarius laughed, despite the pain in his wrapped arm.

Belisarius handed me the carefully wrapped scroll, beaming as he flashed his teeth. "Congratulations, Varus. It seems that you will also soon be a father," he said, patting my hand as my fingers clasped the paper.

"What?" I gasped, unfurling the scroll violently. Belisarius' words spoke the truth, as Antonina told of Mariya's condition.

"My God," I murmured.

My first thoughts were of Mariya's safety, for even women of the higher echelons of society perished in the birthing bed. Mariya's own mother left King Jabalah a widower soon after delivering Mariya into the world. That short burst of panic was replaced by a sharper throbbing of guilt, for I recklessly placed myself in mortal danger with the mere hope that Liberius could be rescued from the Persians. A fever of responsibility and visions of the future washed over me as I half smiled toward Belisarius, who laughed at my reaction.

"Everything will be fine, my friend. Antonina herself is near her time, and I know our children will be close friends," Belisarius said with an air of reassurance. "Although I doubt that Sembrouthes will allow you to go on any further forays on your own."

I nodded, and as I did, Belisarius bellowed the news to the room, soliciting another series of cheering and applause. Solomon scowled and spirited himself out of the tent, though few seemed to notice his absence.

"I see you did not delay at all, eh, Varus?" Baduarius ribbed, joking with Ascum.

My veins grew hot as I looked away from my friend, preferring silence and a change of subject.

As the men shared their news and jokes, I gazed at the vast lambskin map of the Empire that stretched over a low wooden table. The Empire's borders were burning with activity, including new developments that I had not been aware of. The northern army under General Sittas had been evicted from Persian Armenia, his remaining forces pushed from Iberia back into Roman Pontus. To the south, the Vandal incursion into Egypt had been halted by Domnicus' newly arrived forces. However, the Vandals, under their warlord Gelimer, flooded across the western Libyan desert, as Domnicus lacked the force to evict the fierce Vandal warriors.

Most striking of all were the Persian armies. Wooden figures representing Xerxes' army remained near Thannuris, their numbers easily twice those of Belisarius'. Perozes' forces, now pushing west from Assyria, were larger still, including large numbers of armored cavalry. Additional Persian armies had been stationed just west of Tigranocerta and in Iberia, boxing Roman and

Allied armies into a tight confinement along the eastern coast of the Euxine Sea.

Further alarm was due to another huge force forming near Ctesiphon, the Persian Capitol near ancient Babylon, which had been labeled as belonging to Astabadh Azarethes. Large numbers of Lakhmid Arabs reportedly flocked to Azarethes' forces, which packed enough force to cleave Rome's Empire in two.

"From this angle, the situation does not bode well for us," John said, almost in my ear.

"How can we beat them?" I asked. The sheer magnitude of trained and hardened men now facing Belisarius' army was daunting.

"We can't," John admitted, "but we could bloody them enough to sue for peace, if Hermogenes would allow for such a strategy."

"You mean Hermogenes is still forcing Belisarius' hand? What could the Emperor want now?" I asked.

John nodded. "Nothing for certain, but Hermogenes will address the officers in a week with Imperial orders. Whatever they are, it won't be good."

Sighing, I turned away from the map and mingled with the others, gaining an idea of the overall status of what remained of Belisarius' army. Despite the loss of thousands of Ghassanids, the Roman core of the army remained largely intact.

Leaving my side, John went to begin a heated conversation with Belisarius, gesturing toward Belisarius' injured arm and pained movements.

"Lord, as we spoke of privately earlier, it is essential that you appoint a chief bodyguard," John said, his voice lined with worry. "If that mace had hit you a handsbreadth higher, I doubt you would still be here to lead us."

Belisarius groaned and eventually nodded. "Very well, John. If I am to be watched over like a child, it might as well be by someone I trust."

Other conversations in the room dulled as Belisarius scratched at his beard. Bessas was the first to break the silence, offering several names for the role. Ascum soon followed, arguing that it should be a man not unduly influenced by the Emperor. Belisarius chuckled at that comment, insisting that all of his soldiers would always be loyal. Simmas rolled his eyes in silence. Marcellus shifted uncomfortably and glared at Ascum, though he did nothing to intervene on behalf of the excubitores.

"What of Uliaris, Lord?" Troglita suggested. "Wasn't it he that slew your attacker before another blow could be struck?"

Others nodded, with John acknowledging the decision particularly.

Belisarius nodded. "Yes, that is so. Send a messenger to bring him here."

Not long after, a short Frankish man entered Belisarius' tent, his face flushed and panting from the exertion of arriving so quickly. His dark hair was allowed to flow wildly, yet his beard was neatly plaited—the customary style, according to Liberius, of the Frankish tribes. On Uliaris, the braids looked at once hygienic and savage. A guard demanded the Frankish man's weapons, and Uliaris scrambled to unhook the francisca and short sword that hung at his belt. Satisfied at the measure, John signaled for Uliaris to enter and introduced him formally to the gathering.

A deep scar running across Uliaris' right eye flashed white against his face as he looked nervously at the army's commanders, standing awkwardly straight as he saluted Belisarius with a stiff right arm. I could hardly guess at his age, though Baduarius, who was then his commander, later informed me that Uliaris had seen at least twenty summers. Uliaris kept his helmet tucked under his left arm, its plume showing his rank as a dekarchos of spearmen.

Belisarius smiled warmly at Uliaris, offering his lone good arm in a wide greeting.

"My friend, I owe you my life, and all here are grateful for your service," Belisarius said formally. "My fellow lords have advised me to form a bodyguard, and I would like to appoint you as its head. Think hard on this, Uliaris, for it is a position that does not come without significant danger, and you will be encompassed by violence and death."

Uliaris shook his head, prompting curious glances from several officers. "No need to think about it, Lord, it would be my honor to serve you," he said, his eyes fixed on the ground even as he relaxed slightly, but not entirely, at the compliment.

Belisarius smiled again, but it was John who spoke next. "Very good. You will be raised to the rank of a centurion and will have command of five other bodyguards who will be selected from the ranks. It will be your task to ensure that Belisarius is guarded day and night, and to protect him on the battlefield before even yourself. Is this acceptable?" John asked, his eyes fixed on Uliaris' stiff gait.

Uliaris nodded. "On my life, Lord. I will protect yours over all others," he said, finally daring to bring his eyes square with those of his new charge.

"I trained him, you know!" Baduarius cried, breaking the solemn moment with his bragging. John looked at the Gothic tribune in annoyance before giving Uliaris more immediate orders to follow. Belisarius' new chief bodyguard was commanded to gather his possessions and take new quarters that adjoined Belisarius' own, and to visit the army's armorer soon thereafter for equipment more befitting the heightened role. Uliaris saluted stiffly and disappeared into the streets of Dara, leaving the remaining officers laughing lightly at his eagerness.

Belisarius soon dismissed the officers, reminding us to assemble promptly and respectfully for Hermogenes' inspection and orders upon his return from Odessa. Germanus grumbled at this, insisting that he could have the legate sent away and leave the armies to fight the war more properly.

"The Emperor is my cousin, after all!" Germanus cried. "I'd think he would trust my opinion that following Hermogenes equates to suicide at this point." There were nods and murmurs from the men; even Marcellus showed signs of agreement.

Belisarius shook his head. "I will explain our position to Hermogenes, but he is to be treated with respect and deference. In the meantime, make sure your men treat the city dwellers with equal respect... especially those who have been billeted in private homes. All expenses will be paid with army silver, and any crimes or violence will be dealt with harshly," Belisarius said, desperately seeking to maintain order in a city that had already experienced a vicious siege.

After I took leave of the others, excitement gave way to exhaustion that crept through my bones and made my boots feel as if they were filled with heavy liquid. Soon, I discovered the makeshift barracks for my foederati, which contained private quarters that had been constructed by my men. Despite my overwhelming desire for sleep, Rosamund organized several servants to heat a bath and prepare a variety of foods to nourish my body. My protestations went unheeded as she led me toward their progress, with many of the Herulian men shouting their welcomes as I passed by. Fulcaris, already cleaned and wrapped in softer cloth, called out his support.

"Believe me, Lord, you will feel much better," Fulcaris said. "Eat slowly, though. My stomach could only handle so much at first."

Grudgingly, I went along with Rosamund's plans and dictated a letter intended for Narses and Theodora back in Constantinople. I detailed my capture by the Persians, noting all details that I could remember of Nisibis, its soldiers, and its people—though I left out my encounter with the magus Hakhamanish. The magus' curse haunted my sleep as I worried for Mariya and my loved ones, my mind replaying the prophecy of the end of the Roman world.

"I am more than an instrument of death," I muttered to myself, startling the confused servant, who asked if he should include such a statement. Smiling weakly, I shook my head, silently perturbed by that deep, rasping voice that branded me as an agent of the darkness that crept around us, the darkness that grew nearer each year, snuffing out more and more of what little light of civilization remained. Banishing such thoughts from my mind, I scratched a note to Mariya in my own hand, telling her of my safety and expressing my burning desire to be reunited with her soon. I handed the two scrolls to Rosamund, who carried them to a courier who was to depart Dara for Antioch that evening.

Dark thoughts haunted my dreams, although that sleep was still far more restful than what I could get on the filthy stone floors of my jail in Nisibis. My body jerked awake as I struggled to make out my surroundings in the darkness, forgetting that I was now in the relative safety of Roman territory. Hearing the thumping wood and growing noise in my room, Rosamund burst through the door.

"Everything is okay, Varus. You are safe, and your friends are here with you."

As my eyes adjusted to the darkness, and I made out Rosamund's silhouette, my breathing slowing as I sat back down on the bed. Rosamund ferried cool water and small cuts of fruit that I gnawed at, struggling to calm my mind and return to sleep.

As I alternated sips of cool water and breaths of the light air, I nodded at my servant. "I don't know what to do, Rosamund."

"About the dreams?" she asked.

"About anything—everything," I said. "How am I supposed to be a father like this, waking in fits and spouting anger?"

"You shall do everything that you can, and more," Rosamund shot back immediately. "More importantly, you are not alone for when you fail. There are dozens who would step in front of a soaring arrow to protect your child, girl or boy."

She spoke the truth, I knew, but the meaning still puzzled me. Even then, I still did not fully understand the full extent of the life I'd chosen, full of suffering, hardship, and responsibility. "Why?"

"Because life is not living unless we have friends to share our burdens," Rosamund replied. "It has nothing to do with Roman concepts of duty or requirement. In times of plenty or of famine, you are my family, Varus. That means your child is my family. And we—all of us—will do what we must to survive."

Rosamund sat with me for a time, waiting until I returned to the rest long denied my body. The extent of her care made me feel childish, almost ashamedly so, yet it left me feeling whole all the same, with the rumble of the magus' voice fading to a dull and distant murmur. Sleep came, and blessedly, without dreams.

As dawn broke, Perenus led the Herulian foederati outside of Dara's walls for the day's training, leaving me in the relative isolation of the storage building. Judging by the remnants of cut grains and seedlings, the building used to be some sort of granary, and I offered a small prayer of thanks that our foederati had not been assigned to some rank tanner's shop or that of a similar pungent profession.

Once Perenus departed, Cephalas emerged with my armor and weapons and began to secure their straps. Though not a poor fit, the steel scales and hardened leather of my armor fit loosely over my body, feeling oddly heavy. Later, I found Fulcaris in a similar exercise, laughing as his mailed armor swayed against his thin frame as he jumped from one leg onto the other.

Cephalas next brought my weapons, while Rosamund handed me the pouch that held my cross and dragon. Embarrassed at my forgetfulness the evening before, I quickly threw the chain around my neck and slid Theodora's ring firmly onto my shield hand. Cephalas helped to secure my belt and weapons, while Rosamund again yielded the dagger that had been one of the four gifts that I received from Father Petrus and Emperor Justin. Once belonging to Aetius, the dagger was a gift from General Godilas, my old master-at-arms, who fell in the Thracian Army's initial battle against the Avars.

My weapons secured, I ran my gloved hand over the decorated pommel of my sword, drawing a macabre sense of reassurance from the blue-tinged blade that hung at my hip. Several servants prepared a training yard, where Fulcaris and I forced our bodies into the motions of training, our muscles straining after the initial effort. Though we had been captives for only a matter of weeks, we would require significant time to regain the strength and endurance to assure survival on the battlefield. Belisarius ordered that no expense be spared to nurse Fulcaris and me back to health, and his servants frequently deposited packages of rich foods that Rosamund carefully tested before preparing for my consumption.

Our first day of training was agony. A week of hearty meals and sound rest, however, saw Fulcaris and I regaining some of the bulk that had wasted from our frames, and we extended our time in the training yard each day. By the end of the week, we were able to rejoin the foederati, and I led Ignis on a gallop around Dara's surrounding countryside as the Herulians trailed closely behind.

With my days spent training with swords, bows, and spears, and my early mornings still given to Father Petrus, my evenings were spent in Belisarius' offices, scouring maps of the nearby region and identifying the next best course of action. Neither Liberius nor Father Petrus deigned to attend these meetings, although Liberius did meet privately with several officers and made his counsel known.

In a meeting early in the first week at Dara, Belisarius remarked that our ideal strategy would be to wait for the Ghassanids to reform under their new king, al-Harith. The other officers disagreed.

"The Persians won't delay that long," Bessas said. "They know they have an advantage now and will come for us sooner rather than later."

Grimly, Belisarius nodded and opened the floor to other avenues. Baduarius suggested attacking the Persians head on as we had done with the Avars, a strategy John cautioned against.

"The Avars were fierce but poorly armed or disciplined," John said, "while the Persians have some of the world's most elite military formations. Besides, their scouts will be monitoring our every move at this point."

Others suggested that Dara and Mesopotamia in general be abandoned to the Persians, but Belisarius shook this notion away. "The Emperor has prioritized Dara, and we cannot evacuate without direct orders," he said dutifully, to groans from his followers.

It was not an unexpected reaction. Our anxiety gradually ran riot at the anticipation of Xerxes' next move. Though Bessas dispatched scouts to keep eyes on Xerxes' army in the aftermath of Thannuris, few reports trickled back into Dara in the weeks following the battle. It made little sense for Xerxes not to immediately re-besiege the Roman fortress city, given that its walls were already weakened by recent attacks and its stores of food largely depleted from siege and hungry Roman soldiers. Still, despite the ill omens that plagued daily life in Dara, Xerxes' Zhayedan did not flood across the Mesopotamian lowlands, and Belisarius was slowly able to bring his forces back into fighting order.

Our news of Xerxes' next move came the day before our inspection by Hermogenes. In the darkness of evening, as Belisarius was nearing the end of another planning session with his officers, a Roman soldier was granted entry into Belisarius' offices, his face beaded with sweat as he saluted Belisarius.

"Yes, soldier?" Belisarius asked.

"My lord Belisarius, Xerxes' army has retreated northeast," the soldier reported, "with parts being absorbed by Perozes a half day to the east of Nisibis. Xerxes himself was seen being led away in chains through Nisibis' gates."

"You're joking!" Germanus all but shouted, startling the soldier.

"I am not, Lord Germanus," the soldier said respectfully. "Xerxes no longer leads the Persian assault on Mesopotamia."

Belisarius' eyes closed for a moment. Gasps and murmurs filled the room until Baduarius at last broke the silence. "Why would the Persians make such a foolish blunder?"

"Because the gods smile upon us," Sunicas drawled. "It does not matter why. The Persians made a move, and we now have an enemy who is not fresh from battle victory."

Belisarius opened his eyes. "Did you or your men get close enough to view the composition of Perozes' army?" he asked the soldier.

The soldier nodded. "Two of my men were captured, but I and another were able to circle the Persian camp. With Xerxes' men, Perozes commands at least fifty thousand trained soldiers, not counting those currently garrisoned in Nisibis. We recognized the armor of the Immortals and saw a large contingent of Hephthalites based upon the glyphs that Lord Bessas instructed me to look for," he said, quickly adding, "although I said nothing of the Hephthalites to any others, per your orders."

Belisarius nodded. "You have done well. Give the remainder of your report to Lord Bessas and see Procopius for a reward," Belisarius said.

The soldier saluted crisply and followed Bessas out of the rooms. John immediately went to Belisarius' map and moved the pieces: the Persian figures near Thannuris to Nisibis, and then Perozes westward to meet the mass, creating a huge force that dwarfed the forces remaining to Belisarius.

"Fifty thousand..." Baduarius said, his voice taut with concern.

"Immortals and Hephthalites too," Bessas added. "Elite cavalry and armored infantry, let alone any archers of elephants."

"I saw elephants at Nisibis," I put in. "Although there did not seem to be many."

John shot me a look of surprise but did not reply, adding a strangely carved four-legged figure to Perozes' forces. Marcellus scrutinized the map, tracing distances between the two forces.

"My excubitores can hold any Immortal, but there are far more of them than there are of us," Marcellus said. "I'm not sure that we can withstand such a force."

Ascum agreed. "Our men will follow you to Hell and back, Lord," he said to Belisarius, "but if that many Persians come crashing into our lines, the men will break hard."

"We all agree," Germanus said, with nods from both Mundus and Troglita from the Thracian Army. "We can't fight the Persians in open battle, and we cannot last long in a siege in Dara. We need to evacuate the area soon before the Persian vanguard moves westward. It will take them a day to reach us."

Others began to clamor their own opinions, but Belisarius called for silence. "As I have said, I will speak with Hermogenes tomorrow. If any of you would like to leave with your men tonight, I will not stop you. I release you from your oaths to the Emperor and will pray for your safe passage as you seek safety."

"But what will you do, Lord?" Marcellus asked.

"I will await the Emperor's judgment," Belisarius said. "Whatever comes, I trust that good sense will prevail this time."

"Then I'm staying," Baduarius growled. "Even if I have to thump that senile fool myself."

"Us too," called Sunicas, with a confirmatory grunt from Simmas. "We did not swear our oaths lightly."

"And the Herulians," I called.

Others followed our lead, one officer at a time vowing his loyalty until all present reaffirmed their faith in Belisarius. Listening intently, our general's eyes welled.

The solemnity of the moment was only broken by an outburst from Uliaris, who stood armed at the entrance to the room.

"I just got this job, and I'll be damned if I'm going to desert you so soon!" Uliaris cried, to raucous laughter from the room. Baduarius and Ascum began thumping on a wooden table nearby, with others clapping in a cacophony of friendship.

"Thank you, friends," Belisarius said at last. "Thank you." He dismissed his officers on a high note, our spirits rising despite the growing desperation of our situation, for we held a belief that Rome would not allow its commander to suffer needlessly at the hands of the Persians.

The next day, we discovered how wrong we were.

Belisarius' officers assembled prior to Hermogenes' arrival, patiently awaiting the Imperial legate as afternoon gave way to evening. Belisarius unbound his injured arm and carried it stiffly as he wordlessly paced his rooms, deep in thought. Most of the men trained throughout the day, yet Belisarius made a point to ensure that each of his senior officers arrived bathed and cleaned, a task some were considerably more accustomed to than others. Notable, that morning, was Solomon, whose uniform and armor shone without a speck of dirt as he stood alongside Germanus. Little had been seen of him since my return, and when he was in attendance, few asked for his opinion.

Hermogenes entered, eyeing Uliaris suspiciously as he did so. "Dismiss your guard. I will not allow weapons in my presence," Hermogenes ordered.

Uliaris refused to move but was ordered by Belisarius to accede to the legate's orders. "Please wait outside, Uliaris. I will be safe with Legate Hermogenes," he said.

Once Uliaris departed, Hermogenes scanned the room, a vein in his temple visibly pulsing under scant cover from his thinning hair. He began to pace, stopping at Belisarius' map and taking note of the positions of each army.

"After our ignominious defeat at Thannuris, one of your officers has expressed a willingness to abandon Dara altogether for the Persians to sack. I am extremely concerned about your loyalty to the Empire, Lord Belisarius," Hermogenes said, his voice unmistakably mocking.

At that, my eyes shot to Solomon. Of the men present, only he would ever betray Belisarius' confidence and speak to the legate. Harrumphing loudly, Germanus shuffled away from Solomon, who looked to the floor as his face bloomed a brilliant red.

"This cowardice is intolerable. If the Persians take Dara, there is nothing stopping them all the way to the Mediterranean Sea. The Emperor has stressed upon me that the Empire depends on wealth from Syria and Egypt to survive, and I will not be the one to let these provinces fall!" Hermogenes spoke sharply but with condescension, as though disciplining schoolboys.

"Mesopotamia and Syria are indefensible!" Ascum barked, ignoring John's furious glance. "You're asking us to sacrifice ourselves to protect the estates of pampered nobles and simpering courtiers."

Though far older and slighter than most of the men present, Hermogenes carried himself with an air of strength and authority. He strode over to Ascum, glowering at the Alan.

315

"Marcellus, arrest this man," Hermogenes said, his scowling face inches from Ascum's. "I will deal with his insolence later."

Marcellus hesitated. As a direct servant to the Emperor, Marcellus was legally obligated to follow the instructions of Justinian's legate, regardless of how asinine such commands may be, and now he looked around as though he sought someone to prevent him from doing his duty.

Sunicas was the one to oblige him. "Like hell you will!" he cried, striding toward the legate.

Hermogenes cast his eyes at Sunicas and flared his nostrils with distaste. "Treacherous bastards, you Huns. I never did understand why Anastasius allowed you into our army, but so it is."

Sunicas glowered but said nothing further. Marcellus took a tentative step but halted as Belisarius intervened.

"Legate Hermogenes," Belisarius began formally, "allow me to apologize for my men. They have lost friends in battle and suffered the deprivations of the soldiers' camp. Emotions are high. Surely you remember what similar moments are like."

Hermogenes grunted. "Very well, but I will not tolerate further outbursts. They are uncharacteristic of Romans."

"Thank you, Legate," Belisarius replied. "We have no intention of abandoning Syria and Phoenicia, my lord, only to withdraw westward into a more defensible and easily supplied position. Dara is neither of those things, having recently suffered under siege, and is low on supplies for yet another."

Hermogenes nodded. "Listen, I do understand the difficulties that I am asking of you," Hermogenes said, "but my orders are clear. As one of the most important fortresses of the Empire, Dara, under no circumstances, is to be allowed to fall in the hands of the enemy without a fight."

John, who looked utterly surprised, stepped forward. "Legate, are you aware of the forces arrayed against us under Perozes?" he asked.

Hermogenes' eyes narrowed, his tone even. "My reports are likely the same as yours. Xerxes was dismissed from office, with the remnants of his army massed with Perozes. I fully understand the size and character of the Persian army that you will soon face."

"And do you have any notion of when their advance may be?" John pressed further.

"It is difficult to say for certain, although Perozes will want to attack while the summer is young so that his campaign can continue beyond his attack on Dara," Hermogenes replied. "The Emperor's spies give the Persian invasion another month before commencement, but not much more than that."

"And will the Emperor dispatch any reinforcements, Legate?" Marcellus asked, his tone diplomatic.

Hermogenes shook his head. "Recruits are in training now, but available forces have been sent to Sittas in the north, or to Domnicus against the Vandals. No detachments can be spared for Mesopotamia until the next year."

"Forgive me, Lord, but with no opportunities to maneuver, and with no hope of additional spearmen or cavalry, we will simply repeat Thannuris on a grander scale," John said. "Except this time, we will not be able to retreat with an intact army... Perozes will come to annihilate our army and have free rein all the way to Egypt."

Hermogenes rubbed his temples, his skin flushing in frustration. "Then, Tribune John, I suggest you find a way to stop him. We will not be leaving Dara. That is my final decision."

At that, a hush fell over the room. Ascum scowled, while bulging muscles tensed along Baduarius' thick neck. None dared broach Belisarius' peace, leaving it to Belisarius to respond to the

Emperor's commands. Before Belisarius could reply, the door to his offices slammed open with a crash.

"My Lord Hermogenes, if you wish to kill us all, it would be easier to bring up the hangman now and save the Persians the effort." Liberius strode in casually, his voice cool and drawling as his eyes narrowed at the legate.

Hermogenes sighed. "Lord Liberius, it pleases me to find you safe and returned to Rome," he said. "Though perhaps your time in the desert heat has allowed your mind to wander about who commands this expedition."

Unaware or unperturbed by the tension that had built in the room, Liberius only laughed, bristling the hairs of his beard where the black dye gave way to thick gray roots. "You mistake me, Lord Legate. I would never question your right to dictate Justinian's will," Liberius said. "Instead, I only ask as a representative of these gathered miscreants and castaways that you message the surrounding cities for additional support, including laborers and siege equipment, to arrive in Dara with all haste."

"A helpful suggestion, Lord Liberius. It will be done immediately." Hermogenes inclined his head, and John's eyebrows shot up in surprise. "I will leave you with the assembled commanders to identify other requests to facilitate your efforts, provided that the army remains in Dara."

Liberius returned the slight bow as Hermogenes left the room. Soon thereafter, Uliaris rejoined our gathering, and the dam that had held back the peace of the room broke in a flood of complaints and anxieties. Belisarius stood wordless, looking pensively toward Liberius.

"My lord!" Germanus' voice rose above all others as he addressed Liberius. "My lord, is there anything you can do to sway the legate's mind in this matter?"

Behind him, Mundus nodded.

Liberius shook his head. "Hermogenes is an idiot, but he is not wrong. In this instance, at any rate. If we don't find a way to stop Perozes here, multiple Persian armies will sweep over the Eastern provinces, massacring thousands and extinguishing entire cities in their wake."

Germanus nodded slowly, his eyes falling back to the map that betrayed the huge mass of Persians threatening our position. None countermanded Liberius' words; even Ascum looked onward at this final assessment of our situation.

Liberius' gaze fell upon me as he smiled sadly. "This is an unfair request to ask of each of you, and I have worked this week to find alternative solutions," he said. "Yet, none exist. Belisarius must make his stand here, and I will do all that I can to support you in the time remaining to us."

Now Belisarius spoke out. "I agree and understand, Lord Liberius. Your counsel will be invaluable in the weeks we have to prepare for this fight."

With that, the gathered Roman armies in Mesopotamia were set on a course for war. John immediately dispatched additional scouts to track Perozes' movements and relay additional information about the equipment that these advancing soldiers would bring into Roman territory and the composition of their ranks. Additional riders were sent to a dozen nearby cities seeking help in preparing for the battle.

Belisarius and Liberius spoke privately of Belisarius' concerns, leaving John and the other officers to begin preparations for Perozes' forces. Our first week was spent strengthening Dara's walls and hardening its gates with stones and mortar stacked under the baking Mesopotamian sun. When asked why the walls needed to be heightened, John yielded a simple explanation.

"Elephants," he said, ending all debate.

Still, with their skin reddening and peeling under the unforgiving heat, Perenus and Samur managed to complain.

319

"At least when we were slaves to Justin, he did not command us to field labor," Samur muttered.

Fulcaris, however, was cheerful. "Just be grateful we don't have to do this alone," he said as he and Irilar lathered mortar along another line of stones. "All units are equally required to share the burden, not just the foederati."

The truth behind Fulcaris' words was likely the main reason why many foreign segments of Belisarius' army did not mutiny outright. Where other Roman generals would have forced the Herulians or Huns into such undignified work, Belisarius assigned each segment of his army to the work of improving Dara's outer defenses on a rotation throughout the day, ensuring work never ceased and no man was exempt from his share. Testament to this was Troglita and Mundus, who labored with the Thracian spearmen farther down the line and occasionally called out crude jokes to their Herulian comrades.

When our shift concluded, Belisarius himself led the next contingent of laborers, which included Solomon—although where Belisarius relaxed and laughed in his exertions, Solomon always seemed to shy away from the dirtier tasks, leaving them to his second-in-command, Marcian.

By the end of our first week, Dara's walls had been repaired and raised the length of a man. Outside of the city, Belisarius ordered a vast moat be dug ten paces wide and half again as deep. Disturbed earth from such exercises was used to create another makeshift wall of dirt that ringed the city, offering another impediment to any Persian attacker who wished to scale the walls with ladders, elephants, or any other tricks.

As our labors for Dara bore fruit, our messengers returned from nearby cities. Representatives from Constantina were the first to arrive, offering over a hundred laborers and a dozen wall-mounted ballistae. Edessa and Hierapolis came soon thereafter with their own men and weapons, including a vast caravan of grain that would ease Dara's slow starvation. Others, like Martyropolis, were less sanguine, citing the need to prepare for their own defense and offering nothing except well wishes and a fresh horse for our riders.

Last to respond was a contingent from Melitene. Rather than laborers or siege weapons, the city sent a hundred trained spearmen under a young centurion named Valerian. Gates were thrown open as the Romans galloped inside, gathering in Dara's forum as Belisarius hurried to greet his only reinforcements.

Valerian saluted Belisarius, his features distinctively Italian in the manner of the old Caesars. "General, the city of Melitene shows its gratitude for protection against the Persians. We would be proud to fight at your side in the battle to come," Valerian said, his voice carrying off of the forum's stone streets.

"Gratefully received, Centurion. See your men rested and cared for, and report to me later tonight for orders," Belisarius commanded, though not unkindly, a light smile breaking the otherwise solemn character he presented in public.

Amidst the more positive news of reinforcements and assistance in securing Dara, scouts from the east began trickling back. Using a relay system, John's scouting network could receive fresh reports of Persian troop movements within a day of hard riding, allowing Belisarius to adjust his defenses to meet the threat at hand.

Report after report brought no news save that the Persians kept camp and gathered their forces and vital supplies, but by the end of my third week in Dara, they were beginning to show signs of preparing for march.

"Another two weeks, maybe three, until they're ready," one scout said. "After that, they will only need two days to reach Dara's walls."

Belisarius accepted this account, which was further confirmed the following day by another messenger. Most unusual of all was a rider from the Persian camp bearing a flag of truce, stopping just outside of bowshot of Dara's eastern gates.

My foederati was assigned sentry duty that afternoon, and I hailed the Persian rider as he planted his flag in the ground. Sending Alaric to retrieve Belisarius, I descended Dara's walls and mounted Ignis, trotting through the gate. Always close behind, Sembrouthes followed me through the gate, his spear looped tightly across his back.

The Persian waved a hand in salute that I returned in kind. Approaching cautiously, I found the man armed only with a light dagger and a confident look on his face. Most of his head was masked by a thick metal helm that opened at the eyes and chin, allowing the man's curly beard to fall to his chest.

"Well met, Greek. Do you command here?" the messenger asked in stilted Latin.

I spat off to the side. "You face Romans in Dara," I growled in his own Persian tongue. "That is all you need to know."

The messenger smiled and switched smoothly to Persian. "Greeks, Romans, whatever you call yourselves now—it hardly matters. Where's your commander? I am here to negotiate."

"Throw your dagger to the ground, and we will talk then," I commanded.

Rather than resist, the Persian disarmed himself in full view of Dara's walls. Belisarius trotted out of the gate thereafter, flanked by John and Liberius, who rode hard behind Belisarius.

The Persian scoffed at the arrival. "Who of you leads here?" he asked, returning to Latin.

"That honor is mine," Belisarius replied coldly.

"Then listen well, Leader General. Spahbad Perozes comes for you. He does not make the mistakes of Prince Xerxes. He does not show leniency. You open your gates and surrender your arms now—the Spahbad, he treats you with all proper honors. You refuse to do this and...."

322

With a grin, the Persian made a slashing motion across his throat. John gritted his teeth at the display, yet Belisarius' dispassionate expression did not so much as flicker.

"Tell your leader that we will not be cowed, and that he faces his death in Dara," Belisarius said, his brow furrowing only slightly as he spoke.

The Persian laughed, the scales of his armor shaking as he moved in the saddle. "You are all servants of the Great Lie," he spat. "Perozes drives your darkness from here. And me, I am so blessed to see this happen in my life. Your armies are pathetic. We come for you and you run like sheep."

Liberius responded in Persian, his voice as deep and even as Belisarius'. "Darkness comes for us all, friend. I wonder which is worse: a heathen Roman who pays no respect to Ahura Mazda, or a soulless Persian who consorts with Hephthalites and massacres women and babes?"

The Persian snarled but offered no denial. "You have one week, Romans," he said in Persian, abandoning all pretense at diplomacy. "After that, you will find no mercy from the armies of Perozes."

He dropped from his saddle, quickly gathered his dagger and flag, and remounted to return to Persian lines. I loathed his demeanor and was tempted to ride him down with my own blade, but I dared not disgrace Belisarius with a breach of truce.

"One week, then," Belisarius muttered.

"Earlier than expected," John observed. "But it is enough time to plan."

The five of us trotted back through Dara's gates, and Perenus ordered the bridge raised and bars closed. Iron creaked and wood groaned as Dara's eastern gate resealed itself, leaving the Persian interloper to fade into a barely perceptible speck along the Mesopotamian horizon.

Belisarius ordered the officers gathered immediately. Most rushed toward the governor's palace in varying states of dress, with Belisarius and John speaking in hushed tones. Bringing Perenus and Samur, I walked inside and stood near Sunicas, whose beard dripped with grease and fat from the roasted haunch of goat he gnawed upon messily.

With the men assembled, John unfurled a map of the surrounding area, showing the hills, streams, and roads that linked Dara to Nisibis. "The Persians will be here in a week, maybe slightly more, but we *must* decide on a strategy now." John was vehement.

"No change in Hermogenes?" Ascum asked.

"None," Marcellus answered, resigned in his role as an intermediary between the Emperor and the army.

"We have enough supplies to last several months under siege, and the numbers to make it difficult on Perozes to take the city," John said. "Yet it will be difficult to last through the planting season, let alone another winter."

"And while we wait, Perozes will burn and plunder the countryside, and every Roman in it," Troglita added.

Valerian, leader of Melitene's soldiers, nodded at Troglita. "The man is right. The Persians have demonstrated a desire to kill all Romans they come across. Even if Dara remains in safe hands, most other cities outside of Antioch will fall by the year's end."

Dark tidings sat uneasily with the men. None of them relished the thought of a siege at any rate.

"So we bring battle to them!" Baduarius bellowed, slamming a meaty fist into a wooden pillar.

"But how?" asked Germanus. "I fear no man, but I don't want to willingly sacrifice my men for Hermogenes' hubris."

"Hubris."

It was Belisarius who spoke, and all discussion halted. "That is our weapon against Perozes," he finished.

Many murmured, but none spoke outright.

"Lord?" I asked at last, giving voice to the confusion that all seemed to feel.

Belisarius smiled. "It's almost poetic. Perozes is certain that we will be beaten, and Thannuris only reinforces that belief." At the thought of disgrace, several officers grimaced.

Belisarius was unperturbed. "Perozes will use his numbers to try to punch a hole straight through our army in hopes of encircling and killing us all. He cannot afford to allow a Roman army to escape, even if only partially intact."

John agreed. "There does seem to be odd dissent and tension amongst the Persian leadership. If Xerxes remained at the head of the invasion force, we would be in far bigger trouble right now."

Belisarius nodded. "And that is our advantage. He does not want to suffer Xerxes' fate, wherever that Zhayedan prince is chained up. Perozes will charge at us, and all we need to do is stay alive long enough to separate detachments of his army and kill them off one by one."

"Easier said than done," Mundus interrupted. "All Perozes needs to do is to send sections of his army to hit both flanks simultaneously, and our lines will buckle before cutting off individual Persian detachments."

"I will deal with one of the flanks," Liberius said, finally adding his voice to the war council. "Just tell me which one you want to protect."

"How, Lord Liberius?" Belisarius sounded polite but curious.

"Let me deal with the particulars," Liberius said with a wave. "All I ask is that you gather all of your ballistae and onagers in the city forum this evening."

Siege weapons. I shivered in spite of myself, envisioning the destruction our onagers could wreak as they catapulted heavy stones over huge distances.

John nodded. "Done," he said. "They would not be useful outside of the city anyway… we'd hit our own men."

Liberius grinned wickedly. "Don't worry about that," he said and fell silent again.

"So we bring battle to the Persians, then?" Baduarius said, repeating his question with equal force.

Belisarius laughed. "Yes, my Gothic friend, we will face the Persian lines after all."

None of us was confident that such a strategy could succeed, yet between Hermogenes' stubborn orders and the losses we would surely suffer from a siege on flat terrain, little choice remained. We would attack Perozes and the Persians in open battle, just beyond the easternmost gates of Dara.

DARA

DARA GREW INTO A hive of frenzied action in the aftermath of Belisarius' decision. John led the loaned laborers of nearby cities to two hundred paces outside of Dara's walls. The commander ordered deep trenches be dug in the shape of a bucket, two hundred paces farther out into the eastern horizon and four hundred paces wide, with its base the closest point to Dara's gates. Short trench lines were marked perpendicular to the sides of the bucket, extending outward another hundred paces in each direction. Each trench was littered with sharp wooden spikes that were dug diagonally into the soil, their points facing the likely route of Persian attack.

John explained his strategy to Troglita, who assumed leadership of the effort as John next led the leaders of the Herulian foederati over a steep hill that blocked our view of John's prepared lines. Sembrouthes followed as a representative of the few Aksumites in Belisarius' army, who refused to allow me to venture off into battle without a bodyguard.

"Your task is to lie in wait well beyond our left flank," John said. "No matter what happens, do not enter the battle until you receive Belisarius' signal."

Perenus grunted. "We are not to fight, Lord?"

John shook his head. "Believe me, we will need you. But your role is one of ambush, whenever that moment will be."

"And what if the Persians ride over the hill and discover us?" I asked.

"They won't," John said. "Perozes cannot been seen running from a fight, and Liberius will make sure that no large detachments of Persians reach your position. Just stay hidden behind the hill and send a careful scout to watch for Belisarius' signal."

Our orders received, we trotted back over the hill, finding a small group of men painting thick white lines into the soil. Seeing my confusion, a laborer walked forward.

"Distance markers for Lord Liberius," the man explained.

Inside, along the city's northeastern walls, I found Liberius in deep conversation with Ascum, who was running his hands over various parts of our siege equipment as he spoke. I watched as he carefully demonstrated the assembly and operation of Belisarius' ballistae and onagers to Liberius, then gestured for his men to load a huge iron-tipped bolt into one the of the ballistae. The machine fired its projectile hundreds of paces distant, and Liberius cackled at the display before asking Ascum to provide enough men and munitions to operate these wicked devices in the upcoming battle.

Trenches formed and walls were secured within our final week of peace at Dara. As the days progressed, I found many of the Herulians laughing nervously to one another, eager for a break in their tedium yet also fearing the unbeaten Persian forces that opposed us. I ordered Perenus to drill the men each day, hoping they might find calm in the routine, and made sure each man received hearty meals each evening as well.

Servants polished armor and tended to Roman horses while running hundreds of errands for the army's officers, all under the scrutinizing eye of Hermogenes. It came only as a slight surprise when word spread that Solomon, a komes of the Thracian spearmen, was injured in training and would be temporarily replaced in the upcoming battle by the centurion Marcian. Seemingly wishing to appear helpful, Solomon was often seen trailing Hermogenes' steps as the legate inspected each section of the army, his arm wrapped in a tight sling.

As our preparations drew to a close at the end of that week, thick clouds of dust rose over the horizon, reinforced by a low rumble that spread across the horizon.

"The Persians have finally arrived," Mundus said as we peered over the city battlements.

We sent Belisarius warning of the incoming enemy, squinting as we fought to make out any figures in the distance. As the sun fell in the sky and light grew scarcer, the Persian vanguard rose into our field of vision, the banners of Shahanshah Kavadh flying high into the heavens.

The Persians' progress halted a few miles distant, leaving only a few their forces visible to the sentries of Dara. Thousands of fires were gradually lit in the darkness and illuminated the Persian lines, the fires dancing as they rose in the Mesopotamian night.

I ordered Dara's guard doubled, and all bridges across our moat raised for the evening. More than a few city residents complained, yet I shrugged off their concerns at each turn, as though it was truly a mere inconvenience and not a coming apocalypse.

"Why do you not hear them out?" Fulcaris asked me.

"We can't afford for any to run to the Persians and let them know how desperate our situation is," I said coldly. Fulcaris nodded, eyes wide.

Upon returning to my foederati, I asked Father Petrus to offer prayers over the men, which were gladly received despite the fact that most of them remained ardent pagans.

"It doesn't hurt to have another god's favor," Alaric reasoned. "And the Christian God is native to these lands, so your priest's words can only help."

After my own words with Petrus, I ordered food distributed and the men to return early for sleep–a command that was almost universally ignored as most were too excited or anxious to rest. I pretended to not notice their noise as I retreated to my own quarters, mentally preparing for the challenges ahead.

Rest, however, was impossible. I arrived to find that my rooms were not vacant. Instead, Rosamund was sitting at my desk, clad in her softer robes instead of her armor.

"Varus, if we move silently, we can leave Dara and escape to the far north where none will find us," Rosamund whispered. "We can bring others, if you want, but we need to leave soon before the Persians come."

My stomach clenched. I should have expected she would propose as much, yet in all the preparations for war, I had forgotten the ongoing battle waging within my own household.

"Rosamund, I don't want to hear talk of this again," I said sternly. "I am not abandoning Belisarius or the army. We will win, and then we will all go to Antioch and find Mariya."

"Again?" Rosamund cried. "What do you mean, *talk of this again*? This isn't like with the Avars. This isn't like anything else. The Persians are trained killers, and the Hephthalites enjoy nothing more than war."

"It is already done, Rosamund. I will make sure you are safe in Dara while we are in the field," I said.

It was as though Rosamund had not heard me at all. "I can find Mariya for you," she said. "I will take her north, too. Just please don't go. Please don't go out into that battle—"

The sound of Mariya's name struck me like a bolt to the chest. "Don't you dare invoke my wife!"

I did not realize I had shouted until I saw the ashen look on Rosamund's face.

"I—" she started.

"No, listen." I cut her off, impatient in the growing ache of my fatigue. "If you will not yourself swear allegiance to Rome, then so be it. Keep your gods. Keep your witchcraft and potions. I begrudge you none of it." I raised my palms to her, surrendering.

"But know that it is a Roman soldier's money that keeps you in fine clothes and sees you fitted with your own set of play armor. You may not swear to Rome, but you gladly suckle from her, Rosamund. And I will not have my own family used as a wedge to divide me from my sworn duty."

Rosamund gasped, and I saw her face was wet with tears. Instantly, I knew I had pushed too far. Shame flooded me, weighing my body heavier than the exhaustion had, but my feeble words were silenced by Rosamund.

"You are right." She paused to gulp for air. "Though I did not know you could be so cruel." Once again, I made to speak, and she brushed me off. "But this is not about Rome, Varus, I swear to you." Wiping tears with the heel of her hand, she surprised me by hugging my chest tightly. "You promised not to leave me," she said. "You cannot die. I have no one if the Persians kill you."

"They won't." Yet even as I said it, I fought back visions of the magus' curse.

"You are my family, Varus." Again, she spoke as though she had not heard me. "I will attend to Mariya as I attend to you. That is all I meant." She let me go.

"Rosamund, I am sorry."

Defeated, Rosamund simply nodded. "Let me be the one to prepare you for battle. Not Cephalas, just me alone."

"Very well."

Rosamund embraced me one final time and disappeared out into the dark storage yard, seeking out her own private quarters that I ordered constructed on our first days in Dara.

My sleep was disturbed by visions of Mariya's suffering and the magus' laughter, his curse repeating in my mind. It was not until my dreams took the form of the red-eyed conqueror, his hand burning into my flesh, that I awoke. Covered in sweat, I left the building for the cooler air of the night, sitting against a stone wall until my mind slowed from fatigue and exhaustion.

My sleep was not disturbed again until just before dawn. Relaying that Belisarius wished the army formed up outside of Dara, Rosamund brought a light meal that I ate slowly, and laid out fresh clothing that I would wear under my armor. She left for a moment as I dressed, and returned when called for.

Rosamund slid my chest piece over my head and secured its leather straps. As I adjusted the scaled armor, Rosamund knelt down and gingerly secured the thin greaves that protected my shins from blows below the shield wall and tugged my thick leather boots over each foot and ankle. With that task completed, Rosamund stepped away as I fastened my cloak and tied my belt around my waist, my weapons hanging reassuringly from the thick leather.

Unstopping a small dark pot, Rosamund dipped two fingers into its contents, withdrawing a viscous black ink. Placing her unmarked hand on my chin, she ran the ink in a thin vertical line below each eye. The substance seemed oddly warm against my skin, although Rosamund cautioned me against moving my face for a few moments as I placed a hand near my jaw.

"What is this?" I asked.

"A ritual from my people," she said, "to keep you safe in battle." She flicked a gaze up at me as if challenging me to stop her, and I all but winced, remembering my harsh words from the night before.

"Thank you," I said, and though I was skeptical, I truly meant it.

The task complete, Rosamund wiped her hand clean before handing over my shield, spear, and helmet.

"How do I look?" I asked, standing straight.

"Like a god," Rosamund whispered, her hollow voice nearly absorbed by the wooden paneling of my makeshift rooms.

She straightened my plume and handed me Aetius' dagger. "Bring this back when you return," Rosamund commanded. "I'm expecting it."

Not waiting for an answer, she hugged me one final time, and I could only suppose our argument was, if not forgotten, at least forgiven.

Rosamund led me out to the Herulian foederati. The building had already been vacated, with Perenus leading the Herulians into Dara's forum. With help from other servants, Cephalas fed and saddled Ignis, and I patted the stallion's neck as I vaulted onto his back. Ignis was bedecked with a light coating of dark iron scales, making him easily fit in with any of Belisarius' cataphracts. Atop his armor rested the white wolf pelt I had taken from my fight against the Avars, tied to the rear of the saddle so that it would not fall or appear obvious plunder to be torn away in battle.

"The horse armor is a gift from Lord Belisarius," Cephalas explained. "His men said that the armor is made lighter, so Ignis will not tire as easily."

I smiled at Cephalas, resting a gloved hand on his head. "I wish you could come with us, my friend," I said.

Cephalas simply nodded with a stony face, although I thought I caught a tear forming at the corner of his eye as I nudged Ignis out of the high doors of our quarters.

The Herulian army glistened in the dawning sun, row after row of armor and blackened shields that made them appear more like soldiers from Hell than any mortal army. I grinned in satisfaction as I took my place at their head, nodding to Perenus as he took his place at my side. Sembrouthes urged himself forward, his Aksumites forming two short lines immediately behind me.

Father Petrus, astride an older mare, straightened in the saddle as he blessed the army.

"Go with God, my sons, and do what you must to preserve the last light of Rome against the vast array lined against you. For the sword of our Lord is greater than fifty thousand Persians, and his shield offers protection to all who seek it out," Petrus said, one arm held toward the sky.

I thanked Petrus, who laid a hand on my decorated shoulder plate as he drew close. The old priest ignored the dark marks on my cheeks and instead offered only warmth before we parted.

"Justin would be proud of the man you have become, my son," Petrus said. "Take care of your men."

"I will, Father." Raising an arm, I commanded the foederati forward, and we trotted toward Dara's northern gate.

Rather than follow the same route as the rest of the army, John's insistence on discretion inspired me to depart via a more indirect route, using the hills to Dara's northeast to disguise our approach. As we moved northward, a fur-clad warrior galloped toward my location, his horse's hooves clicking against the cobbled streets.

Samur saluted me briefly. "Stay alive, brother." He offered his arm from the saddle, and I grasped it, drawing Samur as close as I could while staying mounted and clutching my spear in an opposite hand.

"If anything happens to me," I whispered in Latin. "I need you to care for my family. Promise me, and I'll go into battle with a clear mind."

Stern faced, Samur nodded. "You need not even ask. You have my oath as you have my blood."

"God be with you, Samur."

Samur said nothing, only flashed his wide smile as he departed, driving his horse back toward Sunicas and the Huns.

Before the sun rose full into the sky, the Herulian foederati cleared Dara's northern gate and hooked eastward, careful to mute our progress and prevent large plumes of dust from rising into the air. Soon thereafter, we reached the nadir of three hills that blocked our view of the Persians. I ordered the men to dismount and summoned Fulcaris as we crept across a hill for a view of the Roman forces.

Belisarius' plan unfolded beautifully. Much of the Roman cavalry occupied the forward trenches on either flank, with Marcellus and Valerian on the forward left and Bessas and John on the forward right. At the center, Baduarius led Belisarius' infantry toward the center-right, while the Thracians under Germanus, Mundus, and Troglita held the center-left. Ascum's foot archers stood in two long lines behind the spearmen, while a large reserve of cataphracts under Belisarius stood closest to Dara's walls and behind Baduarius and Ascum. A curiously unarmored horseman stood attentive near the white-plumed Belisarius: Uliaris, shadowing his commander, never allowing Belisarius to move more than ten paces from his position.

Sunicas and Simmas each led their own detachment of Huns that floated inside the bucket of Belisarius' formation, their horses able to effortlessly weave between gaps of the trenches. Sunicas moved toward Bessas' position, affording me a glimpse of Samur riding close behind his leader.

As impressive as Belisarius' plan was, the Persian lines still dwarfed our own.

The rich purples, yellows, and reds of Persia's ancient royal standard flew throughout the lines, the Derafsh Kaviani that terrorized Greece a thousand years prior waving high above countless bodies of men and horses. Persian commanders whisked through the ranks, using long spears and war banners to set infantry and horsemen alike in clean lines.

At the center, three monstrous elephants towered above the troops, with the tallest bearing a gold-armored Persian. This, surely, was Perozes.

For all their mass and might, the elephants seemed to stand somewhat lazily before the Persian ranks, with one using its trunk to search for food along the ground.

"Not enough to attack with, I think," Fulcaris whispered.

"It seems so. They are probably for scouting our positions," I replied.

Resisting the urge to gawk at the massive, armored beasts, I surveyed the cavalry, a mass of mounted Zhayedan at the center of Perozes' formations, with heavy scaled armor covering man and horse alike. Thick-linked mail hung from each Immortal's helm, giving Persia's elite soldiers a faceless and emotionless gaze.

A larger body of lesser-armored Persian cavalry faced the Roman left, with a vast reserve of spearmen and bowmen lined behind. My eyes traced the seemingly limitless ranks from left to right until I finally arrived at the far Persian flank. Where the Derafsh Kaviani billowed over the Immortals, crude black banners bearing the glyphs of the Hephthalites rose over those men facing Bessas and John.

It was impossible to count the Hephthalites precisely; there were, easily, thousands. In their thick furs, they did not look too different from our own Hunnic foederati, but the addition of Persian mail confirmed Sunicas' assurance that any kinship between his people and the Hephthalites had broken centuries before. They cast dark figures compared to the polished Immortals, their wooden shields clashing against the thick wicker favored by Persia's men.

The sun rose over Dara, promising another scorching day unless a rare sweep of clouds arrived to spare us the worst of the typical heat. Rome's soldiers stood silently as the Persians finalized their preparations, the banners of a dozen commanders lining the nearby walls of Dara as well as within a small staff of soldiers that stood amongst Belisarius' cavalry. At Dara's walls, I spied Liberius, who stood alone atop the stone battlements as he scanned the Persian ranks.

Dozens of horns blew from the Persian lines as Perozes, atop his elephant, dropped his right arm. Persian officers scrambled to obey, wasting no time to order thousands of riders forward to face Marcellus and Valerian. Led by black-plumed Persian commanders, the lesser-armored Persian cavalry moved forward, trotting slowly as they broke away from Perozes' lines.

A cacophony of horns blared as the Persian cavalry gained speed across the plains outside of Dara, closing distance against the Roman left flank. Marcellus barked orders as the excubitores took their places at the front of the flank, their horses standing over the shallow trenches that offered a small degree of protection against a Persian charge.

"Do we go help?" Fulcaris asked, eyes wide as Persian hooves thundered in the distance.

"No," I said shortly. "We need to wait for Belisarius' signal, no matter what happens."

The Persians closed in, and my eyes darted again and again to Belisarius, hoping and fearing the sight of the banner to signal our charge. While the Persians lowered their lances, the signal never came.

The first Persians to reach the Roman lines stumbled into the trench, with several thrown from their horses and quickly butchered by an excubitor. Others were more cautious, slowing their charge as they guided their horses carefully down the trench and urging them upward to hit Marcellus' ranks. In support of the excubitores, Valerian commanded his men to throw their spears, launching a thick volley of iron and wood that drove dozens of lightly armored Persian men and horses to the earth. Despite the growing mound of death that filled the Roman trench, the Persians began to push Marcellus and Valerian back.

Seeing this, Sunicas signaled his half of the Hunnic foederati forward, unslinging his bow as he trotted forward. Sunicas' bow quivered in his hand as his arrow shot forward with wicked force, and his men followed soon thereafter. I saw Samur draw and release arrows in perfect harmony with his Hun comrades, raining death upon recoiling Persians.

The clash surged as the Huns curled forward, blanketing Persian riders with three and four arrows at a time. Pressure against Marcellus lightened as the center-most Persians cowered from the Hunnic assault and evaporated entirely when a Persian commander was cut down by a well-timed sword stroke from Valerian. Horns blew from the Persian lines, and the bulk of the attacking cavalry turned around and galloped back to safety.

"That was it?" Fulcaris exclaimed, seeming to forget the need for quiet.

I was just as suspicious. "Something doesn't make sense," I said. "But keep your voice down."

No flags were raised by Belisarius, and I scanned the Persian lines in confusion. A single horn blew from the center of the Persian lines, and an armored Immortal emerged from the massed Persian ranks, galloping forward but stopping a hundred paces before the Roman lines.

A roar went up from the Roman infantry as Baduarius, commandeering a horse, galloped to meet his challenger. Meeting his Persian adversary, Baduarius dismounted and unslung his massive shield. The Immortal did the same.

Affronted by the Roman lines, Perozes raised his arms with energy, drawing cries of support as the Persian champion strutted forward. Like a cracking whip, the Immortal moved from a standing position into a deep lunge with his spear, its point ramming toward Baduarius.

The massive Goth was barely able to react, caught off guard by the Immortal's speed. Unable to lift his shield in time, Baduarius swept his own spear downward, driving the Immortal's spearpoint away from its target's heart. Even still, Baduarius reeled back as the Immortal regained his balance, slipping a hand just below his armpit in obvious pain.

"I've never seen anyone that fast," Fulcaris said in a hushed voice, his mouth slightly agape and eyes intent on the duel.

"I have." For a moment, my mind drifted back to Tauris, beyond the Euxine Sea. "And keep your eyes on Perozes. This could all be a trick."

From our distant post atop Dara's hills, it was difficult to see the finer details of the fight, yet I could make out a liquid, shining red in the lines of Baduarius' heavy gloves. With a roar, he charged the Immortal, jabbing his own spear toward the armored torso. But time and again, the Immortal pivoted, and Baduarius struck only air, wasting his energy with each missed blow.

Then, noise from the Persian lines grew. The Immortal appeared to be retaking the initiative, hurling his spear toward Baduarius, then drawing a long blade. Baduarius' shield absorbed the spear but sent him stumbling left as the missile stuck in the buffer's wood. With desperate speed, Baduarius dropped his spear and drew his own massive blade just in time to parry the Immortal's strikes.

As the Immortal sought a killing stroke, Baduarius swung his shield square with his body, facing the Immortal. As he did, the Immortal's spear, still protruding stiffly from Baduarius' shield, swung violently toward the Persian and cracked against his helmet with a sickening sound that even Fulcaris and I could hear over the din. Baduarius cut down with his sword, and a mass of groans swept over the Persian ranks as he dispatched with the Immortal in a single, heavy thrust to the neck.

Tugging the spear from his shield, Baduarius raised his arms in challenge to the Persian lines. Behind him, Rome's forces cheered wildly for the victory that, despite its unorthodox ending, was our first auspicious omen since Thannuris. Baduarius reveled in their cheers as he spat toward Perozes, then picked up his spear and slammed it heavily against his shield.

But the battlefield does not rest. As our champion triumphed, a lone arrow sailed high from the Persian ranks. I watched it crest toward Baduarius, nearly screaming a warning even though my voice would not carry far. Instead, I looked on helplessly. The arrow fell toward Baduarius, lined perfectly for the man's head.

Baduarius was no fool. Rome's champion took two paces to the right and watched the arrow slam into the turn where he had once stood. Picking the arrow out of the earth, Baduarius laughed at Perozes and grabbed lewdly at his groin as he snapped the Persian arrow with one hand.

Cheering rose again throughout the Roman ranks as Baduarius returned safely. Across the battlefield, Persian horns blew in a differing pattern, bringing their massed ranks into an orderly withdrawal back to Perozes' camp.

"Is this part of the trick?" Fulcaris asked.

I was unsure myself, and wary. "It makes no sense," I said. "But they seem to be retreating."

We eyed the Persian ranks for a time, watching their vanguard as it grew tiny along the horizon. The battle had lasted less than a morning, but it seemed that Perozes was finished for the day. Scouts were deployed from the Roman ranks as Belisarius called his own men back into Dara, its eastern gates swinging open to accept the Roman defenders.

Signaling to Fulcaris, we crept away from the hilltop and walked to the Herulian foederati. Sembrouthes looked me over with concern, while Perenus asked if it was finally time to charge in.

"It's over," I said. "We're headed back into the city."

Confusion rose in the ranks, with some laughing as Fulcaris told excitedly of the Persian retreat. I mounted Ignis and led my men back into Dara, where I allowed Perenus to return them to the comfort of their own quarters for the time being.

I called for Sembrouthes, and the two of us left the foederati for the governor's palace, seeking Belisarius and whatever answers he might provide. Sembrouthes seemed to share none of the joy felt by the Herulians upon their return to the temporary barracks.

"This was no victory," he said. "Only the opening maneuvers of a more brutal fight to come."

His expression was startlingly grim. "What makes you think this?" I asked.

"I fought the Persians in Himyar many years ago, before joining Princess Mariya's household guard. Mark my words, they are never beaten... only temporarily set back until they can find a new strategy to gain victory."

Belisarius' officers, it turned out, shared Sembrouthes' opinion. Most of the officers had already rejoined Belisarius, with Hermogenes and Liberius both observing the meeting on behalf of the Emperor.

"It seems that the Persians are fearful of attacking," Hermogenes said, with no small amount of smugness. "Why are we not pressing our advantage by attacking their camp?"

"Perozes was testing us," Sunicas said. "He never intended to fight this day."

"Agreed," said Germanus. "We'd only be charging into fresh Persian spearmen who are better armed and trained than most of our own."

"But why would he waste so many men for so limited a purpose?" I asked.

John grimaced. "Because Perozes has plenty of men to burn through, and the strategic advantage of discovering our strategy was worth more to him than such losses. That's why he sent his least-important units."

"Jesus Christ," muttered Baduarius, earning an angry look from Belisarius. A healer worked at Belisarius' flank, bandaging a shallow wound that bled copiously toward his waist.

"Tallies show about a hundred Persians dead, and maybe twice as many wounded." Marcellus had absorbed the brunt of the Persian assault.

"Any captives? Officers that we could torture for information?" Hermogenes asked, paying little mind to the angry looks from Belisarius' men at his suggestion.

"None, Legate Hermogenes," Valerian answered. "Any survivors rode back to the Persian lines or fought until they were slain."

A half dozen conversations sprang up at once as men sought answers for the confusion of the battle. Rome suffered few losses, yet had seemingly betrayed its own battle strategy, giving the Persians time to regroup for the following day. Hermogenes tried to order a sally by the foederati out of Dara, which only stirred up further arguments from Ascum and Sunicas, who considered these missions suicide.

"We will wait patiently," Belisarius said at last, bringing the din to a close. "Perozes thinks he has learned of our strategy, but in truth all he knows is our organization. In our advantage, Perozes now *must* attack tomorrow, or look weak and cowardly before his men."

Even John seemed skeptical of this, but Liberius called out in support. "Belisarius is right. Nothing has changed. Perozes needs a fast victory and will strike soon now that he believes he understands our intentions."

John nodded. "Very well. Everyone should go to their respective units and keep the men's spirits up. I'll have scouts posted throughout the day in case a detachment of Persians return. Plan on another early-morning fight tomorrow."

Dismissed, Sembrouthes and I went back to the foederati. The men gazed at me excitedly as I ordered them to discard their armor and rest for the day, and prepare for combat again the following morning.

"The Persians don't seem so tough to me," Fulcaris was boasting to Irilar. "If that's the best they can do, Belisarius will wipe them from Mesopotamia with no problem."

"Don't be foolish," Irilar replied. "Did you see how that Immortal moved? Baduarius is lucky to be alive."

I ignored these spirited arguments and returned to my quarters. Rosamund used cool water to clean my face, while Cephalas unstrapped my armor and hung it safely across from my bed.

"Looks clean, Lord," Cephalas remarked.

His comment made me laugh. "No fighting today, if you can believe it," I explained, seeing his confused look.

The remainder of that day was spent resting and eating, with messages flitting between different camps throughout Dara. Samur served as a Hunnic courier and greeted Perenus and Rosamund before stopping to chat idly with me on how the battle looked from a higher vantage point. No messages told of a regrouping Persian army, and by sunset the foederati was finally able to relax.

However, I was not so lucky. As I prepared for rest, a winded rider burst into my camp, demanding to deliver a message to me.

Sembrouthes thoroughly searched him, and, finding nothing other than a scroll, warily allowed the messenger inside, where he delivered me a sealed lambskin.

Sembrouthes' words earlier shone true. Perozes had received another batch of reinforcements in the late afternoon, the message reported, and had even sent a courier to Belisarius to demand the Roman surrender. If Belisarius did not surrender, the message went on, he ought at least to draw a bath in the governor's palace come daybreak, for Perozes would soon have control over the city, and it was only polite.

I dismissed the messenger with a fresh horse and a silver coin and placed a corner of the scroll over a lit brazier. It took to the flame, blackening the skin and turning the ink to ash as it curled in my hand. As the fire drew closer to my skin, I dropped the remnants of the letter into the brazier, watching Belisarius' wax seal bubble and melt.

"Trouble?" Perenus asked, growing curious at the sudden disruption to our evening.

"It's nothing," I said. "Tell the men to rest. We're likely to dispatch at dawn."

And, true to Belisarius' predictions, as night gave way to the stubborn orange light of the morning, messengers from John spread throughout Dara. A heavy wind blew from west to east, cooling the Mesopotamian heat and driving heavy clouds that promised to muzzle the worst of the sun's blistering rays.

I led the Herulians in a repeat of our previous day's preparations, from my private meeting with Rosamund to a blessing by Father Petrus. My foederati rode through Dara's northern gate in the same manner as before, albeit with slightly higher spirits as men whispered boasts of how many Persians each would kill that day.

Upon arriving at our predetermined waypoint, Fulcaris and I again crept to the crest of our hilltop and found Belisarius' battlefield below.

Under John's instruction, we Romans again preceded Perozes' forces on the battlefield. Where the day before, Perozes' men hurried into lines, however, each detachment of Persian spearmen or cavalry marched carefully into order, adopting a similar formation as they faced Dara's defenders. Then, finally in order as clouded light illuminated Dara's eastern expanses, dozens of Persian horns blew in stunning harmony, calling their forces to order.

As the horns finished their song, the sound of spears thundering into the ground filled the air. Huge billowing banners tilted forward and back to the rhythm of the Persian staccato, with thousands of voices chanting in unison as the Shahanshah's emblem returned to an upright position. After several moments of this, the ranks of the Persian center parted, with Immortals allowing a thin passage through their ranks.

"Looks mostly the same," Fulcaris said. "Maybe they won't want to fight again?"

I waved Fulcaris silent as a dozen Persians flooded through the passage, stacking thick wooden logs thirty paces before the Persian lines. Their work quickly completed, the men disappeared back into the gap left by the Immortals, which remained open for a time. Then, soon thereafter, an old man hobbled forward, leaning on his cane as he cleared away from the Immortals and reached the logs.

"No," I said, finally responding to Fulcaris. "The Persians mean to bring the fight today."

Even from that distance, I could make out the scarred eye and distorted features of Hakhamanish. The magus halted before the logs, leaning heavily on his cane as he bowed his head for a time. Then, Hakhamanish discarded his cane to the earth, throwing a powder in the air that engulfed his face. He yelled in an indiscernible tongue, his clenched hands beckoning toward the heavens as his face purpled. Bending over, Hakhamanish placed his hands upon the logs, and soon after, a roaring fire sprouted that called upon the favor of Persia's god, the Ahura Mazda. The Persian ranks cheered wildly at this display, and Hakhamanish gathered up his cane and brought it level with Dara's eastern gate.

Rome's own ranks began their war chants, banging spears against shields in an attempt to deafen the Persian rumbling. A cataphract emerged from the Roman reserve and galloped along the staggered Roman lines, raising his spear to tap the weapons of each of the men that he crossed. As he drew closer, I made out the white plume of Belisarius, calling on his men to fight as brothers against their hated enemy.

Another horn rang out from the Persian lines, its harsher notes interspersed with brief pauses as Perozes, atop his elephant, communicated with his army. From between the cavalry lines, men walked forward and formed two long lines before the Persian center.

"Archers," I grunted to Fulcaris.

Carrying two flags at the heart of their lines, the archers marched forward, unslinging their bows as they took a slow pace in the direction of Belisarius' army. The Persian flags dipped forward menacingly toward their enemies, urging the men farther out into the battlefield.

In response, Belisarius' horn blew its own commands, prompting the flags lining Dara's walls to signal in response. Ascum's black bear fluttered in the heavy winds atop the city walls as he moved his own archers and skirmishers between gaps of the rearward trenches and forward to meet the Persian lines. A second flag waved above Dara's walls, a white cloth with a yellow crowned bird that was carried by Sunicas.

As Ascum led his foot archers forward, a detachment of Huns fell back behind Belisarius' reserves and snaked along the city walls. Most of their movements were hidden by the mass of Romans and sloping hills that stood as bulwarks between the Hunnic riders and Perozes' army, and once beyond our hill, the Huns curled and formed up near the Herulian foederati.

Sunicas and Samur dismounted and crept toward my position. Their furs dragged across the ground, gathering a layer of dirt that would have made most Roman officers irate, but Sunicas seemed to not care, and Samur diligently followed his commander's lead.

"Thought you could use some help," Sunicas said as he reached me. "Belisarius wanted to double the ambush, and my brother has the rest of the Huns toward the Roman right."

I greeted them both in hushed tones, and the three of us, along with Fulcaris, watched as the orderly Persian and Roman lines continued to close the gap between their forces. The wind was blowing hard at Ascum's back, and slightly more than one hundred paces distant, the Persian lines halted with a horn blast. Ascum, too, commanded his own men to stop. Ascum's men were more heavily armored than Perozes' skirmishers, and they duly slammed the rims of their wooden shields into the ground, where they stood upright without any support. I recognized them for the tall, modified shields that Baduarius and Dagisthaeus had prepared for our battle against the Avars, with iron spikes digging into the soil and holding the shield upright.

"So many of them," Samur said, his eyes scanning the hundreds of Persian archers that formed into long skirmish lines. His simple observation made real to me the depth of the threat we faced.

"Jesus Christ," I muttered. "Mariya, forgive me for what we must do."

Sunicas smirked. "Ascum knows what he's doing here. This won't be where the army runs into trouble."

"Oh? And where will that be?" I asked.

Sunicas turned to offer me a wicked grin. "When Perozes sends thousands of men down against our left, and we're all that's available to stop them."

At the center of the Roman lines, Ascum wasted little time in engaging the enemy, thus beginning the second day of the Battle of Dara. With the Persian commander still barking orders to his men and using a long spear to straighten his lines, Ascum bellowed a command to attack, and a disciplined volley of bolts hailed down upon the massed Persian skirmishers.

Many arrows sailed overhead, although more than a few connected against the bodies of the lightly armored Persian archers. Pinned with arrow shafts, dozens of Persian bodies fell forward from their orderly lines, while others recoiled in pain and shock as sharpened iron tips dug through boiled leather and into ribs, arms, and eyes. The Persians responded with their own volley, their huge war bows curling backward before loosing their own bolts onto Ascum's men.

That single Persian volley sailed high into the air, yet quickly lost speed as the westerly wind seemed to catch most arrows mid-flight. Most fell to the ground twenty paces from the Roman archers; others collided harmlessly with the line of shields dug into the soil. A handful reached Roman soldiers, and I did see one man scream as he tugged hopelessly at a wooden shaft buried at the junction of neck and shoulder.

Ascum spurred his men onward to shower volleys at a faster rate, making the release of the fourth Roman volley timed with the landing of the second. The Persian commander threw a thick wicker shield over his head as the Roman barrage hit. He willed his men on to a second and a third volley, yet the intensity of the Persian volleys lessened as their junior officers fell from wounds and the Persians inched back. Preferring the relative safety of their shields, fewer Persian archers continued the volley, making the skirmish a one-sided affair.

After the tenth Roman volley loosed into the air, Perozes' horns called again. Turning back toward the thick lines of the Immortals, another dozen Persians took arrows high in the back, falling into growing pools of blood that swirled dry Mesopotamian dirt into mud. As the last of the Persian archers disappeared into Perozes' ranks, Ascum's men cheered until they, too, were called back behind the core of the Roman spearmen. In a hurry, the Romans jogged away and slid behind Baduarius' lines, leaving behind only a handful of motionless bodies, a stark contrast to the dozens of Persians that twitched and bled in neat rows, their corpses illuminated by the magus' fire burning fiercely behind them.

"Well, at least we won the skirmish," Fulcaris said cheerfully.

"Whatever that means," Samur murmured, his eyes fixed upon Perozes and the other Persian commanders.

Belisarius' men, however, had little time to celebrate their minor victory at the battle's opening: Perozes' horns soon sounded once again. Flags facing the Roman left thumped against the ground and dropped diagonally forward, signaling for the Persian right flank to advance. Yet, where the prior day had been a mad scramble by ragged lines toward the Roman left, the Persian cavalry moved slowly and orderly forward.

Their unity was kept by a thin line of Persian Immortals, their heavy coat of armor marking them as the Persian military elite against a backdrop of leather and mail-clad light horsemen. They rode Niseans similar to my own Ignis, but these mounts were clad in thick armored scales that glittered in what limited sunlight shot between the clouds; the added weight to their charge was intended to shock an enemy into breaking outright.

I beckoned to Fulcaris. "Tell the men to prepare to ride in and wait for further instructions."

"How do you know it is time?" Samur asked.

Sunicas grunted. "John wants the Persians to focus on our right flank, so we need to hit their left hard, with everything we have," he said. "The Herulians will charge first, and I will lead my Huns from a distance closely behind."

Fulcaris and Samur both nodded at the instructions and slid back down the hill. While still slow, the Persian cavalry line rose to a trot. Dozens of banners showed the Derafsh Kaviani leading at least three thousand Persian riders toward that far less numerous Roman left side. Marcellus' excubitores lowered their lances in anticipation of the Persian charge, with Valerian's more lightly armored men filing in close behind.

Fifty paces out, the lead rank of Immortals surged forward at a gallop. Some drew bows and fired at the Roman left, with the force of such efforts blunted by heavy shields and stubborn wind, while others urged their horses forward in a maniacal jump over the Roman trench, leaving several of those men and horses impaled on wooden trench spikes or stuck through with a Roman lance. Nevertheless, their example spurred on the second and third lines of the lighter Persian cavalry, who dismounted just before the trench and skidded handily between its sharpened stakes.

Marcellus bellowed commands to his men, and hundreds of Romans dismounted to form a shield wall before their trench. Many of the Immortals, now reinforced with swelling ranks behind them, did likewise, and abandoned their horses to throw up a shield wall that bristled with heavy armor and short spears. Marcellus pushed his men forward, with Valerian following, and the Melitene men formed a right flank and rearguard of the Roman left.

The sheer force of the massed Persian lines put unbearable pressure on the Romans. Valerian's shield wall buckled mightily as his men dug in against three to four times their own numbers. It was too much. Slowly, the Romans slid away from sections of the trench, offering small but growing openings for the Persian wall to safely cross to the southern end of the defensive line. Even as our defensive line ruptured, I saw many Persians gutted by masses of Roman spears and lances, with most struggling to raise their shields as they crawled up the narrow trench that rose to most men's chests. One Persian stumbled and dropped his shield, leaving him unable to block the thrust of a spear as its shaft rammed through his exposed mouth and out the back of his helmet. Blood fountained into the air as men exchanged blows, their screams melding into the din of wood, iron, and horses all writhing for what little space could be found on the Persian left.

As Valerian's spearmen drew gradually back in disarray, Marcellus' excubitores kept tight ranks. A half step at a time, they edged back to absorb another blow from the growing Persian wall, though they seemed to remain undaunted at the rising swell of iron-cased men and horses. Persian Immortals swarmed around Marcellus' high plume, weapons blurring as the elite of both nations fought for the honor of their commanders. Twice Marcellus was hit in his armored shoulder, yet the thick excubitor's armor absorbed the worst of each blow and allowed the grizzled commander to return with his own force. Marcellus' shield neighbor drove a spear clean through an armored Immortal, lifting the Persian several handsbreadths into the air before thrusting the screaming body back, temporarily disrupting the Persian shield wall.

As the excubitores were driven back, Belisarius' horn sounded in the distance. Black cloth waved in the air as the ouroboros danced against the winds, joined quickly by Sunicas' Hunnic sigil.

"It's time," Sunicas said, rising to his feet and running back toward our joint foederati. Readjusting my helmet, I followed closely behind, half running as Belisarius' horn blew more urgently.

The foederati had already mounted, and their eyes were wide as the Roman horn carried into their shallow valley. Perenus ordered our banners raised and the Herulians to form into columns, then nodded to me as I leaped atop Ignis to face my men.

"We've got one chance to win this fight," I yelled, "and it's right now! I'm going over that hill to kill some of these damned Persians, and I'll remember every man who joins me."

351

A great cry rang out from the Herulian ranks. The Huns echoed our calls, stringing their bows and reading for our next attack. Sunicas raised a fist, signaling his readiness, and I closed in alongside Perenus and Sembrouthes.

With my own bow ready, I raised an armored fist in the air and dropped it violently forward.

"Advance!" Perenus cried.

"Move! Forward!" Opilio shouted, his cry taken up by my collection of dekarchoi.

Our horses jerked forward, and we quickly grew to a canter as our mounts ascended Dara's highest hill. Battle noise flooded over our ranks as we crested the hill five hundred paces from the Persian attack and Marcellus' hard but flagging ranks.

"Steady!" I called, echoed by Perenus and the other officers. The Herulians kept a tight formation, closing our gap to three hundred paces as the Persians slowly realized the incoming ambush along their exposed flank.

At two hundred paces, our horses slowed ever so slightly. "Nock and draw!" I yelled, with Perenus and the other centurions echoing the command.

Our canter surged forward. At around a hundred and fifty paces, I raised my bow in the air. I counted out a few heartbeats, drawing on all that I learned from Perenus, all the training I'd worked into the fibers of my body, and released my arrow.

"Loose!" I yelled.

The Herulians obeyed, firing forth their own rain of death.

Though we were a ways distant, our arrows connected with the outermost Persian ranks. Our horses slowed to a trot as I ordered another volley, which grew thicker from another wave of arrows that sailed high overhead. Sunicas' Huns shot at an impossibly long distance for horse riders, yet their arrows sailed high as they were carried by the westerly wind, finding their marks with an equal measure to my own Herulians. Now fully aware of the incoming attack, the Persians formed another shield wall to face our ambush. Persian officers, still mounted in the rearward ranks of their wall, barked instructions across their lines, and a bristling wave of Persian spears jutted and flew in our direction.

With the Huns now in their effective range, I ordered my foederati to dismount and form our own wall to rival the Persians. Herulians and Aksumites slipped to the ground, depositing bows and withdrawing their spears and shields for the inevitable wall to come. A small detachment of ten riders rounded our mounts and led them safely away from the fight, keeping them nearby in the event that the foederati needed to retreat and regroup for further orders.

Herulian shields slapped together in a show of cohesion, with my dekarchoi inspecting the wall for any gaps and centurions yelling orders for the line formation. Sembrouthes muscled his way to my right flank, his dark-yellow shield guarding my exposed right arm. Opilio's detachment formed along my left, with Fulcaris taking his place next to me at the front of our shield wall. Other Aksumites formed in the second rank behind Sembrouthes and me, their long, serrated spears and flowing yellow robes marking them as unique from my Herulians.

Our line secure, we edged forward, kicking plumes of dust into the air. Hunnic arrows sailed overhead as we made slow progress, closing in to forty paces from the Persian lines. Several of the lighter armored foe threw their own spears at our ranks, which clattered against a thick line of shields and fell harmlessly to the ground. A narrow line of Immortals formed the Persian front, staring down their latest attacker through the dark, bloodstained eyeholes of their helmets.

At twenty paces out, the rearward ranks of the Persian line began to fall back in good order — their officers were ordering them to regroup away from the joint attack of the foederati and the excubitores. Lest we be outflanked, I drew our forces to a pause, allowing Sunicas to order forth another barrage of arrows that easily found targets in close range. While the front rank of the Persians continued to engage Marcellus and Valerian, over half of the Persian forces moved away from the Roman trenches, their banners flying rearward to safety. Indeed, they had nearly reached it—until hellfire rained down.

"Cover!" I called, seeing flaming stones and great bolts flying from the corner of my eye.

The Herulians obeyed. In the interior lines, each spearman threw his shield above the heads of his neighbors, waiting for the imminent pummeling attack. It was not long in coming; the ground rumbled and shook under our feet as huge objects collided with the ground. Through the thin gaps of the shield wall, I peered out at sheer carnage as it tore through the rearmost ranks of the Persian lines. I witnessed two Persians nailed together with a single bolt the size of a small tree: one killed immediately, the other crying in desperation, unable to pull his gore-spattered body from the wood buried into his guts.

"What is happening?" Fulcaris cried.

"We should fall back," Sembrouthes barked, his shield sliding to cover my body.

Glancing back toward Dara, I shook my head. "Liberius is keeping the Persians penned in. This is our chance to annihilate their flank," I yelled over the din of screams as men and horses alike were torn apart by ballistae and onagers. Not every bolt hit its mark, either; I saw at least one stone fall into Valerian's front lines and blast a Roman spearman's torso from his legs in a mist of blood and viscera.

"Fresh hell," Alaric gawked.

"Be thankful it's targeted at the Persians, and not you," I snapped. "Concentrate!"

I took a deep breath and shouted an order that I prayed would not doom my men to a death of writhing agony. "In lines!" I shouted. "Forward, into their wall!"

Perenus repeated my commands, and the Herulians reluctantly dismantled their protective shell. The shower of flaming stones and ballista bolts let up somewhat, but not enough to allow the Persians an orderly escape from the maw of Rome's attack. Instead, the Persian officers ordered their men to return to the fight against Marcellus, presumably hoping to cleave Belisarius' forward-left flank and fight into safety.

Our lines connected with a half-formed Persian wall that had been disrupted by Liberius' sudden and ongoing assault from Dara's walls. An Immortal, eyeing my plume, pushed hard into my shield, attempting to drive me to my feet and leave my foederati leaderless. But Sembrouthes cut forward in the same breath, viciously thrusting his spear through the iron scales on the Immortal's stomach. The Persian hit his knees, a wet red gash streaming his lifeblood as he howled in agony.

A hole appeared to be forming in the Persian lines. Acting quickly, I jabbed my spear at the Immortal's neighbor and cut through his exposed calf, tearing at the wiry leg muscles. Blood spilled down the man's boot, and he crumpled to the ground, his cries cut short with a swift stroke from Fulcaris to my left.

Onward, forward, was our only option. The Persians may have outnumbered us, but their shield wall lacked the force and pressure that would allow them to stand firm in the face of an advancing enemy. My Herulians pushed forward into the Persian second rank and well into the Persian rearguard, where there were fewer, if any, Immortals. The nearby excubitores, too, surged against the buckling Persian lines.

Our forward force appeared to be working. A rearward detachment of Persians remounted their horses and galloped away from the field, leaving their comrades to fight against the swords, spears, bows, and siege weapons of Belisarius and Liberius' ambush. Our press drove the Persians into the spiked trenches that now swelled with the bodies of the dead and dying. As we pushed inward, relentless, their resistance stiffened, and they reached the outer terminus of Marcellus' trenches only for men and horses to stumble over ragged limbs and wet entrails.

All the while, arrows fell overhead. I shuddered as one sailed just over my helmet and jammed into the neck of the Aksumite behind me, the pressure from his shield at my back slipping away as he, and countless others, called out in fear and pain. But I could not let up; my own shield was locked against a squat Persian who was himself distracted by the indiscriminate arrow fire falling on our dueling lines.

"Shields up!" Opilio yelled, seeing his commanders unable to shout in the intense press of the shield wall. The Herulian ouroboros and the yellow Aksumite shields formed a loose shell as another volley struck, the iron tips of the arrow shafts digging into the wooden panels that protected us. Sembrouthes slashed his spear forward at a Persian of the second rank who swung a curved blade at my head, the twisted edge of the Aksumite's spear getting caught in the crude iron strips that lined the Persian's neck. Sembrouthes drew his sword and growled, stabbing forward to create space between us and our enemies.

"Who is Perozes firing at?" Fulcaris yelled, swearing. "Us or the Persian spearmen?"

"I don't think he cares," I managed to call back, "as long as the arrows find Roman targets." I could speak no more, for my brief reprieve ended when another Persian slammed into my shield.

We pushed farther into the trench, our boots sloshing through thick blood and severed limbs that rose mid-calf. Foul scents invaded my nose and mouth as we trod forward, finding several men with exposed bowels lying half submerged in the foul stench of death.

Even now, poems and songs tell only of the glory of battle, of the beauty in fighting and dying for one's country. If there was beauty in that mess of blood and dung, I did not see it. And yet, I will tell you: in those few short moments of blood madness when a man seeks to topple his enemy, when no pain can slow him nor any obstacle stop him dead, there is a kind of bliss.

Resistance against our assault crumbled as Hunnic arrows flew against the undiscerning Persian volley. Thin lines of Immortals bolstered our enemy's resistance, battering at our shields with snakelike reflexes that nearly made the foederati balk. I would not have it; I bellowed for my men to push onward. As the last large detachment of Persians escaped eastward to the safety of Perozes' immense army, my lines curled around those unlucky to be trapped on three sides. I slammed my spear into an exposed shoulder of one Immortal who stood half a head taller than me, the shaft snapping close to its iron head as the man roared and jerked away. Fulcaris impaled the Immortal on his own spear, ending the man's fading strength with a swift thrust through the weaker iron scales at his neck.

Their lines all but failed, but no Immortal offered their peaceable surrender. Even those who were grievously wounded still brandished spears or swords with a feeble hand, slashing aimlessly at approaching Romans, who dutifully crushed them. As I cut down upon these last entrenched Persians, I grimaced, yet I felt no reluctance as I dispatched fallen men to whatever afterlife they believed in. If they would not surrender, then it was our duty to fight them to the last.

As we hacked our way forward, my section of the foederati came face-to-face with what appeared to be some sort of senior Immortal officer, his cloak and clothing heavy with colorful embroidery and his scales run through with golden thread now cut in half a dozen places by Roman blows. I slammed my shield against him, and though I could only glimpse my enemy, I saw that he had once been a man of strength and athleticism. Inside his armor, his beard was speckled with the gray of a man grown exhausted from constant fighting on endless bloody fronts. He slashed with a thin blade that I caught plumb with my shield. Then, with my own sword, I hacked at his arm, severing it just below his elbow. He recoiled in shock, and the brief drop in his guard allowed me to lunge forward and dig the sharpened tip of my blade into his chest. He jerked once, then slumped forward, dead before hitting the ground.

We pushed forward a few more paces but soon ran into our allies in Marcellus' and Valerian's ranks. I yelled for Perenus to take command of the foederati and inspect for any signs of life amongst the Immortal ranks and wove through the excubitores to find Marcellus. Rome's elite guard held gaunt expressions, all of which were caked in blood and bearing cuts and wounds of their own. One excubitor stood upright and saluted as I passed, an arrow shaft sticking out of his shoulder. Amongst the excubitores was Valerian, panting and sweating as he held an arm over a spear gash in his hip. The bodies of at least a dozen excubitores surrounded the young Roman centurion, who hung his head and sobbed as one of the excubitores placed a hand over Valerian's helmeted head.

I found Marcellus at the center of the remaining excubitores, his helmet off. He winced as he placed weight upon his shield leg. Marcellus' armor had been dented in several places, and the splinters that were once his shield bore witness to the hundreds of Persian slashes that could not take him down. Marcellus nodded to me as I approached and removed my own helmet to greet the man.

"For a moment there, I didn't think you were coming," he said, extending an arm in friendship.

"Belisarius' horn came later than anticipated," I said, panting, "and I didn't know what to make of Liberius' assault."

"Like an apocalypse, that was," Marcellus said. "Got the Persians to shit their collective trousers."

Now, the stories of Dara tend to speak in hyperbole, with the feats of leaders and tragedies of slain heroes growing more pronounced with each telling. No description I have heard has ever been so apt as Marcellus' words. The fiery thunder of the projectiles launched from the walls of Dara, sending great stones and heavy bolts eastward and blocking the Persians, was visceral, nearly savage. Even at the end of that engagement, several stones from the onagers remained alight, burning several Persian corpses and mixing the scent of charred offal into the usual stink of a shield wall's aftermath. Multiple bodies still impaled upon ballista bolts slowly slid down the shafts, hanging limply as they descended toward the earth.

Persian horns rang out angrily—Perozes signaling his next maneuvers. However, where only several thousand lesser-experienced Persians tested the Roman left, the huge mass of Perozes' army surged toward the Roman right and away from the murderous assault of the Roman siege weapons. In the scrum, mounted Immortals massed alongside a thick wave of dark Hephthalites against the Roman right, while well over ten thousand Persian spearmen marched toward Baduarius and the Roman center. Only a small continent of spent Persians from the previous attack formed Perozes' reserve guard, leaving the commander to commit the full might of his army to sweep Belisarius away from Dara.

Sunicas galloped toward my position and saluted Marcellus, grinning as he surveyed his artistry and remarking with pleasure upon the lack of casualties amongst his riders. Samur followed closely behind, acknowledging his friends in the Herulian ranks.

"Any idea what's next for us?" I asked Marcellus.

He shrugged. "I doubt we're moving. My men are spent, and Belisarius needs us to hold this position always. You and Sunicas probably won't sit idly for long, though." Marcellus then called for horses to be brought to the men, and I ordered the same, preparing my men for the inevitable shift that Belisarius must already be calculating into his new order of battle.

Perozes' lines formed and pressed forward, kicking up clouds of dust that enveloped Dara's eastern horizon. Anticipating our next move, I signaled for Perenus and Sembrouthes, who trotted to my position carefully to avoid tripping over the chaotic spread of corpses.

I signaled Perenus. "What is our status? Are the men ready for another engagement?"

"I think so," Perenus replied. "We have five dead, with another half dozen too wounded to move. Several of the men are bruised but should be fine."

"One of my men was killed," Sembrouthes added, "but the rest are fit to fight again."

"And the officers?" I asked.

"All accounted for, although one dekarchos was speared in the thigh and shouldn't move," Perenus said.

Next to the excubitores, my foederati seemed fresh and hale, even after accounting for the wounded and the various signs of struggle from broken spears and battered shields. Fulcaris looked particularly confident as he scanned our ranks, while Irilar and Alaric stared impassively at the wave of Persians that flooded toward the Roman center and right flank. Several Herulians used the respite to steal gulps of water, with a rare few sneaking wine, which dulled the senses yet could still invest a man with bravery in the face of a frothing enemy.

Horns blared from Belisarius' reserve, while flags flew atop Dara to signal the general's commands to his wide-strewn forces.

"Time to go," said Sunicas. Waving for Samur to follow, he vaulted atop his pony and galloped away, his forces forming a herd behind him as he moved toward Belisarius and his brother Simmas, who kept the other half of the Hunnic foederati waiting for orders.

As the last of the Huns departed the Roman left flank, the Persian infantry closed into the mass of spearmen at the Roman center. An incoming charge of Hephthalites and Immortals thwarted the forward-right flank—the cataphracts under Bessas and John—keeping them from encircling the advancing Persian infantry, bearing down with a measure of zeal that they seemed to be competing to be first to slaughter their hated Roman adversary. As with Marcellus' and Valerian's lines, a row of spiked trenches slowed the approach of both horseman and spearman somewhat, but the sheer numbers of the Persian assault drove attackers forward, smashing into Romans regardless.

In the Roman center, we saw the Thracians under Germanus and the Cappadocians under Baduarius reel in shock, desperately keeping the Persians from crossing the spiked trench line and preserving what limited means of defense was available to Belisarius' infantry. Several Roman efforts to surge forward were mildly successful, although weak points across the shield wall threatened to drive a wedge into sections of the army and tear Belisarius' forces in half.

With the danger of encirclement growing, horns rose again across Dara's walls. Heads turned as we sought our orders, which were conveyed as my banners were crossed with those of Germanus and Baduarius.

"To the infantry," I commanded, ordering Perenus to gather the Herulians for another assault. "Come, Herulians! There's killing to be done!"

"Good fortune, komes," Marcellus said.

He saluted our forces as we massed, and the other elite Roman warriors followed his example. I returned his recognition and kicked at Ignis' flanks, sending my stallion jerking into a run as my Herulians screamed behind me. As we galloped, wind whipped through the openings of my helmet, a mercifully cool breeze that blew away the pooling sweat along my eyebrows and forehead and deafened me to the sounds of the foederati behind me. Stealing a glance at the rearward ranks, I found Sembrouthes kicking his own horse forward, holding a spear reclaimed from a dead Persian. Behind him galloped the Aksumites and Herulians, all fighting for position as we moved swiftly to the rescue of Rome's massed spearmen.

Rather than attacking the Persians head on, we roped around toward the rear of the Thracians. I had hoped to see Belisarius before engaging further, yet as we moved toward the general's position, we found the reserve Roman cavalry galloping toward the Roman right. Both detachments of Hunnic foederati screened the slower cataphracts with volleys of arrows against stray detachments of those more reckless Persians who sought the glory of slaying a Roman commander in the heat of battle.

Ahead, toward the eight lines of Thracian spearmen, Germanus trotted the length of his forces, ignoring the danger that a senior Roman commander held by remaining mounted a mere thirty paces from the front lines. Yelling commands to officers that were carried to Baduarius, or well beyond, he caught my approach and hailed my arrival.

"We were beckoned. What's the problem here?" I yelled, forcing my voice to carry over the deafening clamor of shields and blades of thousands a mere spear's throw away.

"Bastards are trying to push me away from Baduarius!" Germanus bellowed. "Mundus is holding the far left without much trouble, but Troglita is in trouble where my forces connect with Baduarius."

I nodded vigorously. "I can help with that. Any other problems?"

Germanus cuffed away the line of sweat where his helmet pressed against his forehead. "Solomon's lines are continuously giving way," he said. "Not that I can blame them, given the pressure they're under. But Solomon is with the physicians in Dara, while Centurion Marcian has been unable to hold the lines in his absence."

"They won't break, I'll see to it," I yelled back.

Germanus bobbed his head in assent.

"We can't flank them, and we can't kill them all, so the best I can do is hold the Persians back until Belisarius does something," he said. "If he can't turn the flank, then we'll all be dead men before the noonday sun."

I narrowed my eyes but said nothing to castigate Germanus, who was rarely a defeatist despite the tone of his words. As I turned toward the lines of Roman spears, I began to see what Germanus had described, for there seemed no end to the Persians that drove small wedges at various sections of the Roman lines. Various centurions and dekarchos cycled tired and injured spearmen from the front lines with fresher men from the reserves, which, though effective, was only a stopgap solution, as the Persians outnumbered Belisarius' infantry by at least three to one.

Unable to hear any orders, Perenus motioned his horse close and leaned toward me.

"Stay mounted for now," I yelled, "and loose controlled volleys above weak points in our lines."

"Who is worse off? Any about to break?" Perenus called back, nearly screaming.

"Troglita. Toward the right section of Thracians," I began, "and Marcian, of Solomon's banda."

"Fuck them," Perenus said, his words surprisingly clear. "Let them burn."

I shook my head. "No. It's not the men's fault that their commander is an arse. And if Marcian breaks, the Thracian army breaks. Do not let that happen."

Perenus saluted, his face grim. "I won't," he promised, and turned to collect his men for their next maneuver.

Taking half of the Herulian foederati, I signaled the men into a long line fifty paces from the Persian front. Few could hear orders clearly, and I used slow movements atop Ignis to show what I wished to occur next. I drew my bow, plucked an arrow from my quiver and nocked it, and pulled the string back to my ear. The arrow shot forward, driving its iron head through the helmet of a Persian threatening Troglita's position. He stayed upright, the feathered shaft jutting into the air, and for a moment I thought the arrow had been absorbed by the thick armor over the man's skull. With a temporary lapse of pressure from the shield wall, his body crumpled to the ground.

Opilio and my other centurions signaled to follow my example, producing a thin volley of arrows that found targets along a shallow Persian wedge near Troglita. Our first volley was swift and deadly, significantly stunting the Persian advance. Seeing a chance to give his lines a much-needed moment to recover, Troglita turned his head and briefly raised his sword in the air, saluting the Herulians who helped prevent disaster.

Our second volley was weaker. Rearward ranks in the mass of Persian spearmen lifted their shields overhead, causing most of the foederati's arrows to glance across the upturned wicker and fall harmlessly to the ground. Worse still, the remnants of Perozes' archers fired their own volley, and my men jostled for cover as the arrows arced over the shield wall, bearing down right on us.

I, too, needed cover. As I struggled in the saddle to unstrap the shield at my back, my ears filled with the grating sound of grinding metal, and I felt an arrow scrape across my helmet. Another arrow struck Ignis near his haunch, and though it was safely deflected by the hardy cataphract's armor covering much of his body, he reared in fear at the sudden thud, and it took several heartbeats before I was able to calm him and better protect both of us with my shield.

"Injured?" Sembrouthes called, trotting closer.

"No, just scratched armor," I yelled in return.

But as I looked down the line, others of the foederati began to fall from arrows and spears that flew toward our ranks. While our standing gave us an easy view and target of the Persian lines, that advantage was also shared by the Persians. Several spears flew in my direction, and I was able to move out of the way of one while catching another with my shield. Fulcaris and Alaric yelled at their men to continue firing yet looked to me with concern.

"Foederati, dismount and form up!" I called, and was eagerly obeyed. Again, a small number of men guided our horses safely from the battle, while my banner carrier held the ouroboros high to communicate my position to Belisarius' other officers at their own scattered positions along Dara's plains.

Perenus copied our movements and sent Irilar to request further orders. As I watched the Roman lines begin to strain backward again as Persians surged over the staked trenches, I devised my plan.

"Tell Perenus to take his men and back Mundus on the left," I barked. "I'll keep my contingent here, between Marcian and Troglita."

Irilar repeated the orders back to me, diligent in hearing me correctly over the booming noise, and I sent him back to grant Perenus his own semi-independent command. As the ranking centurion of my half of the Herulian foederati, Opilio had already formed the Herulians into lines, leaving space for the Aksumites in the center. I took my place once again beside Sembrouthes and Fulcaris and scanned for our next target.

Germanus' Thracian lines were battered by the ceaseless Persian onslaught. While a few dismounted Immortals led the Persian assault against our Thracians, that assault was comprised mostly of lightly armored and lesser-trained spearmen of the Persian Empire's poorest classes. Thickly bearded and with skin tanned from constant exposure to sunlight, they lacked neither courage nor a willingness to kill, yet their shoddy iron and torn leather afforded our heavily armored Thracian lines some advantage in the melee. However, by the time we dismounted, the sheer weight and momentum of thousands of Persians had almost annihilated the first and second Roman lines.

Of this, the Thracians were the least seasoned of Belisarius' men, having been largely recruited in the preceding autumn and winter to replace our thousands of losses in the defense of Tauris. Troglita's position somewhat improved due to our initial volleys, although Marcian's banda had been reduced to a mere four lines of healthy spearmen. Looking right, I judged Baduarius' and Ascum's positions as relatively safe, with the Cappadocians holding firm against their trenches. Thus, my decision was made—we would rescue soldiers in Solomon's retinue.

I motioned my arm toward Marcian's thinning lines, prompting Opilio to yell for our detachment to push forward. Within moments, our lines bolstered those left by Solomon, with battered and blood-soaked officers in their rearward lines giving a light cheer at their improved fortunes.

Marcian, however, did not share in their momentary joy. Pulling back from the shield wall, Marcian stomped in my direction, his mail armor covered in gore and his helmet showing a heavy rent in its left cheekpiece. A vein pulsed in his neck as he gritted his teeth at our arrival.

"I won't have a bunch of unwashed barbarians stabbing us in the back!" he yelled. "Take your men from my command, or I will have my men string you up like you deserve."

Sembrouthes growled, and two of Marcian's men to rush to their commander's defense, albeit with hesitant looks in their faces.

"We don't have time for this!" I all but screamed. "As a komes and a liaison of the Empress, I outrank you. Place your weapons against our enemy and accept my help or be the cause that this army falls this day."

366

Marcian scanned my men and judged his own, the noise of the shield wall perilously close to our position.

"Fine," Marcian said, "but if any of your precious foederati run, I'll butcher them myself."

But another surge from the Persians drove Marcian's lines back, effectively ending his resistance. Marcian returned to his lines and pushed forward with his shield, while I ordered the foederati to lock their own wall and slide into the rearward Roman lines.

We arrived in formation as a Persian wedge drove deep into Marcian's remaining forces, reaching the third line as several Roman spearmen were gutted with short spears. The Persian advance was momentarily slowed as two men tripped over a fallen Roman body, giving Marcian's centurions a quick moment to shift their lines.

"To the front!" I called, and our wall slid between Marcian's ranks. The remnants of the forward wall fell behind as we reached the front, our blackened shields locking as each Herulian arrived in that maw of battle.

Where the battle with Marcellus and Valerian seemed apocalyptic, the view of Belisarius' center trenches was a vision of Hell itself. Hundreds of men moaned and twisted on the ground, crying out in a dozen tongues for their mothers. One Persian wept as he held a hand over a gaping wound, his bowels slipping through his grimy fingers as he begged to be saved from death.

I could only oblige. I shot my spear forward, and its tip cleanly severed the man's spine, killing him instantly.

We were hit almost immediately by a fresh contingent of Persians armored in little more than leather tunics, their swords made of a poor steel that could nevertheless hack off an arm or a head with enough force. Spurred onward by a more luxuriously attired officer, three Persians rushed at me. One threw a spear that was easily deflected, while another crashed into my shield in hopes of toppling me over. Sembrouthes quickly dispatched the spear thrower, while I gutted two others with rapid strokes that cut through the leather lining of their stomachs as if it were the softest cheese.

More Persians filled their places, but I used the opportunity to push forward. My incoming adversary slipped on the sheet of viscera that caked the ground, stumbling just long enough for Fulcaris to drive his spear into his exposed neck. The Herulian wall moved slowly forward, and we arrived at the edge of the trench only after dozens of Persian dead were added to the floor of bodies; with each step, I fought to place the sight far out of my mind.

Though the trench here was dug into a greater depth than on the forward flanks, most of its stakes were shattered or had fallen over from constant disruption by the living and the dead alike. The officer of the wall opposite our own yelled his men onward, forcing them to trudge through a sludge of bloody remains that were knee-high and only rising as more bodies filled the trench gap. A thin volley of arrows sailed from behind our position and took several Persians high in the chest, and I turned briefly to find a detachment of Ascum's archers lining the rear of Marcian's position.

I halted the Herulian wall at the lip of the trench, stabbing slightly downward as the Persian wall continued their assault. Arrows continued to fall from the sky, yet rearward Persians again lifted their shields and prevented easy kills by Ascum's men. However, between the horrific conditions of the trench and the arrow fire, it seemed for a moment as if we had stalled the Persian advance into Marcian's position.

The Persian lines parted as the foederati grew confident in their position, allowing a detachment of cavalry to approach close to our trench. Each rider threw a javelin toward my lines before I could command my men to cover. I lifted my shield to protect my head, aided by Sembrouthes, who continually pressed his shield over my exposed right side.

Checking for losses, I thought the rush ineffective, until word came from several paces down the line.

"Centurion down!" Herulian voices called out.

"Who?" I shouted back. My mind raced, praying it was not Perenus.

"Opilio," the voices answered. I nodded, feeling both a shameful relief and a thorough chill at the news.

"Carry him from the shield wall," I yelled back, and several in my ranks departed from their vigil at the front to treat the centurion's injuries.

As the Persian wall closed back up, more heavily armored soldiers formed the first two lines of their wall. Where most of our enemy seemed more members of a levy or upjumped peasantry, these men bore status as professional warriors more befitting the cavalry of Kavadh's elite Zhayedan.

"Immortals!" I yelled. "Be on guard!"

At that, my lines seemed to tense, Sembrouthes and the Aksumites most of all. Sembrouthes snarled as the Immortals formed their wall and began their push forward.

"Hit their legs, knees, or armpits!" Sembrouthes called out. "The Immortals are mainly cavalry, and these are the weaknesses in their armor."

I nodded and commanded the word be spread across the lines. The Immortals wasted little time rushing our formation, closing the distance with disciplined speed. Several Immortals wavered on unsure footing as they entered the trench, yet they moved carefully as they fought to keep their shields even and eliminate any easy targets for the foederati to exploit.

Unhesitating, the Persians charged uphill, scaled the trench wall, and clashed into our own shields with a vicious crack. Wood and metal rang out once more down the lines as we Romans fought desperately to hold our advantage along the incline, spitting and slashing at our thickly armored enemies. An Immortal across from

369

me tried to stab from underneath my shield and sever the tendons along my ankles, yet Fulcaris darted forward and thrust his spear to the earth, pinning the Immortal to the ground. Fulcaris likely saved me from a grievous injury but opened himself up to one of his own.

The Immortal across from Fulcaris jabbed his spear forward, pushing the young Herulian's shield aside and exposing his chest. Before I could react, the Immortal dropped the spear and stabbed a curved short sword toward Fulcaris' chest. I pushed my shield to throw off the man's aim, but it was not enough; the blade dug deep into Fulcaris' shoulder and sent him sagging to the ground.

"Fulcaris!" I screamed, rushing forward despite Sembrouthes' pleas for me to remain in the safety of the wall. I drove my spear at the attacking Immortal with all the strength remaining to me. It was not much, but the tip dug a handsbreadth deep into the Immortal's shield, weighing him down, and in that split second I drew my heavy Avar axe and chopped at his helmet. The sharpened blade cracked through the steel and into the soft brains beneath.

Sembrouthes slew the pinned Immortal at my feet while I hacked at another struggling to drive a wedge into where Fulcaris had fallen. My axe cut through his shield and into his fingerbones. As he fruitlessly attempted to pull his arm away, I drew my sword and cut at his armpit, slicing through the joint of his armor and into flesh.

As he sank to the ground, I sheathed my sword and collected my axe from the Immortal's shield, then dragged Fulcaris into the third rank, allowing others to take our places.

"Lord, it hurts," he said, holding a gloved hand weakly over the blood that pooled from his shoulder.

"You'll be just fine!" I yelled, and hoped it was the truth. Pointing to one of Fulcaris' men, I ordered him to find two others and carefully take Fulcaris into Dara, then seek out Rosamund to bind his wound.

"Go, quickly!" I ordered, and they obeyed.

Fulcaris disappeared within the press of bodies, and I pushed my way back to Sembrouthes' side as the Persians assembled for another charge. I stole a glance down the foederati's lines, finding the men in varying degrees of condition due to the savagery of the Immortals' assault. My banner remained aloft, and other than Opilio, my officers remained in firm command of the ragged and exhausted lines.

"You all!" I yelled to the more rested lines of Solomon's banda. "Rotate out!"

With the command given, I tried to move back but collided with one of the Aksumites, who also was unable to move to the rear of the Roman position. Cocking my head for a view of our reserve ranks, I found Solomon's banda still and unmoving, blocking our passage.

With the Persians charging in, I ordered my men to reform lines and moved to our third rank to face Solomon's officers. Snarling at their stupidity, I demanded the reason for their treachery and was met with only reluctant faces that avoided my gaze.

"Apologies, Lord, but Centurion Marcian ordered that we not allow any further changes to the lines," the dekarchos said. "For our safety."

"Marcian?" I cried, furious. "Bring that horse's cock to me, now!" The man politely saluted, and Marcian arrived soon thereafter, a confident smirk on his face as he approached me.

"Rotate our ranks, now," I growled. "That is an order, centurion."

Marcian spat. "I take orders from Solomon or Germanus, not you," he replied, "and I've decided that I can't trust you at my

371

back. I'll let your wounded through, but your job is to fight off the Persians and give my men the rest they deserve."

I surged forward, blocked by two Romans who held me back. "I will see you dead for this, Marcian. Even if the Persians spear me down, I will make sure that someone is left to slide a knife between your ribs."

"And this is why you're staying where I can see you," he scowled in return.

Drawing my sword, I turned back to the battle, finding my men embattled in another wall along our trench lines. I shoved forward to Sembrouthes, where I drove my shield into the nearest Persian, knocking him off balance enough for me to thrust into his exposed knee. Tendons snapped, and he fell, leaving an awkward gap in the Persian lines.

"No way out?" Sembrouthes asked.

"Not right now," I said. "Pass a message to our right. Tell Troglita that Varus' foederati will need reinforcement soon."

Sembrouthes did as he was told, sending my message down the lines. Except not quickly enough, for a massive wedge of Persians formed and began to push forward. To my left, several of the Herulians gasped for air, eyes wide as they stared at death that came tirelessly for them.

"Steady, Herulians! Shields high and tight!" I yelled, breaking many from their trance and fatigue. Still the Persians came, and no amount of words could will a battered collection of warriors to face a foe of this kind. Twenty paces out, fresh Persians lowered their spears and moved forward.

As they pushed into the trench, however, the ground thundered once more. Massive bolts cut through the Persian ranks, impaling several of the tightly packed Persians in a single blow and dashed their wall to pieces.

Turning back, I found an elderly figure directing a small number of Roman ballistae against the Persian lines. While most of our siege equipment lay facing the Roman left flank, the ballistae still packed force against our enemies and were quickly reloaded for another strike.

"Forward!" I yelled, rushing forward for the first time.

My boots kicked aside pieces of bodies and remnants of weapons and shields as I charged at the shattered Persian lines, hoping that my men were close behind. I cut down at a Persian officer who desperately sought to reknit the Persian wall, my sword cutting into the man's windpipe and severing his spine. Blood bubbled through his skin as I dragged my sword free, cutting at other Persians who reeled in fear at the sight of a heavily armored lord possessed by battle lust.

I killed two others before my shield wall reached me, while others rushed toward the easy killing of the confused and frightened Persian lines. Other ballista bolts flew overhead, wreaking further carnage and allowing our ranks to surge deeper into the Persian lines. As I cut at another Persian leader, I saw one of the more poorly armored men swing a mace toward my head, connecting with a section of my helmet just below my ear.

My world went dark. Yet I could feel hands tugging at the collar of my armor, heard a horn blowing somewhere. Still, my vision dimmed to a blur. From that point, I cannot be certain of the passage of time; I can only guess that it was long minutes, at least, before I came to my senses.

"Varus! Can you hear me?" Sembrouthes' accented Greek called out.

It felt like blood had pooled in my eyes, yet somehow, I could make out the dark Aksumite standing over me.

"Yes," I croaked, my ears ringing and seemingly muffled against most sounds. I reached a hand inside my helmet and withdrew a glove wet with blood, looking around in confusion.

"We had to pull back," Sembrouthes explained. "The bastards haven't attacked yet, but they will soon."

I struggled to my feet as Sembrouthes and the Herulians fought to keep me still.

"Pick me up. *Now*," I said, forcing the vigor back into my voice.

"Lord, you need to regroup," Alaric called out. "I will cut through Marcian myself if that's what it takes to get you back to Dara."

I shook my head. "Pick me up. If we don't keep the line intact, it doesn't matter whether I'm in a sickbed or bleeding on the battlefield."

Alaric sighed but helped me rise to my feet. I nodded to the man and ordered him to find a way to get a message to Perenus of our need for reinforcements. Alaric saluted and left, while I hefted my shield and shuddered in pain.

"You are insane," Sembrouthes said, "and not making my oath any easier. Princess Mariya will have me flogged if you leave her a pregnant widow."

"It won't come to that," I said confidently, yet my ringing mind fell upon a vision of Mariya's face. A wave of guilt flooded over me. My child would have a father, I convinced myself, and I would not allow myself to die that day. I had to escape this bloodied plot of hell.

"Form lines!" I yelled, my voice hoarse and uneven.

Shields slapped together once again, many now cut or dented. Off near my banners, I caught Alaric's gaze, and he nodded to me, a sign that Perenus would soon receive my message. The endless wave of Persians came crashing into our ranks once more, and I leaned my bruised and aching shoulder into the shield that had kept me alive thus far.

Despite our exhaustion, the lines held desperately. Ascum's archers began focusing their efforts on our section of the Roman line, offering brief moments of rest as the Persians shielded themselves from the aerial attack. Persian arrows had largely ceased by this point, but whether this was because they ran out of ammunition or because they could no longer cleanly target our forces, I do not know. All that was clear was that for the moment, no break in Germanus' or Baduarius' spears emerged to send Belisarius' army in a disastrous rout.

Another horn blew in the distance, far to my right. The silvery notes of Belisarius' signal sounded with growing urgency, soon echoed by the sentinels atop Dara's vast walls. After dropping another Persian opponent with a sword thrust into the man's bowels, I stole a look back at the city banners, finding mine waving toward the Roman right flank.

"Belisarius needs us to shift," I shouted to Sembrouthes. He speared another Persian in the weakened armor above the knee, then spat.

"Nothing we can do if we're stuck here," he replied. "Any word from Mundus or Troglita?"

"None." Another horn sounded behind our ranks, and I forced it from my mind. I could think only of staying alive, despite cramping legs and a dull pounding in my head and anything else around me.

We held for another half-hearted Persian push, although it seemed that Perozes' spearmen focused their efforts on other sections of the Roman wall. I gathered up a discarded spear from a corpse of an Immortal and inspected its length, satisfied when I found no flaws or breaks in its short wooden shaft.

Another cacophony of Roman horns blew, except this time our vigil along the front lines was disrupted by a rustling at the lines behind us. Slipping into my foederati's rearmost ranks, I turned again to fight with Marcian, yet was met by the steel-clad figure of Marcellus and his remaining healthy excubitores.

"You need to go, Varus! Belisarius needs your horses on the right!" Marcellus yelled, drying blood lining the length of his body.

I looked around, finding Marcian staring toward the battlefield and ignoring my meeting with the excubitor commander. "These lines are too thin," I told him. "I can't leave them in their current condition, and you're supposed to be on our left."

"Leave that to me," Marcellus barked. "The left is stable, and Valerian will hold. I'll make sure Solomon's banda doesn't fall. Go save Belisarius, or we're all lost here."

The excubitores hardly seemed fit for his orders, but none showed the slightest complaint at their leader's pronouncements. I issued a command to Marcellus and whistled for my foederati to shift out of their positions along the shield wall. I passed Marcian as I moved toward the rear, spitting angrily at the officer's feet as I moved along. Marcian made no response, and instead shouted commands for his men to fall in line by the excubitores who took our places at the front lines.

Perenus' forces greeted me as we reemerged in the open Roman rear. I sucked in a lungful of fresh air, a dizzying reprieve from the heat, gore, and constant press of humanity that defined the shield wall. Perenus' men wheeled our horses around and distributed waterskins, which my men guzzled greedily as they waited for their next instructions.

"Mundus sends his thanks," Perenus called out, and I waved at my friend as he approached.

Perenus narrowed his eyes at the gash in my helmet. "Immortal?" he asked.

"Just some lucky peasant with a mace," I replied. "Hurts like hell, but I'll survive."

I possessed little time to take stock of the forces that remained of the Herulian foederati, guessing that Perenus' men had an easier time than my own as they bore fewer signs of pain and battle fatigue. Belisarius' horn blew again, and I snapped to my task at hand.

"Herulians, on me!" I yelled.

The men let up a hoarse cry but did not resist our quick push into a gallop. Germanus saluted as we passed, and we soon scaled past the tightly organized ranks of Baduarius and Ascum as we moved toward the Roman left. What we found made me pull Ignis to a quick halt, and my mouth dropped in horror as I saw our doom.

John and Bessas' right flank fled the battlefield, kicking sand and dust into the air as thousands of Hephthalites trailed at their heels. Instead, Belisarius held the Roman right against a massed detachment of mounted Immortals, with only the Huns and a small detachment of his personal bucellarii, which served as Rome's reserve cataphract cavalry.

Panic flooded me. I began to move toward Belisarius, watching the mass of Immortals strike directly at Belisarius with javelins and maces. When the Immortal cavalry seemed close to colliding with the Roman ranks, Belisarius would draw backward, allowing the Huns under Sunicas and Simmas to shower arrows onto the attacking Persians. My foederati followed as I desperately tried to clear the distance between Belisarius' forces and my own, yet my progress was halted once more by horns that sounded directly from Belisarius' own lines.

Along the rear of Belisarius' cavalry, a black flag rose into the air, its ouroboros unmistakable as my own sigil. It crossed alongside an image of John and Bessas' cavalry, the general's implied message from the flapping banners making little sense given the dire situation that the Roman right found itself in. Perenus and Sembrouthes galloped to my side and also questioned Belisarius' logic as our orders were repeated.

Even so, the message was clear—we were to assist John and Bessas, despite the fact that they were in open retreat as they galloped westward away from the pursuing Hephthalites.

"Belisarius will crack under so many Immortals," Sembrouthes muttered. "What do we do?"

A horn sounded from the Persian lines, a light and angry pitch compared to the low, sweet notes of Belisarius' signal. "We follow orders," I said, resigned to our fate. "Let's engage the Hephthalites."

Sembrouthes spat at the loathed name of the tribesmen and muttered a low prayer in his native tongue. I croaked orders to my men and turned toward the west, squinting in the distance to spy remnants of John and Bessas' cavalry. From the base of Dara's walls to the corner of my vision, all that I could see were the black furs and glyph-strewn banners of the Hephthalites.

Spittle flew from Ignis' mouth as we galloped toward the retreating Roman cataphracts. Persian horns rang out again, yet I resisted the urge to look at the ensuing battle in hopes that the other officers could hold a bit further—for what, I did not know. The Persians to give up? For the sun to set? We had fought throughout the morning and into the sun's zenith, but still Perozes' forces seemed endless in their depth and belief in their cause for the Shahanshah.

However, as we moved about two hundred paces from Belisarius' battle with the Persian Zhayedan, the Hephthalites turned toward our position. I raised a fist in the air, bringing the remnants of my foederati to another halt as my officers formed a semicircle around me. While still distant, the Hephthalites came fast toward us and showed no signs of stopping.

"Bows!" I called out. "Form columns!"

Perenus drew close as the Herulians took to their formation. "Varus, there's too many of them," he said, his voice thick with concern as the massed Hephthalites closed fast upon us.

"We don't have a choice but to try," I called back. "Don't become tangled in an exchange of blows, and keep our men mounted as long as possible."

Perenus saluted and returned to the head of his column, barking orders for the Herulian men to keep their formation tight and aim true. As the Hephthalites came into focus at three hundred paces distant, I made my move.

"To the south!" I cried.

Hundreds of horses kicked behind me as I led my column forward, with Perenus angling to my left and away from the constriction presented by Dara's walls. We rode diagonally toward the Hephthalites and toward open land, with those White Huns quickly coming into range.

At two hundred paces, I gave the order. "Nock and draw!" The Hephthalites were a mass of swirling chaos, following in jagged numbers behind a leader who seemed far larger and more heavily armored than his countrymen.

I aimed my bow toward that man and drew into the outer extent of our effective range. Steady my breathing, I fought to clear my mind of its distractions and focused on the Hephthalite leader's movements as he rose and fell in the saddle.

"Loose!" I commanded.

Both columns released at my signal, their arrows slamming into unarmored horses and fur- and mail-clad riders moving at a full gallop. About half of my men connected with their targets, yet my arrow sailed just over the Hephthalite leader's helmet. As I grew closer to the man, I saw that twin horns protruded from the helmet's crest, with a skull resting between the horns as a macabre protector of the wearer's safety.

A dozen Hephthalites were thrown from their saddles, their bodies trampled by the thundering hooves of ponies that galloped closely behind. Other men remained atop their horse yet slumped in the saddle, arrows protruding from their chests and necks. Several horses collided from the jerk of a half-conscious rider at their reins, instilling further disorder in the Hephthalite charge.

"Loose!" I ordered again, trusting the rhythm of the foederati's drill to continuously nock and draw arrows after the initial volley.

Again, more arrows fell into the Hephthalites, with my foederati scoring more hits as our range diminished. The Hephthalite leader blocked two arrows that sailed toward his body with an oversized shield. Body unharmed, he growled his followers forward.

"Form a wedge!" I yelled. "Spears!"

Now at a fast canter, I quickly holstered my bow in a saddlebag, then unslung my shield and spear. Our two columns formed separate wedges as we cleared more distance to the Hephthalites, coming fifty paces from their own reckless charge. I could now make out our enemy's features, finding them somewhat similar to the Avars in their physique, furs, and cavalry weapons.

At twenty paces, I lowered my spear. Sembrouthes and Alaric, on either side of my wedge point, had lowered theirs. As I bore down upon my enemy, I screamed Mariya's name, praying silently that Ignis would not throw me.

I found my target. My spear ripped through fur and bone as it tore into the Hephthalite rider's chest and out his back, only to shatter as it lifted the man clean from his horse. I dropped the splintered shaft in favor of my axe. Another Hephthalite slashed a crude blade toward Ignis' chest that caught in the thick scales of the cataphract armor, and I chopped my axe in a sweeping arc that severed my attacker's arm just below the shoulder.

The force of our charge drove us deep into the Hephthalite ranks and spurred us onward due to the loose and undisciplined formation that the thousands of riders adopted in their pursuit of Bessas and John. Refusing to stop, I chopped wildly at riders arrayed before me, wounding several and driving more than one to the ground.

Soon enough, however, I was hindered. A Hephthalite rider drove a spear toward my chest, and I swiped my shield a fraction of a second too late to deflect fully. The spear's edge cut into my armor and grazed my ribs, sending stinging pain webbing throughout my body. Gritting my teeth, I snarled and chopped at the man's neck, killing my attacker but unable to wrest the axe free from the gaping wound of his neck.

Our advance slowed to a crawl at that point, a mixture of Persian and Roman horns blaring in the distance. I drew my sword and cut at the uncovered face of another Hephthalite. The blade edge found a naked eye and sent the man screaming to the ground. Sembrouthes speared another man that charged toward me, ordering his Aksumites to prevent any dark rider from hitting our position at a gallop.

Hephthalite riders drew back from our formation, allowing our wedge to continue forward at a slow pace. Several threw javelins as we rode past, and I heard one Herulian scream in pain as a spear connected with his body. Despite it all, we pushed forward until the Hephthalite ranks began to thin, with flat open ground a mere twenty paces away.

Pain racked by body as an iron mace collided with my unshielded shoulder. Gasping, I fought to steady myself atop Ignis. I felt Sembrouthes' hand trying to steady me, but as I dropped my shield low, something slammed into me: a well-placed dart that drove me to the ground.

Dirt and dust choked my throat as I fought for air, a metallic taste filling my mouth. Using my shield, I managed to plant a leg and stand, even as blood poured from multiple gashes and wounds sustained throughout the day. The scales of my armor had prevented the arrowhead from digging further into my body, although the pain burned along my flesh. I screamed as I drew the arrow out of my shoulder and threw the blood-drenched bolt to the ground, thankful at least that the thin iron lacked any barbs to catch upon skin or bone.

Sembrouthes wheeled his horse about, leading the foederati into a tight ring around me as I gathered my senses. My shield arm felt weak, yet I was able to lift the heavy wood with significant effort. Alaric dismounted and inspected my condition as the second Herulian column swarmed around us in a protective circle. One of Alaric's men led Ignis toward where I stood, his eyes wide with concern as he found his komes spitting blood and leaning heavily to one side.

"I'm fine," I grunted. "Help me onto Ignis."

The two men lifted me into the saddle, and I nearly toppled off the other side from the effort. My shield hung low, and my sword felt unnaturally heavy in my hand, yet I sat upright and surveyed our situation.

Perenus had given us a moment of respite, his circle driving the rearward Hephthalites away and allowing our twin columns to reform as a single cohesive mass. Several within my group drew their bows and fired arrows at more courageous enemies, although few challenged us beyond an idle javelin or spear.

Looking to the west, I found another detachment of riders dashing quickly toward our position, yet I could not determine whether these were Roman or more of Perozes' thousands of mounted men. Still drawing ragged breaths, I took stock of the men who still flocked around my lone banner and judged that we lacked the force to pierce through the Hephthalites and break through toward Belisarius on the other side.

Then, their movement stopped. A roar rose through the Hephthalites, and I saw their leader trotting to the front of their massed riders. Against Sembrouthes' urging, I moved Ignis through my men to view the enemy commander, forcing my body to show few signs of pain or weakness as my men looked on.

The Hephthalite commander raised a hand, silencing his ranks. He lifted the horned helmet from atop his head, revealing a ferocious beard cross-hatched by a half dozen scars. His appearance struck me: at first, the man's head only seemed unnaturally large, until I realized that, somehow, his skull had been shaped into an inhuman point.

The commander spoke words in a harsh tongue, which drew no response from my foederati. He switched to Persian, spitting in disdain.

"Throw your weapons to the ground, Romans, and we will only cut off a hand before enslaving you," he boomed. "Resist, and any who survive will have their cocks removed as well."

"You bleat like a goat, savage," I responded in Persian. "Leave Roman land now, and I won't dismember your corpse for dogs to gnaw at."

The Hephthalite laughed. "You think you can defeat Khingila? I have killed a thousand men with my own hand and burned a hundred cities. My women play with the bones of the kings I have slain."

"That's because Khingila fights only women and children!" I called back in return.

The Hephthalite leader holstered his bow and drew a long blade, pointing it in my direction. "You will not go to the children, I think." Khingila chuckled mirthlessly, signaling his men to form up behind him. "I will keep you for myself and cut pieces of your flesh to satisfy our gods." Khingila led his horse to his formation and slid the skull-tipped helmet over his pointed head as the Hephthalite attack recommenced.

I drew back from the Hephthalite formation and ordered our forward ranks to dismount and form as tight a circle as we could with our remaining fighters. Sembrouthes muscled his way to my side, his yellow robes soaked with gore, while Alaric joined me at the front of the formation. Led by Perenus, fifty Herulians remained mounted, drawing their bows to support our wall for as long as they were able.

Khingila bellowed orders to his men, who swarmed past their leader toward the Roman lines. Alaric handed me a stray spear as we formed our wall, Herulian arrows sailing overhead and quilling horse and rider alike of our nearest attackers.

"Hold the line!" I screamed.

Alaric yelled, and as his anger flowed through the Herulian lines, the rest of my men bellowed the same at the charging Hephthalites. We lowered our spears once more and were met with a crush of ponies and men who would sweep us from the Mesopotamian plain.

I shot my spear toward a horse's chest, goring the iron point deep into the beast's heart. It stumbled, sending its rider vaulting into the air, and when the horse's weight snapped another of my spears, I drew my sword to cut down another Hephthalite that pushed toward my position. The torn bodies of men and beasts provided a small but swelling wall around my circle, giving my mounted archers opportunities to strike down those who threatened to break our lines.

Soon, the Hephthalites began to follow our example and used our fixed ranks as an easy target for light spears. Sembrouthes screamed in pain as one of those spears dug into his hip but yelled an equally loud protest when another of his Aksumites dragged him to relative safety. His place was taken by Wazeba, a younger Aksumite who nonetheless exhibited the unflagging discipline that Sembrouthes demanded of his men.

"Fill the lines!" I yelled back toward Perenus. Nodding, he signaled half of his riders to dismount and push forward. The remaining riders abandoned volley fire altogether, loosing arrows as quickly as they were able.

Hephthalite riders curled around our circle, attacking our position from three sides. Our ranks crushed together as the rising mound of bodies blunted our enemy's charge, forcing several riders to dismount and scale the writhing mass of dead and dying. Their attack seemed to falter, until another roar rose from thousands of Hephthalite throats as Khingila took his place among the front lines.

Dismounting, he hefted a shield and barked at his men, who formed a wall to match our own. Under the cover of raised shields, small detachments of dismounted Hephthalites dragged several corpses away from our front. Perenus' bowmen attempted to impede their progress, yet Roman arrows and spears merely glanced off the tightly connected shields.

Khingila marched his men forward, the skull atop his helmet swaying against the continuing wind. As he drew closer, I saw that the charms at their throats were not mere necklaces, but garlands of fingerbones, which rattled sickeningly as Khingila and his officers walked in their shield wall.

As the Hephthalite wall snaked around our shrinking circle like the waves of a storm against a rocky shore, Khingila's shield slammed into mine. He snarled and spit at my face as he lashed out at me, battering the rim of my shield. Khingila was near my own height, close enough that I could see a mouth of teeth rotten and brown with decay, and shocks of gray within the tangled mat of his hair and beard.

Attempting to keep the circle tight, the Aksumites behind me pushed hard at my back, forcing me into a nearly immobile position against Khingila. Sembrouthes raised a blade to slash at my attacker but was confounded by his own adversary. While Khingila cursed and growled in no language that I could understand, a spear from the Hephthalite second rank was thrust over Khingila's shoulder and toward my face.

I managed to shift my shield upward to block the blow, but Khingila bashed forward with his own bulwark, and I tumbled to the ground. A mass of boots and filth thundered around my prone body, and I felt Khingila's foot smash into my ribs. Spitting blood, I struggled to rise to my knees, swinging my shield to deflect the litany of boots and spear butts that slammed down around me. Vision blurring, all I could muster was a wave of my blade vaguely in my attacker's direction, lacking any measure of force.

Khingila roared in triumph. He dropped his spear, drew his sword, and stabbed downward. I managed to catch the first thrust with the boss of my shield, the iron covering scraping heavily against Khingila's grinding blade edge. Again and again, he slashed with his blade, cutting deep and sending splinters flying into the air, and it was all I could do to prevent him from hitting flesh.

With Sembrouthes pinned by his own adversaries, Alaric pushed forward to my position, striking sword blows at Khingila's body and face. Khingila drew back in surprise of the sudden attack, allowing the men of my second rank to drag me back to the safety of Roman lines. Screaming in frustration, Khingila lashed out at Alaric, bashing aside the Herulian's shield and slashing deep into the man's armored chest. Khingila followed the blow with another, goring Alaric just below his rib cage.

Alaric stumbled backward as I rose to my feet, lunging toward Khingila and pushing Alaric back toward safety. The Hephthalite leader laughed as I attacked, his eyebrows arching as he mocked my display.

"Pathetic!" Khingila grunted in heavily accented Persian, froth dotting the corners of his mouth. "I'll be sure to find your woman once I'm done here—show her what a real man feels like!"

Bitter hatred subsumed me. Teeth clenched, I threw my shoulder hard into my shield, hoping I could throw Khingila off balance and open him to attack. He backed away, seemingly concerned, yet, as I broke away from my shield ring, he feinted to one side and sidestepped my attack, driving his blade into my thigh. I screamed and could only slash pitifully at Khingila's body before stumbling back to my lines.

"Truly pathetic! I've pulled turds out of my arse that had more ability than you!" Khingila taunted, spitting on the narrow clearing between us. The Hephthalite attack momentarily withdrew as Khingila and his fellow chiefs took measure of the battered Herulian lines, judging our growing weaknesses for their final attack.

Their arrows spent, the last of the Herulian riders dismounted and took their places along the shield ring. Sembrouthes held me upright as Perenus rushed forward, his eyes widening as he inspected the gash in my leg. I tried to stand unaided, yet quickly sagged; my diminishing strength simply could not support the weight of my body.

Perenus leaned forward, his grime-soaked brow wrinkled with concern. "This is bad, Varus. We need to take you back to Dara."

"Soon enough." I grimaced. "Bring me Ignis."

Perenus sighed, wiping the sweat and blood that hid his features, but obeyed. Hell itself radiated through my lower body as I was helped into the saddle, rising to face the thousands of Hephthalites that remained against us. Ignis' wolf pelt was lightly spotted with red, blood that could have come from any number of Persians, Romans, or even myself.

Khingila carefully arrayed his lines as the Roman ring grew tighter, our wounded and horses in the center of the formation. Eyeing me, Khingila mounted his own horse and smirked at the rabble that remained against him.

As we stood hurt, outnumbered, and overwhelmed, horns blew from the west. Their echo was distant at first but were returned with a great boom from the walls of Dara. Rising over my men, I turned toward the deafening sound.

John and Bessas had returned, and with them galloped a huge mass of cataphracts. A mighty cheer rang throughout our ragged ranks, and I turned to Khingila in my own private triumph.

"Surrender, Lord Khingila!" I shouted hoarsely, my voice bearing none of a Roman commander's strength and confidence.

Even so, the words sank into the Hephthalite commander, who yelled in frustration and charged forward. Perenus reacted immediately, commanding the men to hold the wall for one final charge in the butcher's fields of Dara.

At this point, aside from surrender, the Hephthalites retained few options. They could retreat, of course, but that would show cowardice on Khingila's part. Even worse, they might run unawares into another Roman detachment and be obliterated in the process. Instead, Khingila bet his rule, and the lives of his people, upon breaking the foederati and facing down John's forces once more.

Their wall hit with the desperate savagery of a warrior who knew that time was an enemy. Likewise, Perenus did all he could to hold back the Hephthalite spearmen, parrying blows and offering resistance only to discourage further assaults. I commanded the remaining officers to slowly back our ring toward the west, and the men obeyed, shuffling their feet a half pace with every other heartbeat.

Mounted, Khingila used the weight of his pony to press against the backs of his men, pushing the Hephthalite lines forward to force a breakthrough. Perenus leaned into the rising swell of enemies, yet our lines lacked the necessary force to fully turn back the Hephthalites' superior numbers. Khingila yelled encouragement to his men, using his horse to shove his way to the front lines and exploit the gap in our shield wall.

I moved Ignis forward, my leg throbbing and head heavy from swelling wounds and blood loss. Biting my lip to help attune my attention, I pressed toward Khingila, slashing against his shield and distracting him from Perenus. As we tangled together, the Roman horns grew closer, and the Hephthalites grew all the more anxious and vicious in their assault. Our ring continued to bend despite our gradual steps backward, although the foederati's dark flag still flew and told of our continued survival as a cohesive unit.

Khingila turned his fury toward me, hacking at the remnants of my shield and even jabbing at my stallion. Though protected by his heavy scale armor, Ignis grew fearful of the dull pain at his side and struggled to move away from the press of men. His skittish movements left a small hole in the Roman lines, which Khingila flooded through soon thereafter. Our ring began to crumble under the torrent of Hephthalite men, with my Herulian and Aksumite warriors fighting desperately to stay alive.

Khingila laughed in triumph as spears flowed around him. Perenus organized a makeshift resistance to stem the Hephthalite attack, yet still they came into our circle, the foederati crammed into fighting back to back as we were slowly swallowed by our fur-clad enemy. Khingila edged his pony forward, slashing again at Perenus and forcing him back as he fought for control over his lines.

My shield arm sagged from fatigue, and I knew it was now only a hindrance. I used my sword to sever the shield's leather straps, sending it tumbling to the ground. Then, I gathered Ignis' reins with my vacant shield arm and urged my mount to one final charge, aiming directly at an unsuspecting Khingila.

The Hephthalite leader did not see the thrust until it was too late. Ignis rammed into the unarmored pony, sending me vaulting toward Khingila. I tackled the Hephthalite to the ground in a cloud of dust and gore. Holding tight to his body, Khingila broke my fall as I rolled to the side, struggling to sit up as I gasped for air.

Stunned, Khingila also fought to sit up, sticky blood pooling into his eyes and further matting his hair. Stiffly, he turned to meet my gaze, his eyes unfocused yet somehow full of disdain. Khingila drew a dagger from his belt and stabbed into the air, finding no target as I slammed an armored hand across the Hephthalite's square jaw.

Khingila's head jerked violently as his back hit the ground once again. With my sword in my right hand, I shrieked with equal measures of pain and hatred as I brought the point down into his chest. Despite the dullness brought on by a day of killing, my blade split the leather and fur with ease. Eyes bulging, Khingila gave a gurgling wheeze as the dragon-hilted sword pierced his heart and pinned him to the ground. With a vicious scream, I spat blood into my enemy's slackening face.

A small collection of Herulians formed a wall around me, with one grabbing me by the collar and dragging me back into the relative safety of the remaining foederati lines. I stole a glance over my shoulder and found Ignis rushing back toward the west, moving away from the howling Hephthalites that now paused in confusion as their leader lay sprawled in the Mesopotamian dust.

Though several still pushed forward into the breach in the Roman lines, many of the Hephthalites wavered and began to fall back, jumping on horses and heading east toward the Immortals fighting Belisarius. Perenus led a sortie to expel Hephthalites from the Roman circle, yelling encouragement as our men found their second wind amidst the rising tide of John's booming horn.

More Hephthalites abandoned the attack, turning their determined assault into a desperate route to escape. John's horses thundered past our formation, earning exhausted cheers amongst my men, who collapsed onto the ground. Perenus and Sembrouthes propped me up in the center of the formation, and I found myself looking upon a torn, familiar body — Alaric.

Eyes brimming with tears, Alaric bit hard on his lip. His fingers reached for wounds cut fresh by Khingila's blade, caking armor and cloak alike with a paste of congealed crimson dust. As I dragged myself closer, faint and nauseous from my own injuries, he turned his lolling head to me.

"Did we win, Lord? Did I fight well?" he bleated in Greek. A tear cut through the grime of his cheek.

"Yes, my friend. Without you, we would all be lost," I replied softly. I took Alaric's hand into my own and squeezed hard, his blood squelching between our interlocking gloves.

Moaning, Alaric spat thick globs of blood. "Lord, the pain is too much," he said. "Please don't let me suffer."

"We will fetch a physician immediately…" I began, yet was cut off by another ragged cough from Alaric.

"I've seen these wounds many times, and they always mean a slow death," Alaric said, and when he moved his free hand, I saw beneath it the bits of intestine that threatened to spill onto the earth. "I don't want to end like that, screaming and twitching."

I felt faint. "Let me bring you back to Dara," I wheezed. "Rosamund can sew these wounds."

It was a lie, however, and Alaric knew it. Needle and thread might be able to stop any further bleeding, but Alaric's wounds were deep, and he had lost too much blood. No matter what we did, death would come in a few hours at most.

"Varus, please!" Alaric yelped in pain, gritting his teeth as his body stiffened and writhed.

I looked up toward Perenus, who cast his gaze to the ground and sighed deeply. Sembrouthes simply nodded, saying nothing as Alaric put his remaining strength into our clasped hands.

"As you command." I drew my dagger with a free hand.

"Thank you, Lord," he mumbled, forcing the words between spasms. Alaric grabbed his sword with his other hand, his fist gripping the pommel tightly as he faced death. His eyes turned to mine as he spoke in Herulian, for the final time. "It has been an honor to serve under you."

My throat felt thick as I struggled for my mother tongue. "It has been an honor to fight at your side," I replied at last.

I struck hard, burying the length of the blade into Alaric's neck with all the speed I could muster. The dagger's point severed Alaric's spine, giving him barely a moment to jerk and squeeze my hand before falling motionless to the ground.

Alaric died quickly, his sword clenched in his hand and his countrymen standing in silent vigil.

After a few heartbeats, I released Alaric's limp hand and sheathed my dagger. I collapsed into a heap, surrendering to a failing body. Perenus tried to slap me awake, but my flesh would not obey any further commands. As my eyes closed, I heard growing shouts of jubilation and disbelief in Greek and Latin voices, calling out from Dara's eastern expanse. Their words were the last I remember of that day.

"Roma Victrix! Roma Victrix!"

THE SIN OF PRIDE

M Y MEMORY OF THE battle's aftermath is a haze. I do not recall being carried through Dara's walls, nor—thankfully—the dangerous task of stitching and bandaging my wounds. Instead, for all I knew, I slept, my mind a darkened void as I embraced the solace of oblivion.

At last, under the cover of darkness, my eyelids tore apart, revealing the converted storage yard that served as the foederati's barracks in Dara. The smell of piss and death hung heavily in the air, although my immediate surroundings seemed clean enough. Moaning from sore muscles and itching cuts, I tried to rise yet found my movements restricted by layers of tight bandages that wound across my shoulder, waist, and leg.

"Varus!" Samur exclaimed. "Sit back! I'll get Rosamund."

As my eyes adjusted, I propped myself up with my one unbandaged arm, fighting against the throbbing pain that radiated up my arms and into my chest. In the cot next to me lay Fulcaris, his upper body heavily wrapped and soiled bandages piled on the ground. His skin seemed waxy and pale as a corpse, yet thankfully his chest rose and fell in a relaxed rhythm.

Light flickered into the barracks as three figures rushed toward me. One was clearly a returning Samur in his Hunnic furs. Running after him was Rosamund, torch in hand and white hair flowing loosely behind her. The third figure's face was masked by a heavy hood, the clothing bobbing up and down as the figure moved closely at Rosamund's side.

Rosamund handed the torch to Samur and peeled off her thin leather gloves. Her hands pushed against my skin, seeking any corruption that too often follows battle injury. Rosamund examined each wound, nodding in approval at my shoulder but

393

sucking air through her teeth when she ran a finger along the slim gash on my thigh. Slowly, she withdrew several bandages caked in blood and replaced them with others, binding the cloth tight enough to make me wince.

At last, the third figure withdrew his hood. Liberius' brow furrowed as his eyes flicked up and down my body. "Will he recover?"

"No fever," Rosamund answered. "The wounds are healing and the stitches are taking hold."

"Good. Please allow me a moment alone with him," Liberius said, silencing resistance brewing from Rosamund and Samur.

"I'll be just outside," Rosamund assured me, dark circles under her eyes. She handed the torch to Liberius and walked out of the building and into the open air of Dara's streets.

"Lord," I croaked, my throat cracking from a desire for water. Liberius offered a wooden cup, and I sipped slowly, gradually sitting up with what little strength I had available to me.

"I am surprised to see you awake so soon," Liberius said mildly. "It has been little more than a half day since the battle ended, and most of your men are either resting or making themselves ruinously drunk."

"What happened?" I asked thickly, my mind slow to emerge from the fog of unconsciousness.

Liberius explained the aftermath of the battle as he had seen it atop Dara's walls. Far from retreating in fear, John and Bessas had lured the Hephthalite horde away from Perozes' forces, allowing Belisarius to focus solely on the mass of mounted Immortals. Linking up with distant reinforcements, John was slowed by a number of Hephthalites that did not turn to face the arrival of our foederati. After defeating these forces, John rushed toward my position, where he found little resistance in the aftermath of Khingila's death. Passing my men, John and Bessas joined

Belisarius in encircling and routing the Immortals, sending what little remained of the Persian cavalry scurrying away. Pcrozes' spearmen and archers held formation for a time until they, too, were hit along their flanks, and their formation disintegrated into frantic scrabbling for survival.

"And our losses?" I asked.

"Minimal, save the excubitores and your foederati," Liberius said. "Although the Thracians took a noticeable licking."

"So we won?" I asked, the haze of my mind flitting back to my last coherent memories on the battlefield.

"My boy, would I be speaking with you right now if that were not so?" Liberius asked, his eyes twinkling against the low torchlight.

I chuckled, then moaned, as the rise and fall of my chest caused stitches to stretch. To the extent that I could take a measure of my old teacher in that moment, Liberius seemed jovial; despite the fatigue he undoubtedly felt, he showed none of the heaviness of exhaustion I'd seen in Rosamund moments earlier.

Liberius held the torch level to his face and away from my cot, its light casting shadows against the far wall. After stewing in silence, I at last summoned the courage to ask Liberius the questions that had burned in my mind over the past two years I had spent in service to the Empire.

"Lord, there are things that I would like to know that have been kept from me since I was freed," I began. "Emperor Justin promised to provide answers when I returned from Cherson, but he perished before I was able to make it back."

Liberius sighed. "I understand," he said. "Ask your questions."

As I gazed into Liberius' stony face, I temporarily faltered in my courage. I began with a question that was presumably easy but had confused me on the fields of Dara.

"When we charged against the Persian attack on Belisarius' left flank, how did you know that you wouldn't hit our foederati, Lord?"

Liberius broke his trance and grinned slyly. "I didn't," he said, "but it worked out in the end. But," he added, "I do not think that is what you truly wish to know."

I shook my head, emboldened by Liberius' seeming invitation for the true question. "Lord, why have I been granted so many privileges throughout my life? Emperor Justin, or Godilas, even you... all since I was a boy. Who am I to deserve such blessings against the millions of others who live and serve in the Empire? What do you want from me?"

Liberius smiled weakly. "I cannot provide that answer for you today, and it was inappropriate for Justin to have made such a promise when he did. I believe that he knew he was nearing the end of his life and wanted to offer as much good to the world as possible in what time he had left."

"But Lord—"

"I promise. You will know when the time is right. But for the time being, allow me the sole responsibility of bearing the burden of the truth," Liberius answered. "For now, all we ask is that you live a life of strength, of leadership, and of goodness. Qualities that singers praise and philosophers lament, both laughably simple and hopelessly impossible to achieve. All I want for you is to rise above the darkness around you, and the rest shall be revealed in time."

I groaned at the answer but knew better than to press Liberius further than he was willing to go. In his way, Liberius yielded a glimpse into a much fuller answer, however generic that glimmer may be. In recalling my last moments with Justin, I saw that Liberius' insistence upon delay at least proved to me that there *was* something more, far more, than merely a distribution of priceless gifts and an education rivaling any in the world.

Something great, and possibly something terrible. I prayed it was not the latter.

"Very well. My second question, then, is about the gifts that have been promised to me—I have received four of seven so far. Who are they from, and what do they mean?"

"You already know the answer to half of your question," Liberius said. "The cross is from Father Petrus, the dagger from Godilas, and the sword and gold are from Emperor Justin. As for their meaning, that, too, must wait for another day."

I had guessed at Liberius' response and showed no disappointment as a result. "I understand. One final question for now, then."

"Ah, finality," Liberius said, his tone lightly mocking. "Choose wisely, then."

"How do you know Father Petrus? I did not meet him until my first day of training in the army, but it seems like you have known him for a considerable time."

"Contrary to what you may believe, I do have many things that occupy my day outside of checking in on your well-being," Liberius said. He preemptively held a bony finger in the air to silence my response before adding, "Petrus has been a servant of the Roman Church for some time, but I knew him even before his service, when we were boys."

"In Italy?" I asked.

"Yes. Our families amassed considerable wealth and power that even the Goths could not fully destroy," Liberius added. "Petrus followed me to Constantinople decades ago, but he preferred a more private life, save a rare intervention in what he felt were the most important political issues. He has known of you since you arrived in Constantinople, however."

"He was your friend? And Emperor Justin's too?" I propped myself further upright, curiosity prodding me despite the pain in my stomach.

"Long before Justin became Emperor, yes," Liberius said nonchalantly. "And Godilas, and Basilius as well," he listed off.

"Basilius? I remember him engineering Justin's rise to the purple, but I never took them as friends," I said skeptically.

"Oh, yes," Liberius said. "*Lord* Basilius was never one for emotion or empty friendship, yet there are few more loyal than he. The five of us served together under Emperor Anastasius, and Emperor Zeno before him."

"But why?" I asked. "What made the five of you wish to serve together for so long?"

Liberius made a clicking noise with his tongue. "Varus, if there is one thing I have desperately sought to beat into the skulls of you youngsters, it is that Rome is an idea worth fighting for. Worth dying for, if need be, and it often is. The price of service can be terrible, as you have seen in Tauris and now in Dara, but it allows countless thousands to live in happiness and prosperity, ignorant of the great darkness that stalks every corner of our Empire."

With that, Liberius paused for a time, allowing the torch to waver as its low warmth glided over his face. Then, with a note of finality, he added, "I miss them terribly—Godilas and Justin. They deserved a greater measure of peace in their ends, but it… was not meant to be." He sighed. "The price of duty is a terrible one, Varus, but the alternative is far worse. Far, far worse than anything imaginable. Take what joys you can, and as much as you can, but never forget that duty lingers on, even after we go to the afterlife."

I wanted to pry further, but Liberius stood and drew his torch away. "Accept your well-deserved rest, Varus. Tomorrow, your duty begins anew, and many will place their trust upon your shoulders in the days to come," he declared. "I am proud of you, the sentimental senile fool that I am."

He swept out of the room, only to be replaced by Rosamund, who again checked my wounds with meticulous care despite her own manifest exhaustion. She spread a paste, its odor sharp and sickening, upon my wounds, insisting it would help my skin reknit itself. Once again, she mixed powders into a clay cup of water, then bade me to drink, and I fell back into a dreamless sleep.

I awoke well into the morning, my body hot and stiff despite the additional rest that Rosamund's potion had granted me. The stitches lining my thigh itched—a phenomenon that meant that the body was healing itself from the inside out. Resisting the urge to scratch at the wound, I propped myself into a sitting position and swung my legs out to the floor, my bare feet brushing the rough stone.

My knees immediately buckled. Struggling to support my full weight, I kept myself upright with an unbandaged arm against my cot, drawing Sembrouthes' attention.

Though he, too, bore cuts and bandages from the battle, Sembrouthes seemed indefatigable. As ever, he fretted over my safety, arguing that I should return to sleep. Seeing I would not be convinced, Sembrouthes relented and helped me walk around the barracks halls. Several Herulians called out as I passed by, offering a low cheer that seemed absurd given my physical condition. Yet I waved all the same, stopping to visit those who bore serious wounds and making notes to ensure their care and comfort. Fulcaris was one of those men, although he still rested peacefully and woke only in short fits for water and food. Perenus was absent for much of the day, although Sembrouthes assured me that he was well enough, just busy meeting with Belisarius in my absence.

With my movement as limited as it was, the next several weeks followed a similar pattern: I awoke, lurched heavily about the barracks, supported by one of my men in an attempt to regain stamina in my legs, and rested. With what little vigor remained to me, I wrote letters to Mariya and to Theodora, telling them of our exploits in Dara and assuring them of my safety. My words to Theodora were both formal and overly detailed, recounting lost souls and weapons broken like lines in one of Procopius' ledgers. It would make for dull reading, perhaps, in comparison to the raw clash of the actual battle, yet Theodora was not one who required — or, indeed, appreciated — too much poetic embellishment.

But for Mariya, I struggled to find words at all. I said little of my injuries, and nothing of the desperate struggle to live as Khingila overpowered and outmatched nearly every maneuver I could muster. How could she understand such wanton violence? What could I say that would accurately depict its horror? No, in my discomfort, I neglected these subjects altogether, and wrote only of my desire to be reunited. On that subject, I was effusive. I would have traded half of Croesus' gold to brush the soft skin of her cheek with my hand, to embrace her and the child she carried within, to leave behind the itching pain of my healing body — and, with hope, the visions of death that clouded my sleep.

My only foray outside of the barracks in those first days after the battle was to view the bodies of my men and ensure that their rites were respected in death. Whereas in Tauris, Belisarius lacked the easy access to priests and burial plots for his fallen soldiers, here, a detachment of laborers dug graves for each of the Romans, treating officers with the care befitting their rank. Opilio and other Roman officers from my foederati were buried alongside two of Sembrouthes' Aksumites, all blessed and acknowledged by Father Petrus as he followed me to stand before each of the men's burial plots. Though an old man, Father Petrus provided a shoulder to assist my pained steps, offering specialized words for each soldier's service to the Empire.

The Christians were not the only men given their own rites. Most of the Herulians, following their older pagan beliefs, were given pyres. While a dozen graves had been dug and filled in for my officers, over a hundred bloating and stinking bodies rested atop wooden pyres, ready for the flames. One man suggested that we use wood from Hakhamanish's charred logs that had been lit at the beginning of the battle as a sign of conquest, but I denied it. We were burying our dead on the merits of their own honor, not as a petty show of force.

Sembrouthes and Perenus took turns holding me upright as I lit a torch and offered what words I could for the fallen Herulians. I strode unevenly across the orderly ranks of bodies and kindling, solemnly looking upon the dead. Each face told of a man who'd spent months training for this mission, laughing and cursing at each session with a horse or in the shield wall, and each face carved its memory upon me until my progress halted at Alaric. His face, despite the crusted blood that lined much of his body, seemed peaceful. I lit my torch, dropped the flames onto Alaric's feet, and stepped back as the dry kindling caught quickly. Along Dara's walls, I found many of Belisarius' senior officers standing silently at my display, momentarily allowing none to leave or enter Dara's gates until the ritual came to a close.

At the end of the first week after Dara, I still lacked the strength to join the meetings of the senior officers, and so Belisarius came to our barracks. As he walked over our threshold, he made an effort to speak with each of my men, checking on their wounds and listening to their stories from different moments in the battle.

"You look much improved, my friend," he told me. "I was worried that you left us as the battle ended, but Rosamund assured me that you would recover."

I nodded, straightening my back as I struggled to put on a strong face in front of my commander. Belisarius smiled and bade me to rest as he updated me on the army's activities.

"Hermogenes sent messengers to Perozes and Kavadh, but we have almost no prisoners to bargain with," he explained.

"No prisoners? Even with the Persian army routed?" I asked.

"Very few," Belisarius admitted. "Even those who broke fought rather than surrender, and the few that we took captive were already wounded. Most gravely," he added.

"And the Hephthalites?" I asked.

"Broke and ran, after your assault," Belisarius said. "Scouts say they ran all the way back to Ctesiphon... and John killed those too slow or too injured to escape. He blames himself for not reaching you sooner, and for the loss of your men."

"There was nothing he could have done," I said firmly.

"You won't convince John of that," Belisarius said. "And we do owe you a debt, for what your foederati were able to do throughout Dara. That man you slew, Khingila, was the sole Hephthalite leader who agreed to serve Kavadh. The White Huns have little love for the Persians by any measure, and Khingila's death may have taken their forces from the Persian army entirely."

I nodded. "As long as my wounded are cared for. But in the final attack, we took no Persian leaders alive?"

"None of note." Belisarius shrugged. "The remnant of the Immortals retreated after Uliaris used his francisca to kill Barsamenes, their commander, and the Persian infantry was annihilated. We are still combing over the bodies, but it will be a few more days before we can get a full account of the outcome of the battle."

"The war is over, then," I said.

"We hope so," Belisarius replied. "Although the final decision is largely left to Kavadh, Hermogenes, and our Imperial Court. We have, at any rate, bought ourselves a few months of rest."

After the battle, Belisarius had written his own missives to Antioch in hopes that Antonina could be escorted to Dara, although a subsequent reply from Sergius argued that reaving Persian bands were still a threat to the interior Syrian provinces. Regardless, Sergius said, Antonina's condition was unsuitable for extended travel over bumpy roads, so she and Mariya were to remain situated in the relative comfort of Antioch. Belisarius promised to continue to send messages to that great city on my behalf, and I in turn grudgingly promised to not take leave for Antioch on my own.

Summer gave way to autumn as life in Dara grew lighter in the absence of the Persian threat. While Hermogenes continued his dialogue with Kavadh, John took responsibility for leading raids deep into Persian territory, targeting specifically the supply wagons that brought food and weapons into the strongholds around Nisibis. Belisarius took pains to acquire necessary supplies and reinforcements for his army and promised to issue a request to Narses for more Herulians to fill my foederati. Procopius remained busy in those months, scratching a quill onto scrolls by candlelight as a steady stream of couriers flowed into and out of Belisarius' quarters.

Our success at Dara reverberated throughout the Empire, spurring other Roman armies into action. In Armenia, Sittas scored a considerable victory against a smaller Persian army, forcing a stalemate along the Iberian and Lazic borders as they had been defined prior to war. In Egypt, Domnicus fought slowly west as he expelled Gelimer's Vandals from Roman territory, sending the Vandal armies back to their African kingdom. In their wake was the charred and depopulated husk of Roman towns in eastern Libya, which Domnicus was rebuilding as autumn progressed.

Through all of this, my strength slowly returned as rest, food, and inspections by Rosamund sped my recovery along. Father Petrus resumed our meetings just the second week after Dara, no matter that they required me to lean on Sembrouthes' shoulder as I met Petrus in a small city church. Soon thereafter, Perenus adopted the task of rebuilding my strength, using what various weapons of mine had been found on the battlefield and returned to me. As part of the spoils of our victory, my men delivered a massive composite bow to my private quarters, which

Perenus explained had belonged to Khingila. It stood half the height of a man when held upright, its stout body built from several types of wood, with a thin layer of buffalo horn on the bow's interior to provide greater strength and dyed a deep maroon color lined with silver glyphs and runes. Initially, I lacked the power to draw and hold under the extreme force of the bowstring, yet by mid-autumn, I was able to fire an arrow well beyond the typical range of a Roman archer.

A flurry of letters from Antioch and Constantinople broke up my daily ritual, with each scroll bearing mixed tidings and instructions for the months to come. With their crisp, precise Latin letters, Mariya's messages were crafted from her own hand, the script so intricate that a clerk would be considered a wasteful luxury. Perhaps it was my imagination, but I swore the vellum held the faint memory of her perfume, its floral scent piercing through the stench of blood and piss that wafted throughout my quarters. The sensation made me weak, for in those moments, I wanted nothing more than to escape my duties in the army for a warm bed and soft company.

In her letters, she offered welcome news of her continued good health in the early stages of pregnancy. Mariya was not satisfied with my initial reports of the battle and asked for a more honest account of my injuries at Dara—even going so far as to inquire about the possibility of me requesting a transfer back to the Capitol.

Whether you tell me of your battles or not, I know what you face. You must not make me a widow, she wrote. *Theodora will recall you if you just ask.*

I curled the scroll and placed it over a low brazier, a pang sweeping over me as I burned Mariya's words. I then scratched a response, assuring her again of my safety and that we would be reunited soon. For a moment, I was even tempted to ask for temporary leave to visit Antioch myself, yet guiltily rejected the idea; Belisarius would likely approve the request, even though he himself could not do likewise, and I could not force him to suffer that.

Additional notes arrived from Narses, expressing the Empress' delight at our success in Dara and requesting information of further needs of my foederati. True to his world, Belisarius helped reply to this missive with a request for additional Herulians to be enlisted and trained, noting that our considerable losses in Dara were due to the near-constant fighting instead of any concerns of quality or courage of the men.

A month of slow exercise and rich food helped restore my strength, and soon thereafter I was also able to rejoin the other senior officers in Belisarius' planning sessions. Mundus was the first to acknowledge my presence as I entered the room, bobbing his head once in my direction as a sign of respect. Ascum and Baduarius offered heartier greetings—their tight embraces threatened to leave fresh bruises, and they only released at growls from an overcautious Sembrouthes. Solomon, I noted, was not present at the meeting, which Mundus later attributed to a lingering ailment that kept my old rival from his duties in the officers' gatherings. However, where Perenus was permitted to represent the Herulians in my absence, no replacement was made available for Solomon, who, as a mid-level officer in the Thracian Army, lacked an independent command.

Of all the officers, John alone greeted me with solemnity. A strained look worried his gaunt face, the premature gray speckling his hair and thin beard making him appear much older than his age of some thirty years. His deep-set eyes gazed sadly into mine as he offered a hand in recognition, seemingly unsure of how I would react.

"I'm so sorry, Varus. I wasn't able to reach you soon enough, and you nearly died with your men for my follies.

Whatever you ask of me, I owe you a great debt," John said formally as I took his hand.

I shook my head. "No man can control all stages of battle," I said, "and you did all you could."

Eyes welling, John embraced me, breaking away only when Belisarius called the meeting into order.

The mood of the room quickly darkened. Hermogenes seized Belisarius' place at the head of the table, where he surveyed the officers with a pinched expression that further wrinkled his aged skin.

"Reports from scouts and spies are mixed," he began. "Perozes has been jailed by Shahanshah Kavadh, and the Hephthalites have been banished back beyond the outer edges of the Persian Empire. By all accounts, the remnants of Perozes' army were publicly scorned, and its officers punished or demoted."

Bessas rapped his knuckles against the table, joined soon thereafter by other officers, who saw in this a further measure of their unlikely victory in the fields of Dara. Still sour-faced, Hermogenes raised a hand for silence.

"Any attempts at negotiation have been rebuffed. Rather than end the war, Kavadh has commanded a new army be brought to bear against Roman Mesopotamia," Hermogenes declared.

Ascum stifled a groan, while Valerian muttered some disbelief that the Persians would continue after such a devastating blow. "And what is the size of this army? Who commands it?" he asked, noticeably incredulous.

"Forty thousand, or thereabouts," Hermogenes replied. "About half are Lakhmid Arabs, and the other half Persian spears or cavalry. All commanded by Astabadh Azarethes, Kavadh's senior military commander."

"We must send to Constantinople for reinforcements immediately," John sputtered, his eyes wide on Hermogenes.

"I already have tried," Hermogenes said, "but the Capitol is silent, and previous messages have noted the difficulty of transferring large contingents of men in winter. Nevertheless, I have procured local soldiers that can bolster our army here."

"Locals? Why weren't they at Dara, then?" Sunicas arched his brows in suspicion.

Hermogenes glared at Sunicas, offering no challenge in return. "King al-Harith has reformed the Ghassanid armies after the death of his father and has pledged to support us in the event of any invasion," he said, rather formally.

Belisarius cleared his throat, a rare interruption of the legate. "How many men can the King provide us, and of what quality?" he asked.

"Perhaps ten thousand," Hermogenes said. "Though I won't lie to you: They will be raw recruits. The Ghassanids were routed badly at Thannuris, and their veteran core is disbanded or dead."

"And there is... no sign of Xerxes?" John asked nervously.

Hermogenes pursed his lips. "Xerxes is not with Azarethes, and from what we have heard, he remains imprisoned at Nisibis for displeasing Kavadh."

"That's pure madness, isn't it?" Germanus put in with a chuckle. "Shackling the only Persian commander who was able to chase us from the field."

"Take it as a sign of good fortune," Hermogenes snapped. "And be sure that your men are ready to stand and fight this time."

Germanus and Mundus rose angrily from their chairs, yet any protestations were silenced with a swift hand from Belisarius. Belisarius retained a serene expression even in the midst of the burgeoning tension, though his dark eyes were deeply lined from lack of sleep—or, perhaps, sadness.

"It seems," Belisarius said, taking control of the room, "that Azarethes will outnumber us with fresh and veteran soldiers.

Wisdom dictates that we attempt to offer some concessions for peace, especially while we still have the advantage after Dara." Only he would dare to voice the opinion that all the officers hoped for, and only he could voice it so calmly.

"Absolutely not!" Hermogenes bellowed, slamming a fist on the table. "I will *not* cede a single footstep of Roman land to the Persians. If the Persians come, it is your sworn duty to fight them, and to defeat them, and chase them back to the desolate lands whence they came."

"Legate," John said, his voice pitched low and deferential, "if I may, we won at Dara because Perozes was a poor commander who underestimated out capabilities. Azarethes will not make the same mistake."

Hermogenes' nostrils flared as he gazed at John. "No more talk of defeat," he bit out, teeth clenched. "All of you have quivered with your tails between your legs since we disembarked in Trapezous. The Emperor requires another victory of you. Find a way to make it happen rather than mew and complain about how life is unfair."

At that, John blushed, allowing his gaze to sink to the floor. Baduarius flew to his feet, veins pulsing in his muscled neck, but Belisarius jumped to attention first, his voice rising above the grumbling.

"You are correct, Lord Hermogenes, and I apologize," he cut in. "We will determine the best strategy to ward off Azarethes' incursion. But do we have any knowledge of his likely invasion path?"

Hermogenes grunted. "Syria," he said. "Too far south to be reinforced by Sittas in Armenia, yet full of wealthy towns that the Persians will squeeze for ransom and plunder."

"Then we will do what we can to deter an attack," Belisarius answered calmly. "Please give me time to confer with my men about our course of action. I shall write to the Emperor of our progress."

"Good," Hermogenes said, still wary but slightly less disgruntled. "I will be with Procopius if any further consultation is required."

With a flourish of pomp, Hermogenes threw his cloak over his shoulders and left, ignoring the angry stares of officers whom he condemned to the toil and pain of another impossible battle. As the door closed and his footsteps faded, several of the officers exploded. A frustrated chatter of displeasure, even shrouded fear, swelled in the room, with many feeling betrayed that the worst of the campaign had not, it appeared, been laid to rest in the fields of Dara.

"Can we ask Liberius to reason with the legate?" Germanus asked. "Maybe seek the Emperor's direct intervention in the peacemaking process?"

Belisarius sighed. "I can ask discreetly, but I doubt it will come to anything. Emperor Justinian is of a similar mind to Hermogenes, although he will allow the legate to act independently in the event that our army fails to stop Azarethes' invasion. We will need to make do with what we have."

"And what exactly is that?" Bessas asked. "We are just starting to recover from Dara and will need at least another month to bring the men into fighting fitness."

"Indeed," John said quietly. His eyes flicked to the ceiling as he recounted once again the numbers of dead, wounded, sick, and otherwise infirm across the major divisions of the army. My own foederati as well as Marcellus' excubitores were among the worst hit, with only half of each unit remaining hale and prepared for combat in the near future. Our spearmen suffered relatively light losses with only a few hundred unable to march in full kit or hold a shield steady. Most promising of all were the Hunnic foederati of Sunicas and Simmas, who received no fatalities in Dara and sustained only a few minor injuries from a day of hard riding in the saddle.

Regardless of our incredible victory at Dara and the relatively intact forces under Belisarius' command, we nevertheless lacked the men to track down and defeat Azarethes and his troops—even before factoring in his Hephthalite mercenaries or the remnants of Perozes' army. The presence of thousands of Lakhmids was even more disconcerting, for those men were still fresh, unspoiled by months of serious fighting along the Mesopotamian border, and would be better armed and trained than our own Ghassanid Arab allies. Despite Hermogenes' confidence that we would, again, snatch victory one final time, none of the officers could envision an encounter that did not include the wholesale slaughter of our Roman forces.

"One promising note," Belisarius added hopefully, "is the season. Azarethes makes his way west, although our scouts claim that he is under-provisioned and will not attack in winter. That should give us another season to rest and hope for reinforcements from Sittas or the Capitol."

"Yes, and another three months for the Persians to grow stronger," Ascum shot back.

Ultimately, we simply had little choice in our course of action. Belisarius lacked the numbers to pursue his advantage after Dara, and neither could he invade Persian Mesopotamia or Assyria, for fear of being cut off and surrounded by a numerically superior foe. Instead, we wintered in Dara with cool breezes fluttering over its immense walls as our sentries gazed ever eastward for any sign of movement in Nisibis or the Persian frontier beyond.

It was a difficult winter. Not due to any deprivations, for we were well supplied and well fed, thanks to detachments of cavalry from John and Bessas reopening trade lanes between Rome's Syrian and Mesopotamian cities. Nor was training particularly grueling, although the cold did bring an ache to the many wounds I accrued in Tauris, and in the long conflict on the Persian frontier. Rather, it was the tedium of inaction; many men fell into restlessness, with pockets of boredom and anxiety threatening to boil over into fights, whether between members of Belisarius' army or with private citizens in Dara.

To keep the peace, Belisarius doubled the town guard that had been assigned to Dara and threatened any found fighting or destroying property with public whippings and forfeiture of gold. To stave off sloth, he scheduled regular drills outside of Dara's walls that left most men too exhausted for drinking, whoring, or the sundry scuffles of an army at rest. Disruptions still occurred, but they lessened in number, and the citizens of Dara seemed happy enough to be profiting from our presence in their fortress city.

The winter days also brought a different sort of fretfulness. Though Belisarius was known to keep an air of prudent calm when facing his men, as Antonina drew closer and closer to being delivered of his child, the general's private disposition was more worried. By midwinter, Belisarius even called Rosamund to his quarters, asking dozens of questions about the nature of pregnancy, and if anything could be done to ease his wife's difficulties. I did my best to reassure my friend, even though his worry prodded at my own fears for Mariya, who was not too far behind Antonina. So it was that I often found him particularly pensive well beyond nightfall, with neither of us able to find restful sleep. For me, it was a body still healing from a half dozen wounds, and for Belisarius, it was the ceaseless charges of office; for both of us, I see now, it was our incipient fatherhood.

"Would you rather fight your way through childbirth or through the battlefield?" Belisarius asked one such night.

"Lord?" I did not quite take his meaning.

411

"Yes. A ridiculous question," he admitted. "It's simply—I find it odd that we know so thoroughly the ways to end a man's life, yet so little about how it begins."

Still wary, I grasped for reassurances. "The Empire has thousands of physicians, Lord, and well trained in the birthing bed."

Belisarius nodded. "True. But still, with all our learned masters, how many women still die from the labor of birthing—one in five, perhaps? One in four?" He shook his head. "I'm sure those physicians have their explanations, but what poor odds! More deadly even than decimation. Would any of our soldiers follow us so loyally battle if we brought back hardly four score of every hundred?"

The figure indeed left me deeply disquieted, if not altogether unsurprised. The Imperial Palace housed many of the Empire's most vaunted healers, I had often heard tell in my time there of one patrician's wife or another succumbing to childbed fever. To Belisarius, all I could do was echo Father Petrus, hollow counsel though it was. "We can pray," I offered.

"Prayer is good," Belisarius replied, his tone unchanged. "And I pray for Antonina's health every day, and every night. If God grants me the blessing of survival from this war, all I wish is to find a fertile plot of land and build a home for her. No swords, no suffering, just crops and children and a wife to adore."

Though Belisarius' expression was grave, I could not help but smile. "I cannot imagine Antonina as a farmer's wife."

At that, Belisarius chuckled and clapped me on the shoulder. "No, I suppose not. She's most comfortable when attended by servants, and a grain harvester could hardly afford a banda of washers, cooks, and dressmakers. But she makes me happy, even if my impossible dreams cannot come true."

I never understood Belisarius' infatuation with Antonina. True, she boasted a noble bloodline and was comely by any measure, yet she seemed to take no natural joys beyond her possessions, nor any delight in the pleasure of a daylong ride into the hills or a few hours swapping tales with the plebeians. She was an intricate web where Belisarius was a strong, simple through line, desiring little and requiring less. Even so, I understood the larger shape of his longing, for I felt it as well.

"Perhaps I shall join you in that paradise," I said.

"I would enjoy that." Belisarius smiled. "We two are so fortunate. In love and fortune when others have neither. Though if gold could purchase Antonina's safety into motherhood, I would happily beggar myself without a second thought."

"As would I," I agreed. "I will be far happier when Mariya's ordeal is finished, though I have faith in the outcome."

Liberius did little to ease my concerns the following morning. "She's much too small for children, that wife of yours, but you did not consult me before selecting your bride!" he chided. "Now Hilda, that mad Vandal you were to marry, I hear *she* is quite plump... at least before Gelimer made her a head shorter, that is."

I brushed aside his jibing. "Lord, do you really think that Mariya will struggle in the childbed?"

"There's no way to know for sure," Liberius said, his tone a bit more sincere. "I've never found the point to take a wife myself, but I do know there are countless peasant girls who spit out new babes each year and head right back to the fields. I'm sure your princess will be perfectly fine."

Father Petrus, having been childless and chaste for so much of his life, was hardly any assistance, though he did offer to pray for the safety of Mariya and Antonina and both infants. Still, for some reason, his offer only made the situation feel even more ominous.

For Belisarius, at least, it would turn out that his worries were for naught. Shortly after the feast in celebration of the birth of Christ, a messenger rode hard into Dara, his satchel heavy with a sealed brass container bearing an urgent message inside. My foederati maintained city watch that day, and Fulcaris brought the sealed message to me with all haste. Guessing at its contents, we mounted horses and trotted toward Belisarius' quarters and were swiftly admitted by Uliaris and others of Belisarius' growing personal guard. I handed the scroll to the general, who broke its wax and gazed at its Latin script.

"Lord?" I questioned, polite but undeniably curious.

Belisarius beamed. "I have a daughter," he said breathlessly, his teeth flashing as he laughed lightly to himself. "Healthy, both mother and babe."

"Congratulations, Lord!" I truly meant it.

Fulcaris echoed the sentiment. "Any name?" he asked politely.

"Joannina," Belisarius said, the name rolling from his tongue, "after Antonina's mother."

Belisarius grinned like a drunken idiot for a day and a night. Clutching the letter, he thrust the happy words toward any who so much as stopped to wonder at his mood. Most of the men humored him, marveling at the unfurled scroll, even those who could not read any letters at all, let alone the formal Latin preferred by the Empire's dwindling batch of patricians. His only moments of melancholy were upon the realization that he would visit neither mother nor daughter for many weeks, for a weakened yet hale Antonina would remain in Antioch. Similarly, Antonina requested her guards remain close at hand in the event that enemies should venture near the coastal city.

Sergius is taking good care of us in Antioch, and I need to keep our daughter safe and warm while you are away, she wrote, leaving Belisarius with little room to argue the point further.

"More reason to win this war!" Belisarius beamed to me, repeating Antonina's declaration aloud. "By then, we'll both be fathers, and free to enjoy it!"

However, even this happy interruption faded as the wrath of winter gave way to the first signs of spring, and fires blared along our frontier with Persia. Scouts reported growing commotion around Nisibis, with dust clouds betraying an army on the march to the south. The Emperor's peace talks having failed miserably, Astabadh Azarethes gathered his army for war and moved cautiously westward as the Shahanshah's banners fluttered in the Mesopotamian spring winds.

Having already provisioned the army for another campaign season, Belisarius was quick to react to Azarethes' incursion. Sunicas and Simmas led their Hunnic foederati as outriders for the slower march of Romans and were charged with the duty of harrying Persian scouts and foragers that ventured from Azarethes' main army.

"Don't engage them," John insisted, "but make them pay for any mistakes as they move toward Syria."

I hailed Samur as he followed Sunicas through Dara's western gates, their twin black furs enviable in the lingering chill of an early spring. Belisarius' main army departed Dara three days later, leaving behind nearly all servants, staff, and wounded that were unable to bear a spear or shield. Rosamund protested, yet, perhaps recalling our argument before the Battle of Dara, did not insist as vehemently, and accepted her plight as I coaxed her into looking after the several dozen wounded Herulians that we were forced to leave in Dara. She also agreed to attend to Liberius, who isolated himself in separate quarters where he wrote letters to Basilius and others in the Imperial Palace. Servants told me that candlelight flickered under Liberius' doorway deep into the heart of the night, giving my old teacher a reputation as a man who required little sleep in his labors for Rome.

On my final morning in Dara, I offered prayers with Father Petrus and embraced the priest before leaving. He lay thin wrinkled hands on the bronze cross at my throat and smiled when he found the dagger and sword cross-latched at my belt.

"One more fight, Varus, and we can all go home," Petrus said. "God guide your steps."

I allowed Cephalas to accompany our foederati and tasked him with keeping track of our banners and armor on the march ahead. Though he attended this task dutifully each evening, I often found him at Perenus' side during the march, joking and laughing as they passed time in the saddle. Their easy mirth was a pleasant presence, and at times I longed to join my friends, although I forced myself to maintain my position at the head of the foederati to keep watch for any request from Belisarius or the other officers.

We left through Dara's massive western gate, our army snaking in a thick column into the plains of Syria. John organized regular scouts that flitted toward the direction of Azarethes' army, which kicked up massive plumes of dust as they advanced slowly westward from the Saokoros River. Against Hermogenes' wishes, Belisarius largely dispensed with engaging the Persian masses, electing instead to shadow Azarethes' movements south and west.

There was little that we could do to stop Azarethes, even if we acquiesced to Hermogenes' demands in those early days of the campaign. Even so, Sunicas' raids stung Azarethes' outriders and foragers, forcing the Persians to remain in thick columns that were reinforced by the remaining Zhayedan Immortals that had survived the Battle of Dara. After two weeks of a torturously slow pursuit of the hulking Persian forces, massive dust clouds from the west stirred Belisarius' men into a simmering kind of frenzy.

"Persian war bands?" Perenus asked, using his spear to point at the wide plume that formed along the western horizon.

"No," I responded. "They are too close to Edessa, and we would have received warning of their approach by now."

Nevertheless, I yelled for my foederati to form up, our dwindling numbers bolstered by riders from Valerian's light cavalry. Valerian eyed the incoming force nervously, cracking each of his fingers underneath a thumb.

"No banner present," Valerian said, "but they're coming in too fast to be on foot."

As I gazed onto the horizon, the first wave of mounted riders came into view, trotting at a leisurely pace. Above the frontmost riders billowed a great red flag—a familiar one.

"Ghassanids!" I yelled to the men, who visibly relaxed in their saddles. "Inform General Belisarius that our allies are here."

Valerian nodded and took two of his men back to the Roman camp two miles distant. I ordered Fulcaris to keep the foederati in position for the moment and took Perenus and Sembrouthes forward to meet the thousands of Arab recruits who re-pledged their services to Emperor Justinian. As we approached, Perenus flew the foederati's banners, and we hailed the incoming Arabs as friends.

First in their procession was al-Harith, Mariya's older brother and the new Ghassanid king after the death of King Jabalah at Thannuris. Seeing me, he waved and kicked his horse forward to meet our small party.

"Well met, Lord Varus," al-Harith said. "I hear that I am to be an uncle soon."

"God willing," I replied. I lowered my head. "I grieve for the loss of your father. He was a staunch ally of Rome."

Al-Harith gave a weak smile in return. "Yes, he was. And he died fighting. A fitting end for a warrior, if there ever was one."

Formalities observed, King al-Harith greeted Sembrouthes warmly and gave stiff courtesy to Perenus. The king asked of Mariya once again and rode at my side as we slowly made our way back to Belisarius' camp. Conversation soon fell upon grimmer subjects as Sembrouthes asked about the nature of our Persian foe.

"Reports from Dara are incredible," al-Harith conceded, "and what you all were able to do is nothing short of a miracle. I

417

will regret to my dying day that the Ghassanids were unable to take part."

I waved off the king's apology, much more curious about news of our foes.

"Azarethes is an accomplished warrior," al-Harith responded, "not of Prince Xerxes' caliber, but he has a mind for strategy honed by the Shahanshah's campaigns in the far east. He will not make the same mistakes as Perozes at Dara, nor will he underestimate Belisarius' command."

"And the Lakhmids? Will we be able to turn them back with your forces?" Perenus asked.

I winced—even as al-Harith's brother-in-law, I would not have spoken so frankly. Perhaps Perenus felt such candor was acceptable due to his own status as a distant Lazic prince; more likely, however, he simply did not care for the petty decorum of conversation with nobles.

Al-Harith eyed Perenus for a moment but made no sign of indignation at having the fitness of his soldiers questioned so. "Many of my men are young and untested," he admitted, "but they understand that our survival depends upon killing our Lakhmid enemies, and upon supporting Rome."

King al-Harith relayed a similar message to Belisarius and Hermogenes, arguing for caution in engaging Azarethes and the fresh Persian army.

"They seem to be following the original plan of Xerxes and Perozes toward Syria," he declared, "and will need to secure fresh supplies to feed and water their army. Al-Mundhir of the Lakhmids can provide some support"—here, al-Harith wrinkled his nose at his hated rival—"although my war bands will harry any Lakhmid supply train that moves through Mesopotamia."

The struggle for supremacy in Arabia ran deep. Though the Ghassanids had enjoyed an advantage in numbers and wealth over the Lakhmids for a good while, recent events in the war made al-

Harith's position atop the Ghassanid throne a precarious one. Indeed, few in Belisarius' command felt confident that their Arab allies would hold under the intense pressure of a Persian assault, no matter the assurances from King al-Harith.

Regardless, given Hermogenes' admonishment and the deteriorating situation in Roman Syria, Belisarius had little choice but to trust al-Harith. The Ghassanids composed near a third portion of the healthy forces available to Belisarius, making it impossible to use them as a reserve-only force behind more seasoned yet exhausted Roman soldiers. Besides strategy, there was diplomacy to consider; to relegate al-Harith's men to also-rans would be grossly insulting—and would only provide further ammunition for Hermogenes to hurl at Belisarius' staff of young officers.

Even with reinforcements, however, Belisarius still lacked the force to assault Azarethes directly. We shadowed the invading Persian force for weeks, staying fifty miles distant but keeping close watch of all Persian movements to the southwest. The Persians slowed their pace as they approached Barbalissus, seemingly unable or unwilling to siphon off raiding parties from their larger army. Belisarius and John sent regular missives to settlements as far away as Antioch and Palmyra, ordering them to store grain and closely guard their walls, only for such precautions to turn out unnecessary as Azarethes left the surrounding countryside unmolested. Other than the giant dust plume that clouded the countryside that linked Syria and Mesopotamia, the Persian astabadh left little sign of their malicious intentions altogether.

At last, when the noxious boredom of waiting for action had reached its unbearable peak, Sunicas stormed into the Roman camp. Thick spittle frothed at his pony's mouth as he galloped forward, not ceasing his haste until reaching Belisarius' position. With the sun at its midday peak, we heard the news that would change the direction of our Persian war forever.

"The Persian supply train... we burned it," Sunicas panted, gasping for air as the rest of the Hun foederati thundered in behind him—including , I noticed, Simmas and Samur. Their furs were thick with sand and dirt, and all seemed ragged from weeks of ranging out into the Syrian flatlands on their low ponies. Though weather-beaten and filthy, most still grinned with excitement as Sunicas continued his tale of their unanticipated success against the Persian column.

Belisarius ordered waterskins brought for the Huns and offered a hand to help Sunicas dismount, which Sunicas only shrugged away before dropping down on his own, albeit on weak and bowed legs. After drinking deeply from the skin, Sunicas continued his report, telling of the foederati's activities of the previous weeks.

"We trailed the Persians and Lakhmids since leaving Dara," Sunicas explained, "but Azarethes made little effort to disguise his intention or throw out false trails. We split into groups of fifty and picked off small foraging and scouting parties of a half dozen or so at a time."

"And the Persians never tried to ward you off?" John asked.

Sunicas shook his head. "A few war bands challenged us, but we killed several and otherwise kept our distance," he said, grinning wickedly. "No Persian can match a Hun on horseback."

Simmas joined his brother in the tale. "Our smaller bands moved continuously to disguise our numbers and position, so Azarethes or al-Mundhir struggled to anticipate our movements even if they mounted a serious defense," Simmas said.

"And the baggage train?" Belisarius asked.

"Destroyed," Sunicas replied. "Or most of it, anyway. The Persian oxen were poorly suited for soft Syrian soil and lagged terribly behind the army. We simply swooped in when the whole train was guarded by no more than fifty auxiliaries, killing their oxen and torching anything that would burn."

Hermogenes, who joined the meeting late, rubbed his hands in excitement. "Azarethes will be desperate—no food or water with that many bellies to fill! This is our chance to fulfill the Emperor's demands!"

Bessas scoffed. "More like this is our opportunity to watch Azarethes' men wither from thirst and hunger while we sit safely back. Why fight when their army will sicken and die on its own?"

"Agreed," replied Ascum. "We can block all the major watering holes, and it is far too early for harvest for Azarethes to replenish his grain stores. Let them wilt in the desert."

Optimism rose across the officers as men voiced their agreement. Azarethes' considerable loss seemed to be a gift from God: The setback would spoil his invasion before it even really began, seeing as their forces captured only a few villages on their march from Mesopotamia. By luck or skill, Belisarius again seemed to have acquired the upper hand for his men.

Yet this, still, was not enough for Hermogenes.

"The Persians have invaded Roman land, killed Roman women and children, and threatened to tear our Empire in half. And you would simply let them walk away?" he bellowed. "The Emperor will not stand for cowardice, nor will I."

"Legate—" John began.

"I've had enough of your honeyed tongue, Armenian," Hermogenes snapped. "All you offer are excuses and complaints. I have held your hand each step of our campaign, and I will do so again if it means keeping Roman honor intact. This army will take advantage of Azarethes' growing desperation and will sweep the Persians from the field, just as it did at Dara."

Dumbstruck, the officers simply stared at Hermogenes as his face purpled with indignant rage. All eyes then fell upon Belisarius, but our general merely nodded and threw a stiff salute to the legate, his face betraying no emotion.

"As you command, Legate Hermogenes. We will obey at all costs," Belisarius said, his voice resigned yet firm.

Brow still furrowed, Hermogenes adopted a look of triumph. "See that you do," he said crisply, and left our makeshift gathering to return to Procopius and other clerks.

Silence descended upon the officers. Again, we all turned to Belisarius, waiting. The general looked thoughtfully around at his men, a slight frown breaking an otherwise emotionless expression. At last, his deep-brown gaze came to a rest upon a banner showing the Imperial Eagle, and he rubbed his forehead with grimy fingers. Taking a deep breath, Belisarius opened his mouth and issued an order that would forever alter the course of history.

As a gray-haired and crook-backed man today, I still cannot forgive Hermogenes' intransigence. With time, however, I have come to understand it, even if I disagree. For a hundred years, the Empire's generals shied from Persian attack, losing mile by mile of territory. These losses were humiliating and infuriating to both patrician and plebeian alike, imbuing us all with a sense of inevitable defeat at the hands of a leviathan. Further defeat would cost us the Levant, and with the Levant would fall Egypt and the vast quantities of grain, gold, and men that sustained our armies and cities.

After Dara, it would have been difficult for Hermogenes to insist upon anything other than outright slaughter of the Persian invader. Defeat Azarethes, and the east would be finally free of war for a generation or longer. In Hermogenes' eyes, Belisarius' men seemed to have everything they needed to extinguish the enemy entirely—save the old Roman courage. However, Hermogenes, like so many Roman commanders before him, misjudged his adversary. And for that, I spit on his memory.

"Break camp and set a direction to intercept the Persian vanguard. We will attack them along the Euphrates River," Belisarius commanded.

Many in the room muffled hisses at the order, yet only John dared offer an alternative path. "Lord Belisarius, should we discuss this further? Perhaps something could be done?"

"We have our orders," Belisarius said firmly. "Based upon the pace of the armies, where would we meet the Persians?"

"Near Callinicum," replied Sunicas. "We ranged by there several days ago. It is a larger town at a junction on the Euphrates."

"Then Callinicum it is," Belisarius declared. "Send couriers to warn the town leaders of our advance. I will prepare additional instructions to be carried with the messengers."

Belisarius' words were met again with awkward silence. True, there was some logic in facing the Persians on the banks of the historic river, but we simply lacked the numbers to hold off any encircling advancement on our flank not covered by the river. Even worse, the flat ground was perfect for the Persian and Lakhmid horsemen, and our enemy would be doubly motivated by the need to defeat our army with all haste.

"Well? Is there any confusion amongst you?" Belisarius said darkly.

"No, General. We will do as you command," John answered. "I will see to it."

And so he did. We made our way to Callinicum, a backwater town on the Syrian–Mesopotamian border so insignificant it was not even registered on most Imperial maps in Constantinople.

In our wake, that would be forever changed. Fools that we were.

Immortal

THE WATERS OF CALLINICUM

As PREDICTED, THE Persian army changed direction after Sunicas and Simmas' attack, and they were now heading east, with their right flank hugging the Euphrates River as a reliable source of fresh water. Under the baleful watch of Hermogenes, Belisarius ordered the army to double its pace to beat the Persians to Callinicum, which followed a southeasterly bend in the course of the Euphrates. Germanus ordered the Thracians mounted on spare horses for that exercise, while Bessas distributed mounts to Baduarius' spearmen—to Baduarius' wild protest. If the gods intended for him to travel on a horse, he argued, they would have made him a smaller man to make mounted travel comfortable. Still, grumbling and grunting, Baduarius joined his men atop a pony that panted and sagged under the man's weight.

Even at that late stage, nearly all of us hoped that battle could be avoided. Mundus even suggested that Belisarius' haste to reach a predetermined battleground was meant to dissuade Azarethes further from engaging in battle, and instead force the Persian masses to seek shelter at the border fortresses around Nisibis.

"Too risky, I'd wager," Mundus argued, "and even with the numbers, Azarethes would be wary of losing so many men on enemy territory, and with little food or water to keep the survivors moving forward."

"Perhaps Azarethes assumes he can rout our army and take our own stores?" I suggested unhappily.

"Aye, perhaps, although that's a desperate gamble. And one that will cost the Persians thousands of lives," Mundus replied, showing his teeth in distaste.

The Roman Army reached the outskirts of Callinicum a mere three days after Hermogenes' insistence upon our need to combat the invading Persian forces. Men slid from horses to tease at stiff muscles and sore legs and drink deeply from waterskins. Even more seasoned riders like Perenus grunted in relief at a rest for his chafing thighs, only to be harassed by Huns who saw moaning as unbefitting a warrior.

Belisarius informed the town of our peaceable arrival yet ordered John to form our camp outside of Callinicum's stone walls. Within hours, neat rows of white tents were arrayed along the plains, with men collapsing in exhaustion and filling the once-tranquil surroundings with the croaking snores of thousands of unwashed bodies. As the men slumbered, Belisarius called his officers in for a survey of the battlefield and the creation of our plan to face down Azarethes' massive army.

Even Solomon made an appearance at this meeting, although he made something of a show of gingerly holding his heavily bandaged arm as he stepped into Belisarius' tent. At the peril of my immortal soul, I wished the injury both painful and poisoned until the limb withered with rot. But either I was not so lucky, or Solomon far too blessed, for he would neither be truly injured nor suffer mightily from it.

More vexing still—to me—was that few enquired about the source of yet another serious injury to the commander and allowed the charade to continue despite its likely conclusion being Solomon's excusal from the upcoming battle.

"Keep watch over him," I muttered to Perenus. "Bastard tried to kill us once; he'll do so again if given the chance."

"Want me to return the blessing?" Perenus offered. "Painful or peaceful, I'll let you choose."

"No," I said, though not without temptation. "Just keep watch on Solomon's every movement. If Marcian carries his waste bucket to the latrine, I want to know of it."

Other officers filed into Belisarius' tent, which, despite the absence of Hermogenes, remained tense due to the watchful eye of Procopius sitting in the corner and scribbling notes on a cleaned animal skin.

Belisarius cleared his throat and scanned his officers, offering a light smile of encouragement. "Let us begin. Tell me of the surrounding area," Belisarius said, prompting several officers into lively reports all at once.

"No natural impediments or landmarks to slow Azarethes down, other than the river," Bessas noted, "and the terrain is generally flat, with small stones that are easily avoided with a careful eye."

Still covered in gashes that slowly healed in the months after Dara, Marcellus offered his own assessment. "Good cavalry ground, although the soil nearest the river will break hooves and snap legs, as soft as it is."

The Huns grunted agreement, arguing that even the light ponies would struggle on such terrain.

"Then the river flank is mine," Baduarius said with a sniff. "More's the better."

Unusually for these meetings, Belisarius interrupted the discussion with his own thoughts. "The riverfront must be held at all costs," Belisarius said. "No retreat. If our river flank falls, the army will be encircled."

"I will not let my lines falter, Lord," Baduarius said, his tone serious. "We will give those Persians a good licking."

Others laughed. King al-Harith, too, interjected with his own proposal. "I request the right flank, General Belisarius," he said in his accented Greek. "The Ghassanids are the largest contingent in your army, and as a cavalry unit, we will benefit from having the firmest ground."

"Are your men prepared for that?" John asked, his voice betraying more skepticism than would have been polite before one's allies.

"They are," the king said pointedly. "And if there are issues with my lines, we have substantial space to maneuver and reform to support the army."

"Granted," Belisarius said. "Bessas will command a third of our cataphracts that will be stationed on your left, Lord King."

"We will bring honor to our alliance." Al-Harith nodded, appearing grateful at the trust shown to him, although Bessas and John shared a look of concern as the position of the men was drawn out on a makeshift map.

Belisarius continued. "I would ask Lord Marcellus to join the excubitores as well as the spearmen under Valerian to reinforce Baduarius on the left," he said, adding more pieces to the Roman left flank, "and John will command the remainder of my cataphracts in the army's center."

John sat upright at the mention and grinned. "Of course, General. I would request the Huns be stationed in an auxiliary role to fight off any Persian archers or light cavalry."

Simmas snorted a laugh. "Leave it to the Huns to fend off your nuisances, eh?" he said, eliciting a barking laugh from his brother.

"We'll kill them all," Sunicas declared. "No Persian or Lakhmid can match our range."

Belisarius nodded. "And Lord Ascum will have command of our foot archers and what few ballistae are available to us, with his attention focused upon protecting the riverbank."

"The riverbank, Lord?" Ascum asked.

Belisarius traced a finger along the crude outline of the Euphrates that lined his map. "Azarethes will hit us hard here and try and push Baduarius away from the river," he explained. "You are our guarantee that their pressure will not become too great."

Ascum nodded. "Saving your arse again, Baduarius."

"Like hell you will!"

Marcellus rolled his eyes, and Belisarius raised a hand to stop the banter. "I also ask Lord Germanus and Lord Mundus to protect the center-right of our formation, with the Thracian Army's spearmen plugging the gap between John and Bessas," he said. "I will primarily station myself with our main body of cataphracts, and will be accompanied by Uliaris and a small retinue of couriers."

Side conversations began to break out amongst the commanders, who jostled for position or voiced concerns of their assignments to others. Curiously, I saw no place for my foederati on the map. In the midst of the cacophony, I raised my voice.

"Lord, what about the Herulians?"

Solomon snorted at my interjection but quieted after a stern look from Germanus and a nudge from Troglita.

Belisarius smiled at me. "Varus, I would like you to keep you and your men in reserve. After your sacrifices at Dara, I think this is a sensible maneuver."

"Agreed," said Baduarius, and thumped the wooden table.

"Absolutely," Marcellus chimed in. "I agree with Belisarius."

Hot shame crept up my neck. "But Lord, we would be wasted as reserves... We... my men won't disappoint you," I replied clumsily, fighting to keep my eyes locked on those of Belisarius.

"I am depending on it," Belisarius said. "And reserve does not mean that you will not be needed. I would just like for your men to stand with me at the beginning of the battle and deploy where help is most needed."

A deflection, and expertly phrased to disarm any slight to my honor. Still, young and prickly as I was then, I lacked the grace to accept it, feeling the assignment an insult to all that I'd bled and sacrificed, to my hard efforts in bringing the foederati into elite fighting form. Philippi. Armenia. Dara. All seemingly meaningless as Belisarius' army took order against the most critical engagement.

"But, Lord, please!" I insisted. "The Herulians will win this fight. They want to serve you and send these Persians back into Assyria."

"The abilities of you and your men are unquestioned, komes," Belisarius replied, his voice steady. "Which is why I require you at my side to heed my instruction as our forces clash against Azarethes."

I nodded, knowing I could not continue to refuse Belisarius without seeming petulant and disobedient. "Of course, Lord Belisarius," I said formally. "It would be an honor."

The planning session ended soon thereafter, with men departing for their tents for a much-needed night's sleep. As I slipped through the tent flaps with Sembrouthes, Belisarius called out, bringing me to a halt.

"Varus, would you speak with me for a moment?" His tone was light, as though the request was a mere suggestion rather than a command. Reversing my momentum, I bade Sembrouthes to wait for me outside of the tent and rejoined Belisarius in his command post.

Absent the other officers, the space seemed oddly dark, with low fires illuminating the tent walls and giving the quarters an overlarge look. Alone, Belisarius sat by one of his braziers, dipping a rag into a wooden bucket and lathering the wet cloth over his face. Belisarius rubbed his temples as the cloth hid his features, taking several moments before revealing a warm gaze. He invited me to sit, scratching at the growing stubble on his chin before he spoke.

"You seem troubled by my decision, Varus. What can I do to put your mind at ease?" Belisarius asked, inviting response.

My eyes immediately fell to the floor as I gathered my thoughts. A sudden streak of courage brought me to sit straighter as I responded.

"I'm worried that you do not trust my men to do their duty, Lord, and I want nothing more than to serve you," I replied, meeting Belisarius' gaze. "I have little else in this life beyond my family and my honor. Emperor Justin trained me my entire life for service to the Empire."

"Ah." Belisarius clapped his hands. "Varus, I apologize for giving you that impression. The other officers and I have been incredibly impressed with your leadership against the Avars and over the Herulian foederati. It is rare to see a young man rise so quickly without the benefit of money or influence."

"But... then... Lord, why am I not being entrusted with a portion of our line?" I stammered.

Sighing, Belisarius pushed on his knees and stood to walk to a low desk, where he withdrew a small scroll whose wax seal had been broken some time ago. He handed the parchment to me, and I unfurled the document to find my wife's own neat handwriting. I read as Mariya begged Belisarius for a reprieve from my duties, asking if anything could be done to spare me from those more dangerous assignments our foederati often engaged in.

Again, shame flooded through my body. I reread each word, the heat of dismay building as Mariya begged special favors to protect me from harm. Now, with the wisdom of age, I see that such requests were as sensible as they were predictable—for who would not wish to protect their beloved? Yet at that age I lacked that wisdom and had only a clumsy understanding of the bond of marriage. I could only see Mariya's entreaty as a strike against my honor. Worse, I could only see that both she and Belisarius thought me incapable of fulfilling my duties without dying, such that others were forced to take losses in my stead. The thought that others would die so I might live was too much.

431

I lowered the scroll. "Lord, did my wife convince you to remove me from harm? To put another in my place against the Persians?"

Belisarius shook his head. "No, Varus, despite my heart's desire to ease Mariya's fears for you. Do not vex Mariya for worrying for her husband, or the father of her soon-to-be child. Love makes us do things that inflict pain upon those we care deeply for in hopes that a greater loss may be averted in the future."

"Then why?" I exclaimed, my eyes beginning to well. "Do you not trust me?"

"Quite the contrary." Belisarius narrowed his eyes. "I know you better than you could ever realize."

His insistence took me aback. "What do you mean?"

"I was never a slave," Belisarius confessed, "and I could not know the pain that has caused you or your brother. But I, too, was an orphan, and an impoverished one at that. I know what it means to not know one's mother, or father, and question whether the kindness of strangers would one day expire and leave you inches from a slow death by starvation."

"Lord—"

Belisarius interrupted. "I served a local governor in Macedonia, eating scraps from his table and scraping dung from his chamber pot. If it wasn't for the actions of a Macedonian commander, I would likely still be there, or more likely deceased from disease or bodily neglect."

I gazed into my general's large, sad eyes. "Who was the commander, Lord?" I asked.

The answer left me stunned.

"An excubitor by the name of Justin," he said. "Even then, he was an older man, and rarely visited his home in Macedonia, but he found me on one of his visits and asked if I wished to live out my days as a scullion or if I burned for something more."

Belisarius' words flowed over me as I sat, dumbstruck by the revelation. A spring chill swept into the tent as the last light of day disappeared over the horizon. Belisarius shuddered and stretched his gnarled fingers over the brazier, gathering what warmth he could in the callused flesh. I'd heard only faint details of this tale before from the lips of others; Belisarius' own telling left me awed at all that we had, somehow, shared in life.

"I was fourteen, but Justin bribed a local recruiter to assign my age as seventeen in order to enlist me into the ranks of the Roman Army. Justin paid for my arms and armor, and I was trained in the same unit as his nephew, Flavius Petrus," Belisarius said.

"Justinian?" I asked, my eyes wide.

"The same." Belisarius nodded. "And I would appreciate it if this story was kept safely within your own knowledge."

I swore to keep Belisarius' confidence, and he told me of his extensive time with a younger version of Emperor Justinian. "Many in the Senate and the Capitol speak poorly of him today, but that is because they do not know his heart," Belisarius said, enunciating each word. "Justinian is a man of vision and burns with an ambition that can shape the remnants of our empire toward something better. His passion gave me and the other men real hope that our lives may return the Empire back to its former glory and provide a sense of purpose and safety that had been absent since even before Attila ravaged Europa."

Nodding in understanding, I sat, transfixed, as Belisarius pulled his hands away from the flames and drew a cloak over the exposed skin of his arms and neck. "Just think of it!" he exclaimed. "A world where men and women of a hundred peoples could all live in peace, fat and happy, under the security of Rome once more."

"Emperor Justin spoke of this often," I said, "as did others in his immediate circle."

Belisarius smiled. "Yes. Justinian and I joined the Imperial cavalry, which even then was under-strength and engaged in war with dozens of tribes. Our detachment was led by a tribune named Godilas, whom you knew well at the Imperial Palace."

"He was a good man," I said, "and an excellent master-at-arms."

Belisarius nodded. "Godilas and Justin continued to work with me, convincing me that the army represented my only real opportunity to rise above my pitiful station in life, to leave a mark upon the world that makes a positive difference in the lives of the common people. Through hunger and cold and battles with dozens of enemies, this fire is what kept me striving forward, striving to rise to the highest stations in the Roman Army. So when you ask how I know you, it is because you and I share so much. I was raised on the same words, by the same teachers who raised you from lonely orphan to a force to be reckoned with. I know the fire that burns within you, Varus."

A tear fell down my right cheek, which I hurriedly cuffed away. Pressing my eyes with thumb and forefinger, I let my face fall toward the ground as my mind rushed back to the late Emperor's final command to me.

"Come back from Cherson, and I'll tell you everything. I promise," Emperor Justin once said. He swore to provide answers to all the questions that left a hole in my heart. Who am I? Where do I come from? And why did the Emperor and his friends provide special treatment to one who grew up a slave? However, the old Emperor died before he could yield the truths that he held all of those years, and I remained in darkness as I continued to serve the Empire that he had loved and fought for.

A hand came to rest lightly upon my shoulder as Belisarius continued.

"You have done more than enough to earn a place of honor and wealth at the Emperor's table. With a single letter, I could have you transferred back to serve Empress Theodora and place all of this hardship behind you," Belisarius said. "You will probably grow fat and be surrounded by a herd of small children, and you would live in peace. It would be a life you have earned, and none would begrudge you that choice."

My chest rising and falling with deep breaths, I wiped my eyes and stared into Belisarius' face. "Is this a choice you have considered yourself?" I asked, thinking of our conversation earlier—his dreams for a simple life, of Antonina and farmland.

"Yes," Belisarius admitted. "Many times."

I pressed further. "What keeps you from retiring, of leaving war behind?"

Belisarius offered another weak smile, his wide lips arching just barely upward. "In spite of everything, I still believe in Justin's lessons, and in Justinian's vision. The possibility is a faint one, but if enough loyal and capable men and women pledge themselves to that cause, it will give Rome its best chance to rise above and out of this present darkness."

I could no longer hold back and let slip all the nagging concerns—of Rosamund, Samur, and admittedly myself. "But are you not dissuaded by the Emperor's commands? Of Hermogenes? Of a capital that seems to care little whether we are maimed or killed on some distant battlefield?" I asked.

Rather than answer, Belisarius paused, then asked his own question. "What do you think makes a great leader, Varus?"

"A love for his men, and a willingness to sacrifice one's own safety for theirs," I replied instantly, though I wished that I had taken more time to craft a more eloquent response.

Nevertheless, Belisarius nodded and chuckled at my answer. "Yes, my friend, this is a rare quality that separates normal men from the perilous few that make the world a better place," he said. "But it is not enough. What makes a leader great?"

I shook my head. "I couldn't tell you, Lord," I replied, my eyes rising to meet his own.

Belisarius gave another light chuckle, lines forming at the edge of eyes that grew dark and sunken from a lack of sleep. "A great leader is one who is willing to make decisions that seem cold and uncaring by many, yet are designed to foster the best possible outcome for the army and the Empire," he said. "It is the ability to send a man to suffer and die without question or doubt if their lives will tip the balance toward our survival and success. To seek the advice of even those who would scorn or mock you but be willing to stand confidently alone and shoulder the burden of the terrible losses that come from one's decisions. It is the ability to live with your failures and still have the courage to risk more in the service of one's duty and convictions."

Belisarius coughed and sipped from a wooden cup that had been prepared on a nearby bench. "In essence," he concluded, "it's a willingness to place duty over love, and honor over desire. It is the simplest command that there is, yet the most difficult path available to any person living."

"I think you are a great leader, Lord. All of your followers do," I replied.

Belisarius laughed. "That is kind of you, Varus. But I fear that I will never live up to the legends of Caesar or Hannibal. I strive to be everything that my teachers wished of me, yet I am weak, and I fail. And in my failures, I turn to my brothers under the Imperial banner and let their strength shoulder my weakness. John, Baduarius and his late brother, Ascum and Marcellus, and Sunicas and Simmas," he recounted, speaking each name with reverence. "And now you as well, if you'd believe me. When my journey clouds, and the road ahead is uncertain, I put trust in those I love. And it has made all the difference."

Belisarius paused again, warming his palms against the brazier. His words seemed to flow so easily from him, as if from his very soul, yet they rooted me to the ground. Enraptured and spellbound, I felt all that Belisarius described resonate within me, made all the realer by admission of his human flaws and limitations. Lacking words of my own, I waited for Belisarius to continue, feeling more at ease than at any point since departing Constantinople.

"But more importantly, is this a path that you would choose for yourself? Or shall I see you safely back to Antioch and then Constantinople, with all the love and friendship that I can muster as a parting gift?"

My eyes fell upon the fading brazier, its last embers giving way to the cool breeze that flooded into the tent despite all attempts to seal it from the world. The faces of others filled my mind as I considered both paths, knowing that Belisarius would honor either. Taking a final deep breath, I gave my answer.

"I would serve you, Lord, and the Empire. I believe as you do," I replied.

Belisarius face broke into a wide smile as he nodded. "I thought so," he said, "as did Lord Liberius. But this also means that you must take care to protect yourself, even as you look after your men. A sign of a leader is to know your limitations, and to understand when it is time to ask others to shoulder a piece of the great burden that you carry."

I nodded. "I understand, Lord. My foederati will begin the battle in reserve, at your side."

As we concluded our conversation, Belisarius embraced me, dismissing me with a blessing upon my safety and for those of my wife and unborn child. I thanked Belisarius and returned to my men, my mind awash in hope for the future, even when all good sense suggested we'd be dead men in just a few days' time.

The army worked furiously to prepare the area around Callinicum for the following two days. Scouts worked in teams to track the progress of the Persians, whose vanguard closed in on our position as they followed the course of the Euphrates River eastward. Baduarius ordered that replacement shields and spears be available to all of Belisarius' infantry, while Sunicas and Ascum ordered all fletchers in Callinicum to prepare additional arrows for mounted and standing archers alike.

Two days later, our labors were finally interrupted. The Derafsh Kaviani, borne by Azarethes' outriders along the Syrian horizon, crested the horizon, and throughout the day, more Persians continued to flood across the expanse, with thousands of mounted Lakhmids taking their place toward drier land and opposite their hated Ghassanid enemies. Hermogenes, impatient as always, urged Belisarius to harry the Persian forces with our mounted cavalry, although Belisarius convinced him of the need to keep our foederati fresh for the inevitable battle between the two forces.

Thus undisturbed, Azarethes pitched his camp several miles from his Roman counterpart, and the evening passed with little disruption other than fast-fraying resolve and the idle-yet-fearful chatter of men who would soon be placed in the bloody horrors of the shield wall.

Dawn broke, and horns blew. All rose, though few from any kind of restful slumber. Some men gorged on wine—a practice that was formally discouraged yet rarely condemned; no officer could truly begrudge borrowed courage for men about to suffer in the crush of battle. Driven by the lessons, if not the example, of Godilas, I drank only water as I stirred Perenus and the Herulians awake to ready for the uncertainty ahead.

A thunder of hooves and horns bellowed from the direction of the Persian camp, their fires still blazing despite the growing light of the morning haze. Their rising intensity produced images of Hakhamanish, and I saw Fulcaris shudder as his eyes fell upon the preparations of Azarethes' men.

"So, here we are again," Samur called out to me. "I've heard that you'll be in the reserves to start the fight."

I admit it still smarted to hear, even from my own brother. "Yes, until Belisarius orders us into the line," I responded curtly.

"Good," Samur said, with not a hint of scorn or sarcasm in his voice. "I mean it."

We quickly embraced as my men struggled to assemble their armor, and as Sunicas' banners rose into the air. Samur waved to Perenus and Cephalas before departing, and I whispered a quick prayer that my brother would return safely to me at the conclusion of the battle, and of the war.

"Your brother is right about one thing," Perenus put in. "The Persians seem to have enough men to keep this war going forever."

Sembrouthes snorted. "No army is invincible, and the Persians are no exception. One more victory, and we can all go home as rich men."

"I'll settle for happy and whole," Fulcaris answered, his normal mischief gone from his face. I had requested Fulcaris' promotion to centurion and gave him command of Opilio's remaining men and was pleased at Belisarius' quick acceptance of such an order. Fulcaris beamed at the honor yet took to his heightened responsibilities with a grave manner that, it seemed, even Perenus could hardly transform into mirth. The young Herulian had lost considerable weight since taking a wound at Dara, and while he insisted that he was physically strong enough to fight, he looked slight, even gaunt, in his place alongside his cousin Irilar. More than that, however, Fulcaris seemed to have lost the carefree joy that he carried to Philippi so long ago.

Our last visitor was Troglita, who commandeered a pony and galloped toward my ouroboros banners. Troglita formally saluted my men and dismounted as he found my position amongst my remaining forces. The komes curled his arm into my own and professed his best wishes for the fight to come.

"Belisarius will be counting on you to plug any gaps in the line," Troglita warned me, "and I'd be a poor commander if I didn't ask for you to look out for my men."

"For the man who saved my arse against the Avars? Of course." I smiled, hoping to reassure him, but Troglita offered only a perfunctory smile. He drew close and whispered in my ear.

"It's the Thracians. I don't trust Solomon, or Marcian," he said briskly. "Dara was a debacle for them, and their pettiness almost brought our lines to collapse. If you see them buckle or run, I'd ask you to come and reinforce me as quickly as you are able."

"Do Germanus or Mundus share your concerns?" I asked.

Troglita gave his head a quick shake. "They are aware of it, but there's nothing they can do. Solomon is protected by his father, and Marcian by Solomon. Oh, Marcian is a decent enough soldier, but he's excessively cruel and not one for self-sacrifice."

"I will keep an eye on it," I promised him. "And I will keep your confidence."

Troglita embraced me and departed for the Thracian banners, disappearing into a swirling press of men and horses that comprised Belisarius' cosmopolitan army. Ghassanids mixed with Goths, Alans, and Huns, who all jostled for position or sought one final bag of supplies or arrows. Officers barked orders and did what they could to maintain order in the camp, with John leading efforts.

Cephalas helped me into my armor, which had been hastily repaired in the aftermath of Dara. "You'll need to get repairs from the master smith in Constantinople," he observed, knocking a knuckle lightly against the scales, "but this should hold for another battle."

As I tugged the leather-and-scale armor over my head, I winced at the still raw and healing flesh that covered my shoulder and thigh. Cephalas helped fasten my cloak and held Ignis still as I vaulted onto the stallion's saddle, checking its stirrups with my boots out of habit. Cephalas next handed over my sword, dagger, and axe, and I placed them along my belt and handed over Khingila's massive recurve bow. Lastly, I was handed my shield and spear, which I secured across my back using the shield's leather straps as a holster against my armored shoulders.

Securing my helmet and plume, I sat high in the saddle and assessed the army as I made myself visible to my men. "How do I look?" I asked Cephalas.

"Like Ares himself, Lord," Cephalas answered. I smiled at my friend and bade him a safe and uneventful day, guessing that my wishes were unlikely to manifest themselves.

I nudged Ignis forward with my knees, and we trotted in tight circles as I reacquainted myself in the saddle. Perenus and the other Herulians looked on for additional orders, while Sembrouthes and his Aksumites stood silently as perhaps the deadliest force within the entire Roman Army. With an outstretched arm, I saluted all of them and commanded the foederati into formation.

"Mount up!" I called, spurring the remnants of my men into action as they heeded my words with urgency. Despite the constant chaos of the Roman camp, within a few heartbeats, all were on horseback and ready to move.

Finding Fulcaris and Perenus, I gave the order to move out. "To the General!" they cried in unison. "To Belisarius!"

We moved toward the center-left of the Roman lines, finding Belisarius atop his own horse behind an array of cataphracts led by John. Belisarius acknowledged our presence and issued his compliments.

"Herulians, Aksumites!" he called out. "Keep your wits honed and your swords sharp, for I will need you this day!"

Perenus unsheathed his sword and cheered, earning a ragged but determined cry from the men. Fulcaris began chanting

Belisarius' name—a call that was gradually picked up first by John's cataphracts and then down the line toward the Cappadocian and Thracian spearmen. Men beat their spear butts and shield rims into the ground, head bobbing slightly to the rhythm. Despite himself, I caught Belisarius in a disguised smile, raising an arm to acknowledge the cheering.

It was at this time that I gathered a clearer view of the Persian forces. As Sunicas and Simmas guessed, Azarethes wasted little time arraying his men into battle, seeking a decisive end to the conflict before his men's vigor exhausted itself from too little food or rest. Blazing fires had been lit before the Persian army as Zoroastrian priests extolled the Persian and Lakhmid soldiers to destroy the insipid Roman dogs and claim the food and gold that was rightfully theirs. Scanning the flames, I saw several priests but no Hakhamanish, and unintentionally let out a sigh of relief that the magus would not be able to torment us this day.

Where the Roman ranks were a hive of organized confusion, the Persians were orderly and neat. They moved as if possessed by some omniscient spirit, spears glittering against the rising sun as mounted Zhayedan Immortals—presumably those who survived the carnage of Dara—led them forth. Far across from the Roman right stood thousands of Lakhmid horsemen, their lighter and unarmored ponies standing in contrast to the elite Immortals that formed the disciplined core of Shahanshah Kavadh's vast army.

The murmur of Zoroastrian prayers suddenly ceased, and a great shout went up throughout the Persian masses. The heavily armored lines of Immortals parted, making way for a lone horseman with an immense horsehair plume and heavy scaled armor covering soldier and horse alike.

"Azarethes," Sembrouthes muttered.

Indeed, it was. While Perozes at Dara had adorned himself with the trappings of wealth and princely power atop a great war elephant, Azarethes was hardly discernable from the ranks of his Immortals. But as I looked more carefully, I saw small differences: gilding that lined the thick scales of his armor, and a personal standard that hung from a small pole at the rear of his horse. Otherwise, Azarethes appeared as typical a warrior as the men he led.

From his sheath, Azarethes drew a huge blade that was curved near its tip, and with a thrust of the sword into the air, began galloping along the Persian lines. Thunderous cheers and growls arose again from the Persians while officers shouted for order across the lines.

Here, again unlike Dara, no pageantry, duels, or insults served as a precursor to battle. Instead, as Azarethes returned to the center of his lines, he simply lowered his sword for a quick blessing from a nearby priest, then raised the blade level with Belisarius' cataphracts across the Syrian expanse.

Then the Persian officers barked commands, and the earth rumbled.

Spearmen thundered toward their Roman enemy. Azarethes held back his Lakhmid allies and mounted Immortals in reserve and watched as his forward ranks eagerly closed the two hundred paces that separated them from Baduarius, John, and the Thracians.

On horseback, beside Belisarius, I heard the general lean toward a courier and issue his first order of battle. "Tell Baduarius to advance to meet the Persians, but venture no farther than ten paces from our main body," Belisarius said, yelling over the din to be heard clearly. The courier repeated the order, saluted, and galloped away toward the Gothic Dux.

Moments later, another boom echoed from the Roman lines. The curious sound of laughter followed, and the Roman far left advanced forward only to halt soon thereafter. Joined by Marcellus' excubitores, Baduarius' rearward ranks now stood just a pace farther than the frontmost of John's cataphracts. The great mass of spearmen slapped their shields together and lowered their spears, Belisarius' wolf and the Emperor's eagle flying high in the air. With the Persians just one hundred paces away, a chorus of harsh Greek voices rose high in song, soaring to a crescendo as the Cappadocians joined in the resistance against their looming death.

Belisarius nodded in approval and summoned another courier. "Tell Lord Ascum that he may fire his ballistae when ready," Belisarius bellowed, each word clear and measured. As with the first messenger, the second darted through the ranks toward a body of archers and heavy wooden siege engines, neatly arrayed and positioned to launch their massive bolts over the heads of the Roman Army.

Only seventy paces separated the armies now. I made out the sound of Ascum's screaming voice far behind our position as he ordered the ballistae to fire. Flaming missiles whistled overhead, showering embers upon the field and trailing a scent of brimstone that made me shudder with gratitude that such weapons were not levied against our own forces. They sailed in a jagged line toward the tightly clustered Persian ranks, which began to separate and scatter in anticipation of the barrage.

It was of little use. The massive wooden bolts showered into the heart of the Persian formation, with several bursting into thousands of pieces that punctured armor and left men and horses cut and bleeding. I saw a horse decapitated by one unlucky bolt, its rider crying out in shock as he fought to free himself of the saddle and the husk of a body that began to topple over. Other bolts impaled one or more soldiers, with the lucky ones dying upon impact rather than writhing in agony as their blood pooled in the Syrian dust.

The smell of burning flesh filled the air as the second volley hammered into the Persian lines, scattering spearmen and sending more than one horse on a frantic gallop toward safety. A banner rose within the Persian lines, signaling their thousands of bowmen to return fire. Baduarius ordered his men to take cover, and the rearward Cappadocian ranks layered their shields in a thick impenetrable shell high over the men's heads. With more warning, Germanus' Thracians followed Baduarius' example, firming the Roman front. As an added measure to bolster our defenses, John's armored cataphracts shuffled to the front to absorb any stray arrows, using the reinforced shields that the elite Roman horsemen carried into battle.

Several Persian arrows found their targets, but most clattered against wooden shields and scaled armor without inflicting any real damage. Ascum answered the attack with his own, bringing the Persians to raise their own wicker shields to stay the barrage of arrows. The exchange of fire dramatically slowed the Persian advance, yet after four or five volleys, both sides ceased, and the Persian commander opposite Baduarius ordered a charge.

From a safe vantage point in Belisarius' reserves, the synchrony of the Persian lines was nothing short of awe inspiring. Even with a slow hail of flaming ballista bolts falling overhead, the Persians maintained their discipline as they closed the final forty paces, their officers chanting a cadence to maintain order across the lines. With the front ranks led by more heavily armored and dismounted Immortals, the Persians lowered their spears and gathered speed, driving their weapons home into the painted sigils of the Roman shields.

Baduarius' and Valerian's spearmen met the wave of Persians with a crack of wood and wicker, with the Romans giving only half steps at a time as they leaned into their shields for the second and third ranks to stab viciously with spears and swords. Shouts of agony soon filled the expanse, nearly drowning out the clamor of wood and metal and the recurring shouts of various officers who kept order along the lines.

Marcellus' excubitores flooded in to replace the wounded and sore men at the front of Baduarius' ranks, and their effect was as immediate as it was temporary. The Persian advance stalled as Marcellus' expert swordsmen cut deep gashes into the Persian lines, but Azarethes led more than enough reinforcements to overcome his rising losses, and fallen soldiers were replaced almost as quickly as they fell. Immortals and excubitores traded lightning-fast blows across the lines, each bearing heavy lamellar armor that could absorb the few sword or spear strikes that snuck around their shields.

As Baduarius and Marcellus held the Roman ranks adjacent to the Euphrates River, the center of the Persian lines snaked toward John's cataphracts. Rather than wait for their attack, John's banner dipped as he signaled the cataphracts forward, crashing into the Persian ranks and sending dozens toppling to the ground. Rather than further his assault, however, John called the cataphracts back, reforming neat rows of armored cavalry that formed the core of the Roman center.

Ballistae continued to fire as the Persians closed in on Belisarius' right flank, bringing Germanus to strengthen his shield wall and resist the press of mounted Zhayedan and Persian spearmen alike. Another crash of shields sounded toward my position among the Roman reserves—the sheer pressure of the Persian advance jolted the Thracian wall backward.

Sensing the danger, Sunicas ordered the Hunnic foederati to blanket the second and third Persian lines with arrows, relieving some of the pressure on the Roman spearmen. I saw Troglita's plume dance high in the air as he fought in the most aggressive center of the fighting, his shield wall holding firm despite the continuous Persian attack.

It was at that moment, from the vantage point of the reserves, that two curious realizations befell me. First was that, although the bulk of the Persian army was engaged in direct assault upon the Roman lines, and especially our left flank, the Persian reserves were almost entirely made up of Lakhmid light cavalry, who sacrificed heavy armor in favor of speed and agility in battle. I watched as Belisarius eyed the Lakhmids warily, frequently turning his gaze to our own Ghassanids, who had only suffered light combat in the opening stages of battle. Yet we could see little further, as pillars of sand and dust kicked high into the air where Lakhmid and Ghassanid lines clashed.

The second realization was that ships with Roman masts filled our left flank along the Euphrates. Most of the vessels were no larger than barges or skiffs, holding one or two dozen men that bore bows and small shields on the ship's deck. However, as the battle progressed, several larger vessels appeared, their shallow hulls able to navigate that ancient river even as its tide shrank and ebbed from poor rainfall. I watched as they took anchor at a safe distance from Azarethes' bowmen.

The nearest craft fired several volleys into the mass of Persian spearmen, quilling their exposed bodies and sending many falling into the river and the sweeping current. I noticed several twitching and splashing as they called out to their comrades for help, their heads falling into the river in a swirl of blood and viscera that painted the Euphrates the color of death.

"What of the boats, Lord?" I yelled to Belisarius, who turned and nodded at the development.

"All planned," Belisarius said. "Don't worry."

The truth of battle is that few encounters last more than moments: One shield wall buckles, then runs in fear, and it is done. A small number of encounters, like Dara, last an entire morning, if both armies persist in their faith that they will succeed in toppling the other with just a bit a struggle.

Rarest, though, are the battles that last an entire day, and one such was Callinicum.

As the hours wore on, Rome and Persia alike fell into wanton depravity as exhausted and bloodied men fought for survival as much as a victory. Perhaps most shocking was the bitter Persian resolve to continue their assault on our left and center despite the many obstacles Belisarius had lain before them. As the sun reached its peak and began to fall in the sky, mounds of gored and trampled bodies lined the front of the Roman wall, with the dead and dying further soiled by churning mud, guts, and rank piss that frothed under the growing spring warmth. What once had been trails of blood in the Euphrates formed into a stagnant, almost fleshy sludge; I remember distinctly being put in mind of the plagues that God had wrought to punish Pharaoh's pridefulness against the Israelites. Floating limbs lapped against the skiffs and boats that remained anchored along the riverbank, with occasional surges from splashing bodies sending filth onto their decks.

Belisarius' men inflicted horrific casualties upon those of Azarethes. Wave after wave of Persians scaled their fallen comrades to assault the Roman lines, whose swords had been dulled by the repeated hammering against metal and bone. Azarethes did not deviate from his original strategy, and Belisarius did not deploy the Herulian foederati toward any section of the Roman lines, despite my repeated questions. Finally, Belisarius glowered at me and reminded me that our Ghassanid allies remained fresh and largely unused despite the length of the day.

"You will know when it is time," he barked. "I promise."

So we sat and waited. Messengers ferried updates to Belisarius from across the lines, and the few servants available to us carried water to the ranks. Wounded Romans were carried away from the battlefield, with some slumping over unconscious. Most remained awake, with many screaming in agony as their wounds oozed and tore past the point of repair from even the most gifted healers in the Empire. They should have counted themselves lucky to die there, swiftly; those who survived the night would win

448

nothing beyond the itch and burn of the green rot that killed a man over the course of days.

Then, as the sun hung low in the sky and the layers of Persian dead grew thick, the battle turned. From our vantage point, the shift was almost imperceptible at first, a mere whirling of dust clouds in an otherwise tumultuous stretch of torn Syrian landscape. Soon, however, the sound of hooves thundered in our ears.

Belisarius widened his eyes with fear. "Find Ascum, and tell him to send a flaming barrage as soon as possible," he said hurriedly, and I galloped hard toward the position of the Roman archers.

When I relayed the order, Ascum took up the command with vigor, ordering his teams of ballista operators to load bolts onto the spring-operated engines. That step completed, the tips of the bolts were covered in naphtha and carefully lit with a long torch, instantly spawning an inferno.

"Fire!" Ascum screamed, his voice hoarse from an entire day of commands over the din of combat.

I paused and gaped as the bolts flew into the sky, illuminating the darkening horizon and temporarily brightening the sky over the Persian lines. All seemed in typical order—until the bolts traveled over the ranks of spearmen and Persian cavalry and fell toward the reserves that Azarethes had kept at bay.

"Oh God!" I yelled. Not stopping to even salute Ascum, I kicked Ignis forward and galloped toward Belisarius, desperate to reach him to warn of the tidings.

For Azarethes had sent the entirety of his Lakhmid forces toward the Roman right, finally deigning to challenge our Ghassanid allies as dusk emitted a cruel twilight near Callinicum.

"Lord Belisarius!" I yelled. "The Lakhmids! They're coming for our right!"

Belisarius nodded. "I've sent a warning to al-Harith, and for Bessas to reinforce him. You may need to take your men there soon, though."

"Can the Ghassanids stand against such a heavy assault alone?" I asked. "Will the Herulians truly be necessary?"

Belisarius shook his head. "If it were earlier, with better light, the Ghassanids would fare well on their own. But in the dark when most of my men are spent..."

Belisarius trailed off, his eyes frantic as he searched for any opportunity to drive the Persians back and end the battle while our army remained operable and orderly. The choices were few. Despite the incredible casualties the Roman spearmen and cataphracts were able to inflict, more Persians pressed forward and prevented Belisarius from repositioning his units for fear of breaking the security of the broad Roman lines.

Another flaming volley fired overhead, lighting the sky over the Lakhmid cavalry that rose to a breakneck gallop as they closed in upon their rival Arab enemies. I saw King al-Harith recognize the threat and order his own horsemen into a defensive stance. But the undertrained Ghassanids toward the center and rear of his formation began to panic and mill nervously backward. The Lakhmid charge rammed hard into the Ghassanid right flank, which disintegrated as if turned to ash under the force of a great maul. Al-Harith tried to turn the charge back upon his opponents by hacking and slashing at the Lakhmid officers nearest his position, and his hardened front ranks even had some success at breaking the Lakhmid lines for a few moments. Panic consumed the core of the Ghassanid army, with small numbers fleeing the field with all haste. Panic, indeed, was all that was required to bring the Ghassanids into a rout.

In my time as a young boy in Godilas' training yard, the old general was asked one day what the most dangerous opponent was that a Roman army ever faced. Samur immediately suggested

Attila, while others recalled Hannibal or Mithridates, or the Persian Immortals, yet Godilas shook his head at each answer.

"Panic," Godilas answered. "That is the single most dangerous foe that any Roman can face in battle. Stand confident and disciplined, and no enemy is too great. If even one man throws down his weapons and runs in fear, that loss will infect the army quicker than any disease and cause more casualties than the most vicious barbarian to have ever crossed into the Roman Empire."

It was not until Callinicum that I understood the wisdom of these words. The trickle of Ghassanids fleeing their assault quickly grew into a torrent as men's courage waned. With their wall broken and discipline flagging, few men would willingly sacrifice themselves when their friends and officers ran to save themselves, tempting even the most hardened of soldiers to flee. King al-Harith fought for control over his army, yet the Lakhmids poured into growing gaps in the Ghassanid lines and massacred our allies dozens at a time.

"Tell Sunicas to send a contingent of Huns to reinforce al-Harith. Ranged attacks only, do not dismount!" Belisarius yelled to a courier, who saluted and galloped toward Sunicas and Simmas. I saw Sunicas receive the order and take a hundred of his more hardened soldiers toward the Roman left. Among them was Samur, his thin frame and short hair standing out amongst the shaggier and burlier Huns.

Even the steady stream of Hunnic arrows could not deter the Lakhmids. As they pushed forward, unflagging, I saw further reserves of Azarethes' armored cavalry shoring up the Lakhmid rear, with several Immortals ensuring discipline in their continuous push forward. Bessas helped to anchor the leftmost Ghassanid units, with his cataphracts slowing the Persian advance and protecting King al-Harith, who refused to vacate the field with the bulk of his army, but this only caused the Roman right to curl inward, and the more daring Lakhmid riders encircled the Roman ranks, threatening to end the battle for good.

At the height of the assault, Hermogenes trotted toward Belisarius, his face crimson with fury.

"What are you doing?" he screamed. "We're all dead if you don't turn that back!"

Belisarius turned his head toward Hermogenes, leaning slightly toward the older man. "Lord Hermogenes, you wanted this battle. Please allow me the freedom to prosecute it," he said calmly. "One of my men will see you safely to the other bank of the Euphrates."

Hermogenes blustered but did not refuse the offer. Belisarius summoned Uliaris, who identified a courier to escort the legate toward the riverbank. The legate kicked his pony forward, not deigning to look back at the continuing struggle of shield walls, arrow fire, and bodies roasting from still-lit ballista bolts.

I still did not see the full sweep of the plan. "Do the boat captains know that they will need to ferry Romans across the river, General?" I asked.

Belisarius nodded, his face gaunt. "Yes. This was planned for, in the event of disaster."

Disaster. My gut sank. The battle was lost. Despite the Romans in good formation and condition, Azarethes sacrificed huge numbers of his men to exploit our weakness: the untrained and underequipped Ghassanids. Our left and center held strong amidst a continuous assault, although our dire situation further unveiled itself as the rightmost ranks of the Thracian Army began to buckle.

Perenus trotted forward and leaned toward me. "Is that Solomon?" he exclaimed, pointing toward a contingent of Roman spearmen that retreated in a middling state of order. Indeed, a komes' plume sailed above the men and turned only to answer a harangue by the stout figure of Mundus.

"Likely yes," I answered, thinking of Troglita's warning. I pointed out the growing crisis to Belisarius, who nodded and issued more orders to his remaining couriers.

"Find Lord Germanus and order him to pivot the Thracians parallel with the river. Stop the Persians from encircling us at all costs," Belisarius bellowed, his orders carried over to the Thracian command.

Germanus quickly acknowledged the order and executed a masterful maneuver of the Thracian lines. Keeping their battle formation, the remnants of the Thracian right flank swung backward, their shields held tight against the Persian and Lakhmid assault. King al-Harith copied Germanus' example, ordering his remaining forces to gallop behind the Thracians and reinforce the hole that Solomon and Marcian had left on the Thracian right. In a matter of moments, Germanus' lines were perpendicular to those of John and Baduarius, forming a crude square that boxed Belisarius' army against the riverbank.

Even with the impressive maneuver, however, the Thracian shield wall began to warp and bend. Azarethes sent in his remaining reserves of veteran Persian cavalry, and Persian and Arab archers fired into the mixed ranks of cataphracts, Ghassanids, and Thracian spearmen. The combined effect was far deadlier than at the outset of the battle. Now, encroaching darkness was broken only by ballista flames and bonfires that Belisarius ordered lit at regular intervals behind the Roman lines, yet this served to make the battlefield appear more ghoulish. Belisarius shook his head as the thinned ranks near Troglita and Mundus threatened to fall and turned to me.

"Give the order to reinforce the Thracians," Belisarius commanded. "I'm going with you."

I thought of protesting, worried that Belisarius would expose himself to unnecessary danger. However, Belisarius' insistent tenor brooked no opportunity for debate or refusal, and so

I merely accepted the order. Signaling Perenus and Fulcaris forward, I directed the centurions to prepare the men for their engagement in the battle, noting that Belisarius and his personal guard would be joining us.

"Gods," Perenus said, showing the same signs of worry that I felt.

I raised a hand to stifle further discussion. "Protect Belisarius regardless of risk or cost. Uliaris will help, but it is on us to keep him alive."

Perenus and Fulcaris nodded and ran to pass along our charge. Waterskins were quickly distributed amongst our men as they hurriedly stretched stiff muscles and loosened themselves for battle. The ouroboros banner and the yellow-gold Aksumite crest was joined by Belisarius' wolf and the Imperial Eagle, with Uliaris leading a dozen of Belisarius' household guards as the general's primary protective force.

Belisarius trotted to the front of our formation, and Perenus gave the order for silence in the ranks. The sounds of battle sailed over our heads, and my men sat tall in the saddle, their helmets fastened and weapons ready for deployment.

"Men of the Herulian foederati! I rely upon you once again to save our army! For Rome!" Belisarius yelled, and I saw many of my men sit taller at the compliment.

Belisarius gathered his spear and shield as his thick armor glittered against the flames, with his horse Xanthos gulping at a water bucket held up by a nearby servant. Lowering his spear, Belisarius gave the order for his reserves to commit themselves to the fighting.

"Herulians!" I yelled. "To battle!"

"Forward!" cried the officers, with a great cheer rising from the throats of my thinned forces. Sembrouthes jostled toward my right as Belisarius took a position at my left, his household guard forming behind him. Uliaris stood to Belisarius' left and leaned over, nodding to me.

Our foederati surged forward, eager to break ourselves from the idyll of a day spent in still silence. We quickly closed the gap toward the Thracian rearward lines and were greeted by Mundus and Germanus, who personally joined in the fighting to keep the Thracian wall intact.

"Foederati!" I bellowed. "Nock your bows!"

Perenus echoed the order, which was passed along the line with all haste. I plucked my own bow—the massive, monstrous weapon salvaged from Khingila—from a holster against Ignis' saddle, and its blackened limbs reached high above my crest. Based upon the tension of its bowstring, Khingila surely possessed unnatural strength to draw his arrows, as the bow required at least twice the strength of any normal Roman or Hunnic weapon.

"Draw!" I called, which was immediately obeyed by the Herulians. Belisarius' guards and Sembrouthes' Aksumites waited patiently, their eyes darting curiously down my lines as over one hundred bows drew taut with vicious precision.

"Loose!" I yelled.

My arrow hurtled from its bowstring toward the crush of Persians and Lakhmids and pierced cleanly through the scaled helmet of a mounted Immortal, who swayed lifelessly in the saddle before falling and disappearing into our massed enemies.

The Herulian volley followed soon thereafter and inflicted horrible blows against the Persians. The Lakhmid advance was forced to a halt as suddenly as if they collided with a stone wall, with men tumbling from horses and tripping those who followed them. Lit torches flared on both sides but did little to dispel the totality of the dark.

I relayed three further volleys that, while still deadly, diminished in their effectiveness as the Persians and Lakhmids began to anticipate our strikes. Pressure on Troglita's front lines resumed, and the Thracian lines bent to accommodate the swell of attackers. Belisarius waved a spear to grab my attention and gestured toward the troubling sign. I nodded and ordered the next maneuver.

"Foederati!" I yelled. "Shield wall!"

Depositing my bow, I slid from Ignis' saddle and unslung the shield and spear from my back. Within moments, my men followed, joined by Belisarius' household guard as a small number of our riders led our horses a safe distance away. Once again, Belisarius stood snugly to my left, my shield protecting his exposed right arm.

"To the front!" I ordered, bringing our wall toward the Thracian position.

Anticipating our advance, Troglita signaled for the front ranks to rotate out, opening gaps for my men to trickle through the lines in an orderly fashion. The komes called out to me in thanks as I hustled to the front, consumed by the aroma of blood-drenched soil and all manner of filth. In the darkness, my legs felt weak and my stomach light, but I shrugged such weaknesses away in an attempt to focus. At last nearing the front lines, I screamed Mariya's name and burst toward the Lakhmid cavalrymen that fought desperately onward.

Almost instantly, my shield clattered against an Arab pony. I pushed hard at the beast's haunches and threw its rider from the saddle. Filing in behind me, one of the Aksumites speared the Arab through his lightly armored gut, which I followed with another slash to the man's throat.

Hands grabbed at my cloak and pulled me back into the lines, my shield slamming reassuringly into those of Belisarius and Sembrouthes. Even in the darkness, Belisarius' crest made for a handsome target, and several Lakhmids made an attempt to slash at Belisarius' body. I myself took one spear into the heart of my shield, its reinforced wooden panels shuddering with the impact.

Sembrouthes impaled that man while Uliaris thrust his spear into another, catching the man's armored torso with the tip just long enough for Uliaris to draw a francisca and throw the axe blade into the eye socket of an oncoming attacker.

Belisarius himself jabbed his spear at a mounted Immortal, its blade catching in the man's shield. Drawing his sword, Belisarius rushed forward, cutting a deep gash along the Immortal's thigh and stabbing up into the man's more lightly armored armpit. Even with a heavy helmet, I heard the Immortal squeal in surprise as he fought to turn his horse away from the Roman shield wall.

"Substitute!" a voice called behind me, and our front rank fell behind a fresh wave of Herulians. Perenus shoved his way in front of me, cursing the Persians as dogs and cowards in what little Persian he knew.

"I fucked your mother!" he called out. "Does she miss me?"

The message carried. One of the Persians growled and rushed Perenus, slamming shield against shield. Perenus took a step back as he absorbed the blow, and the Persian careened to the ground as he tripped over a rolling severed limb. Perenus deftly speared him in the neck, mercifully ending his life before even the poor man realized the mortal peril he had placed himself in.

From the second rank, I threw my spear at another mounted Lakhmid, missing the rider and connecting with the pony's exposed neck. The horse bucked in pain and surprise, throwing the man from the saddle and toppling two of his comrades. Our line surged forward, and Belisarius and I jabbed our swords over the shoulders of the front rank as more enemies pressed against my men's shields.

Even as we clawed back small success at our section of the wall, the far right of Germanus' lines fared less positively. A booming cheer rose from the Persian ranks, with fearful shouting echoing from those of Belisarius' own forces. To discourage our enemies from seizing on such energy, I ordered the foederati to push forward, and our third and fourth lines launched a volley of spears that hailed down upon Persian heads. Sheathing my sword, I drew my axe and used the barbed point opposite its axe blade to pierce through the leather skullcap of a Lakhmid entangled on Perenus' shield.

From behind us, a Ghassanid messenger tugged anxiously at Belisarius' cloak, struggling to gather the general's attention.

"General, King al-Harith has been wounded, and his remaining forces are collapsing on the right," the messenger said. "If we are not reinforced soon, the entire line will crumble."

Belisarius nodded and turned to me. "Seek Troglita and inform him of the Herulians' immediate departure for the Thracian right," Belisarius yelled, already motioning to fall into the rearward ranks in search of an open field to move.

I found Troglita, who had anticipated the maneuver. "I will be fine now," the komes said. "Go to the flank, and leave this section of the wall to me."

With Troglita prepared for our sudden departure, I ordered Fulcaris and Perenus to move our men toward the Thracian rear. This was executed flawlessly, with my foederati full of vigor despite their brief foray into the shield wall. Finding Belisarius and his guard, our combined force trotted in orderly lines toward the edge of the army, finding it increasingly ragged and disorganized the farther we moved.

As I neared the Ghassanid remnants, I heard a Roman horn blare in the distance, and I darted a confused glance at Belisarius.

"Are we expecting reinforcements?" I asked.

Belisarius shook his head. "We're the only army between here and Armenia," he answered. "It might be a trap."

But it was not.

Illuminated by torches at the front of a Roman column stood Solomon, his uniform caked with dirt yet suspiciously clean of the gore of battle.

Belisarius galloped toward the column, leaving me to command the foederati. Finding Lakhmids threatening to puncture the Ghassanid lines, I ordered my men to form a wall and charge forward, reinforcing our Arab allies.

Our wall collided upon unsuspecting Lakhmid and Persian riders, who had largely abandoned a coherent formation in pursuit of a rout of al-Harith's forces. I hefted my axe high into the air and chopped into one rider's leg, nearly severing the limb at the hip as bone cracked under the blow and spurted dark blood. He fell screaming, unable to balance himself atop his mount.

Temporarily, the ruin of Germanus' right flank was halted, although the diminutive numbers of my foederati left me uncertain how long we could hold. A Ghassanid bedecked in rich lamellar-and-leather armor approached and offered his thanks as the Lakhmids reformed their lines, joining his men with mine.

"Where is the king?" I yelled to the man in Latin, my voice gravelly with excessive use.

The Ghassanid dropped his gaze. "King al-Harith took an arrow in his arm," the man replied, his Latin stilted. "He did not die, but he is crippled for now. I… I am leader of the remaining forces." His last statement sounded unsure.

"What is your name?" I asked.

"Jafnah ibn 'Amr, bodyguard of the Royal House of Ghassan," the man replied, meeting my gaze with a note of pride.

"Well met, Jafnah. We are depending on your valor to hold these lines as long as possible." I took pains to compliment the man by offering such a difficult assignment. Jafnah's chest rose at the charge, his eyes darting briefly to the Lakhmids who had begun their advance.

"It is my honor to fight with Belisarius' men," Jafnah replied with a salute before returning to his men.

Nearly all mounted, the Lakhmids hit our lines shortly after, attempting to use their ponies to batter our shield wall apart. My Herulians had been well trained for this type of attack, however, and centuries of Roman discipline were solid proof that a well-disciplined shield wall can turn back even the most determined of cavalry attacks. Those of my men who retained their spears thrust toward the exposed necks and chests of the lighter Arab ponies, breaking the integrity of the Lakhmid lines that decayed into smaller pockets of fighting.

As we hacked and cut at our enemies, forming a higher wall of dead and dying that hindered the Lakhmid charge, the Roman horn sounded again a mere fifty paces distant. Alarmed, I gave Perenus command of our shield wall and moved to the rear of our formation, spying the incoming column that formed lines behind my own.

Swaggering in front of nearly four hundred Roman spearmen was Solomon. Belisarius walked close by, keeping his personal guard separated from Solomon's banda as they approached our lines.

"Reinforcements!" Solomon yelled, a grin on his face.

"Fucking coward!" I yelled in return, moving faster as I closed the distance between us. I came a handsbreadth from Solomon's face before Marcian drew his blade and shoved himself between us.

"Sheath your sword, centurion, or I will have you whipped for threatening a superior officer!" Belisarius roared. Turning to me, Belisarius changed to a lighter, but still firm, tone. "Lord Varus, now is not the time for recriminations, and I would ask that you step away from Komes Solomon."

Snarling, I backed away as Solomon smirked in triumph. "Coward," I muttered, too low for Belisarius to hear.

"Savage," Solomon replied under his breath—bold, now that he was assured I would not respond with violence.

Belisarius drew closer, followed closely by his household guard. "We need to hit the far right immediately. Lord Varus will have command, and Komes Solomon's banda will serve as the rearward ranks."

"With respect, it's Lord Solomon, General Belisarius," Marcian said, his voice honeyed and innocent.

Belisarius spun around violently. "That is news to me, centurion. Komes Solomon lacks independent command, and I am certain I did not bestow such honors upon him myself. Nor, judging by your banda's actions, is an honor deserved. Fall into line immediately or surrender your plume to someone who will follow my orders without further insolence."

Surprised at Belisarius' anger, Marcian bobbed his head in deference and commanded the banda to form into a shield wall. My own foederati moved into their own wall several paces before that of Solomon, with Perenus and the other officers wary of further treachery. In that moment, a wave of regret swam over me—I should have sought punishment for Marcian's actions at Dara. At this point, though, there was little I could do.

The Lakhmid whooping and cheering grew as a small number of riders broke through the remaining Ghassanid forces. As Belisarius moved to my left, I gave the order for the foederati to charge, and we leveled our weapons and moved toward the crumbling Roman flank.

Our impact was immediate, with the few Lakhmids who threatened to turn the Roman flank killed by spears and other blades while the exhausted Ghassanid spearmen and cavalry were given a reprieve from the shield wall. Belisarius led the advance against our enemies, using a long blade that would have been better suited upon horseback to pierce through a wicker shield and disembowel a Lakhmid who ventured too far from the safety of his

461

own shield wall. Unlike at Dara, when the time came to rotate my men for those of Solomon's, Marcian made no sign of protest, although Solomon himself came no closer to the shield wall than the third rank of Thracian spearmen.

At the rear of the formation, a pillar of light rose behind our lines, followed by a wave of heat. Distracted by the ongoing chaos of battle, my only impression was a general pleasantness brought by that sudden warmth, especially given the creeping cold that haunted the Syrian riverside. My mind soon snapped to attention at the screams of pain that followed.

When I turned, it was to view another fresh horror.

Flames shot high into the air, three or four times the height of a man. The fires pulsed in spurts as they licked at the lines of Baduarius and John, which still held despite the inhuman effort required to hold discipline for so long. At the center of the fires stumbled a mess of bodies, all being devoured by the fire's maw.

I was only able to piece together the cause of such disturbances well after the battle. Despite Ascum's better judgment, the ballistae were ordered to continue firing at the massed Persian army throughout the day, placing considerable strain on their wooden arms and thick horsehair rope that launched each machine's massive bolts toward the enemy. Ascum had gone to extensive lengths to keep each of Belisarius' twelve ballistae in working order—applying olive oil to the wooden body, pouring water over the rope when it began to overheat. By nightfall, only two had been deemed inoperable, with one's rope snapping and the other splintering under the tension of its bolt.

The failure of the third ballista proved disastrous. The weapon likely possessed cracks along several of the boards that angled the bow upright—a fatal flaw that the chaos and darkness of the evening battle kept unseen. The crew did not hesitate to ignite another bolt with a heavy layer of oil that burned searing holes through Azarethes' forces, but as they fired the machine, the ballista toppled, shooting forth its massive iron-tipped spear as it fell.

The lit bolt collided with a small pyramid of clay oil pots that easily burst upon impact, catching fire soon thereafter. That fire spread to other ballista teams, throwing Belisarius' siege engineers into their own personal hell.

My eyes could hardly bear the searing white heat of the inferno, although I could make out the agonized shouts of Ascum amidst the anguish of his men. Belisarius immediately called a nearby courier to execute fresh orders.

"Find Ascum and any survivors and ferry them across the river immediately," Belisarius ordered. "There will be a small camp a short distance on the other side, and there will be doctors present. Take ten Ghassanids with you to help carry those who have some chance to live."

The courier left as a fresh attack cut deep into our lines, ripping Solomon's men apart. Their shield wall was poorly constructed, the men spaced too far apart, and the Persian and Lakhmid attackers broke through easily. My foederati turned them back, but we, too, were pushed back under the swelling mass of the enemy attack.

Then, disaster struck again. Marcian was hit by a stray arrow—a light wound, but enough to leave him incapable of fulfilling his duties as an officer, and left Solomon without his closest sycophant. Panicking, Solomon ordered the banda to fall back but left it to his remaining officers to determine the pace of retreat. Confusion followed, with Solomon's banner toppling into the muck, driving the jittering men of the shield wall into an unruly mob. Several in Solomon's rearward ranks trickled through gaps between my men, while others milled about helplessly as they looked to officers for orders.

As more Persians collided with my lines, we fell perilously backward. We'd become separated from the other groups of

Thracians under Troglita, Mundus, and Germanus. I saw Jafnah lead a counterattack to plug that gap, and my spirits lifted, only to plummet as a Persian spear lodged itself in the Arab guardsman's throat. Perenus yelled for the men to keep their wall high and tight, yet I could sense the Herulians' confidence waning as they came perilously close to encirclement.

Belisarius sent several of his guard to reinforce my left and remained with me as I ordered the foederati to retreat ten spaces back. Given that space, I hoped that our wall could regroup and reorder itself and dissuade the exhausted Persian attackers from pressing farther into our spiked wall of death.

Yet I was wrong. The Persians came again, and it was all we could do to hold ourselves together for a few more heartbeats.

"Go now, Lord, while there is still time!" I yelled to Belisarius.

"Not a chance," he called back.

Anger overtook me. "Goddammit, this is it!" I cried. "In a matter of moments, we'll be surrounded, and you'll be cut off from the army!"

Before Belisarius could respond, a silver horn blew far behind us in short, urgent notes—enough, it seemed, to give my men a second wind.

"Not yet!" Belisarius called out in return, offering a rare toothy grin.

The Persians made one final desperate push against my men, driving a wedge between our lines that threatened to pierce directly through toward Belisarius' center, which still smoldered from Ascum's ballistae. One massive Persian drew close, swinging a mace at my head, only to be skewered by Belisarius' sword. Two other mounted Persians charged at our plumed figures, their lowered spears poised to knock us clean off our feet. Belisarius and I braced for the attack, but it never came. Our assailants' world came to a sudden end.

A volley of arrows flew over our heads and quilled the riders to a point of paralysis. Dozens upon dozens of Persians and Lakhmids were thrown from saddles, ending their charge, and the lucky survivors scrambled for the shelter of their own shield wall.

Seizing the moment, I ordered our wall to regroup, to join the larger Thracian lines, and turned to face my savior.

I was greeted by the sweat-strewn, grinning face of Samur.

"Thought you could use some help!" he cried. "Sunicas and Simmas have the bulk of the Huns. But I've got fifty riders to protect the Thracians."

Samur's Hunnic riders sat awkwardly in the saddle, their legs burned raw from a day and night of hard riding. Several had blood dripping from their hands, evidence of bowstrings that slashed at exposed wrists and hands. None complained, and several saluted Belisarius, who nodded in gratitude.

"You have my thanks, Samur. You have saved the army," he said. "But we must evacuate. Quickly—as soon as possible."

"Evacuate, Lord?" I said. "Evacuate who?"

"Everyone," Belisarius replied. "I commandeered those boats for this purpose, in the event that Azarethes would not sue for peace or leave us alone."

"But you can't evacuate them," Sembrouthes rasped, wincing as he spat a gob of blood from his mouth. "Hermogenes will arrest you, or worse."

Belisarius nodded sadly. "That is my burden to bear." Turning to two of his bodyguards, he issued the command that would finally end the battle. "Order Bessas and the Thracians to fall back, slowly shrinking our area of operations. Valerian's men will board first, then Marcellus, then Baduarius."

"And what of our horses?" I asked. "There's no time to load so many onto the ships."

Belisarius pointed south, toward Callinicum. "Anyone with a horse will ride toward the city to seek shelter and man the walls.

This is the best that we can do, given the circumstances," he conceded.

His bodyguards galloped away to convey the missives to the various commanders, and as they disappeared into the darkness, a shout rose over my men once again.

"Incoming! Shields up!" Perenus screamed out, and the Herulians ducked into place, cowering under the great bulwark of a hundred shields joined together. Arrow fire struck hard at my men, with several cursing as an arrowhead pierced through a shield's wooden panels and tore at the skin on their hands and arms. I joined them, more for self-defense against the stinging hail than to solidify their ranks, and permitted Perenus to issue the orders.

"Recover!" Perenus shouted again as the volley subsided. Looking around, several men praised their good fortune at remaining untouched, while Fulcaris yelled out that the Persians were not following their arrows with another charge.

Behind me, however, sounded a thick gurgling noise, and the thudding of boots as men dismounted their horses.

I spun around again to see Samur, pale-faced atop his horse, two arrows stuck fast in his torso.

"Samur!" I yelled, running to my brother as he tried in vain to pull one of the shafts from his flesh. Sembrouthes followed close behind, while Belisarius remained to command the foederati, and I dove to Samur's side as two Huns gingerly laid him upon the earth. Seeing me, Samur tried to speak, but he choked on a viscous glob of blood that stained his lips and pooled crudely around his head.

"Samur!" I shrieked again, easing my hands under his head and cradling his body with my legs. I looked around frantically for help, for anyone, desperate.

"Find a medic, now!" I screamed in rough Hunnic at one man.

"Lord, there are no medics here," the Hun replied in a worried voice, wary of my rising anger.

I screamed wordlessly again and saw Samur's eyes grow wide with fear. He shook his head. "Varus, leave me before it's too late," he choked, tears cutting through the dirt caking his nose and cheeks. "Don't die here."

"No!" I yelled. I looked to Sembrouthes for assistance, but he only closed his eyes and shook his head. There was nothing he could do.

Roman horns sounded—the signal of an army about to march. Belisarius' order was unfolding: Germanus' collective bandae fell back, while in the distance Valerian's surviving spearmen had already begun to board the smaller transport craft to reach the safety of the other side of the Euphrates.

"Take him to the boats!" I yelled. "Belisarius stationed doctors there. They will help him!"

The two Huns shrugged but obeyed, and lifted Samur with the help of one of my foederati. I ran to Belisarius, who slowly retreated toward the coast with the rest of the Thracian line.

"Lord, my brother—"

"I know," Belisarius said. "We will get him across, and I will do everything I can to help him."

I nodded in gratitude, fighting back hot tears that massed at the corners of my eyes. "The Persians will assault us soon, one way or another."

"Yes," Belisarius said with a look that poorly masked the worry in his voice. "We need to cross the river as quickly as possible. The boat archers must keep the Persian attackers at bay."

I nodded and fell alongside him to follow the men carrying Samur toward the riverfront, stepping through the occasional arrow-riddled body and the mound of smoldering ash that had once been Belisarius' siege weapons. Dozens of freshly lit torches dotted the riverbank, guiding men to their embarkation points at craft of all sizes. Valerian's spears and all the excubitores had departed, and the first bandae of Baduarius' remaining men lined up for rescue as the Roman formation continued to shrink.

Even with dozens of boats ferrying ten to a hundred Romans away from the battle, it became easier to defend our formation as our shield wall condensed and had less ground to guard. Detachments of Persian horsemen still tested potential weak points and forced our remaining men into a defensive wall, yet the deadliest attack option remaining to Azarethes was his remaining bowmen and their seemingly inexhaustible supply of barbed arrows.

We were just fifty paces from the Euphrates when John galloped toward us with a crisp salute. Belisarius returned the gesture, visibly relieved to see his boyhood friend safe. "Link up with Bessas and gallop toward Callinicum," Belisarius ordered, "and stop for nothing. Take the Herulian ponies with you, but don't lose lives over them."

John nodded, panting. "What of the other cavalry?"

"They have no heavy armor to slow them," Belisarius replied. "They'll move quicker than any Persian. Leave now, before the Persians close our last lanes to the south."

John acknowledged the command and immediately relayed it to his surviving followers. Soon, thousands of armored horsemen moved south, bruised from blows and painted with the blood of friends and enemies alike. I saw one cataphract carrying a severed hand as he galloped south, and it took a moment to register that the man had a stump where his sword should have been. Amidst the cataphracts ran several riderless horses, and I hoped that Ignis would be found in their number.

As the moon came into clearer view, the last of Baduarius' men boarded ships. The great Goth found me in the press of men and beckoned for me to follow, and I yelled that I would wait for the next boat with Samur.

He shook his head violently. "Get the hell out of here!" he cried, panting from exhaustion. When I refused, he shrugged and limped onto his boat, with sailors using oars to push their heavily laden craft into the river and away from combat.

Belisarius' remaining archers fired volleys to dissuade approaching Persians as the wounded within the Thracian Army began to be loaded onto the boats. Among their number was Troglita, who was half carried onto a boat as he leaned heavily upon two other spearmen, his hip crusted with blood that had already begun to dry. In the midst of the chaos, Germanus approached Belisarius' position for further orders, his face deeply furrowed.

"With a few thousand, we can hold the riverbank," Germanus said, "but once we get to a small enough number, the Persians will overwhelm our ranks and kill hundreds, maybe even a thousand."

Seeing a meeting of the remaining officers, Sunicas and Simmas trotted forward, the rest of their Hunnic foederati firing over the heads of Germanus' spearmen. Sunicas' gaze fell to Samur, and his eyes grew wide as he dropped from the saddle.

"What happened?" he asked me, his voice grave.

"Arrows along the flank," I said, feeling foolish at such a simple explanation.

"Get him out of here, now," Sunicas barked at the two Huns at Samur's side. The men grunted in assent and picked Samur up, sending his head lolling to one side. Samur's waxy face focused for a moment, moving his mouth barely above a whisper.

"Is Varus coming?" he asked.

"Yes, little brother, in just a moment," I lied.

"Good," he said serenely. "What about Sunicas?"

"Me as well, Samur," Sunicas answered, grabbing my brother's limp hand and offering a squeeze.

The men carried Samur away and onto a low galley, careful to not aggravate the arrow shafts that still protruded from his furs and leather. As I followed, there was little else that I could do beyond hold Samur's weapons until I could entrust them to one of Samur's bearers after he was secured on the boat. The boat waited for additional passengers, and I grew more and more impatient, seething in frustration as I struggled in vain for any means to ease my brother's pain. But I had none; all I could do was pace and wait for the end.

Soon, however, others called for my attention. Resigned that there was nothing I could do for Samur under the current crisis, I allowed my brother to be cared for by others upon the raft. As they prepared for departure, Germanus gestured toward me, raising his voice as he spoke to Belisarius. "Someone will need to stay behind to guard the retreat."

"You mean someone will need to stay and die," Sembrouthes countered, warily eyeing the shrinking territory held by the Romans.

Belisarius raised a hand. "I am the commander here. I will stay with volunteers from my bodyguard and hold the beach until you are all safely off."

"Like hell you will!" Mundus arrived as Belisarius made his death pact. "I've seen more wars than any of you, and I'll make sure those Persian bastards don't take me too early. By my count, I should have died long ago."

"Me too!" I called out. "My men are freshest from the reserves and can fight with a bow as well with a spear or sword. I demand to stand in General Belisarius' place."

Germanus glared at us, his eyes narrowed with affront. "Varus is still young and will soon be a father, and I am Mundus' commander. I will be damned to the deepest Hell if either of you fights while I flee. I will hold the beach," Germanus barked, his general's plume standing nearly as tall and grand as Belisarius' own.

Belisarius began to argue with all of us, and our conversation descended into cacophony. Belisarius attempted to pull rank and command us all to leave, but none of us would abandon our general to the enemy.

"It must be me," a dark voice said, breaking the deadlock. All turned to face Sunicas, who removed his helmet to unveil wet hair and a deeply lined forehead where the metal helm dug into his skin.

"Explain," Belisarius said, his voice already suggesting resistance.

"Whoever stays must be able to shoot a bow, as Varus suggested," Sunicas said, gesturing to me. "Yet he must also be able to maneuver, and be steady enough to avoid panic, as Mundus explained."

"Any man present would fulfill each of these requirements," Belisarius countered, "including myself."

Sunicas smirked. "Yes, my lord. But who fulfills them better than the Huns?"

"None," Simmas answered for Belisarius, his face tired and resigned to his brother's words. "None can and none ever will. The only thing preventing the Huns from ruling the world are other Huns."

Belisarius began to object until Sunicas continued. "Belisarius, I have served you for years. It has been the honor of my life to do so. I will not see you die this day."

"Me as well," Simmas added. "And besides, we might escape on our ponies. Persians are fat in the saddle and know not how to ride on no food or sleep."

Sunicas laughed at this. "It must be us, Lord. You bear the burden of leading the remnants of the army after this, to see the men safe."

471

Belisarius paused for a moment, disturbed only by the Persian horns that grew ever closer. After a time, he nodded, his eyes wet with tears.

"Rome owes you an incalculable debt," Belisarius said, "and I will pray for you."

"Just make sure the Emperor knows that Huns died to save Roman sons," Sunicas said. "Take one hundred of my men and leave me the rest."

With the strategy sealed, the other senior officers embraced the two Huns. Simmas offered a tight grip, while Sunicas placed a hand upon my shoulder. Sunicas' eyes fell to my sword hilt as he spoke his words to me, his voice slow and morose.

"Take care of Samur," Sunicas said. "He shows a face of stone to the world, but inside all he desires is love. This—what we're about to do—will be difficult for him to understand. But it is important that he knows that his story will not end here."

"I promise," I replied, and with that, Sunicas departed.

Belisarius was the last to offer his goodbyes, and he tightly embraced his two longtime commanders. "The moment we are away, gallop hard to the south. Get yourselves out of here," Belisarius said, his face buried in their furs.

Though laced with honey, the words were pointless. All present understood the truth: There was no escape for Sunicas and Simmas. Many today insist that their sacrifice was unnecessary, or that the Huns might have galloped free from Persian confinement, at which I can only scoff. I was there, and I saw a force of the finest soldiers that Rome ever fielded delay the Persian victory at Callinicum so that others might live another day. Sunicas and Simmas did not flinch at their fate, and for that, they deserve far more than the latter-day strategies of soft clerks and feeble-minded scholars.

A shout amongst the Persian lines broke our meeting. Germanus and Mundus ordered more of the Thracian bandae aboard boats that had recently returned from depositing other men and quickly filled to capacity as Romans nervously clung to hopes of survival. Among their number was Solomon, who removed his helm and disguised his komes' plume with the hem of his filthy cloak.

At last, the boat carrying Samur finally pushed away as the last few hundred Romans remained on the Syrian beach. A contingent of a hundred Lakhmids charged at our diminished lines only to be stuck fast with arrows from Huns and ship archers alike, killed by the dozen. Belisarius, Uliaris, and the rest of the general's household guard boarded an open boat. I assured Belisarius that I would follow suit in a larger craft able to hold my more numerous foederati. Belisarius' boat quickly departed, his gaze unblinking as he stared at the carnage of the battle.

The final two boats arrived, and I ordered my foederati aboard. "Move faster!" Sunicas yelled to me as his remaining men fired as quickly as possible, slowing the Persian advance to a slow creep. Fulcaris and Perenus hustled the last of their men onto one boat while Sembrouthes and I shepherded ours onto the other.

Finally, we were boarded. Throwing a salute to the Huns, I nodded to the ship captain, who pushed away from the shore and rowed toward the opposite side.

"If Hell is real, it can't be too different from Callinicum," Irilar said as he leaned against the boat railing.

I agreed in silence. As we drifted, a moan rose above the chaotic noise of Belisarius' army along the Euphrates River. It began low and pained, yet soon I recognized it.

"Sunicas! Sunicas! No!" It was Samur who cried out, though his voice was garbled, undoubtedly from blood filling his mouth. I watched as men fought to lower Samur back to the deck of his boat, his head rising and falling as he fought his caretakers to stand.

"No! Send me back!" Samur called out, weeping, seeming to forget his injuries. "Sunicas! Why did you leave me?"

If the Hun heard Samur's calls, he showed no recognition. Torches along the river gave my men an uninterrupted view of the battlefield as we drifted away, and we watched as Sunicas ordered his riders to break hard to the south, loosing arrows at a full gallop and carving a hole in the Persian ranks. He reached the end of Persian resistance and seemed to clear through without losing too many men in the struggle.

A volley of Persian arrows and stiffening spearmen forced the Huns back into a trap of Persian and Lakhmid men and horses, with dozens falling as they reached their shrinking half circle of safety. The Huns fired more arrows, yet a Persian horn ordered a charge of armored Immortals that rammed into the Hunnic formation.

Of the few dozen Huns remaining, Simmas fell first. His sword cut clean through the chest of one Immortal only for the spear of another to gore and drive him to the ground.

The Immortal slashed down, and I looked away. I only hoped that his death was a mercifully quick one.

Roaring at the death of his brother, Sunicas rallied his last dozen defenders, backing up slowly as his boots splashed into waters of the Euphrates. He used his bow to down two attackers, then drew his sword to cut a long gash into the sword arm of a third. But then his head flew back, and his spine arched at an awkward angle. A half dozen arrows thudded into the Hunnic commander's chest, leaving him jerking in the saddle as he fought to keep from falling over. He managed to raise his sword one final time despite his grievous injuries, but a Persian spear stuck into his chest. He fell into the river, his hand tightly gripping the sword pommel as his body made a violent splash in the shallow water.

I heard Samur wail. Two Persians took Sunicas' body and raised him high into the air, their eyes manic and gleeful. One held Sunicas' limp body upright as the other hacked at the Hun's head, at last severing it from his body with a fountain of deep crimson.

With a laugh, the Persian hurled the head toward my boat, and it floated for a time before falling into the murky depths of the river.

We reached the other side of the Euphrates, which was at most three hundred paces from the Persian position. I disembarked amongst hundreds of moaning Romans strewn along the dirt and sand, completely spent from an entire day of battle. I do not doubt that a single banda of fresh Persians could have annihilated most of Belisarius' survivors in that state, and it was only Azarethes' lack of ships that saved us.

As I walked through the disorganized mass of men, I found the makeshift tents that housed the dozens of doctors that Belisarius paid to follow his army. Prying my helmet free of my head, I strode inside the first, hoping to find Samur already receiving the attention of a healer. Instead, I found someone else I had not thought to see so near Callinicum.

"Varus!" Rosamund called out, sprinting toward me. She was bedecked in mail and leather, yet her long white hair flew freely behind her body. She jumped at me, squeezing her arms around my waist as she buried her face into my blood-soaked armor. I embraced her, but only briefly.

"Why—how are you here?" I asked, looking distractedly for my brother.

"Belisarius called for healers, and I asked to be escorted to Callinicum," she said. "I wanted to help you, even in some small way. But Varus, I saw the battle from the riverbank. It was horrible—"

"You can help me," I interrupted. "It's Samur. He's been hurt badly."

"Samur?" Rosamund paled. "I haven't seen him come in. He must still be outside."

Grabbing a torch, Rosamund ran outside, yelling for Samur as she sprinted through the army, with me at her heels. Shortly after, we found him sobbing in pain not far from the riverbank, mumbling Sunicas' name, ignoring the world around him.

Rosamund ordered Samur's caretakers to convey him into the medical tent, and I followed close behind, stopped only when Rosamund put a hand to my chest.

"You won't want to see this," she warned. "I'll send for you when it's over, or if... if anything changes."

I motioned to resist but thought better of it. "Keep him alive, whatever gods you must bargain with to do so."

She nodded, and after I watched Samur disappear into the tent, I wandered aimlessly through the Roman camp. Sounds of misery and suffering flew all around as even those untouched by Persian arrows or blades agonized over torn muscles and parched bodies that cried desperately for waterskins that were passed through the camp.

I stole another look at the battlefield, where hundreds of Persians whooped in victory as they taunted us from across the river. I wanted to scream, to empty my lungs of all the foul spirits that enveloped this cursed battle that Belisarius so adamantly warned against. More so, however, a painful knot formed in my throat as the image of Samur's torn body clouded my senses, tears streaming uncontrollably down my grimy cheeks. Like me, he came so far, farther than any palace slave could hope for, and now, through injury and loss, he had again fallen into a luckless, brutish existence. And God damn it all, there was not a thing I could do about it.

My melancholy was broken by Mundus, who laid a gloved hand on my shoulder. "Belisarius is looking for you," he said.

I found Belisarius with his helmet off, and though he looked haggard and pale, he still threw himself into his work, dispatching orders via couriers and inquiring with officer after officer on the status of his men. As I neared, he ordered several boats to travel west toward Barbalissus and Hierapolis in search of supplies and other aid, which were obeyed immediately. Belisarius nodded to me as I squatted beside him near a low fire, asking whether Samur was being tended to, which I confirmed.

"Good," Belisarius murmured, and he glanced at me with a half smile. "He is fortunate to have you for a brother, Varus."

What the true purpose of our meeting was, I would never know. For it was then that Hermogenes, flanked by two dozen guards with shields bearing the Imperial Eagle, strode into view.

"Arrest General Belisarius," Hermogenes barked, "for the crimes of incompetence, dereliction of duty, and cowardice."

Hermogenes' guards drew their swords, but Uliaris and a half dozen of Belisarius' household flung themselves forward.

"You can take that pretty prick and stuff it up your ass, you bunch of painted whores," Uliaris bellowed. "I doubt any of you've ever even raised a blade in anger."

Hermogenes was undeterred. "And take this... mustachioed Frank with him," he added. "The Emperor despises such skulking creatures."

Uliaris snarled, teeth bared at the threat. "I'll die before I let you take Belisarius."

"That will not be necessary," Belisarius said calmly, rising to his feet. "Legate Hermogenes, forgive my men. They have been through an ordeal and are only seeking to perform their sworn oaths."

Hermogenes grunted. "Fine, as long as you come quietly now, with no trouble."

Belisarius nodded. "Uliaris, watch after the men. Speak to Varus for any further orders or instruction."

I, too, leapt to standing and seized Belisarius by the shoulder. "Lord, don't do this," I murmured.

Belisarius offered another weak smile, his eyes still wet with tears for his fallen friends. "Keep my men safe. That is your duty now."

I nodded, tears again welling in my eyes—from frustration, exhaustion, the death of trusted friends and potentially my brother. After so much death and pain, so much surging anger, Hermogenes' condemnation of my lord was too much for me to bear, and I struggled against an instinct to plunge my dagger into the elderly legate's guts. Few present would have raised a finger to stop me, and none would have regretted the loss.

Prudence prevailed, anchored in the mournful eyes of Belisarius, who needed me. "I promise, Lord," I said aloud.

Belisarius waved to me and had his arms grabbed violently by Hermogenes' guardsmen. As Belisarius disappeared far into the night toward Hermogenes' tent, Romans of all types rose to their feet in anger and confusion. Many threatened Hermogenes with violence, and the scattered mutterings and cries soon gave way to isolated cheers, difficult to understand at first, yet they spread like wildfire from one of Hakhamanish's rituals.

"Belisarius! Belisarius! Belisarius!" the army chanted, their voices cracked and hoarse from overexertion.

Hermogenes, eager to escape the precarious situation, scurried away as the cheering reached its apex. As for myself, I was at a loss. My gaze drifted, my mind feeling strangely untethered, and as I stole another glance across the river, where flames from bonfires and torches rose unnaturally high as Persians and Lakhmids galloped in wide celebratory circles, I saw a lone figure in the robes of a Zoroastrian priest.

He stared back at me. Somehow, the man seemed to have spotted me amidst the darkness of Rome's army, and he stood, silently and motionlessly, eyes fixed as his fires cut through the darkness across the river.

Uliaris broke my trance with a disgruntled mumble.

"So, what do we do now?" he asked.

Startled, I gazed back toward the riverbank, but the robed priest had vanished. Fires still blazed heavily, yet the thickly bearded and robed man was nowhere to be found, leaving only an ominous feeling of dread in his wake. Gripping the bronze cross that hung at my neck, I sighed deeply and issued my first orders as the interim leader of the shattered remnants of Rome's Eastern Army. In more than one manner, it was a dark night of the soul.

"Let the men heal and rest for the night," I said, "and then tomorrow, we're getting Belisarius back."

For Rome's struggle had hardly begun. Darkness swept over more than the Empire's east, and Belisarius would be needed again soon enough.

AUTHOR'S NOTE

THIS IS A work of fiction. Characters are adapted and timelines adjusted for the sake of storytelling—this is both a blessing and a curse for an author of historical fiction. The reality of the Iberian War was far more dramatic and far more complex than any novelist can adequately cover. In general, the sixth-century East Roman Empire was rife with struggle, and defined by a complex bureaucracy and military where thousands of people influenced the course of events. As much as feasible, I did my best to keep the spirit of sixth-century life alive on *Immortal*'s pages.

While Belisarius' other wars are discussed by Procopius and others, the Iberian War is perhaps the most well-known to the public. Procopius goes into detail regarding Belisarius' preparations and execution of the Battle of Dara, with a lesser (yet still astounding) description of the Battle of Callinicum. This war made Belisarius famous, and also characterized the type of relationship he would have with Justinian in the years ahead— asked to succeed against unfavorable odds, and at great personal and social risk. Though young—still in his early twenties by his victory at Dara—Belisarius had been thrust into the heights of command.

It is tempting to view Belisarius' victory at Dara, and general success in repelling the Persian attack on the eastern provinces, as obvious or inevitable. Far from it. Over three hundred years, the Sasanian Empire had evolved into a wealthy, populous, and advanced military power that repeatedly thrashed the Romans. Likewise, the Roman armies had been stripped of men and forced to repel attacks along their northern border, leaving paltry formations available to defend their extensive Armenian and Mesopotamian frontier.

Outside of Dara, Roman frontier fortresses had become dilapidated, although Anastasius and Justin expended resources to harden defenses against the objections of Persian envoys. Belisarius and Justinian, recognizing the imminent danger of the situation, instituted changes into frontier fortifications as well as the general composition of the Roman Army (importantly, moving from an infantry-centered force to a cavalry-dominated one). However, such changes are not executed quickly, and the Iberian War caught the East Romans at a strategic disadvantage. Belisarius faced many setbacks, yet through astute battlefield command and extensive trust in his men, he was able to seize one of the more famous military victories of all time.

Drawing from Procopius, many scholars deduce that the bulk of Belisarius' forces at Dara were underequipped, painfully outnumbered, and of generally suboptimal quality. These thousands of infantry were nestled behind a spiked trench near Dara's walls, allowing wall archers to relieve pressure from the lines. The only hardened and reliable soldiers Belisarius could rely upon were the Huns (under Sunicas and Simmas), the Herulians (under Varus, or Pharas), and the bucellarii, his household retainers. Most others were considered unreliable, either because they were undertrained, demoralized, poorly equipped, or a combination of these. Belisarius leaned upon his bucellarii and foederati to execute the more complex maneuvers at Dara. Though few in number, they fulfilled their orders masterfully, and against unbelievable pressure from vaunted Persian forces. The historical Varus played a pivotal role at the Battle of Dara by setting an ambush along the Roman far-left flank—a role he notably succeeded in.

Callinicum had similar limitations, albeit without the protective walls of Dara at the Roman Army's back. Their egos overinflated from Dara's success, Belisarius' army near-demanded a battle with Azarethes' forces, despite the Persians' superior quality. Compared to Dara, few details remain of Callinicum, although we can glimpse the order of battle as well as the overall outcome. Again, Belisarius lacked the experienced and hardened forces of his Persian foes, and was joined by a reeling detachment of Ghassanid allies. The Ghassanids and Lakhmids fought viciously for control over much of southern Mesopotamia and northern Arabia, yet the Ghassanid forces suffered considerable losses (including their king) at the prior battle of Thannuris, and were now led by lesser-experienced officers.

Callinicum was a massive engagement led by two crafty commanders (Procopius describes Azarethes as an "exceptionally capable warrior"), a battle dominated by cavalry and fought along the banks of the Euphrates. In the end, the Ghassanids were routed, and Belisarius' right flank crumbled. Procopius commended Belisarius' strategy for preserving the core of the Roman Army and exacting heavy losses on his enemies, yet Malalas describes Belisarius' decision to depart the battlefield in a more negative light. Significant importance is placed upon the decision of Sunicas and Simmas in holding the remaining lines as others escaped to safety. Nothing is known of the Hunnic brothers after Callinicum, although given their success in allowing Rome's army to withdraw against Azarethes' onslaught, it is very likely that they died during the battle or shortly thereafter.

The Eastern Empire's enemy, the Shahanshah Kavadh, had decades of experience as the Sasanian monarch. If I had to describe Kavadh in a single word, it would be *resilient*. He inherited the Persian throne in his teenage years, only to be deposed by a powerful nobleman and replaced his brother, Jamasp. Rather than fade into the dust of history, however, Kavadh escaped to the lands of the Hephthalites. Later, he leaned upon the Hephthalites to regain the Persian throne, although the Hephthalites remained a separate kingdom that occasionally warred with Persia's outlying eastern provinces. Through the course of his reign, Kavadh bolstered his armies and rooted out potential adversaries, strengthening the Sasanian Empire despite many internal and external adversaries.

Precious little is known of the Hephthalites, and only from their neighbors and foes. They were described as fierce warriors, with the Armenian chronicler Lazar stating that "...the mere sight or mention of a Hephthalite terrified everybody..." and that few willingly engaged in war against any of the Hephthalite kings. They thrived on conquest, carving out a sizeable empire centered around ancient Bactria.

Though sometimes described as the White Huns, scholars are split on whether the Hephthalites had any connection with the Huns of Attila and Bleda. Whether or not a biological or cultural connection exists, the Hephthalites were active in their conquest around the same time as the Hunnic conquests of Europe, and they struck a similar note of terror in their neighbors as Attila's hordes did amongst Roman and barbarian tribes to the west. They received considerable tribute from the Sasanian Persians and were occasionally deployed in battle against the Romans.

Their presence at Dara is fictional, but they did lay waste to much of Roman Armenia in the early sixth century. Their inclusion at Dara is my invention, but not entirely unrealistic—Kavadh had deployed the Hephthalites as mercenaries within his army many times. The Hephthalites practiced cranial deformation, and denoted their presence through customized tagma (what we would refer to as runes or glyphs). Almost certainly pagan in their earlier years (contemporary Chinese scholars suggest that the Hephthalites worshiped foreign gods and demons), the Hephthalites nevertheless yielded considerable religious construction to posterity—Buddhas of Bamiyan—with several of the mural paintings having belted jackets and physical features uniquely favored by the Hephthalite kings. Sadly, the paintings, and much of the site, was destroyed in early 2001 by the Taliban under the orders of Mullah Mohammed Omar.

The Sasanian Immortals, or Zhayedan, were radically transformed from their mythic forebears from the Achaemenid era. Though still as expertly trained and equipped for war, the Immortals had become an elite force of heavy cavalry, intended to break an opponent at critical points in a battle. Persia's armies were vast, comprised of many thousands of armored cavalry, war elephants, bowmen, and great masses of infantry that were generally used as an auxiliary to Persia's mounted core. It was the Immortals, however, that garnered the greatest degree of respect and fear from their enemies, for they remained utterly loyal unto death.

Historical accounts indicate that Kavadh was so enamored with his Zhayedan that he punished commanders who allowed too many to perish in battle, even if the result was a victory. They were a considerable force in the Iberian War, and a constant threat to Belisarius. Their story is not yet complete in this tale, however, so I will not say more at this time.

In many ways, the second entry of The Last of the Romans was more complicated than the first to write. I owe considerable thanks to a team of dedicated professionals who brought this story to life, as well as a number of close contacts who served as test subjects for earlier drafts. Blair Thornburgh is a fabulous editor not only gifted in storytelling and craft, but also in a rich understanding of the early medieval period that this novel strongly benefitted from. Crystal Watanabe of Pikko's House handled all copyediting, proofreading, and formatting. Dusan Markovic provided the rich illustration of the novel's cover, conferring a level of detail and imagination that brings the sixth century to life. The twin maps are productions of Cyowari, who constructed beautifully detailed works despite sparse records of the various peoples of the age. I am also blessed with a wonderful collection of test readers. *Immortal* is incalculably improved from their efforts.

If you enjoyed *Immortal*, please consider leaving a positive review on Goodreads, Amazon, and other review sites. I am grateful for your time in this—such reviews are critical to the series' success and continued production. Ultimately, we have seen only the beginning of Belisarius, of Theodora, and of Varus. The conflagration of Constantinople looms near, as does the long-lost city of Carthage, its distant shores home to a tribe that put Rome itself to the torch, enslaving thousands in their quest for domination.

The novel that follows *Immortal* will address the fallout of Callinicum and confront Varus and Belisarius with the horrific Nika Riots, as well as the pivotal Vandal War. For even after extensive battle in the east, the Empire's foes abound, including some within the Imperial Court itself. The challenges ahead tower above any hardships suffered along the Mesopotamian frontier.

Made in the USA
Monee, IL
16 September 2022

36c13860-bcbc-47a7-9838-f78b12af3d66R01